To Nancy,
Enjoy the journey.

Victor DiGenti

WINDRUSHER

D1267810

Published by The Writers' Collective
Cranston, Rhode Island

Manufactured in the United States of America
Set in Times Roman

ISBN: 1-59411-048-4

Library of Congress Control Number: 2003110786

Printed in the United States of America

Published by The Writers' Collective
Cranston, Rhode Island

THE WRITERS' COLLECTIVE

WINDRUSHER IS DEDICATED to my strong supporting cast, particularly my dear wife, Evanne, for believing in *Windrusher* as much as I did and encouraging me to complete the journey. I am also indebted to my two creative sons, Brian and Greg, for their invaluable assistance; to Brian, who is a much better writer and editor than his father, and to Greg, for sharing his extensive technical expertise and publishing experience. I'm most grateful also to the talented Andrew Robinson for creating the excellent cover art. And finally, I dedicate this book to everyone who believes in the magic that lives within our feline friends.

Some things have to be
believed to be seen.

—Ralph Hodgson

chapter 1

STUFFED INTO A CAGE. Again.

How could he be so foolish? He pushed against the door hoping that this time it wouldn't be locked, that it would give way under his weight and swing open. He would scramble out and disappear before they knew he was gone.

Nothing. It was wedged tight, wouldn't move.

Barely enough room to turn around. Take a step or two, then turn back. Air was streaming through the holes in the box, but his throat felt like it was being squeezed; he couldn't breathe. His eyes grew wide with panic, and an image came to him of the walls of the box pressing in, crushing him. How long until they would mash the life out of him?

He had to get out of here. Had to get out now. The cage moved; he felt its gentle swaying, then the fragrance of a recently mown lawn told him he was outside. Patches of light splashed into the box, and he heard distinctive outdoor sounds—a bird whistling to its mate, a ball bouncing against a wall, distant sounds of discordant mechanical noises.

Vehicles! No, they wouldn't do it to him again. Would they? Unconsciously, he began a low, plaintive whining and turned from one side of the box to the other, feeling it rock with each movement. Then the slamming of a heavy door and he was down once again.

He jumped at the sound of the door, scratched impotently against the sides of the cage; his whining growing louder, more pathetic. Chest heaving, he felt a pulse twitch in his neck and knew he was losing control. Breathe deeply, he commanded his quaking body. Stop this pitiful whimpering, he told himself, nothing bad had happened yet, had it?

Maybe this time would be different. Maybe the noise and terror wouldn't come, and they would let him out before it began. Remember this has happened before, and you survived. It won't be long before they release you, and everything will be as it was. Even while his eyes darted wildly around the cage, searching for an escape route he may have missed, he focused on finding an inner peace, and forced himself to relax.

Peering through the slots in the side of the cage, he saw the snouter, its head hanging from the open window, and the young male sitting next to him. Then the calm, soothing voice of his female was speaking to him from directly above, saying those nonsensical words over and over. Although he didn't understand them, he instinctively felt better. She was here, and she wouldn't let anything bad happen to him.

"Shhh, Tony, it's just a short ride, we're going to Stacy's. I know you don't like it in there, but it won't be long. I promise you."

Kimmy Tremble spoke in hushed, almost reverent tones. She stared into the pet carrier at her cat, and her stomach twisted in pain. Her eyes misted at the sight of the frightened tabby. She knew Tony was on the edge of panic, fearing the ride that for some reason always turned him from a loving pet into a furious, terrified creature. She continued a stream of gentle words, hoping to calm him down before they made the short trip to her cousin's house.

Kimmy was wedged in the back seat of the Bronco with her brother, GT, several bags filled with Tony's food and toys, and Stella, the massive Black Lab that had been part of their family since she was a pup. Stella pulled her head inside the car and studied the pet carrier. The Lab barked once, as if letting the cat know that there was only one of them inside a box and it wasn't her. The dog turned to GT and gave him one of her best doggy smiles.

"That's right, Stella, it's time for Tony to throw one of his hissy-fits, isn't it," GT said.

Anger, guilt, pain, and self-pity swam together in Kimmy's emotional pool. She threw mental jabs at her brother, while trying to understand the terror Tony must be feeling at this moment. And what she would be feeling for the rest of the trip. She wanted to be mature about it, but that might be asking too much from an eleven-year-old in this position.

Kimmy's right arm flashed out and hit her older brother in the ribs before he could cover himself.

Crouching tensely on the floor of the carrier, the cat they called Tony, a gray mackerel tabby with orange stripes subtly woven through his coat, swished his tail anxiously. He was calmer now, his heart rate had slowed, and he was breathing evenly. Although he was still in the box, they were sitting quietly, no noise, no movement.

No cause for alarm, was there? He was confident that if he continued with his best behavior, his Hyskos female would let him out of the box.

But it was difficult to know how any Hyskos would react. Hyskos is an ancient cat term for the humans who were both feared and respected for their size, their vast numbers, and their unpredictability. To be called a Hyskos brought with it an implied derision as well, since they obviously had no cat sense and were largely unintelligible in the grating sounds they made. A cat understood why he did what he did, whether searching for food or grooming himself before a nap, but these creatures with the false fur filled their days with pointless actions.

They were certainly living up to their reputation for strange behavior by imprisoning him in this small box. But everything was quiet now, except for the occasional squawking of the brainless snouter. Curling up on the floor of the carrier, he relaxed enough to close his eyes and pictured himself running free in the grass once again.

He heard the soft murmurings from the young female, and inhaled slowly. This wasn't going to be like the last time after all.

His ear swiveled as both front doors opened, and he felt the vehicle shift slightly, then the sound of closing doors.

Gerry Tremble wedged his rangy body behind the steering wheel and slammed the door, perhaps with a bit more force than necessary.

"This is it, say goodbye to the old family estate," he said, reaching over and patting his wife on the knee. Amy Tremble gave her husband a tight smile and squeezed his hand.

Tremble glanced at the mirror and nodded to Kimmy and GT in the backseat, then cranked up the Bronco and slipped the gear shift to drive. Either the sound of the powerful engine, or the vibrations it sent coursing through the pet carrier, triggered a frenzied defense mechanism in Tony. The frightened cat leaped against the box, scratching frantically at the pet carrier, desperately trying to find a way out.

From the front seat, Gerry and Amy Tremble cast furtive glances at the cat and Kimmy, then turned soundlessly to look at the road ahead. Even Stella had fallen silent.

"Tony, Tony, please settle down. You'll hurt yourself," Kimmy said, her face resting on the box, her hands patting the sides as though she was hoping to transfer all her love and concern through the plastic walls into the cat.

She didn't know why it happened, but Tony reacted with the same terrible panic attacks every time. He had been doing it since he was a kitten. For the cat's first visit to the veterinarian Kimmy made the mistake of holding the young tabby in her lap. He seemed content until her mother started the car and pulled out of the driveway. It was then that the loving kitten became another creature altogether. At the sound of the engine and the movement of the car, a short ride to the animal clinic erupted into a fury of fur and claws as if the vehicle had triggered some primal subcortical reaction of sizzling neurons and sputtering chemicals.

Inside the cage, it felt as though the air had been sucked from the cat's lungs. The grinding roar of the vehicle assaulted his sensitive ears, and the uncontrollable motion seemed to move him inexplicably in ways he didn't understand. His overloaded brain reacted the only way a trapped animal could react and he exploded into a frenzy of fear and frustration.

Several miles later, Tremble turned into the High Hills subdivision. Cold Spring Road was a short street of well-manicured lawns and two-story colonial style homes where Amy Tremble's sister, Jeannie, and her husband lived. Tom Warren worked for the city of Bloomfield, and was fortunate not to be affected by the recession. In fact, the Warrens seemed to be thriving. He was the top financial officer for the city, and they had recently moved into the spacious new home.

Tremble couldn't suppress the tiny bubble of envy that churned his stomach like acute indigestion. Amy's sister had done quite well for herself marrying the parsimonious business major she met in college. During the bitter depressions of his unemployment, Tremble sometimes wondered if his wife had regrets about their marriage. Thinking back on the ordeal they had endured and how their lifestyle had changed, he certainly couldn't blame her if she did.

The bright light that was their life dimmed considerably when Colonial States National Bank traded a century of service to the people of Connecticut for a $23 billion pay-off. LibertyBank moved quickly to merge its three hundred and fifty branches with Colonial's five hundred and realized significant cost savings by cutting corporate overhead. Even though Tremble's shares jumped by sixteen dollars, his enthusiasm was kept in check since he was considered part of that overhead. He joined the rolls of the unemployed along with 3,400 other Colonial employees in four adjoining states. And he stayed there for thirteen miserable months.

The Bronco pulled into the driveway, and Tremble turned off the engine. Kimmy immediately pushed the door open and carefully lifted the pet carrier off the seat, placing it on the leaf-covered front lawn. Kneeling, she opened the grilled door, reached in, pulled Tony out, and covered the cat with kisses. Even though he had been through a terrible ordeal, experience had shown that it wouldn't be long before his loving personality returned.

She was right. The tabby rubbed his jaw affectionately against her neck, his whimper quickly turning into a persistent purring. While the adults hugged each other, Stacy, Kimmy's cousin, scratched him softly under the chin. The cat closed his eyes, the terror of the last half hour apparently forgotten.

The cat they called Tony felt like he was home again. His Hyskos held him lovingly while the other female murmured nonsensical sounds and scratched his head. He lost himself in the girls' attention, and didn't object as they transferred him from one set of arms to another. Since he had selected this family of high-legged beings as his own, his life had changed. Without realizing it, he had grown dependent on them for his every need, trading his independence for the security that came with being a house cat. He understood that this girl, this family, would never purposely hurt him, and they would care for him as long as he chose to be part of their family. That was why he stayed.

Cats never forget any cruelty or harm done to them, but they have a marvelous capacity to suppress unpleasant experiences. And that's what he did. The terror and dread that ravaged him while he was in the box was put aside, and he was swept up in his freedom and feelings for the young female who cared for him.

Outside the box, free to run and play, he thought. With my own loving high-legged being who treats me like I was part of her litter. And for this, he would put up with the strange behavior his mother had warned him about.

This business of naming the kitten Tony is a good example. When the young cat with the piercing green eyes and unwavering stare boldly approached the Trembles' door fourteen months earlier, Kimmy took one look at the subtle M-shaped orange stripes rising from between the cat's eyes and mingling with the dark gray of his coat and announced breathlessly, "Tony the Tiger is here."

Of course, Kimmy Tremble had no way of knowing that *Tony* already had a name. In fact, he had two names. Every cat of good breeding, that is, a cat fortunate enough to be close to its mother until the time of separation, is given a Mother's Name and a call name. To be absolutely formal Tony should have introduced himself as the Son of Nefer-iss-tu. This name told all who understood these things, here is a cat that can trace his lineage directly to the royal family and once was part of the household of Queen Nefertiti.

A cat's call name, on the other hand, is his common name; it is how all other cats know him. Often the cat will take his call name from a physical attribute, the surroundings where he spent his early days, or even a boastful exaggeration meant to impress other cats.

One afternoon when he was still with his mother, the young cat awoke from a dream shaking with excitement and the knowledge that he had found his call name—Windrusher.

"I don't think you'll have to buy anything for awhile, Tom," Tremble told his brother-in-law, stacking the last of the packages on the driveway.

Tom Warren pulled at his ear lobe and studied the cardboard boxes and paper bags stuffed with litter trays, toys, a scratching post, water bowls, and food. He glanced from them to the cat in his daughter's arms and shook his head. "Wonder where we'll put all this stuff," he said.

Tremble gave his brother-in-law a supportive smile, his eyes sliding to his watch. "Well, folks, I think it's time for goodbyes, we have a long drive ahead of us."

Kimmy dutifully hugged her aunt and uncle, then came back to stand in front of her cousin, who was cradling Tony in her arms. She rubbed the top of the cat's head, pulled gently on his ears and massaged the back of his neck. The cat closed his eyes, a loud purr rising from his throat. Kimmy pressed her face against his, tears glistening on her cheeks.

"This is your new home, Tony," she whispered. "I know you'll be good for Stacy, but you better not forget me." A single sob escaped from the girl. "You know I won't forget you."

Amy Tremble led her crying daughter to the car and everyone waved and yelled goodbye one last time.

Windrusher was more confused than ever. His Hyskos female was whimpering like a kitten, and had returned to the vehicle leaving him behind with the other female. It seemed to him that this moving box was about to take his family away from him.

He didn't understand what happened next; how the potent combination of emotions coursing through his strong feline body ignited a feral jungle instinct lying dormant in his brain. His vision seemed to constrict until only his Hyskos family was visible, sitting in their shiny vehicle, the same vehicle that had always frightened and repulsed him.

There was no weighing of options; Windrusher's primal brain spurred him to the only action open to him. With a frightening growl, he leaped from Stacy's arms, leaving a three-inch scratch on her arm, and bounded to the front of the car just as Gerry Tremble was backing down the driveway.

Before Stacy or her parents could act, the cat with the tiger stripes on its head had skidded to a stop, turned abruptly and sprayed a pungent jet of urine across the front fender and tire of the Bronco, then watched it roll out of his life.

chapter 2

TOM WARREN HAD his reservations about the cat. His life was a perfect balance — what did they call it — his yin and yang? Everything was right where it should be: a prestigious job, a new home, and a wife and daughter he adored. What was there not to like?

There was the cat, of course. Warren had been afraid a pet would disrupt the comfortable patterns of his life, and throw it all out of balance. Except for an occasional goldfish, and a gerbil Stacy once brought home from school, the Warrens had remained pet-free until now.

When Jeannie told him that his sister wanted them to take the cat, and that Stacy would take care of it, he reluctantly agreed. It was the least he could do for his hard luck brother-in-law. The poor guy had suffered through a miserable streak of bad luck. First, he lost his job, and now moving to Florida to run a motel, of all things.

He walked toward Stacy's room to check on her and the cat, pausing momentarily to straighten the Calder lithograph on the stairwell wall. Warren glanced over the rail into the living room before going into Stacy's room, making sure that everything was in its proper place.

Wind roamed curiously from room to room that first day. After a careful investigation of both floors to make sure his Hyskos were not playing a game with him, he quickly lost interest in his new surroundings. He located a bare place atop Stacy's five-drawer dresser and laid down, his head between his paws. He moped through the next thirty-six hours splayed out on the dresser, staring vacantly at the opposite wall.

"Do you think he's sick?" Stacy asked. "He's either on the window sill or lying there, hardly eats anything. He's not even sleeping, see, he's watching us with one eye."

Jeannie Warren was standing in Stacy's doorway staring at the prone cat. "No, baby, he's not sick. It's going to take time for him to get used to us and forget about Kimmy."

"He doesn't have to forget about Kimmy, but I don't want him to be unhappy. Do you think he doesn't like me as much as Kimmy?"

"I'm not a veterinarian, but I'll bet he's going through some kind of shock. Imagine how you'd feel if we left you with your Uncle Chet and his family and—"

"Not Uncle Chet, please," Stacy said.

"You know what I mean. Let's give Tony a few days and if he's still acting strange after that we'll take him to the vet."

Sleep and only sleep was the answer. Deep, healing sleep had abandoned him, however, as his Hyskos family had. The chaotic thoughts caroming through his brain barred him from uniting with the Akhen-et-u or the Inner Ear as it was called. Without access to this vital communication tool connecting many felines, he felt lost and even more alone.

Sleep had been an important part of his life since he found his call name in a dream. His mother, Nefer-iss-tu, had encouraged him to take Black Tail as his call name, after the tom she suspected fathered him. For his part, the Son of Nefer-iss-tu wouldn't accept such a dreary call name, but he didn't have a good alternative, not until the dream.

In the dream, he was rushing down the sheer side of a rocky precipice; a cold blast of wind whipping through his fur, propelling him almost faster than his legs could run. Terrifying sheets of lightning threw wild shadows in his path, and in the shimmering rusty yellow haze he saw trees bent nearly double by the furious storm.

Rain pelted his face and, even as he surveyed the hellish scene in his subconscious landscape, he realized he wasn't frightened, but somehow exhilarated by the experience. His vision expanded past his own narrow view of the steep slope, and there, behind him, was a smaller, mottled tabby tumbling headlong down the nightmarish hill.

The Son of Nefer-iss-tu awoke breathlessly from his vivid dream. He lay there with his heart pounding, his ears still ringing with the echo of thunder, savoring the excitement of the wild descent, the feel of the wind at his back, the acrid smell of the lightning-filled air. While the meaning of his vision escaped him, he awakened with his call name.

From now on, he would be known as Windrusher.

Since his momentous dream, Windrusher believed himself to be blessed by Tho-hoth, the great god of wisdom. But now, Tho-hoth had turned his back on him, and he lay exhausted in a strange home, unable to sleep. If he could only connect with the Akhen-et-u he might find an answer.

Since the age of two months, he had received and understood the voices that came to him while he slept. But not all cats are so fortunate. Even Wind's mother was unable to explain why some cats are part of the Inner Ear and others, the poor Wetlos, are not.

"That is something for Tho-hoth to know," she would say, "but thank the Holy Mother, Irissa-u, that you're not one of them."

Many cats held Wetlos in contempt, calling them *not worth a sniff*, but Wind's heart had always gone out to these incomplete creatures. Now that the Inner Ear remained beyond his reach, he had a better understanding of what it must be like to be a Wetlos.

Stacy sat in front of the computer scrolling through the pages until she found the section. "Here it is," she said, leaning to her left so her mother could read over her shoulder. "It says that cats sleep twice as much as humans—at least sixteen hours a day."

"Huh," her mother said, staring at the screen. A photograph of a sleeping calico cat, flat on its back, legs akimbo, was below the title, *Why Cats Sleep...And Sleep.*

"Says there are three types of feline sleep: brief naps, longer sleep, and deep sleep," Jeannie read from the computer screen. "Sixteen hours a day, amazing."

"Right, and Tony isn't sleeping at all. That can't be good for him," Stacy said.

"We don't know he's not sleeping, you're not watching him every minute, are you?"

"Mom, he's just not acting like he did with Kimmy. I used to see him playing with one of those plastic rings from milk jugs that Kimmy gave him, and he'd toss it up in the air and catch it—"

"Well, he doesn't feel like playing yet."

Stacy pushed the chair back and stood to face her mother, one hand tightly gripping the chair, the other balled at her waist. "No, you're not listening," she said. "Right in the middle of playing, he would fall over on his back like he had a heart attack or something and be sound asleep. Ten minutes later he'd jump up and start playing with the ring again."

"So…"

"So, cats need to sleep. Even when they're playing and Tony isn't playing or sleeping."

Jeannie Warren squeezed her daughter's shoulder. She felt the muscle tense beneath her fingers. "All right, if you're that worried, I'll try to get an appointment with Dr. Vaughan tomorrow."

At 8:45 P.M. of that second day in the Warren home, Windrusher finally fell into an exhausted sleep. He rolled over on his side, his ears and paws quivering. Stacy looked in on him and smiled to herself, then ran to tell her mother that Tony was asleep.

They had no way of knowing that at that very moment their cat was listening to his Inner Ear, hearing the voices of thousands of other feline creatures coming to him in a dreamlike roll call. Oblivious to the outside world, he was plugged into an ancient communications system that dated back four thousand years.

The voices rippled through his unconscious in tinny, unceasing waves. At first they nearly overwhelmed him, like being in a cavernous room filled with tens of thousands of talking dolls, each of them programmed to repeat a different phrase, and all speaking at the same time. A primitive fear of being swept away in the rush of voices and not finding his way out lingered in the recesses of his mind, but he put it aside.

Slowly, the waves slackened, and he concentrated on the voices, winnowing out the inconsequential, the parochial. Wind narrowed his focus, and waited for a break, then became one with the onrushing waves. Carefully following the code of Akhen-et-u, he identified himself by both his Mother's name, Son of Nefer-iss-tu, and by his call name, Pferusha-ulis, Windrusher, and shared his tale of separation, his agony at being left behind when his Hyskos emptied the house and went to a place called Florida.

"It happened in the flicker of a whisker, and before I knew it they were gone."

Windrusher's story ended with his spraying of the Trembles' car, and then he was quiet. Fatigue engulfed him and he fell back to accept the inevitable, like a fragile winged insect caught in the viscid tentacles of a spider's web finally realizes the futility of struggle.

After nearly two days of sleeplessness, Wind found it nearly impossible to stay afloat in the roiling sea of Akhen-et-u. He tried to concentrate on the voices in his head, but the internal connection became tenuous and he slowly slipped away, gripped in the arms of heavenly, healing sleep.

"Windrusher."

His name echoed, bouncing off the canyons of his unconscious, drifting down through the murky depths and forcing his dormant mind to make that prehistoric connection once again. He heard his name repeated until a grizzled voice belonging to a cat identifying itself as "Short Shank," broke through the murmuring current.

"Windrusher, your Hyskos have gone to a far place," he growled. "Florida is many long lengths in the direction of warm waters. It would take you nearly twenty night globes to reach it unless you traveled in a Hyskos vehicle."

Shank paused and Wind felt a thumping in his chest. Twenty night globes? He had hunted night creatures before he became a house cat, and understood that the round, glowing globe brightened the night sky only after many visits by Rahhna, the day globe. Twenty night globes must be... Windrusher couldn't comprehend such a period of time, but he didn't believe he was even twenty night globes old. It was an impossible task; no cat had ever made such a journey.

"Of course, no cat has ever made such a journey on foot, and—" Short Shank repeated his unspoken thought before being cut off.

"Except for the Holy Mother, Irissa-u," a female's voice interrupted.

An angry babble followed as Shank and the new voice were joined by hundreds of others arguing every conceivable side of this question.

The first story every cat hears from its mother is Irissa-u's heroic journey from the dark jungles to the civilized world of the Hyskos. Irissa-u and her followers were the first to enter the stone villages of the high-legged beings, and their adventures passed from one generation of cats to the next.

This was a familiar tale. It was told by loving mothers to inspire their kittens, but to his mind it was only a legend, a catnap story for kittens. Short Shank was right: No cat had ever made such a journey.

Windrusher was too exhausted to concentrate on the Inner Ear any longer. The voices whirling in his head were growing unintelligible, and before he was labeled impudent for not responding to his elders, he dutifully thanked Short Shank and the other voices for their advice, then withdrew.

Sleep was delicious, a banquet of aromatic delights placed before a starving creature. Windrusher ate hungrily of the banquet, and plunged into the deepest stages of sleep.

chapter 3

"FOLLOW ME, Pferusha-ulis." Her voice cut through the tangle of brush, into the root-festooned den where he hid. "You have nothing to fear. Have faith, follow me, and I will show you how to live forever."

Wind was dreaming. Or was he? Beguiled by the irresistible voice that beckoned him, he crawled out of his hiding place under the fallen baobab tree and slowly peered out at the source of the voice. A stately queen of burnished gold and black silhouetted against a brilliant indigo sky stood waiting for him. Her glowing copper eyes fixed him with an expression that was bold and arrogant, yet somehow filled with love and forgiveness. The overwhelming presence left him feeling like a tiny kitten dangling helplessly by the nape of his neck as his mother carried him to a new nest.

"Don't be afraid, Windrusher," she said. "You are strong and wise, and ready for a great adventure. Come with me."

Her words seared him like an electric shock. "We will travel many night globes from here. Together we will make history, living forever in the memory of all cats."

She turned away from him and walked into that shining horizon, her sleek, dark tail held high, the burning face of Rahhna, the sun, encasing her in a golden aura. Wind was close behind, prepared to follow her out of the jungles that fed and protected him. He had no choice. This was the Holy Mother herself—Irissa-u.

The light grew more intense and the voice lured him onwards, the words no longer making sense. As the noise bubbled in his brain, he opened his eyes and saw the young female cooing over him, the bright overhead light shining in his eyes. Wind blinked at the light, slowly raised his rump and stretched his front legs out as far as possible, as if bowing down. He yawned extravagantly while his paws kneaded the dresser top.

The girl kept talking to him, and he allowed her to pet him while he thought back on his dream. All cats had heard the legend of Irissa-u. His mother and her mother and all mothers before them had told the story of the Holy Mother's appearance in the jungles. She was dropped from Rahhna, they said, and gathered seven cats around her. Together they embarked on a 2,000-mile trek across jungles and deserts and into the land of the stone-builders. It was an impossibly heroic journey that Wind had always considered only a tale for kittens.

But now, it was more than a fanciful legend. Irissa-u had appeared to him. The story must be true, and if she could make the journey, then what could stop him? That must be his Path.

Wind yawned again. A growling in his stomach reminded him he had eaten little in the past two days. He jumped from the dresser and padded to the kitchen where his food bowl was kept, devouring every morsel, and lapping at the water bowl until it was almost empty. Traveling twenty night globes meant he must build up his reserves. He rubbed his head against the corner of the pantry and wondered if he was about to embark on a holy mission or simply reacting to a bad dream.

Wind spent the next two days eating and sleeping in preparation for his twenty night globe trek before he realized one important thing was keeping him from his journey. Unlike his other family, these Hyskos had yet to let him out of the house. A screened porch was the closest he came to the outdoors, and it was while resting on the cool glass table top that a squirrel presented him with a solution.

The squirrel perched upside down on the trunk of the white oak outside the screen. Chattering brashly, head cocked toward the confined cat, it punctuated each nasal bark with an impertinent flip of its feathery tail.

Without thinking, Wind leaped on the screen frightening the squirrel into a mad dash up the tree, its bushy tail flagging a spasmodic S.O.S. The big cat hung by his claws watching the panicked squirrel with more than a little satisfaction. Then a small opening in the upper right corner caught his eye, a tiny triangle of screen hanging loose from the black gasket. He pulled himself up another two inches and saw the opening enlarge under his weight.

This was his way out.

He briefly considered making his escape right then, but his stomach began grumbling and he withdrew his claws, dropping nimbly to the porch floor. It was almost time for the Warrens to return home, and he might as well enjoy one more night inside before he started. His journey could wait until first light.

Wind jumped on the table, turned around twice until he felt comfortable, and folded his legs under him. Ignoring the scolding clucks of the nervous squirrel safely hidden in the branches of the oak tree, he flicked his ears several times, and laid his head on his crossed paws.

Gerry and Amy stood on the balcony of the King's Bay Resort admiring the sparkling inlet twisting away into the Gulf of Mexico. The Trembles felt a sense of uncontrolled giddiness wafting through the air like a cloud of nitrous oxide. After suffering through thirteen months of hell, this was almost like a gift from above Amy thought.

Amy squeezed her husband tightly. "It's beautiful, isn't it?"

"Yes, and we could have been here long ago if it wasn't for my ego."

"Let's not dwell on that, Gerry. We're here now; you needed to make this decision in your own time. Don't beat yourself up over it."

Amy was right, of course, but he was haunted by the past thirteen months. He turned the pages of his mental calendar, like he had done daily while searching for a new job that never materialized, and thought back to the family conference when they broke the news to the kids.

"Your mother and I made a difficult decision last night, but we think it's for the best."

Tremble gave his wife a kindly glance. "I have a new job, but it isn't going to be here in Bloomfield. And it isn't in Hartford or

Springfield, either."

He let it sink in briefly then plunged on. "You know that grandpa and grandma have that hotel in Florida. Well, they're getting old, grandpa isn't doing too well, and for some time now, they've wanted to retire. They asked us a number of times over the past year to come down and take it over. And each time I said thank you very much, but no thanks."

Gerry, Jr. or GT as he preferred to be called, and Kimmy stared silently; their faces turning slowly from bewilderment to comprehension.

"I thought I had some good reasons— What did I know about running a hotel? Or that going to Florida would uproot us from everything we've known all our lives, but I..."

He paused, running a large hand through his thinning rust colored hair, and swallowed to regain his composure. Tremble looked at his feet and spoke quietly. "If I took over my father's business, it seemed to me I'd be admitting my failure as a father and provider for my family."

Amy spoke up while her husband coughed and wiped his eyes. "Your father tried everything to find a job here, and there isn't anything available. Not just for him, but for hundreds of people who lost their jobs."

She turned to her husband, reached out and rested a hand on his cheek. "It's not your fault, honey, and the kids know that," she said.

"Are we moving to Florida?" Kimmy asked

"Yes, Kimmy, we're moving to Florida. We're going to be the new proprietors of the King's Bay Resort in Crystal River."

That was when they had to tell Kimmy that Tony couldn't come. At first, she couldn't understand why they could take Stella but not Tony.

"Honey, think about it. We'll be driving for four days, and Tony will be cooped up in a carrier all that time," Amy said.

A slow, steady rain beat down on Bloomfield, Connecticut throughout the night. Wind slept deeply and informed the Inner Ear of his plans. Once again, it was Shank who emerged dominant from the whirlpool of voices and congratulated him on his courage.

"It will be a great adventure for you my young journeyer," the grizzled voice cut through the blur of noise. "I do wish you well, although I'm not sure you have the sense Tho-hoth gave a floppy-eared snouter."

Windrusher found himself in agreement with Shank, although a storm of voices urged him on. He quickly tired and excused himself, then was lost in the all-enveloping arms of sleep.

A half-hour later, Wind was still dozing, rolled in a tight ball, his tail twitching to the sound of a branch drumming against the window. The distant rumble of thunder snapped his eyes open, and he bounded across Stacy's bed to the windowsill to look out at a muddy sky lightened only slightly by a reluctant sunrise.

Warren folded the paper and took another sip of coffee. "Looks like rain all day, folks. Are you taking Stacy to Connie's house?"

"Uh-huh," Jeannie said. "Don't forget you're having your teeth cleaned this afternoon. I got the latest appointment they had, but you need to be there by three-thirty."

He shook his head and pursed his lips in mock irritation. "I know, I know."

Warren had what his mother referred to as a low forehead, hair that curled out from just above his eyebrows, giving him the look of a quizzical wolf man. He arched his eyebrows into his hairline and sneaked a look at his daughter. They both laughed.

"Sure, you knew about your last appointment, too, but you didn't make it, did you?"

"Don't worry, I'll be there," he said. "Can't disappoint Dr. Dracula, can I?" He gulped the last of his coffee. "Gotta run. I'll pick Stacy up at Connie's after my appointment and have dinner ready by the time you get home."

He gave his daughter a wink. "Although I'm sure my mouth will be too sore for me to eat anything."

Stacy filled Tony's bowl with hard food and gave him a quick hug. "You're such a good boy, I'll see you this afternoon."

Wind followed closely behind her and watched the girl crack open the door to the screened porch. A cold breeze blew a few drops of rain inside the house before Jeannie rushed over and pushed the door closed.

"Honey, it's too nasty to let him out there. He'll have to stay inside today."

chapter 4

RAIN AND SUN battled enthusiastically through the morning and into the early afternoon, taking turns pelting the Warrens' house. Windrusher awakened from a series of brief naps and stretched his neck with an awesome yawn, then sat back on his haunches and began grooming.

A cat grooming itself can be the equivalent of a human scratching his head, wondering what to do about a situation, and that's what Wind was doing as he licked the side of his left paw over and over, then rubbed it over his ear.

He stopped in mid-lick and noticed the sun streaming through the bedroom windows. As a house cat, Windrusher was protected from the weather and seldom gave it much thought. But now, he realized how uncomfortable he would have been outdoors during the storm. He pondered that a moment then shook his head vigorously.

Old Shank was right when he told me I didn't have the sense Thohoth gave a floppy-eared snouter. A journey of twenty night globes would certainly expose me to all that and more. I can't expect to stay warm and dry once I leave here.

He leaped from the dresser and ran into the living room. The door to the porch was still closed, and he padded from room to room looking for another opening, scratching at windows, and poking a paw under each closed door. Wheeling around, he loped into the kitchen, jumped on the counter and stared out the window onto the porch.

There was no way out unless the female opened the door after she returned. Perhaps the best thing would be to wait until the day globe arose and the Hyskos left him alone on the porch. This didn't make him happy, but he had no plan other than to scratch that nagging itch on his right flank. So he did.

Tom Warren left the dentist's office with sore gums. At one time in his life he had briefly considered becoming a dentist. Remembering that, he scoffed. He couldn't imagine poking around in open mouths all day, looking at the crags and snaggles of teeth, drilling holes and causing fear in kids and grown-ups alike. No, that wasn't for him. He'd rather be a rectal specialist.

Well, maybe not.

After picking up two sacks of groceries, Warren drove to the Lawson's to claim his daughter.

Stacy Warren and Lori Lawson were best of friends, and had been since second grade, a fact that set his already sore teeth on edge. Frank Lawson was a member of the Bloomfield City Council, and an odds-on favorite to knock Mayor Jensen, Warren's boss, out of office next November.

You can't get your kids mixed up in politics, he reminded himself for the hundredth time. He politely greeted the horse-jawed Connie Lawson and swept his daughter up in a bear hug.

On the way home Stacy prattled on about the perfect score she made on her spelling test that day, and how Lori tried to copy from her paper.

Is there any way we can use that in the campaign, he wondered?

Tom parked in his driveway, and pulled the two bags out of the backseat of the BMW. "Did you remember to buy Tony's food, daddy?" Stacy called out as if Warren were on the next block.

"It was the first thing on my list, sweetheart. Bought a bag of those delicious brown pellets that Tony loves to scatter through the kitchen, and we enjoy crushing into the tiles. It's in the trunk, why don't you pull it out?"

He carried the two paper sacks toward the front door, transferred both bags to one arm, inserted the key into the lock, and pushed the door open. Warren turned to look at his daughter struggling to drag the ten-pound bag of Purina One Cat Formula from the trunk.

"It's not too heavy for you, is it Stacy?"

The slick paper sack slipped momentarily from her grasp and the bag almost dropped to the ground before she wrapped her arms around it and hoisted it to her chest.

"No, I've got it," she said from behind the teal-colored bag, never seeing the shadowy form that slipped out the door and was now disappearing around the side of the house.

chapter 5

WINDRUSHER WAS FLUSH with exhilaration as he ran through backyards, scurried under hedges and crossed streets. He was free. The thought filled him with an excitement he had never experienced before.

He was nearly a mile away before he stopped to catch his breath. Overhead, the sky was quickly changing complexion. Wind looked at the open fields on the edge of the High Hills subdivision; six acres of undeveloped land given a reprieve from the bulldozers when the housing market tumbled.

To human ears, the only sounds were those of distant cars blindly charging home. The cat's sensitive ears heard the vehicles, while receiving signals of children playing, an animal chewing diligently, probably a squirrel, the sound of birds alighting in overhead branches, and even insects crawling through the leaves talking their buggy talk.

Wind raised his left rear leg, brought it over his head and began licking the inside of his thigh. He couldn't believe how simple his escape had been. One moment he was lying on Stacy's dresser thinking about the porch screen, the next moment he was running to greet the family at the door. When the door opened and no one came in, he scurried out, unseen, unheard.

A rumbling in his stomach snapped him out of his reveries. He was accustomed to demanding and getting a full food bowl twice a day. On his own, Wind was now responsible for feeding himself and the juices gurgling in his stomach were sending him an urgent reminder that without food, freedom meant very little.

There was food all around him, and, after all, he was the Son of Nefer-iss-tu, taught to hunt and kill by his mother. He knew many Hyskos fed their cats outside, so hunting might not be necessary when he was near the high-legged beings.

The March weather was still unseasonably warm as dusk settled in, and Wind made his way toward a block of homes. Warily, he approached the first house, sniffing carefully for any sign of other animals, food, or danger. A rush of delicious smells overwhelmed him from inside the house, but there was nothing at the front door. He moved on to the next house and heard wild screams and music; the Hyskos were praying to their flickering picture box.

A shifting current of air brought a familiar scent that started his mouth watering. He loped to the front door and found a dish of partially eaten cat food. The scent of a strange cat was all around him, on the dish, and on the food itself.

Wind crouched before the dish, his fur flashing a lighter shade of gray where his hipbones protruded, and greedily gulped great mouthfuls. His head shook with each bite in the unconscious twist of death a cat gives to live prey. Finishing the food quickly, he eased over to a bowl of water and was lapping greedily when the floppy-eared snouter approached from inside the dwelling.

The Basset Hound was only a pup, and it bounded against the screen door with a playful bark. Wind jerked his head from the dish, water dripping from his nose and whiskers. The big cat's eyes opened fully, pupils dilated, ears flattened against his head, and studied the squawking puppy behind the screen. He realized he was in no danger and hissed loudly at the little dog, watched it jump and run away yelping, its long ears flapping.

Windrusher took a moment to lick his mouth clean, the rough, ruddy tongue playing lightly over and around his lips and nose. Then, he left his mark on the bushes by the front door. After all, it was only good manners to inform the cat of the house that she had a visitor while she was gone. Without a glance back, Windrusher walked away, his head and tail up high, looking as if he were on a mission for the Holy Mother herself.

Windrusher paid little attention to the world around him and padded silently and swiftly to the southwest. He gazed at the dark sky noting that the day globe, what the Hyskos called the sun and what cats called Rahhna, had disappeared once again and twinkles of faraway lights poked holes through the night's canopy.

He called upon Nut-atna, the god of the night, to guide his way through the darkness. Nighttime was special for all cats because that was the time to hunt, and he would surely need his hunting skills to help him survive in the days ahead.

The legend of Irissa-u floated through his mind as he walked. His mother had told him the story of the Holy Mother dropping from Rahhna to lead the cat tribe out of the jungle. When she completed her mission, she flew back to live with the other gods.

Could it be true, he wondered, that our gods could live on that burning platter in the sky? He couldn't imagine cats living on the day globe, but it made sense that such a wondrous place should be the home for gods like Tho-hoth, Hwrt-Heru, Nut-atna, and Irissa-u. Perhaps they guided the day and night globes across the sky and made them disappear, playing godly games of hide and seek with one another.

The thought of these heavenly creatures with their unearthly powers filled Windrusher with excitement. Maybe they were looking down at him to see if he was able to complete his mission. Anything was possible, he thought, even that he might join the gods on Rahhna at the end of his journey.

Wind's eyes flashed in the night, his head filled with eerie pictures of life on Rahhna. Running easily along the road, only barely conscious of his surroundings, the big cat never saw the on-coming car until it caught him in its headlights. He froze, confused by the shining lights bearing down on him.

Windrusher heard the hammering of the engine, the whine of the wheels. Fragments of questions flashed through his brain: Should he stay where he was, dash across the road, or run into the woods?

Like a pebble rattling in an empty jar, the questions echoed in his head, but no answer came to his befuddled mind. His legs had turned to stone and his eyes grew wide as he watched the Hyskos vehicle roar by within inches of his rigid body.

Wind stared numbly at the receding lights and commanded his wobbly legs to move. He staggered breathlessly into the tree line, his tail drooping behind him. The cat that a moment before was picturing himself flying to the sun to keep company with the gods now leaned against a tree to keep from shaking.

Windrusher's heartbeat finally slowed to its normal rate and he nervously licked his paws. His journey was nearly over before it even started. Oh yes, I'm going to join the Holy Mother on Rahhna, he told himself scornfully. If I'm not careful, I'll become part of the Hyskos black path and prove that I don't have the sense of a floppy-eared snouter.

The incident with the Hyskos vehicle brought home the lesson that there was more to his travels than finding his way out of a house and stealing another cat's food. Wind resolved to stay off the Hyskos' paths whenever possible, and to never, ever look into the glow of their vehicles' ferocious eyes.

With that firmly entrenched in his brain, he set off into the night.

Preternatural weather continued throughout Connecticut filling the air with ghosts of summers past and whispers of the season to come. It painted the branches with nodules of green, and here and there, pairs of robins searched methodically for food. In the towns and villages surrounding Bloomfield, people energized by the act of shedding coats and sweaters, burst out of their winter gloom and bustled along the streets greeting one another with good humor.

Windrusher saw none of this, but he was the beneficiary of the good weather nonetheless. He traveled comfortably through Hartford County, making good time on the gentle slopes, moving instinctively south by southwest.

On the third day of his journey, Wind scampered over fallen logs deep in a section of forested hills. Acres of pines, hemlock, and spruce trees trapped the rays of the sun, permitting isolated bands of light to slice dreamily through the branches. The excitement of his journey pushed him to travel long distances without rest, but he was learning to gauge the signs in his body and sleep was what he needed. Windrusher inhaled the yeasty aroma of the woods, and lay down in the middle of a shaded clearing carpeted with moss and generations of needles. He waited for Hwrt-Heru, the goddess of sleep, to take him.

The rhythm of his breathing soon matched the waves breaking incessantly over his unconscious, threatening to engulf him, pulling him deeper into the grip of Akhen-et-u. Chirping undulations of the Inner Ear washed over him, and once again the mystical melding of voice and mind overwhelmed him. Wind forced himself to concentrate, found an almost imperceptible breach in the waves and pushed himself into the flow.

His unconscious voice cried out, reciting the ancient petition of entry into the Inner Ear. "I am called Pferusha-ulis, Windrusher, Son of Nefer-iss-tu. My voice, alone, is small and weak, but joined with Akhen-et-u, we become one and unbreakable."

A surge of words came tumbling out as Wind again related his story to the countless felines. "I am following the Path assigned me by the Holy Mother. Assist me, if you will, in my mission. Lend me the wisdom of oneness that only Tho-hoth could provide through his gift of Akhen-et-u."

He completed his entreaty to the Inner Ear and waited for answers.

It didn't take long, and for the first time since he planned his journey, it wasn't Short Shank that responded. Of course, even Shank had to be awake occasionally, he told himself, hoping that nothing had happened to the old cat.

"Windrusher, Son of Nefer-iss-tu, may your journey end as well as it has begun," the intriguing voice of a queen sliced through the babble filling his mind. "You have made us proud. Not since the long-gone days of Irissa-u, has a cat attempted such a journey."

The words tingled in his head, swelling him with pride.

"Thank you for the kind words," Wind replied with as much humility as he could. "I am not yet worthy of them,"

Quickly, he reported on his progress, and asked again for assistance. A new voice broke into the web of sound, speaking timidly at first but gaining confidence.

"You are traveling toward the village of Avon," the young cat managed to burble, making it sound more like a question than a statement of fact. "Be careful, Pferusha-ulis. That is the place where I live, and the Hyskos hunt down and steal all cats that are not part of their households. I know of many who have been carried away, and never returned."

Windrusher thanked him for the advice. He was tiring now, but forced himself to concentrate since more voices wanted to talk to him about his improbable trek to Florida. One voice added a word about the mountainous country he would have to cross. Another jumped in and shared the surprising knowledge that she had located Wind's family in Crystal River. "Your scent is strong still on the Hyskos vehicle," she said.

He couldn't believe that a cat many night globes from here could find his family. This was a cat he had never met, never rubbed noses with, or sniffed its tail, and it was telling him he had located the Hyskos family by the mark he had left on their swift machine. Yet, it gave him hope that his female Hyskos was waiting for him at the end of the journey and would welcome him when he arrived.

He struggled to stay alert and hold his place in the hypnotic circle of the Ear when a harsh voice intruded.

"Wetlos! You are all acting like brainless creatures, believing in things you can't see, and chasing your tails," the grating voice dripped with malice. "We all know that this aptly-named 'Wind-thing' will never complete his mighty mission. He has been lucky so far, but it's only been a few day globes. Believe me; he'll end up as worm meat, if the Hyskos don't destroy him."

chapter 6

HE WAS PICKING his way through tangled underbrush. Suffocating heat penetrated to the floor of the jungle even though a dense canopy of branches blocked most of the sun. An occasional beam of light broke through the trees in chunks of dusty glittering slivers, sliding from branch to branch, leaf to leaf.

Once again, Wind was following Irissa-u. They entered a clearing by a narrow river, and light glinted off the clear green water sending out a halo of fiery sparks that cascaded around the burnished gold of her coat. He was dreaming again. Wasn't he?

This time, though, he wasn't alone with the Holy Mother. Spread out in an uneven arc behind her were six other cats, Wind was the seventh. The seven followers of the Holy Mother.

The legend was passed down from generation to generation, from mother to kitten. The prophet from Rahhna came to earth and chose seven cats to follow her from the jungles to the villages of the Hyskos where they mated and multiplied until they were like the leaves on trees.

Irissa-u and two of the males entered the stone kingdom in the desert where they were taken in and treated as holy ones. Of the remaining followers, a pair was sent to the west and a pair to the east so they might spread their kind to the many tribes of high-legged beings. According to the ancient tale, one of the seven wandered away and was never heard from again. He came to be known as the lost follower. Windrusher's mother said that sometimes, when the night globe glowed its brightest, sharp-eyed cats could see the lost follower looking for the Holy Mother.

It was beginning to drizzle when he entered the town of Avon. Wind had walked for seven continuous hours, and he wanted nothing more than to find a meal and a place to sleep. The sounds of vehicles followed him, and Wind realized a black path, with its treacherous moving boxes, was very near. He broke through the trees, the noise growing even louder, and saw a busy intersection and a long line of stores.

Windrusher sniffed the air, his whiskers measuring the air current, and his tail whisking back and forth nervously as cars passed in front of him. Nose twitching, raindrops running off his coat, he inhaled deeply and decided that food was very near. High-legged beings passed him carrying boxes, and the overpowering scent of food billowing from the containers overwhelmed the hungry cat causing him to whimper and drool.

Wind lowered himself to the sidewalk in clear view of the people going in and out of the fried chicken restaurant. His stomach told him it was suppertime, and he assumed one of these two-legged beings, slow though they were to understand the obvious, would eventually end his hunger.

He sat there for over a half-hour, ignored by more than a dozen people who passed him with barely a look. Windrusher meowed pitifully when a girl, slightly younger than his Kimmy, approached with her mother.

"Mom, mom," the girl yelled excitedly, yanking on her mother's hand. "The poor cat is hungry; can we bring it home and feed it?"

She pulled away from her mother and bent over to pet the hungry cat. Wind reacted as he always did at feeding time and rubbed his head against the girl's leg, purring loudly.

The girl's mother looked dubiously at the dusty animal rubbing against her daughter, and took the little girl's arm.

"No, Treen, I'm sure it belongs to someone near here," she said. "Let's get our chicken, dad is waiting for us."

Wind pulled half-heartedly at a nail on his left paw, watching the mother and child go inside. He debated momentarily the merits of following them, but decided to wait until he found a Hyskos with the sense of a hairless kitten.

Inside, Treen's mother casually mentioned to the manager, a seventeen year-old boy wearing a brown paper hat and a bored expression, that there was a cat outside. He nodded as he fished out her change.

"Yes, ma'am. We get a lot of the neighborhood strays through here. The smell drives them crazy, but animal control comes running when we call."

He handed her the change and tipped his head toward the telephone on the wall. "He won't be around for long," he said.

Wind finally decided to find his own food since he could not depend on these Hyskos to feed him. He walked to the last store and rounded the corner just as a white van pulled to a stop in front of the chicken restaurant. A rotund man in a baggy gray jump suit eased out of the passenger side, and lumbered toward the cat.

Wind heard the heavy footsteps behind him, and turned to see a short, round Hyskos, his hand extended casually, speaking softly in typical human babble-talk.

"Here kitty-kitty. You just sit there for two more seconds and we'll take you for a ride," the animal control worker said in a sugary tone. "That's a nice cat. See, I've got something yummy for you."

He moved closer, his extended hand holding a few fragrant cat treats.

Wind smelled the food in the man's hand and took a step toward him then stopped. He sensed danger on this foolish-looking Hyskos, and turned and ran behind the long row of stores. The animal control worker cursed loudly and ran after him, throwing the cat snacks away.

Wind scampered low to the ground, his tail bushy with fear. A tall concrete block wall brought him to an abrupt stop. It surrounded the entire back of the shopping strip, and there was no way around it. Several trucks were parked in the narrow alleyway, and at the far end, against the concrete wall, was a large, green dumpster. He ducked under a pick-up truck and peered out from between the back tires, searching for an opening in the wall. There weren't any. The only way out was the way he had come in, the same direction that was now cut off from escape by the fat man pursuing him.

The big Hyskos had stopped and was leaning against the building trying to catch his breath. Wind realized he could easily outrun this two-legged being, but as he watched, the man turned and gestured behind him. Almost immediately, the large white van rumbled into the opening between the store and the wall, blocking the exit.

Another Hyskos climbed out of the vehicle. Together, the two men walked down the alley toward the cat. Wind backed slowly from under the truck, never taking his eyes off the two men.

"There he is," yelled the taller one, and they moved quickly toward him.

Windrusher scrambled away.

"You're hurting my feelings, cat," the fat one said, giving his partner a wink. "We just want to bring you home for dinner."

The drizzle had turned to a steady rain, and Windrusher splashed through puddles, the concrete block wall closing in on him. The two men moved forward, holding long-handled nets to their chest like weapons at ready. Wind felt a pulse tapping in his ear and jerked his head skywards as a ragged scratch of lightning etched the sky behind the two Hyskos.

Windrusher backed into the block wall next to the green dumpster. The high-legged beings stopped and stared, murmuring to one another. The fat man stood away from the wall, and Windrusher thought if Irissa-u was with him he could dash by him before the slow Hyskos had time to react.

As if reading his mind, the heavy-set man stepped closer to the wall, cutting off that lane of escape while his partner edged nearer the dumpster. Wind's tail swished nervously, and he hissed defiantly. They moved closer, their nets out in front of them.

Wind was tensed to plunge between the two-legged beings in a last desperate attempt to escape when the high-pitched yowl of another cat froze them all in surprise.

"Up here, b-b-brother."

All three of them looked up to see a small mottled tabby with wide, panicked eyes standing on top of the block wall.

"Don't run. J-j-jump up here and I'll s-s-show you the way out," the cat stammered.

The heavy man pointed at the wall. "Damn, there's another one."

Wind leaped on the dumpster and onto the wall before the men could react. He kept his eyes on the bushy, question mark-shaped tail of the multi-colored tabby scurrying over the wall into a heavily wooded lot.

chapter 7

WINDRUSHER SAT in the hollow of a tree trunk and stared at his unlikely savior. The small cat was shaking with fright, and Wind couldn't believe this pitiful creature actually helped him escape from the Hyskos.

He approached the shivering tabby and sniffed it politely. This was obviously a young cat, perhaps only five night globes old, and a very jittery young cat at that. The kitten wore a longhair coat that resembled the swirl paintings children made at carnivals; oranges and reds flowed wildly into a background of black and gray. He noted the tabby's ears were bent forward in apprehension, and a stream of clear liquid seeped from its left eye.

Windrusher broke the ice by giving his names, and thanking the little cat for his help. "It was beginning to look like my Path had come to an end, my little friend," he said as lightly as possible. "I thank you and the Holy Mother for allowing me to continue my journey. Without your help, who knows where I might be now?"

The small cat remained still, and Windrusher asked him his name. Only silence greeted him. Wind could tell by the distracted look in the young cat's large, chartreuse eyes that his benefactor was having trouble understanding him. Tho-hoth played a cruel joke on this kitten, he thought.

"What name do you go by, what can I call you?"

Again, there was no answer from the kitten. Was it reflecting on the question, or simply deciding whether the older cat was trustworthy?

Finally, he spoke. "Call me Lil' One."

Wind's eyes snapped shut, surprised by a name he hadn't thought about since he was a kitten. He studied the tabby closely to see if he was playing games with him. No, that was beyond his capabilities. Lil' One was serious, and didn't know that he had named himself after a kitten's bedtime rhyme.

Lil' One plays so hard.
Lil' One cries so loud.
Lil' One sleep and grow,
And make your mama proud.

That was what his mother crooned to him after his feeding and before he went to sleep. It was also the last thing he remembered his mother saying before she walked away from him. Could it be the same for this little cat?

Lil' One sniffed the air with a nose that was nearly the same color as the purplish tongue that was now snaking out of his mouth and licking his upper lip. With what seemed to be a major effort, the little cat pulled himself to his feet and took a tentative step toward the cat he had rescued.

Lil' One had not responded to Wind's comments because he was still trying to understand what caused him to get involved with this big cat. He had seldom spoken to other cats, and he found it difficult to shape his thoughts into words. All of his young life had been focused on only one thing—survival. That involved hiding from other creatures, from the high-legged beings, even other cats. Now, he had risked his life to help this strange cat. It didn't make any sense.

The big tomcat suddenly leaned over and began grooming him. He licked the top of his undersized head and the side of his jaw with his great, rough tongue. Lil' One jerked back at first, but quickly closed his eyes in gratitude, and allowed the large dark cat to continue licking.

He couldn't remember an intimate touch by any being. His mother walked away from him when he was only four weeks old, going off to find food in these very same woods, and never returning. Lil' One only remembered living alone, spending every waking moment in fear.

It was a miracle he survived without a mother, but he was fortunate that the first time he ventured out to look for food he found a young squirrel that had fallen out of a tree. That sustained him for several days while he explored his world. His nose quickly led him to the same space behind the Hyskos stores where he found Windrusher. At the time, a wooden fence stood in place of the concrete wall, a fence with several broken boards.

The two-legged beings were careless and lazy, and that proved to be the difference between life and death for the tiny kitten. They often piled garbage in an open container next to the store, instead of depositing it in the enclosed dumpster.

The blotchy longhair ate his fill of chicken on many nights, but the tasty scraps of chicken soon attracted other cats that stayed and refused to leave. The cats quickly grew in number; litter upon litter, competing for the food, fighting among themselves. It forced Lil' One to move deeper into the woods, and find the warm hollow of the half-buried log.

Soon the cats became such a nuisance that the Hyskos changed their careless habits. Food was placed in the covered dumpster, and the dilapidated old fence was torn down and replaced with a tall, sturdy block wall. Most frightening of all, however, were the sudden sweeps by the high-legged beings, picking up cats by the dozen. The unlucky felines were too slow or too trusting and were never seen again.

His wariness and solitude saved him.

A loud, urgent rumbling in his stomach reminded Wind that he still hadn't eaten. He looked at the small cat's den, as if expecting to find a dish of cat food awaiting him. The floor of the log was covered with gnawed chicken bones, brittle and cracked with age, a few bird feathers, scraps of newspaper, and the plastic lid to a juice bottle.

There was no dish of cat food.

"Hungry, find food," he said, unconsciously simplifying his speech as if he were talking to a helpless kitten.

Pale shards of light slipped from behind the clouds, the reflections of the moon casting a ghostly glow over the forest. In the distance, a low rumbling intruded itself on the nocturnal sounds, not so much a threat of thunderstorms as a punctuation mark on the stillness of the night.

The white-footed deer mouse sat up on its hind legs, small round ears erect, seeking signals like a pair of steerable satellite dishes. Its white-tipped snout sniffed the air for danger, dark whiskers sensing the breeze while black beady eyes scanned the shadows nervously. In its paws, the mouse lifted a struggling grasshopper and nibbled delicately on the insect's head until it was still.

The trees formed huge pillars of blackness, splitting the small field of brome grass and weeds that spread before the mouse. Stalks of Queen Anne's Lace and thistle swayed with each puff of wind, and the mouse's head jerked nervously surveying the field for hidden dangers.

Eight yards to the right of the deer mouse, flattened against the ground in the shadow of a large red oak, Windrusher patiently watched. He remained still, silent. Frozen in time, his senses totally focused on the mouse, Wind stalked his dinner in a slow motion, invisible game of hide and seek.

The mouse stopped chewing on the grasshopper's leg and thrust his snout in the air, exposing the soft white neck and underbelly. Thin, dark whiskers flicked left and right as his nose tested the night air. There was no sound, no discernable scent of danger. Yet, something was hanging over the clearing, and the mouse, alarmed, but not knowing why, dropped the grasshopper and began drumming its front feet on the ground excitedly.

A faint crack of leaves panicked the mouse and it turned and dived toward its burrow. But it was too late. In two furious leaps, Wind overtook the mouse, pinning it down with muscular front paws. The terrified deer mouse squealed in the darkness, its eyes wide with fright.

Wind batted at his prey, a low, gurgling growl rising from deep in his throat. Teeth bared, he used his whiskers to guide him to the killing point, then bit hard and deep into the helpless rodent's neck.

chapter **8**

WINDRUSHER GROOMED HIMSELF deliberately, cleaning all traces of blood from his coat. He carefully studied his front paw, holding it up with the digits spread apart like an open hand, then licked between the toes and pads slowly, thoroughly.

Lil' One sat a respectful three feet from the big cat, his eyes following each movement of Wind's head. He had stayed far in the background during the mouse hunt, watching intently as Windrusher patiently stalked the hapless rodent, then striking swiftly to deliver the life-ending bite.

On his own for most of his life, the young cat never had an older role model to show him how to hunt properly. While Lil' One could claim a few kills, they were almost accidental, not the result of any purposeful hunt. His youthful impatience betrayed him each time he ventured into the woods to stalk a meal, and except for stumbling across a baby mouse or bird egg, he usually returned tired and hungry.

The large dark cat was still grooming himself when Lil' One found the nerve to approach the hunter. "You hunt g-g-good," he stammered. "Will you t-t-teach me?"

Windrusher looked at the little cat with bemusement. "All cats are hunters, and when you grow larger, I'm sure you'll make many kills," he said.

He hoped it sounded more sincere to the little one than it did to his own ears. There were some cats that would never be good hunters, and they needed to be cared for by the high-legged beings. Surely, this was one of those cats, although how he had survived all this time by himself was a bit of a mystery to him.

"Stalking and killing takes patience and time. Of course, it helps to have the good fortune of Irissa-u on your side."

He paused for dramatic effect, although Lil' One was hanging on his every word.

"Irissa-u?" asked Lil' One.

Windrusher's right ear fluttered momentarily in an involuntary nervous spasm. This cat was totally ignorant of the Way and Path, and he obviously wasn't receiving help from the voices of Akhen-et-u. There was no doubt he was a Wetlos.

"That is the name of our Holy Mother," he said.

In abbreviated form, Wind told him the story his mother had repeated so many times, as had mothers of cats for thousands of years. "These nursing tales are one thing, but there's not too much about hunting I can teach you that you can't teach yourself," he lied. "Anyway, I must be leaving you soon to continue my journey."

Lil' One's head bobbed as if Wind had swiped him across the ear. "Journey? Where are you going?"

Windrusher hesitated briefly, and then said, "There is something I must do."

Lil' One's huge eyes implored him to continue.

"I'm traveling to a far place to find the Hyskos family I lived with."

He hoped that would satisfy the small cat's curiosity, but Lil' One's large, liquid eyes stared at him in puzzlement. After an uneasy silence, he decided the cat deserved to hear the story, and with a stretch of his large body began the tale of his adventures.

Lil' One sat upright, listening to every word without a motion, except for an occasional shudder of his bushy tail. His large eyes seemed to grow even bigger as he listened.

In reality, very little had happened to Windrusher, and yet, everything was different. He had no intention of sharing each detail, but once he began, he couldn't stop. There was the shadow of Irissa-u beckoning him to follow her through the misty jungles in search of the Hyskos tribes. He felt the droplets penetrating the tree branches, settling on his fur. The smell of rotting foliage under his feet filled his nostrils.

Wind told the little cat about his travels, and when there was no more left to say, he lay quiet, oddly unnerved by the unwavering, reverent stare of the small cat.

"And now, you see, I must move on," Windrusher said gently. "There are many night globes ahead of me before I reach the end of my journey, and find my family."

"B-b-but," Lil' One stammered painfully, then stopped as if the effort of conceiving that one word had worn him out.

"You have been a good friend, Lil' One, and I'm in your debt, but after I rest, I will have to leave."

"L-l-let me g-g-go with you," the small cat blurted out. "I'm young and strong and can help you." Lil' One sounded more determined with each word, and ended by butting his head against the larger cat.

Windrusher resisted the impulse to swat him away. Instead, he stared past the cat with half-closed eyes, his tail swishing impatiently in a negative gesture that even this kitten could understand.

Lil' One's eyes filled with tears. "It's not fair. You knew your mother, you were nursed, loved, taught to hunt, and then lived with a Hyskos family."

Wind noted that Lil' One had stopped stammering.

"Look at me. I've lived alone in these woods all my life, and can't even remember my mother." The young cat's eyes were misty, and his voice quavered slightly. "And when I meet a cat I can learn from, a cat whose life I saved," he said with a penetrating look, "he tells me he's on a great adventure and must leave me behind."

It occurred to Windrusher that perhaps the kitten was not as dimwitted as he thought, but what he wanted was crazy and out of the question. He couldn't undertake such a long, arduous journey dragging this kitten along with him. No, it just wasn't possible. And that's what he told him.

"No, it's not possible. I'm sorry; the journey will be long and dangerous. I've been told this is a hairless idea and the only thing I'll find is an early death." He tried to be as firm as possible, but now it was Lil' One's tail that was twitching irritably.

"Think about it, Lil' One. What I'm doing has never been accomplished, and probably never will. I chose my Path and will accept whatever Tho-hoth in his wisdom has planned for me. If I'm hurt or killed, then it was meant to be, but I can't be responsible for you, too."

Lil' One was standing at his full height, his tail held high and his ears turned toward Windrusher. Looking into his eyes, the smaller cat growled in anger. "You know you won't fail. You told me yourself about the Holy Mother, and how she picked you to make this journey."

His voice was steady and strong, and Wind was impressed despite himself.

"Where did Irissa-u send you? She brought you here. And who was here to save you from the Hyskos? I was!" He said this all in a rush without giving Wind a chance to answer.

"Doesn't this mean we're supposed to help each other complete your mission? Doesn't it?"

Windrusher was amused, but he also saw some truth in the kitten's words. Could that be the reason the two of them had met? Maybe bringing Lil' One along wasn't such a whiskerless idea, after all. The cat had survived on his own practically since he was born. And, as much as he hated to admit it, Lil' One had saved his life.

He looked at the mottled tabby and shook his head. "I'm tired, let me sleep. When I wake up, if you haven't changed your mind about risking your whiskers on such a senseless adventure, then you can come along."

Windrusher sank heavily into an exhausted sleep. It covered him totally, pulling him deep into its healing breast. He resisted the hypnotic tug of the Inner Ear, needing his rest more than communication with the confusing babble of voices.

He awoke hours later momentarily unsure of his whereabouts. Blinking several times to get the sleep out of his eyes, he stretched to his full length, scraping his head against the top of the log in the process. Wind recalled his conversation with Lil' One, and mentally prepared himself for resuming his journey with a traveling companion.

It was past midnight, and no light found its way into the log. Even cats, with their superior night vision, can't see in total darkness, and looking around the cramped, dark den, he sensed, more than he could see, that he was alone.

Windrusher pushed himself through the opening of the log, his pupils instantly constricting in the light of the Gibbous moon glowing above. His nostrils sniffed the air currents, his whiskers alert for any movement. A few branches shifting above in the gentle night breeze caught his attention, his ears strained to hear a sound that might tell him the whereabouts of Lil' One.

Windrusher's tail swished from side to side impatiently. He shouldn't have given in to the kitten, no matter how indebted he might feel. Lil' One had pleaded to be taken along on his search, and now that he was ready to continue his journey, where was the Wetlos? He contemplated leaving him behind, it would serve him right, but he decided to wait a little longer for the young cat to return.

He studied the night globe overhead while he waited, and saw that Irissa-u was playing games again. What had she done with the missing slice of the globe, he wondered, and when would she bring it back again?

There wasn't time to solve the mystery. His reveries were unexpectedly interrupted by a vicious howl ripping the night air. Windrusher's ears were instantly erect, swiveling toward the angry shriek of a floppy-eared snouter coming from the direction of the shopping center. Wind gauged the distance of the snouter's barks and realized he was in no imminent danger, but instead of relaxing, he jumped forward and began running toward the noise. All his instincts told him he should be running in the other direction, away from the mindless fury and slashing teeth that awaited him. The strident growls of the snouter grew louder and now a pitiful whine he'd detected stabbed at his senses, pushing him to run even faster.

For a moment the barking stopped, leaving Wind leaning into the silence, a sudden vacuum sucking him into its void. As his ears strained with anticipation, the silence was shattered by a long anguished scream that impelled him forward.

The scream was just a single word: *Windrusher*.

chapter 9

WINDRUSHER RACED to the shopping center, his head throbbing with the beat of naked emotion. It was almost as if another beast, a ferocious jungle cat that lived eons ago, had taken over his body.

He stopped within sight of the concrete wall—the same one that only yesterday blocked his escape. Lil' One crouched in terror, half-hidden between the wall and a scraggly bush. He was trying desperately to hide from a large, yellow dog. Snarling viciously, the snouter snaked its head into the bush and snapped at the young cat.

Windrusher understood the danger, but realized the small cat was lucky he hadn't tried to outrun the larger animal. Otherwise, the dog would have easily caught him and torn him to pieces. It seemed the snouter, for all its ferocity and screeching, was content to terrorize the young cat rather than harming it. At least, he hoped that was the case.

The dog's ugly head plunged through the bush, closer and closer to Lil' One. Once it tasted blood, there was no doubt it would go for the kill. Windrusher had no choice but to show himself.

He cautiously crept along the wall behind the snouter until he was just yards away. The awful snouter odor was overwhelming, now, and he was close enough to see the hairs standing erect on the back of the dog's neck and feel the breeze from its whipsawing tail.

There was no more time. Wind instinctively transformed himself into his most threatening posture; his back arched up sharply, he stood tall on rigid legs, his fur stood out stiffly making him look several times larger than he actually was. Standing broadside to the dog, Windrusher hissed horribly.

The snake-like hissing grabbed the snouter's attention and it wheeled around to face the intruder. For a moment, the dog seemed confused. It looked at the small cat crouching on the ground, then at the bristling, hissing cat in front of him.

Lil' One was amazed to see the hissing apparition standing up to the snouter, and taking heart from his friend's appearance, he jumped to his feet and copied Wind's threatening display as best he could.

The snouter ignored the smaller cat, still strategically placed behind the bush, and growled menacingly at Windrusher. It took a step toward him, the growling deeper, more intimidating.

Wind stood his ground. His hissing grew louder, then as the dog stepped forward the hissing turned into a low, rumbling growl. The snouter stopped, cautious and uncertain. For what seemed like an eternity, the two of them remained frozen in their most intimidating postures, glaring icily, growling noises filling the night air.

Saliva dripped from the snouter's long teeth, and it pushed its head menacingly toward the cat. Living up to his call name, Windrusher moved like the wind. With a loud hiss, he whipped razor-sharp claws across the snouter's sensitive nose.

The dog wrenched back in pain and surprise, the growling giving way to a wounded whimper. It wiped a large paw across its bleeding snout, whined softly, and dropped its tail. Wind sensed the snouter's insecurity and flicked another paw at the snouter's tender nose. The dog stepped back, barked stridently in Windrusher's face, turned abruptly, and ran away leaving the two cats alone.

In the safety of the hollow oak, Lil' One rubbed his head against Wind's shoulder. He explained how he had awakened from his nap hungry and gone to the Hyskos' place to find food. The only thing he found was the vicious floppy-eared snouter who appeared so suddenly he was unable to run.

"But I was getting ready to show him even small cats can draw blood when you showed up," Lil' One said.

The long, white hairs above Windrusher's eyes twitched as he remembered the helpless kitten crouching behind the bush. He understood they were fortunate the snouter wasn't smart enough to know its own strength.

"Yes, there probably would have been blood drawn if I hadn't shown up when I did," Windrusher said. "Just remember you can't back down or run from a snouter. Your only chance is to show no fear and make it painfully clear that you will fight."

"I guess you showed him. That snouter didn't know what he was tangling with when he cornered me."

The small cat's voice broke slightly, and he continued in a husky whisper. "It didn't know that I had a friend like you, Windrusher. This time, you saved my life."

"Nonsense, that snouter would have tired of its game sooner or later. If anything, we're even."

Lil' One butted the taller cat lightly in the side, pushing him toward the opening of the den. "We've proven we can work together, and there's no doubt we have the luck of Irri..." he floundered momentarily looking to Windrusher for help.

"Irissa-u," Wind said.

"Yes, the luck of Irissa-u is on our side. Now, let's go find your family."

chapter 10

AMY TREMBLE THOUGHT her daughter would be broken-hearted after she heard the news, but now, nearly two weeks after Tony's disappearance, Kimmy didn't seem at all concerned.

None of the Warrens could offer an explanation. They left the cat in the house when they went off to work that morning, and when they arrived home in the afternoon it was missing.

"It couldn't have broken through the screen on the porch," Jeannie explained. "It was raining that morning and we didn't let him on the porch." She said they placed a reward notice in the neighborhood paper, and promised to call as soon as Tony was found.

But no call came from the Warrens, and Kimmy, after a brief emotional outburst in which she cried dramatically for a few minutes, was strangely unresponsive whenever the cat's name was mentioned.

Saturday morning after breakfast, Amy suggested that Kimmy call her cousin to see if there was any news about Tony.

"What's the use? They said they would call us if they found him," she said.

"Yes, but—"

"Tony is fine. He probably found himself another home. And even if he didn't, he was an outdoor cat before we got him. You know he can take care of himself."

Amy was beginning to wonder if Kimmy was actually happy the cat was no longer with her cousin.

"You don't seem to mind that Tony is missing," she said.

Kimmy's eyes drifted from her mother's face, as if she had lost interest in the conversation, then back again. "It's not that I don't care..." she paused and looked down at the book she had been reading. "See, when I first heard he was gone, I prayed every night that they would find him. I even prayed to Tony to return to Stacy. Now…" She shrugged her small shoulders. "Now, I don't think they'll ever see Tony again."

She bit her lip and looked at her mother with shiny eyes. "But that's not bad, really. I think of it as Tony going off on another adventure."

More than once in the past three weeks, Windrusher found himself agreeing with the unknown voice from the Inner Ear that said he didn't have the sense of a floppy-eared snouter. He understood the journey would be taxing, but he wasn't prepared for the tediously slow progress they were making, and the hardships they encountered.

Although he didn't realize it, Wind and Lil' One were making good progress for the conditions they faced. The terrain beyond Avon was difficult for anyone to cross swiftly, much less small animals. Miles of rolling hills filled with thick forests of white pine, oak, and maple trees were cross-hatched with rivers and streams. In between were acres of stony pastureland and fields of vegetables.

Wind's internal beacon directed him on a path that moved them roughly to the southwest, skirting the larger urban areas of New Britain and Waterbury. Their good fortune continued when they found a narrow rock-covered spit of land to ford the Naugatuck River.

The climbing and lack of sleep left Wind fatigued and sore, but at least he didn't have to worry about Lil' One. The little cat seemed to have boundless energy, and as they traveled, he had changed from a timid, frightened kitten to an impetuous creature that bounced from rock to rock. His fearless curiosity helped keep Windrusher moving forward.

Over the course of their travels, Wind shared stories and lessons learned from his mother and from Akhen-et-u. It was time, he decided, to tell him about the Way and the Path.

"Irissa-u's mission was a complete success. The cat had spread from the dark jungles to every village of the Hyskos. Food was plentiful, and the high-legged beings were easily trained to feed us. But before she returned to her home on Rahhna, the day globe, Irissa-u had one more thing to do."

"I know," Lil' One yelled, jumping on Wind's tail with

excitement. "She had to teach us to hunt."

Windrusher carefully removed his tail from under the rambunctious kitten. "That's a good guess, but cats were already the best hunters in the jungle. No, Irissa-u decided that cats must live forever."

Lil' One's large eyes grew even wider. He couldn't have been more dumbfounded if he had just seen Windrusher's ears suddenly fall to the ground and run off on tiny little feet.

"It's not what you're thinking, Lil' One. You and I won't live forever, not exactly, but if we follow the Path we will find the Way."

Lil' One stared at his friend as though the big cat was not quite right above the whiskers.

"I know it's not easy to understand, and I'm not sure I really understand it," Wind said, "but my mother told it to me, and her mother to her, and hers before that. Here's what she told me: Irissa-u was pleased with what she had accomplished down here, but she was afraid that when she returned to her home on Rahhna, cats would forget her and how her love had helped unite them and make them strong.

"Irissa-u was also afraid that without her guidance, the day would come when cats might become fearful and return to the wild jungle ways they had before she came to save them."

Wind paused and bit at a sudden itch on his leg.

"Now, this is the part that may be hard for you to believe, but cats for thousands of years have passed the story on to their litters, so it must be true. Returning to her home on the day globe, Irissa-u gathered her fellow gods: Tho-hoth, the great god of wisdom; Hwrt-Heru, the goddess of sleep; Rahhnut, the keeper of the day globe; and Nut-Atna, the god of night, and told them of her worries.

"After much thought, the five gods provided us with certain rules that would lead to a new life after death. These were known as the Seven Laws."

The itch moved to his shoulder and he scratched it violently.

Lil' One butted his head against Windrusher. "Go on, don't stop," he whined.

"I won't burden you with all seven laws, because they simply mean that if cats follow the Path they can be reborn as a better cat after they die."

"What's a better cat?" asked Lil' One.

"I'm not sure. Perhaps they might be reborn as the lap cat of a loving Hyskos with many rooms, all of them filled with food and pillows for us to sleep on. Or maybe a very wise cat that will help others—"

"Or maybe a cat that gets sent on a great adventure," Lil' One jumped in excitedly.

"Yes, maybe. But it works the other way, too. If the cat is a Setlos, a very bad cat, then that cat will suffer when it returns, if it returns at all. It might be made weak and lame, or it might not be part of the Inner..."

Wind stopped abruptly and began licking Lil' One's head tenderly. Moments later, he continued his story.

"The Setlos might even return as a floppy-eared snouter. But if a cat follows the Path through all of its lives, it may be brought up to the kingdom of Rahhna to live with the gods. That is the Way."

Lil' One's ears twitched and he stared at the day globe, Rahhna. The shining rays stung his eyes and he quickly closed his lids. He inhaled deeply, as if trying to swallow the meaning of the story he just heard, and turned to his friend. "How can I follow the Path?"

Wind shook his head and stretched his muscles, the soreness still nagging at him.

"That is easy. And it is very hard. First, we must know about the Way and believe in it. Then we must avoid hurting other cats and acting in a Setlos manner. If we do this, my mother, Nefer-iss-tu, who could trace her line to the royal family, told me we would find the Way."

He had come to the end of his story and stopped again to pursue the flea biting his shoulder.

Late that night the two travelers climbed a wooded hill, shuddering slightly from a chilly wind that had blown up over the past hour. A smothering carpet of gloomy clouds obliterated the moon and they heard the ominous sound of thunder rumbling behind them.

The hillside was thick with trees, and covered with a lush growth of mountain laurel, but it was unlikely the two cats could appreciate the plant life as they labored to climb the hill. Windrusher led the way, careful not to dislodge any of the loose rocks and send them rolling back on Lil' One.

Near the top of the hill, a blinding flash of lightning ripped open the murky sky. Both cats jumped, their hair standing out, ears pressed down. Seconds later a booming blast of thunder deafened them and Lil' One pressed his head against Windrusher's side. They huddled together while the wind whipped the trees with a savage howl and long chains of lightning cracked overhead.

"We can't sit here like whimpering kittens," Windrusher said. "Let's get to the other side and find shelter."

Ghostly silhouettes sprang up around them with each eruption of lightning and a cold rain quickly soaked through their fur. They struggled to keep from falling, shivering under the bitter, storm-lashed rain, encouraging one another until, finally, standing at the crest of the hill, the two sodden cats had undergone a curious metamorphosis. Instead of shaking with fright, as they had at the start of the storm, Windrusher and Lil' One were stimulated and energized.

"Thanks be to Irissa-u for lighting our way," Wind screamed through the deafening din of the storm.

Windrusher stared through the gloom and saw a series of long, interconnected lakes illuminated by the flashes of lightning. If he were closer, he would have seen the small whitecaps on Candlewood Lake whipped up by the wind cutting across its broad face.

"Are you ready to go on, or do you want to rest?"

Huge raindrops pelted Lil' One's head. "You're the one that needs rest, old one. Going downhill will be a swish of the tail after our climb."

Windrusher nodded, noting the thick trees and boulders in their path. "Then let's go. The last one to the bottom is a floppy-eared snouter."

The ground fell away beneath their feet and they scrambled and rolled down the hill. Overhead, lightning stabbed fiery gashes across the sky, and the wind at their backs propelled them faster than their eight feet could move, bouncing them off trees and rocks.

Strangely exhilarated, Wind had an eerie feeling that this had all happened before. The scene unfolded in his head even as he was experiencing it: the lightning flashing above, the trees bent nearly double by the furious wind, and Lil' One scrambling behind him. Then he remembered the dream in which his name appeared to him that night long ago when he was still his mother's kitten: "Windrusher!"

He tumbled nearly out of control to the bottom of the hill, and skidded to a stop at the edge of a sheer embankment that dropped straight down to Candlewood Lake. The lakefront, bordered by a rocky beach, snaked into the night and Wind thanked Irissa-u for his good fortune in stopping before he plunged into the frigid water. He shook himself, trying to regain control of his body. The excitement of the wild slide down the hill had set his tail to quivering, and he was still flush with the knowledge he had just lived through his dream.

Lil' One would never believe that this was where he found his call name. He turned to look for his little friend, and saw him skid out of control, smash against a large rock with a sickening thud, and roll over the embankment.

chapter 11

WINDRUSHER WATCHED HELPLESSLY as Lil' One tumbled tail over whiskers into the dark waters of Candlewood Lake. He stared through the driving rain, scanning the water below for his friend. Finally, the sputtering kitten emerged next to an outcropping of stone, limbs flailing in a desperate attempt to stay afloat.

Wind crouched on the bank, neck extended, paws gripping the edge.

"Lil' One, are you all right?"

The small tabby coughed up a mouthful of brackish water, scratched furiously at the rocks, then slipped beneath the waves.

"Lil' One," Wind shrieked, and leaped into the icy lake below.

Windrusher paddled madly in the frigid water, making a complete circuit around the rock. He screamed his friend's name but only heard the howling of the wind in return.

The storm-whipped whitecaps slapped over his head and Windrusher was thrust under the water, banging his head against the rocks. He popped up sputtering, gasping for breath, water filling his nose and eyes. Wind looked toward the shoreline and considered swimming for safety when Lil' One's stricken body broke the surface. He plunged through the water to Lil' One's side, bit down on the scruff of the small cat's neck and swam strongly toward land.

It took all of his waning strength to pull the waterlogged kitten through the storm-racked waters of Candlewood Lake, across the rock-strewn shore and deposit him on a sandy stretch of beach. Wind lay there panting, struggling for air, his chest heaving. When he caught his breath, he turned to the sodden body of his little friend and methodically began grooming him, licking Lil' One from neck to jowl. He gently wiped water from his eyes and ears, fluffing and tugging the fur on his neck and under his jaw.

Lil' One waited until his friend had completely groomed his body before he opened his eyes and stood up on wobbly legs.

"I know that Irissa-u has great adventures planned for us, but I pray that this is one we don't have to repeat," the little cat said in a husky voice. "You saved my life once again. Thank you."

"Irissa-u was watching over us, Lil' One, there's no doubt. But she also wants us to care for ourselves, so if you can walk a little more, we must find shelter until this storm passes."

Together, the pair moved off into the wet night. Windrusher's thoughts of the thrill of the slide down the hill and the excitement of his naming dream were shunted aside, buried under his concern for his friend.

Two hundred yards along the beach, the two travelers found an overturned rowboat propped up on a rock. They burrowed under it, and with the wind whipping around them and the rain beating a tattoo on the boat, they fell into an exhausted sleep. Wind curled around the body of the smaller tabby, his large paws crossed over his friend's back.

If Wind thought their adventure at Candlewood Lake was a low point, and that daybreak would bring a brighter promise for them, he was to be bitterly disappointed. After a fitful night in which he was awakened four times by Lil' One's whimpering and shaking, Wind stuck his head out from under the boat to see a forlorn sky. Rain still fell heavily and the temperature had dropped twenty degrees during the night.

It seemed obvious to Windrusher that Lil' One needed more rest, but they also needed food. "Why don't we stay here and regain our strength for another day? You can rest and I'll go hunting in the woods."

"If you're going hunting then I'm going with you," Lil' One wheezed, and tried to push his way past Wind. "I'm just as rested as you are."

The two bedraggled creatures struggled against the wind and rain, their heads tucked in, tails drooping to the ground. Lost in their own feline thoughts, they had no way of knowing they had left Connecticut behind and were now in the state of New York.

Lil' One struggled to keep up with his older friend. In the bitter cold, he suffered with bouts of uncontrollable shaking and alternating waves of burning fever. He plodded behind Windrusher, falling further behind until he stopped and collapsed on his belly. Wind leaned over the small cat and heard him muttering quietly.

"Yes, Holy Mother," Lil' One said. "I am following the Path."

Windrusher prodded him with a paw. "You need some rest, my friend."

Lil' One tried to answer, but his voice was a mere rattle. His slight frame shook feverishly, and a white, gummy fluid flowed from both his eyes.

Windrusher helped him to a nearby tree and lay across his sick friend to keep him warm. He was alarmed to feel how high the kitten's body temperature had risen.

When his friend awoke, Wind said, "We should find a place to rest for a few days, Lil' One. You need to build up your strength. Surely, there is a Hyskos village nearby where food and care are available."

The two weary travelers cautiously entered the small town several hours after sundown. The streets of the city seemed abandoned, and Wind, half pushing half pulling his small friend, quickly spotted an open plaza neatly ringed with trees and bushes. In the center was an old-fashioned band shell, with a small, pond nearby.

Wind left Lil' One under a hedge and scurried over to the band shell. Quickly, he ruled out the exposed stage area noting the rain splashing on the open floor. He pushed through a thick hedge that enveloped the base of the shell and examined the wooden latticework surrounding the crawlspace. Excitedly he ran around until he found what he had hoped for, a break in the wooden slats leading into the darkness below the band shell.

Wind returned and led Lil' One through the break into the warmth of the crawlspace. The stricken cat collapsed in a wet, rumpled heap and settled immediately into a raspy sleep.

Windrusher stood an anxious watch over his friend while listening to the spatter of the raindrops on the roof. He was so concerned with Lil' One's health he didn't hear the low hiss snaking across the black space. As it grew louder, Wind looked up in confusion, his ears rotating toward the noise.

There was no mistaking the vicious guttural snarl tearing through the darkness. Wind whirled around to see a pair of yellow eyes, hot as embers in the dark, searing the night from across the crawlspace.

"Get out," a voice ripe with latent violence rasped. "Get out!"

chapter 12

WINDRUSHER'S FUR BRISTLED and his ears flattened against his head. He stared into those burning yellow eyes and felt his throat constrict.

"We're not here to harm you," he croaked. "My friend is very sick and needs shelter. By the grace of Irissa-u, I ask your help."

The cat had moved close enough for Wind to see its vague outline crouching in the attack position.

"This is my den," the rough voice said. "There is no room for you here. Take your sick friend and go before I make you whimper like a kitten."

Wind thought of what he had experienced just to get to this place; the terrible hardships of their journey, the encounter with the dangerous Hyskos. But most of all, he thought of Lil' One.

"No, I'm not leaving until this storm passes and Lil' One is better, even if it means I must fight you."

The strange cat stopped hissing, and rose to a standing position. The lights of a passing vehicle swept through the crawlspace and Windrusher got a quick glimpse of a mid-size cat with bushy white hair. For what seemed like a very long time, the two felines stared at each other with only an occasional hiss passing between them. Finally, the stalemate was broken.

"I don't have anything to worry about if you fight as well as you care for your friends," the yellow-eyed cat spit out.

Wind felt some of the tension slip away, and concluded from the timbre of its voice that this was a much older cat.

"You can stay until the storm passes," the older cat grunted. "Then you have to find your own den. I have lived alone in this place for six night globes, and I don't need the company of a hairless buttworm like you. Since you're no help to your sick friend, let me see what's wrong with him."

The bushy cat pushed brusquely past Wind and sniffed cautiously at the damp bundle of fur. With a sudden screech, it jumped back as if it had pressed up against a hot coal.

"By the head of Tho-hoth, your friend is very sick, and if we're not careful, we'll soon join him. Claw you for bringing this misery into my den."

The cat retreated several steps into the darkness.

"What else could I do? He's so sick and needs help. You must know what can be done to make him well again."

The long-haired cat glared at Wind, its pale tail flicking back and forth as if keeping time to some internal melody. It turned toward the sleeping kitten, listening to the rhythm of his wheezy breathing before facing Windrusher.

"He must stay dry. At least you had sense enough to get out of the storm, and—"

A tiny sneeze erupted from the kitten, interrupting the older cat.

"Once he's dry and warm we'll need to build his strength with food and drink. Has he eaten in the past two days?"

"No. I tried, but he kept saying he wasn't hungry."

"His sickness knows no hunger, just pain and fever. We must make him take food or he will leave the Path forever. The sooner he is well, the sooner you will move your whisker-less bodies out of here. You stay here and warm him while I find some food, but keep your face out of his, unless you want to suffer the same sickness."

Without another word, the long-haired cat darted toward the opening and into the town square.

Wind lay his exhausted body across his friends, careful not to put his face anywhere near Lil' One's head. The strange old cat left him perplexed. He wondered if he should trust a cat that went out of its way to be so abusive and disagreeable, yet was willing to help two bedraggled wanderers who had invaded its den.

A tiny ember of hope registered as he felt the fragile pulse of life still flowing through Lil' One, like the flutter of a moth's wings against a window screen. As if all of his worries had finally caught up with him, Wind realized how exhausted he was. The two of them had traveled for ten hours since their crazed rush down the mountainside, and every one of those grueling hours suddenly caught up with him.

He tried to recapture the exhilaration of that headlong race against the elements, but the picture quickly faded, first into jagged points of light on the back of his eyes, then into mind-numbing darkness.

Wind moved quickly into deep sleep where a haunting dream of a dog attack battered at his subconscious. Two vicious dogs were chasing him, he could smell the stink of their breath, hear the awful howling ringing in his ears, and see the glint of teeth nearing his flanks. His body twitched convulsively and he ran in a blind panic trying desperately to escape.

"Buttworm, wake up."

The surly voice sliced through his dreams and his head snapped forward in response to a not-so-playful cuff across the back of his head. Windrusher had no idea how long he had been sleeping, or when the bitter old cat had returned, but now he was instantly awake.

"You were whimpering like a lost kitten," the old cat said with a snort. "I would have let you sleep until you found your mommy, but we need to feed your friend if we're going to save him."

The cat pulled at a crumbled white paper bag, shaking it until its contents fell out. An overwhelming smell of cooked meat arose from the litter on the floor of the den.

"How will we make him eat this?" Wind asked. "I don't think we can wake him."

"If he won't eat, then we'll force him to swallow. Grab him by the neck and stand him up. I'll do the rest."

Windrusher took Lil' One by the scruff of the neck and easily lifted him. He shook the unconscious cat, trying to rouse him, but the tabby hung limply from his jaws. The older cat snorted and bent its head down into the discards and began chewing on the hamburger. Wind was so shocked he dropped Lil' One. He leaped at the bushy cat and butted it with his head, trying to move it from the remains of the burger.

"What are you doing? Lil' One needs that food."

The old cat moved back, but kept chewing. Then it walked over to Lil' One and forced a paw into the small cat's mouth, holding it open. Windrusher watched in astonishment as the old cat bent down and spit the food into Lil' One's open mouth, then removed its paw, pushing the sick cat's mouth closed.

Lil' One coughed and gagged, but the old cat kept pushing on the bottom of his mouth until the sick tabby was forced to swallow.

"Don't just stand there looking foolish," the older cat said. "Lift your friend; it will be easier for him to swallow."

After Wind mutely did as he was instructed, the cat repeated the feeding procedure again.

"That's enough for now; we don't want him to spit it all up. After he sleeps for awhile, we'll feed him again then try to make him drink."

Dim rays from the dirty gray sky penetrated the darkness of the crawlspace, and Wind finally saw the cat whose den they had invaded. The shabby, white longhair was napping just a few feet from them, its bushy tail curled around its body.

Wind silently arose and walked over to the sleeping cat. He peered down to examine it more closely, and saw a long-nosed white and black face set in a perpetual frown. The cat was obviously past mid-life, its long white coat was dotted with dirt, and tangles of hair stood out around its neck, giving it an almost clown-like appearance.

Wind thought about the extraordinary actions this strange cat had taken to save Lil' One, and decided that its bitter, mocking attitude was a charade. He also recognized one other thing: this gruff, old cat was a female.

Instinctively, he bent down and began licking the older cat's head. She awoke with a start, and retreated from Windrusher's touch.

"I want to thank you for what you did last night. We were strangers and rudely invaded your den, yet you have tried to save my friend. I am in your debt, mother."

"I am no one's mother, certainly not yours," the cat replied quietly, with just a trace of the bitterness that had infused her speech the night before. "Anyway, no cat deserves to die that way, especially not one so young. And don't get too smug, even though we fed him, your friend still is not out of danger."

"I can tell he is better, though. But forgive me. In the confusion of last night, I forgot the manners my mother taught me. My name is Pferusha-ulis, Windrusher, son of Nefer-iss-tu, and I am grateful for your help."

She looked at Windrusher curiously for a moment before replying.

"My mother was Ana-luru-ru, and I am called Scowl Down," she said. She allowed Wind to sniff her and rub his nose across hers.

Hours later, Scowl Down padded across the crawlspace and sniffed at the sleeping body of Lil' One. "He is still very hot, it is important for him to drink to help chase away the fever that burns at his body. Perhaps we can move him outside to the pond."

Together, they hauled the little cat outside and across the open plaza to the concrete pond. They eased Lil' One over the side until his face was touching the water. The tabby spluttered briefly then lay quiet, his face totally underwater. Scowl Down pulled his head up to let him breathe then lowered him again.

"Drink," Windrusher urged his little friend. "Please, you must drink."

After the third try, Lil' One's eyes opened. Water dripped from his whiskers and he painfully raised his head. The weakened kitten gave a pitiful whimper of recognition, then let his head fall forward, and took a few tentative licks at the water.

Lil' One drank until his tongue refused to move, and they helped him back to the safety of the band shell's crawlspace. The kitten was still hot with fever, but he slept peacefully with Wind lying across his little body.

The young tabby's fever broke after three days. He was still very weak, and the pair of travelers were forced to impose on Scowl Down's hospitality while Lil' One regained his strength.

Wind awoke from a nap one afternoon and automatically looked for his little friend. In the few dusty rays of light that found their way under the band shell he observed Scowl Down crouched over Lil' One. She was grooming him with long, slow licks over his neck and head. With a start, she realized that Windrusher was awake, and quickly stepped back.

"I was just trying to clean your friend so he wouldn't dirty my den," she croaked.

"And I know he appreciates it."

Lil' One grew stronger and more talkative every day. Before long, Scowl Down had heard every detail of their short trek through Connecticut and into New York.

The bushy cat sat quietly, her black and white face set into an impassive frown as she listened to the stories that bubbled forth from the youngster. As much as he tried, Wind couldn't get his friend to stop talking about what Lil' One called *the great mission of Irissa-u.*

Windrusher understood if Scowl Down scoffed at the tales, since Lil' One had a habit of embellishing them until even he had a hard time recognizing what actually happened. The old cat simply listened most of the time, occasionally asking a question, but more often giving a snort that Wind found annoying.

On the eighth day of Lil' One's recuperation, the day Wind decided they would continue their journey, Scowl Down finally spoke about their trip.

"I suppose you'll be leaving soon," the female stated matter-of-factly.

"Yes. Lil' One is strong now, and it's time for us to resume our *great mission,*" Windrusher said wryly, casting a glance toward his young friend. "And besides, we have imposed on your good will for too long."

The older cat stared into the darkness, her whiskers twitched as if plucked by an invisible finger. She turned and peered at Lil' One, then breathed so deeply Wind saw her sides rise and fall.

"This journey of yours sounds like the tales mothers tell their kittens to lull them to sleep. It's a fool's adventure, Pferusha-ulis."

Windrusher listened politely to the old female, his head tilted slightly in her direction.

"You must realize the dangers of trying to travel so far. Already, before you've hardly begun, this snouter-brained scheme of yours has almost cost Lil' One his life."

Lil' One jumped up to protest, but Windrusher quieted him quickly, gently pushing him aside.

"Shhh, Lil' One. Scowl Down saved your life. She is older and wiser, and she deserves to be heard."

Lil' One's ears fluttered violently, but he obediently sat down.

"You're a cat of age and experience, Windrusher, and except for this foolishness, there is no trace of the Wetlos to you. In fact, I'd say you've been given ample gifts from Tho-hoth."

Scowl Down was speaking slowly, picking her words with care.

"If you decide to continue this child's adventure, it will only lead to tragedy. That's a decision you have made knowing the consequences, because, as I said, you are of age and experience."

Windrusher's tail lashed the dirt as he listened to the old female who had housed them and brought Lil' One back from the edge of death.

Scowl Down continued. "But is it fair to take this kitten with you? He is caught up in the fantasy of this *great mission of Irissa-u*, and doesn't realize the dangers."

She gazed lovingly at Lil' One, then turned and boldly looked Windrusher in the eye.

"Leave Lil' One with me, Windrusher. You may have a chance of completing this journey, although I doubt it, but surely you know that this kitten will not."

"No, I want—" Lil' One began, but Windrusher cut him off.

"You make much sense, as usual, Scowl Down. And, in fact, I used these same arguments with Lil' One when he first said he wanted to join me. I know the dangers, and agree that it seems to be the brainless scheme of a floppy-eared snouter…" He paused to see his little friend shaking almost as if he was in the grips of fever once again.

"No doubt that Lil' One would be safer with you," he continued, "but that is a choice only he can make."

There was no stopping Lil' One this time. His large eyes flashed with anger and hurt.

"How can you talk about me like I'm a nursing kitten?" he spit out. "I've been caring for myself and making my own decisions since I can remember, and it is my decision to go with Windrusher."

Lil' One stood between the two adults, arching his back defiantly, then turned toward the female.

"Wind tells me I owe you my life, and for that I am forever grateful. But nothing you say can keep me from going with my friend."

Lil' One hung his head, much of the anger draining from him.

Silently, he lay in the dark shadows, focusing all his attention on a paw that suddenly seemed to be in serious need of grooming.

The two older cats stood looking at the tabby. Scowl Down made a gurgling sound deep in her throat, and tilted her head toward the pouting kitten. "The little one certainly knows his mind," she said.

Scowl Down stood quietly for a long time, then spoke again. "I suppose it wasn't proper for me to give advice without being asked, but you must admit that you're an unlikely team on an improbable mission."

Windrusher snorted his agreement.

"There's no way I can stay in this den now that you two have made it unlivable, and it's been many night globes since I've been outside this Hyskos place..."

Lil' One jumped up and ran to Scowl Down, rubbing against the older cat's hip, almost knocking her off balance.

Windrusher was taken completely by surprise. "Are you saying that you want to come with us?"

"I don't see how you're going to make it on your own," she said. "Someone has to care for you whiskerless buttworms."

chapter 13

IN THE EARLY MORNING DARKNESS, three cats slipped from beneath the band shell and left the town park behind.

Windrusher was exhilarated to be resuming his journey even though he was filled with doubts about allowing the old female to accompany them. Out of deference for her age, he let Scowl Down lead the way, and she set a swift pace in a mostly westerly direction. They walked single file along the road leading out of town; Scowl Down in front, Wind close behind, and Lil' One impatiently at his heels.

As the sun rose to light their way, the three travelers left the road behind for broad fields of brown grass. Mountains beckoned to them from the distance, but for days, they rambled through valleys of apple orchards and hilly pastureland.

After leading the way for the first few days, Scowl Down now lagged behind. Lil' One kept the long hair company and urged her over the steeper grades. In turn, Scowl Down would encourage the small cat when they encountered the many creeks and small rivers that cut through the Hudson River Valley.

Lil' One's memory of his near drowning at Candlewood Lake was frighteningly vivid, and it came crashing back each time they had to swim a stream. The three travelers stopped to rest after crossing a small river, and Scowl Down carefully groomed the squirming kitten.

"Stay still," Scowl Down said, holding the struggling tabby with one paw. "Do you want to get sick again?"

The old female turned to Windrusher. "We should stay here and find some food. After we eat and sleep we can move on."

"This is our third stop, Scowl, let's keep walking while it is cool, then we can rest."

"Can't you see how shaken the little one is," Scowl Down rasped. "We're stopping here, you go on if you wish."

Wind's eyes slid over the old female. She had lost more weight during their travels and folds of loose skin hung from her belly, swaying when she walked like the udders on a cow. He closed his eyes, suddenly overcome with a feeling of impending disaster.

Weeks later, the ragged trio, limping on bloody paws, emerged from the woods south of Beacon, New York and confronted Highway 9. Like a school crossing guard, Windrusher carefully surveyed the highway then tilted his head indicating it was safe to cross.

The night was still, and no one observed the three furtive creatures scurrying across the road. Skin sagged on their rangy bodies, they skulked low, their tails fluffed, eyes wild. Wind led the way through a grove of shag bark hickory, then stopped abruptly. The others, moving sluggishly, just barely awake, banged into the gray cat.

"Be careful!" Wind cried out.

They were standing at the top of a cliff. Lil' One stared over the edge of the steep embankment and let out a whimper. A broad river stretched below them, its surface rippling with a dull shine in the moonlight.

"Let's return to the Hyskos' path," Windrusher said. "There must be a crossing ahead."

The sun was chewing ragged holes in the night sky when they found themselves on a large concrete bridge above the Hudson. Ahead of him, Lil One saw the Hudson Highlands and the narrows of West Point. His chartreuse eyes grew even larger, shining like pools of water in the apricot-hued light.

"You wanted to cross the river. So what are you waiting for," Scowl Down growled. "This path will take us to the other—"

Before he could finish, an on-coming vehicle careened toward them, the engine echoing in the stillness of the morning. The three cats squeezed themselves against the railing, and watched the Hyskos contraption fade into the distance.

On the other side of the river, the trio scurried off the side of the road into the thick underbrush.

"Let's rest here," Scowl Down said breathlessly. "The little one needs some time to get over that adventure." She collapsed on the ground, and before either of her companions could reply, rolled over on her side and was fast asleep.

Windrusher studied the limp form of the sleeping female. Clumps of hair had fallen out of her dirty white coat, and a rusty crust of dried scabs covered her paws. She lay unmoving except for the slight rise and fall of her chest. Exhaustion was part of each of their lives, yet a faceless fear nagged at him like a persistent parasite drinking deeply from his blood.

Wind led them along the Hyskos path to a sheltered valley filled with buildings. The small town was a welcome sight after the days of torturous climbing through the mountainous woods.

Scowl Down surveyed the mountains ringing the valley, and at the greening fields scattered throughout the town. "This Hyskos village is a sight to behold. It looks like a place where we could live happily and enjoy the good fortune that Irissa-u has given us. Don't you think, Lil' One?"

"I'm hungry," the small cat replied.

The mottled tabby had a way of bringing them back to reality. They had walked steadily for the past six hours, and all of them were hungry, but with the sun overhead and in their exhausted state, Wind decided the hunting would have to wait.

"We should rest now," he said, "then we'll find something to eat."

After napping in the cool shade of the woods for almost three hours, the travelers awoke to a nagging hunger that was as strong as any they had faced during their journey. The question now was where to find food. In the distance were weathered stone buildings and ramrod-stiff Hyskos dressed uniformly in gray moved almost mechanically from building to building.

The travelers kept their distance from the strange Hyskos, and made their way past the stone buildings where acres of green offered them ample protection. Typically, cats are solitary hunters, but on this day they spread out across the field of grass and weeds searching for some unlucky animal that would put an end to their hunger.

The three hunters combed silently through the grass, pausing frequently, nostrils quivering, each whisker alive to the possibilities carried on the currents of air. Wind stopped abruptly and dropped to the ground. His ears trembled briefly then pointed forward. The other two cats followed his lead and flattened out on their bellies, sniffing the air to locate Wind's target.

Lil' One slowly lifted his head and peered through the grass. He was momentarily startled by a series of odd man-shaped objects thirty yards away, but he quickly focused his attention on a flicker of movement much nearer to the trio.

The bird was pecking at something on the ground blithely unaware of the three hunters. Its back was to them, revealing dappled feathers of black and yellow, patches of red and gray on its head. The bird bobbed up and down, spearing the ground with a long, wicked beak.

Windrusher bared his teeth momentarily, and then fluttered his ears indicating he was ready for the kill. In the woods behind them, they heard the chirping of other birds and insects calling out to one another, but here a stillness settled over the field as the three cats froze, careful not to disturb their prey. The ancient pantomime of survival had been set in motion.

Stalking was a matter of inexhaustible patience, creeping in millimeters, freezing into inert poses, and being prepared to do it all again when the prey bolts. Both Scowl Down and Lil' One understood that only one of them could take down the prey, and here, in this spot, they must rely upon Windrusher.

The yellow-shafted Flicker was unaware of the danger lurking nearby. It relished its meal of ants, plucking each one out of the top of the mound as they came rushing out to protect the nest. The bird had eaten its fill and now was stockpiling extra rations to bring back to the hatchlings hungrily waiting to be fed.

Windrusher's head started a slow, rhythmic side-to-side motion, as he prepared for the final pounce. All of his instincts were focused on this moment; he visualized landing on the feathered creature, claws fully extended against the pitiful struggle, the fateful bite into the thin neck, and the taste of hot blood in his mouth. There was no way for him to anticipate what happened next.

Sharp metallic clicks and indistinct human voices from the other side of the field caused the bird to raise its head warily. To Wind, the noise was a welcome diversion. As his brain relayed the critical message to leap upon the hapless bird, the jumble of noises in the background gave way to a clear bark of command.

"Fire!"

Immediately, a volley of gunfire split the valley, sending chunks of dirt flying around the four animals. The Flicker spread its golden wings and flew toward its nest on the hillside.

A rush of adrenaline coursed through the bird's body as its wings frantically cut the air, lifting it from the dangers on the ground, and providing a view of the earthly panorama below. Across the field, a line of men lay flat on their stomachs shooting at paper targets. Inside the bird's tiny brain, electronic messages telegraphed an all-clear, and it continued winging toward the tree line completely unaware of how close it had come to never seeing its young again.

On the ground, Wind, muscles coiled to spring, had instead jumped involuntarily with fright at the first sound of gunshots. The explosive sounds echoed in his head, and he was momentarily frozen in shock. He prepared to flee, then paused, suddenly filled with guilt because he had forgotten his two companions. They were the closest family he had; friends who had followed him bravely on his quest, and here he was thinking of his own safety. His concern overshadowed his fear and he turned to see if they had been harmed.

At that moment, Scowl Down and Lil' One nearly knocked him over in a wide-eyed, desperate dash for safety. They ran past him, ears flattened in fright, tails tucked between their legs.

chapter 14

DESPERATION AND FEAR fueled their escape. Scowl Down and Lil' One ran so far and so fast Wind was afraid they were lost. He found them hiding below a fallen hickory tree in a wooded area a quarter-mile from the firing range.

Laughter is strictly a human trait and there is no scientific evidence indicating that the feline species is capable of such a reaction. Irony, however, comes naturally to many cats that have developed a keener sense of the incongruities of life. When he found his two cowering companions, their backsides sticking out from beneath the log, Windrusher recognized the irony of the situation.

Wind regarded the quivering rears while he caught his breath. He had chased them across the field, through the woods, and into this shaded thicket. He crept forward, gave each of them a solid swipe across the rump, and watched as they yowled loudly, jumped back in fright, scraping their heads against the tree.

"Thanks be to Irissa-u that my two brave companions are unhurt," Wind said and rubbed against the two distressed cats. "It does my heart good to see that you were so concerned for my safety."

Scowl Down, still shaken by the fusillade of bullets, looked crazily at Windrusher. Without warning, she struck out with unsheathed claws. Wind drew back a heartbeat before the swooshing claws dug painful furrows across his nose.

The old female stood broadside to him hissing loudly, back arched, grimy fur standing out in matted clumps. The last thing Windrusher wanted to do was fight the old female, but he had to protect himself. He tensed his muscles to absorb her charge then felt a gentle push on his flank.

Lil' One rubbed against him affectionately, then turned and did the same to Scowl Down.

"Our meal flew away, and since you can't fly, Windrusher, I guess you're going to have to find us something else to eat," the young tabby said.

For ten difficult days, the trio traveled in a southerly direction, roughly following the Hudson River while the final days of March were left behind. The sun slid away from them in a slow silvery arc while they moved in fits and starts, over hilly, nearly mountainous terrain. Occasionally, they crossed black ribbons of deserted country roads, and more frequently were forced into fearful sprints across wide highways throbbing with the smells and sounds of Hyskos vehicles.

The hardship of their travels was increasingly evident on Scowl Down; she grew gaunt and morose, snapping at her two companions bitterly, much like she did when they intruded on her den. Windrusher knew he couldn't keep pushing them; they all needed a long rest.

They rested on a shaded hillside for three days while Scowl Down regained her strength and eventually shed her foul mood. Late on the third day, she awoke from a satisfying nap to find Lil' One grooming her, working patiently at one of the knotted clumps of fur on her left side. The old female lay there for a minute enjoying the attention from her young friend then reached out and licked him across the head.

"This is a fine place, isn't it?" she asked, staring into the distance.

Rahhna, the day globe, had migrated across the sky while she slept, slipping magically through a change of colors that now cast a pumpkin-hued glow over the grove. Scowl Down stretched her long legs in front of her, claws digging into the ground, her mouth opened wide in a gaping yawn. She walked slowly to the little stream, hung her head and lapped at the water for what seemed an interminable time.

Scowl Down shook her head brusquely, her ears slapping loudly against her head, little droplets of water flying from her whiskers. She settled next to Lil' One and nuzzled him.

"As I said, this is a fine place we found. We have food and water; there is no one here to threaten us. No Hyskos doors to lock us in. Are you sure you want to return to that high-legged family of yours,

Windrusher?"

"Yes," Wind replied. "You know this is something I must do. And you don't have to tell me that it's a Wetlos errand I'm on, I realize the foolishness of this journey."

He cocked his head to one side, one ear pointing at Lil' One on his right, the other tilted toward Scowl Down, as if embracing them both.

"You must admit, though, that this is a grand adventure we've undertaken."

Lil' One bounded to his big friend. "Tell me about the Hyskos female that cared for you, Wind," he said excitedly. "How you trained her to bring you food when you were hungry, and open doors when you wanted to go out."

As he did almost daily, Wind related the story of his life with the Trembles. There were so many things he took for granted at the time: a food bowl that was always filled; a loving Hyskos who scratched his head and throat for as long as he wanted her to; a warm house that protected him from the rain and cold. Sharing these memories with Lil' One made the pain of this grueling trek more bearable, and reinforced his need to again find that warm house and loving family.

Scowl Down lay flat as if gravity had suddenly increased tenfold, her head down between her outstretched front legs, eyes closed. The aging female had heard the stories so many times she could recite them as if they were her own. She always remained silent, but she had listened to the boring tales of Wind and his Hyskos female one time too many.

As Windrusher finished, she looked up from between her paws and said, "You would think that you were the only cat who ever lived in a Hyskos home."

She pushed herself up, ignoring the way their heads had swiveled toward her in surprise.

"I've lived in three of them, and my memories aren't nearly as glorious as yours."

Wind and Lil' One eyed one another briefly then turned to the older cat.

"You've lived with three different Hyskos families?" Wind asked incredulously.

"Three different times I was thrown into the world of these long-legged beings," Scowl Down said.

Speaking softly, she told this story.

Whimpering cries of her four brothers and sisters greeted the two-week-old kitten. They clamored over each other, stepping on her head and soft belly, grasping for a foothold trying to reach the sweet smell of milk that impelled them toward the weary mother's nipples. Overshadowing the kitten's cries were other sounds the newborn kitten did not recognize. Strange squeals, oohs, and ahhs, emanated from above the box of cats.

This was Scowl Down's first memory. She tried to focus her newly opened eyes on the source of the squeals when suddenly she found herself lifted into the air.

"Oh, look at this one," the girl said to her little sister, cupping the infant kitten in both hands like she was bringing water to her mouth. "It looks like a fluffy snowball, doesn't it? It's so cute."

The two girls fussed over the kitten for a while, then another, deeper voice cut through the squeals.

"Put that damn cat down," the gruff voice said in a tone that caused the fine white hairs on the infant feline's tail to stand on end. That was Scowl Down's introduction to the world of the Hyskos.

"You know I told you to get rid of those things. Shoulda unloaded that bitch before she had her brood."

He glowered at the cats and absently scratched his stubbled chin. "Cats ain't good for nothing, besides we can't afford to feed them so I don't want you getting too attached."

Over the next month, the kittens were given away, but the two girls kept Snow Ball and her mother, hiding the gangly white kitten in their bedroom whenever the ugly Hyskos was near.

Scowl Down paused to bite at an itch on her left haunch then looked up to make sure Wind and Lil' One were still paying attention. She noted with more than a little satisfaction that for a change it was her story that was keeping Lil' One mesmerized.

"The giant high-legged being who lived there was loud and unpleasant, not worth a sniff, but my Hyskos females loved me every bit as much as yours loved you."

Scowl nodded at Wind then continued.

"Yes, they fed me and loved me. And my mother was still there to groom me and tell me the stories of Irissa-u. When the Hyskos were gone, I played for hours on their bed, sleeping under the covers until they came home. It was as good a life as a cat could hope for."

Scowl Down stopped suddenly and put her head down on her paws as if telling the story had completely exhausted her.

"Ohh," Lil' One squealed. "Don't stop. You had a home with two Hyskos to care for you. Why did you leave?"

"It was a fine life but it was over within two night globes. I didn't leave, I was discarded like a piece of bone," she growled and closed her eyes.

The sun was dipping below the tree line now, and the old female was thinking of that long-ago nightmare when she awoke from a deep sleep to find herself in a Hyskos vehicle for the first time. She and her mother were in the same cardboard box that had been her home for the first few weeks of her life.

With a loud squealing noise, the vehicle came to a sudden stop. A door opened, and the box dropped to the pavement. Scowl Down and her mother huddled together squinting at the blazing sun shining down on them.

"I was too young to be truly frightened. That would come later," Scowl Down said.

A stillness had crept over the clearing as Lil' One and Wind somberly wondered what would happen next.

Scowl Down and her mother remained in the box for a short time before they became aware of the terrible noise of the Hyskos vehicles. They passed so close they could smell the choking fumes from the engines, and feel the vibration shaking the box. Then a wrenching collision sent the box tumbling sideways, launching Scowl and her mother painfully across the pavement.

"It was only then that we realized what he had done," Scowl Down said softly, her eyes closed as if reviewing the horrible pictures in her mind. "He had dropped us in the middle of the black path with the great-wheeled vehicles screaming by in every direction."

She paused and surveyed her two companions who were still as the trees around them, staring at her in horror. Scowl Down didn't wait for them to ask, but took a deep breath and continued her story.

"Irissa-u must have been with me that day because the next vehicle passed completely over me but left me unharmed. Somehow, in my blind panic to get off that evil path, I made my way to the side and out of danger. I climbed on a walkway and lay there trembling and whimpering like the kitten I was."

Even though she had been very young at the time, the memories of that day stood out like an ugly red scar in her mind. More rapidly now, as if she needed to get her story out before she changed her mind, Scowl Down told them of lying there on the Hyskos walk path while high-legged beings passed by.

The bright orb of Rahhna shone brightly that day as the vehicles continued to speed by. The kitten scanned the black path in panic, searching for her mother. There was the box that was her home for the first month of her life, the box where she and her siblings had nursed at her mother's side. It was flattened, and one car after another was passing over it.

"Then I saw her," Scowl said quietly, looking away at a fallen tree as though it held some hidden secret.

"She was lying on the other side of the black path. She was so still she could have been sleeping, except for the blood that ran from her broken body."

A sudden gust of wind, like the sneeze of an invisible giant, rippled the branches above their heads. Lil' One looked up and made soft mewling sounds in the back of his throat. With great tenderness, he began grooming Scowl Down.

Wind was transfixed watching his two traveling companions. The enormity of Scowl's story had left him speechless; he was unable to respond to the trauma his friend had experienced. Finally, Wind joined Lil' One in the sympathetic grooming of the old cat.

Scowl Down's smoky yellow eyes seemed to turn inwards as amber streaks spread across the sky above her. There was a time not long ago she would have used her acid tongue and lashed out at the two friends trying to console her. Now, she lay there quietly, lost in thought, but very much aware that these two creatures were the closest things she had to family.

The traumatized kitten stumbled across the sidewalk, bumped from one high leg to another, and recoiled as a huge shoe flipped her whiskers over tail into the wall of a storefront. Her eyes were squeezed shut, but there was no way she could block out the sight of her mother's crushed and bleeding body.

Scowl Down lay shivering on the sidewalk, haunted by her mother's death, until she felt the hands lift her into the air. She smelled the tart odor of a male Hyskos and tried to summon the strength to get away before she found herself in the street like her mother.

"Hey, there," cooed a soft voice. "It's all right, I'm not going to hurt you."

The kitten meowed miserably and slowly opened her eyes. An elderly man cradled Scowl carefully in hands that shook faintly with a slight tremor. He raised the cat and snuggled it against his red and green flannel shirt, gently stroking the fine white fur.

"What are you doing here?" the man asked, as if expecting an answer from the tiny feline. "Don't you know you could get hurt hanging around street corners? I think you better come with me, and meet my Francesca."

The old man's soft voice and gentle hands soothed the young cat. Slowly, she relaxed, and for the first time since being placed in the box with her mother, the little kitten stopped shaking.

Scowl Down paused again and closed her eyes as if trying to remember the sequence of events in her sad tale. Her two companions remained silent, their gazes fixed upon the old female.

"These two Hyskos were kind and treated me much like they may have treated one of their own young," Scowl Down finally said.

"After my experience with the first Hyskos I thought I could never trust high-legged beings again, but these two were kind and loving. I'm not sure how many night globes passed, but I was no longer a kitten when the bad thing happened."

Lil' One jumped to his feet. "Bad thing. What bad thing?"

The old cat looked nervously at her two friends. She hesitated a moment, then continued.

"It was still the dark of early morning when outside sounds woke me, and the old woman let two strange high-legged males in the house. They rushed into the back room where the Hyskos slept carrying bags and a rolling thing. I could tell by their voices that something was not right, and I heard my Hyskos female crying. When I tried to go into the back room, one of the high-legged beings pushed me out and closed the door.

"It wasn't long before the door swung open and the two strange Hyskos pushed the rolling thing across the room. The old Hyskos male was laying on it. His head rolled over towards me and I saw his face, it was almost as white as my fur, and a long, shiny thing hung from his arm."

Scowl Down was still for a moment; she examined the treetops and watched the leaves drifting towards the ground. Her two companions lashed their tails nervously, ears twitching, eyes wide.

"That was the bad thing, wasn't it?" Lil' One asked with a quaver in his voice.

"That was the bad thing," she repeated quietly. "My female rushed after them and left me alone in the house. I don't know how long I stayed there, but I grew very hungry since my food bowl was empty. The old Hyskos had never let me go hungry before and I paced in front of the door whining and looking for them to return. Finally, I fell asleep.

"The sound of the door opening must have awakened me and I ran to greet them. A strange Hyskos female entered the house calling 'Sasha,' the name my family had given me."

Scowl Down never saw the old couple again, but her life had changed once more, and now she was living in another house with another high-legged female.

More than a week passed since the young cat went to live with this new Hyskos and her house filled with antiques. The old woman, perhaps in fear her precious furniture might be damaged, allowed the longhair to play in her backyard for a good part of the day. There the young cat chased butterflies, stalked insects among the high grass and flowers, and believed she had the perfect life.

Late one afternoon, while watching a squirrel in the chestnut tree, a wave of warmth spread over Scowl Down and she was overcome by a strange excitement. She felt a warm tingling coursing through her as if her blood had been heated on the stove and then injected back into her body. She meowed loudly several times and began rolling in the grass beneath the tree.

The young female was overcome by an emotion she did not understand, and found herself running in circles. Almost exhausted, she dropped to the grass once more and lay still.

Even with her eyes closed, the outline of the burning day globe over head was visible, and she sensed a shadow fall across her face. A sleek gray and white male stood over her, watching patiently, almost submissively.

Scowl Down thought she heard her heart beating as she watched the gray male slowly circle her. Her breathing became shallow, her tail twitched high in the air. The young Scowl Down could only rely on her instincts, and they were telling her that this male wasn't to be feared. Still, a growl emerged from deep in her throat, low and persistent.

The male stepped closer and lowered his head in front of Scowl Down. The young cat didn't understand why she did it, but she growled loudly and clawed at the older cat's neck. He quickly jumped out of reach and froze while Scowl rolled in the grass. Each time she looked up, it seemed the male had moved closer.

Still growling, she lowered her head and raised her back end toward the male. He clamped both claws on her back, and Scowl Down's head spun dizzily. She didn't know what to expect, but it wasn't the sight of the old woman running out of the house waving a broom and yelling.

Frightened by this screaming apparition, the tom cat released the young queen, scampered through the hedges, and disappeared. Before Scowl Down could move, she was scooped up and carried inside the house by the broom-waving old Hyskos.

Scowl Down paused, a far-away look in her faded yellow eyes. "The next day I was taken to a room filled with the yapping of snouters. I cringed in my box and stayed very quiet. Then I was taken out and immediately went to sleep.

"That's all I remember of that visit, but when I awoke something was different."

"What was different," Lil' One insisted.

Scowl Down patiently licked the top of the young cat's head for a moment.

"I'll tell you what was different if you stop interrupting me. For one thing, I woke as if from a sleep of several night globes with a sharp pain in my belly. A patch covered the spot where I felt the pain.

"It passed quickly, but I didn't feel the same sense of excitement and wonder when the old Hyskos eventually let me go outside again. There was no thrill of anticipation, and somehow, I knew that my adventure with the gray male was a thing of the past. Later, I left."

Scowl Down's story had begun in late afternoon, and darkness now enveloped the trio. Slivers of pale moonlight filtered through the trees and flickered across the backs of the three cats. This time it was Wind who spoke up.

"Was it difficult to leave the Hyskos house?"

Scowl Down looked at Windrusher curiously for a moment then answered flatly.

"Difficult? No, it wasn't difficult. The old woman let me out in the yard the next day and I walked away. That was the last time I trusted a high-legged being."

chapter 15

SCOWL DOWN'S STORY left a depressing pall hanging over the clearing, and Windrusher's stomach knotted with sadness for his old friend. Her earlier experiences were in the past and beyond his control, but he could make sure that nothing else happened to her.

Wind rolled on his side and saw the star-spattered canopy above the trees. All around him, night creatures engaged in an endless survival ballet; rodents and frogs stalked insects and in turn, birds swooped silently from the sky hunting the smaller creatures. Somewhere out there, prey was waiting for him, as well. He was tempted to join the hunt, but his fluttering eyelids persuaded him that sleep was infinitely more enticing than food.

At least for now.

Windrusher bobbed in the currents of sleep, like a leaf swept along in a tumbling brook. Here and there, a face from his past greeted him. Kimmy cooed unintelligible sounds and called his Hyskos name as he silently slid below her outstretched arms.

The stream picked up speed, and carried him around a bend. An old man stretched palsied hands toward him, and tried desperately to pluck him out of the water. Tubes ran from the man's arms, and slowly, very slowly, the Hyskos fell to the ground the tubes trailing above him like ribbons of seaweed floating in the surf.

One more twist in the stream and, without warning, Wind was caught in a whirlpool that sucked him deeper and deeper into its vortex. Immediately, he heard the roar of voices surrounding him, and understood he had traversed the bridge from deep sleep into the Inner Ear.

"The TDC works to bring more people to Crystal River to stay in our hotels, eat in our restaurants, and make us lots of money, especially during slower times," Tremble said.

Amy was listening to her husband's excited conversation about the Citrus County Tourist Development Council. She smiled as he moved maniacally around the small kitchen, a glass of chardonnay in one hand and an oversize green and blue oven mitten shaped like a fish on the other. He wore a pair of khaki Duckhead shorts and an old YMCA T-shirt.

"That's why there's an extra six cents tax on each dollar our customers spend at the hotel," he said, rubbing his thumb and forefinger together with the oven glove and rolling his eyes in a way that reminded Amy of Harpo Marx.

Tremble had worked until 3:30 P.M. before rushing home to make dinner. His Thursday dinners had become complex affairs, inspired by the new cuisine served at the Crystal Grille, the hotel's upscale restaurant. Amy watched with wry amusement as he scurried about juggling pots, referring to recipes, and sipping his wine, all the while keeping up a steady stream of conversation. He was as excited as a kid at Christmas.

Tremble stuck a glass of wine in her hand when she entered the house, planted a wet kiss on her cheek, and launched into the story of his appointment to the TDC. A whiff of citrus and alcohol told her he was into his second glass of wine.

Amy still wore her white nurse's uniform, although it wasn't nearly as crisp as when she left for a nine-hour shift at Seven Rivers Community Hospital early that morning. She leaned against the kitchen counter to take the pressure off her aching feet; careful not to put her elbow into any of the puddles Gerry left in his wake.

He bent over to check the corn soufflé in the oven, and then peeked under the lid of the oversize frying pan on the stove. Clouds of white vapor tumbled out of the pan filling the room with fragrant layers of garlic and basil.

"Ahh, this is going to be so good you'll have to start calling me Wolfgang and pay me in very special coin," Tremble said.

He took another sip of wine and wagged the ridiculous fish mitten in her face. Amy laughed out loud despite the dull pain that was slowly working its way up her ankles into her knees.

"Hold that thought, Wolfgang. Let me get out of these shoes before I collapse."

She walked toward the bedroom. "Is GT going to be home for dinner?" she asked.

"Yeah. Thursday means track practice, so I expect his swift bod to make an appearance in time for dinner. We hardly see him these days, and it isn't even football season."

The excitement of moving to a new city and living in a hotel suite had carried them for a few days. The kids enjoyed the swimming pool, the tennis courts, canoeing in the bay, and everyone especially appreciated having a staff that cleaned up after them.

With only two bedrooms in the suite, they were forced to pair off with the two males in one room and the two females in the other. Stella had her choice of rooms, but usually stayed in the living room. The novelty of this arrangement soon wore off, and after one week, they all agreed it was time to look for a house. The next week they found a three-bedroom rental about six miles from the hotel.

Tremble was waiting at the bedroom door with the bottle of wine when his wife emerged. She had pulled her hair back into a ponytail, and flicked a strand out of her eye as she held out her glass for a refill.

Amy smiled broadly and looked into her husband's flashing green eyes. She ran the tips of her fingers tenderly down his flushed cheek, and the pressure of the day slipped away.

"Gerry, we have been blessed, haven't we?" Her voice suddenly deserted her; and she felt her eyes glisten.

He put a long, lanky arm around her and kissed her gently on both of her wet eyes.

"Baby, sometimes I think I've died and gone to heaven. And I promise you it's only going to get better."

Windrusher settled himself in the chaotic pipeline that was Akhen-et-u, the Inner Ear. Experience had taught him to be patient and wait for calm to overtake the rush of voices buffeting him. Eventually, he sensed a gap in the stormy procession, identified himself, and quickly brought the listeners up to date since his last visit.

Almost immediately, the familiar voice of Short Shank broke in.

"Ah, Windrusher, you've returned once again. I thought you might be worm meat by now."

"Only through the grace of Irissa-u, and not on my own merit," he said.

"Nearly three night globes have passed and you're still on the Path to complete your mission. Do you realize that you have become the main item of communication among the sleep-speakers?"

Wind wasn't sure if Short Shank was teasing him once again, but inside his sleeping body he felt a pleasurable shiver of pride pass through him. Was it true that he could be the center of attention among the hundreds of thousands of cats fortunate enough to be plugged into the Inner Ear? He found it unlikely.

"You are wise and respected, Short Shank, and I would be honored if you counseled me. The days have been difficult, and my two friends sometimes slow me down. But I know that I am on a holy mission from Irissa-u and will continue until I reach my goal."

Wind felt his grip weakening and knew he would soon be swept away, drawn deep into the dark, warm folds of true sleep.

"Follow your heart, my friend," Shank replied. "We are with you on your great adventure, and all cats will be blessed if you complete your journey."

There was a hint of real emotion in the old tom's message, and Wind was touched once again.

"Thank you for your kind—"

Wind was abruptly cut off by the same biting voice that had attacked him in the past.

"Is there no sense left in your heads? Above all four-legged creatures, aren't we alone supposed to have the gift of wisdom given us by the great god Tho-hoth? Yet you babble among yourselves like the brainless Hyskos."

The unspoken rule of the Inner Ear called for civility not cruelty, but this voice was harsh and condemning.

"How can you give any credence to the drivel of a foolheaded buttworm, old one? His head is filled with ridiculous tales that make less sense than the ramblings of a female kitten."

The voice became ever more strident, stabbing cruelly at Wind, scraping at him like a sharp claw across his nose. Desperate to leave this accusing bully behind, he released his fragile grip and dropped into the blackness of the caverns of sleep.

chapter 16

SCOWL DOWN LED THE WAY through the shadows of the narrow alleyway. Lil' One was right on her tail, and Wind a few paces behind. With ears pivoting to catch any hint of danger in the strange landscape, the three travelers heard the clanging of machinery and the occasional blast of a boat horn.

The weeks of punishing travel through Hyskos villages and the incredibly rough terrain of southern New York had taken its toll on each of them. Incessant traffic, lack of food and vicious dogs proved a constant danger. It was Scowl Down who convinced them that a short stay in a Hyskos village would have certain advantages. She had lived most of her life in cities, where food was readily available, and hiding places plentiful.

Through the Inner Ear, Scowl Down learned of a large colony of abandoned and feral cats living in a large city not far from their present location. According to her source, the colony's leader, Wild Tail, welcomed travelers in need of a place to rest.

The tired trio stopped at the end of the alley where stacks of rusted iron containers were aligned in a huge L. Beyond the containers stood a rotting warehouse that had obviously lost the battle to the forces of time and weather.

Scowl Down sniffed the air. "I believe this is the place."

Hugging the shadows, they padded to the warehouse entrance. Wind peered through broken doors and saw cats of every size and shape lying among piles of debris. Sensing no danger from within, the exhausted trio entered the warehouse, found an isolated spot next to a concrete column and quietly lay down. They saw hundreds of eyes watching their every movement, but were too tired to care.

Scowl Down soon heard steady breathing from her two friends

and was envious of their ability to find sleep at will. Recently, sleep often eluded her, while pain was a constant companion. She tried not to dwell on it, but it was difficult to ignore the sharp twinges in her hips and knee joints or the sore muscles that made it impossible to find a comfortable position.

With an effort, she pushed the pain into the background of her mind and found pleasure in the minor victory she'd won. They had agreed that this was the best course, followed her through frightening city streets, dodging the roaring Hyskos vehicles, and trusted her judgment.

Her age was a hindrance in the rocky countryside, and the two younger cats could move faster without her, but she had shown her mettle more than once, and now her intelligence and fortitude had delivered them to this place of safety. After they were rested and regained their strength, her two friends would thank her for bringing them to this colony.

Shards of morning sunlight streamed through the broken warehouse roof, cutting dusty swaths in the shadows. The vast warehouse overflowed with mounds of trash, broken crates, flattened cardboard boxes, and the feline denizens of Wild Tail's colony. None of them bothered the three new arrivals, and they stayed to themselves near the front of the warehouse.

Wind was cleaning the inside of his left hind leg, Lil' One chasing specks of dust floating on the rays of sun, and Scowl Down was still sleeping when she approached.

"And these must be our visitors from last night."

Wind turned to see a female of middle years standing over him. Her sleek, shorthaired coat was a light charcoal gray, with patches of white on her front paws, chest, and the tip of her tail, which was bent at an acute angle as if it had been caught in a door. She was definitely well fed, showing more than the hint of a belly.

Windrusher stood quickly to face her. Even though he was half a head taller than the female, she looked evenly and coolly at him. A musky redolence embraced her like a second coat, stirring something deep inside.

Before he had a chance to consider the strange feelings, a

movement in the shadows behind the female caught his eye. It was a shapeless, hulking form, and Wind sensed that this thing was watching him much like he would watch a defenseless rodent in the moments before he leapt. This must be Wild Tail, Wind assumed, the leader of this colony of free cats.

Forcing himself to concentrate on the female, Wind responded. "We heard of the hospitality we might find here, and hope that we can spend some time resting before resuming our journey."

Wind was careful not to show any sign of aggression, and sniffed the female politely.

"I am Pferusha-ulis, Windrusher, Son of Nefer-iss-tu. My friends and I have traveled a far distance. We would like to ask Wild Tail for his indulgence and let us stay here for a short time."

The female hesitated, seemingly uncertain of what to say, and turned toward the shadows then back to Windrusher.

"Ah, Wild Tail," she said with a trace of sadness in her voice. "You knew Wild Tail, did you?"

He tilted his head at Scowl Down. "Not at all, but my sleepy friend over there was told that this was a place to find refuge, and that Wild Tail was a wise leader who wouldn't turn away cats in need of shelter."

Wind's discomfort was growing under the steady gaze of the female. Or was it the mysterious creature hiding in the shadows? Maybe it wasn't the best decision to enter the city and come to this place, he thought.

The conversation awakened Scowl Down and she scrambled up on aching legs to join her friend. She instantly sensed the tension between Wind and the strange female, and realized that the warehouse was suddenly still. All the other cats were watching as if awaiting some sign from their leader.

"My name is Scowl Down. We were hoping to rest here until we have the strength to travel on. We heard through Akhen-et-u of Wild Tail's hospitality. Perhaps we're in the wrong place."

Wind saw the female's shoulder muscles relax. "Forgive my rudeness, but we must be careful, you understand? Certainly, you are welcome to stay with us until you regain your strength and can move on."

The female's tail swished several times and she moved forward to brush noses with both Scowl Down and Windrusher.

"My name is Swift Nail. Sorrowfully, I must tell you that Wild Tail died in his sleep three night globes ago. He and I were...." She paused in mid-sentence as if searching for the proper words.

"We were together for a good while and I have come to be protective of the outcasts that live under this pitiful excuse for a roof."

She glanced up as if expecting the roof to fall in on them at any time. Then she looked past the two visitors and said, "I see you have another companion with you."

Both Scowl and Wind turned together to see Lil' One standing behind them quietly observing the interaction between the adult cats.

"Yes, Swift Nail, this is our friend Lil' One," Wind said, butting the small cat playfully. "Lil One has been part of many adventures, and I'm certain that he'll be happy to tell you all about them. More often than you wish to hear them, no doubt."

Now it was the kitten's turn to butt his older friend, which he did with a loud purr. He was preparing to launch into one of their adventures when a large form emerged from the shadows and moved menacingly toward the group. The sight dried the spittle in the young cat's throat and made his hair stand on end. He scurried behind Windrusher with a whimper.

Both Wind and Scowl stared in disbelief at the approaching animal. If they did not know better, they would have sworn that this wasn't a cat at all, but a snouter. It was the largest feline either of them had ever seen. The animal moved with a stealthy gait that was at once deliberate yet furtive, slinking forward behind massive shoulders and a neck thick with ropey muscles.

The male cat had a coarse coat of long black hair flecked with hundreds of specks that shone with tortoiseshell iridescence. The stringy hair was matted with knots of messy and painful-looking tangles, and standing out against the blackness of its hair, like slimy white maggots feeding on a corpse, were a series of gaping scars.

As unsettling as it was to look on this cat's body, the face was so disturbing they had to look away. The huge head seemed too large for the enormous body, and hung down slightly, causing the cat to look up at them as if from a lower depth. One bright yellow eye stared out like a venomous lemon drop from a face that was flattened ludicrously. A viscous scum the color of rancid oil drained from the other sickly white and sightless eye.

The cause of the hideous cat's injured eye was readily apparent by following the livid line of thick scar tissue tracing itself like varicose veins across the big cat's face. The scar ripped through the cat's left ear, leaving it flapping in two distinct pieces, then continued across the crown of the cat's head before making a jagged turn through the eye itself, slitting one nostril of the ridiculous pug nose before disappearing.

An oversize lower jaw held two wicked canine teeth that protruded over its under slung upper jaw, painting the cat's visage with a cruel and wicked smile. There was no way this creature was happy to see them, Wind was sure, certainly not in any normal sense.

Swift Nail did not seem surprised by their reaction. "This is my friend, Bolt," she said, rubbing her head affectionately across the hulking cat's neck. "He does know how to make an entrance, doesn't he? You'll find him to be a cat of few words, but I would trust him with my life."

Swift Nail paused for dramatic effect, her whiskers flickering slightly, and gazed fondly at the brutish Bolt, then turned back toward the newcomers. "Of course," she added with a soft purr, "others may not share my sentiments."

She turned abruptly, her wiry tail brushing across Wind's face, and padded away followed closely by Bolt.

chapter 17

LIL' ONE'S MOUTH dropped open. He watched the unlikely pair saunter away and disappear inside a large packing case without looking back. There was a time not so long ago when such an experience would leave him shivering with fright. Not anymore. He was a different cat than the one that hid in the woods afraid of his own tail. Besides, he had his friends.

Lil' One looked at his traveling companions and saw Wind's tail swishing nervously. He leaped on it, and grabbed the end of it in his mouth.

"Look at me," the young cat growled in mock anger; showing his teeth around the bushy tail, "my name is Bolt."

Wind and Scowl brightened immediately, and tumbled together in a playful wrestling match that left the smaller cat lying on his side in surrender. This was the first time Lil' One could remember his two older companions actually playing as if they liked each other. He purred loudly feeling the closeness of his new family.

Later, Lil' One said to Wind. "You once said that a bad cat, one that didn't follow the Path, was called a Setlos. Do you think Bolt is a Setlos?"

Wind looked at his friend, then toward the crate. "I don't like to judge a cat by one meeting, but this time I believe you may be right. We must be very careful with that one, I'm afraid."

A handsome young orange tabby and a small black and white cat approached them. The smaller cat, whose ribs terraced out of its chest, spoke first.

"That Bolt is enough to give you nightmares, isn't he," the black and white said with unexpected strength in its voice. "Be careful with him, he's even uglier than he looks."

This last was said while looking over his shoulder as though he expected to find the brute standing behind him.

"My name is Big Rock," the small cat said, holding his head up defiantly. "And this one we call Sister, since she had no name when she was left here with her litter mates. We don't know what happened to her mother. She went out for food one day and never returned."

Lil' One felt an instant kinship to the orange tabby. He promptly stepped forward and sniffed the two cats, offering his own nose to be sniffed. Sister purred a quiet greeting in return, and before long introductions had been made.

Big Rock was the more inquisitive of the two and asked questions non-stop about where the trio had been, what they had seen, and how they found their way to the warehouse. Windrusher kept his answers brief and vague. Lil' One, on the other hand, was as talkative as Big Rock and began telling his two new friends how he had rescued Wind from the Hyskos.

The enthusiastic youngster would have recounted the journey from beginning to end if Wind had not butted his little friend playfully, but insistently. "There will be time for you to bore everyone with your tall tales later, but we should find ourselves something to eat, don't you think?"

"Come with us," said the orange tabby, speaking for the first time. "We'll show you where there's lots of food."

It turned out that the docks were literally crawling with rats and other vermin, providing relatively easy meals for the more than one hundred feral and abandoned cats living in the warehouse. For a more exotic menu, they only had to travel three or four blocks to find dumpsters laden with choice morsels thrown out by nearby restaurants.

After eating, Lil' One praised Scowl Down for her foresight and persistence in convincing them to come into the noisy Hyskos city. Not a cat to limit himself to one topic, he chattered on about the food, the other cats, even the protection the warehouse offered until Wind ventured this advice.

"This may seem to be a fine place to rest and eat our fill, but I worry about the Hyskos finding us when there are so many cats in one place. Remember the food place where you found me, Lil' One?"

"Sometimes I think you're the old one here and not me," Scowl Down teased. "You worry too much. Why not enjoy the situation and let's concentrate on healing our pads and getting fat before we return to our travels?"

Wind had to agree that the situation was better than he expected, although there was still that nagging feeling that something wasn't quite right here.

"I must admit that this is far more comfortable than climbing hills in the rain," he said.

"Or crossing the black path with the deadly Hyskos vehicles," Lil' One added.

For the next five days, the three travelers slept and ate, regaining their strength. Lil' One's stories quickly spread throughout the colony and there was seldom a time when knots of cats couldn't be found gathered in front of the new arrivals.

Again, this morning, Wind was forced to reiterate the tale of leaving his home to go off in search of his high-legged beings. Cats of every age clustered at his feet. Some he had never seen before, others who apparently couldn't hear enough of Windrusher's adventures.

"Yes, it's true, the Holy Mother showed herself to me in a dream and said that I should travel twenty night globes to find my Hyskos family."

"Tell us about how you ran down the mountain during the storm and found your call name," one of the kittens called out excitedly in a squeaky voice.

"Yes, I'd like to hear that one myself." This was a voice he recognized.

Swift Nail approached, Bolt walked beside her like an evil shadow, his lemon yellow eye glaring malevolently at the cluster of cats surrounding Wind and Lil' One. Hurriedly, the cats scurried back and let them through.

"Go ahead, and tell us the story of how you got the name Windrusher," Swift Nail insisted. "I've been hearing so much about your exploits from others that I would be honored to hear them from the hero himself."

"You know how the young ones exaggerate," Wind said, trying to deflect the attention. "We did have a few close calls, but nothing more than most of you have faced, I'm sure."

"You are much too modest, my friend," Swift Nail purred, sidling next to Wind. "I understand that Irissa-u, the Holy Mother, has sent you on a mission that no cat has ever accomplished. Isn't that right?"

Wind wasn't sure what to say. Should he deny what had happened to them in their travels or say the stories were exaggerated and hope they would be left alone? That might be the wisest thing to do, he thought, as he looked at Bolt's menacing stare. But it would not be true to the cat that was the Son of Nefer-iss-tu and one thing he had learned in his travels was that he had to face his fears or they would overtake him.

"It's true that my friends and I are on a quest to find my Hyskos family. And it is true we have found ourselves suffering because of it, having traveled for four night globes before coming here. Yes, it's also true my call name came to me in a dream that later came to life with Lil' One here."

Wind's right ear twitched nervously, but he continued.

"I have been fortunate to find two good friends in my travels. They have helped me to understand that we draw strength from each other while pursuing what is surely a hopeless quest."

He pawed Lil' One lightly on the back of the head.

"More than once I've been told that I don't have the sense of a floppy-eared snouter, and that's probably the truth as well."

"By the great god Tho-hoth, you know that's the truth, you worthless buttworm," Bolt suddenly interjected.

Wind recoiled as if he had been struck on the head by a wooden plank. The cruelty of the voice rang in his ears like the echo of a recurring nightmare, and raised the hair on his back. It was the voice from Akhen-et-u. The one that had attacked him and Short Shank. The surprise must have registered in his eyes because Bolt let out a grating sound that was a mixture of a hacking cough and a cackle.

"You recognize me now, do you, Wetlos? After hearing your miserable whinings in the Inner Ear for so long, I finally get to meet the cat that has befooled so many."

Bolt lunged at Windrusher without warning, a low growl gurgling out of his throat. Wind reacted instantly; hair bristled, his tail stuck out stiffly, and an immediate infusion of adrenalin prepared him to fight. These were all involuntary actions; deep in his bones he was certain that any fight between them would be a brief one.

Swift Nail lived up to her name and quickly jumped between the two cats.

"Now, now, there's no need to act this way over a few stories." She pushed her body against Bolt's and began licking his face. "You just have too much energy you big old brute," she teased. "Let's go back to our box and leave these cats alone."

She continued pushing Bolt away from the other cats until he whirled around and ran to the packing crate.

"My friend must not have the same love of storytelling I do," Swift Nail purred. "I'm sorry for his bad manners. We'll get together when we can be alone and you can tell me of your adventures."

She turned and walked slowly toward the crate.

The cats were silent, still in a state of shock over the near violence they had witnessed. Big Rock, who was rolling with the other cats in front of Wind just minutes before, was the first to break the silence.

"Didn't I say you had to be careful around that one? You would rather have warts on your rump than have Bolt take a special interest in you. I have seen him chew cats to pieces just to prove he could do it. Wild Tail would never have put up with it, but Swift Nail and Bolt are different cats."

Scowl Down, who slept through the entire encounter, awakened from her nap. She yawned, displaying her yellow teeth and pink tongue.

"By the Holy Mother, that was the finest sleep I've had in many night globes."

She glanced at the cats sitting around Wind and Lil' One and shook her head.

"You two should really stop all this foolishness and take more naps. You'll live longer that way."

chapter 18

S<small>WIFT</small> N<small>AIL</small> <small>WAS</small> two months old when she watched her mother and two siblings die. Her mother was only eight months older than her litter, and was nursing when the crafty snouter burst into the thicket of bushes that passed for their home. Fortunately for Swift Nail, her mother was on her feet instantly, and had the presence of mind to run, drawing the mongrel away from her litter. The three kittens watched the brown and yellow dog with the overly large head and lolling tongue tear after their mother.

Within moments, the dog clamped its jaw on the cat's back and began shaking it viciously from side to side. An arc of blood and saliva swept from the dog's mouth, her mother's head hanging limply like a broken doll.

To this day, Swift Nail can see her mother's lifeless body flopping back and forth in the dog's mouth. She can hear the obscene growls coming from the snouter, and the small bounce her body made when the dog finally released it. If she tried, she can also see her two siblings (oddly, she couldn't remember if they were male or female) walking on rubbery legs toward their dead mother. She can hear the pitiful whimpering noises they made. And then, like a bad dream, Swift Nail can see the two kittens brutally crushed by the rampaging snouter.

It was a lesson that stayed with her as she grew into a cat with the wiles and ways to survive. Wherever she went over the next two years, and she moved frequently, she chose protected environments with at least two escape routes.

She also learned that males were relatively easy to manipulate and made certain to befriend the strongest. When Swift Nail happened upon the warehouse colony, she quickly realized that Wild Tail was the leader of this pack of wayward cats and became his regular mate.

Unlike Bolt, who enjoyed instilling fear and pain in the other cats, Wild Tail was a wise protector of the colony. He never instigated himself into the cats daily routine, but when problems arose it was Wild Tail who moved to resolve them.

If fighting over females grew so nasty that it threatened to disrupt their peaceful existence, Wild Tail would intervene, and the unruly males would find themselves another place to live. Wild Tail was slow to anger, and Swift Nail often pushed him to provide the necessary discipline to the offenders. When provoked his angry claws dispensed harsh punishment.

The colony grew for more than two years, each day bringing more cats and more litters. Some cats stayed for several weeks or a month then disappeared as suddenly as they had appeared, others remained part of the permanent population.

The warehouse colony enjoyed a relatively carefree life until Wild Tail sickened and died. The end came suddenly, and Swift Nail was caught unprepared to be left alone, without her protector. Many of the cats naturally looked to her for counsel since she had been such an integral part of Wild Tail's life. Others were not so open-minded, and she found herself frequently challenged, particularly by more belligerent males.

Swift Nail found herself in need of another strong, yet malleable, male to help her maintain a position of authority and impose her will on the colony. Few of the cats surrounding her fit the role she had in mind, even though it wouldn't take much coaxing to wrap them around her tail for life.

Then Bolt walked through the door.

It was dusk, and the air was heavy with the odors of nearly sixty cats. Flies buzzed above fetid lumps of food, vomit, and excrement, a perfect backdrop for Bolt's entrance. Silence descended upon the warehouse as the menacing brute skulked through the door and padded his way slowly to the middle of the rotting structure. Cats in every corner, involved in everything from grooming to fornication, suddenly froze to stare at this creature that was unlike anything they had ever seen.

Swift Nail watched Bolt, the effect he had on the rest of the colony, the fear and respect he demanded, and immediately realized that this intimidating creature was exactly what she had been searching for.

Bolt paced furiously inside the large packing crate, his anger building like a storm front.

"Just look at how the others are rallying around him. I tell you, if we don't do something this Windrusher will have the entire colony on his side and you'll be outside scavenging for your food like some abandoned snouter."

Swift Nail stepped in front of him.

"You're right, Bolt," she said. "The other cats are drawn to him, but he is planning to continue on his foolish journey soon, so let's be patient for a little while longer. I'm afraid that if you take care of him in your usual way, the others might turn against us and where will we be then?"

Bolt was probably right, but before she turned him loose she wanted to see if Windrusher was as predictable as most males. "I know you can be very persuasive if you want to be," Swift Nail said. "See if you can find a way to convince the others that he is just an ordinary cat, but do it without causing too much pain."

She was lost in her own thoughts now, licking at the fine dusty hairs near her belly.

Bolt ignored Swift Nail's suggestion and began pacing again. "My way is an easier and more permanent solution. The rest of these whiskerless kittens would run at the first sight of his blood."

Swift Nail recognized the incipient violence bubbling inside her protector. Shifting over to face him, she began clawing Bolt's back and sides roughly. A provocative humming throbbed deep inside her, worked its way to the surface, and filled the crate. She licked the plum colored scar running across his face then fiercely bit him on the neck. Now, she knew she had his attention.

chapter 19

A COLD NOR'EASTER blew off the river, whipping up white caps on the water. The dumpster smelled of garlic mashed potatoes and last week's Friday night special. Inside, the three cats chewed on remnants of baby back ribs.

The trio was finally alone, something that was increasingly impossible inside the warehouse where they would awake from naps to find themselves surrounded by a ring of cats. Even when they ate, more than a dozen felines gathered to watch them chew as if this was something they had never seen before.

Windrusher had grown accustomed to the obsessed cats and their hero worship, but Bolt was another matter. "This cat is unpredictable, and he's close to erupting," he said to his friends. "It is time to move on."

"As usual, you're overreacting," Scowl Down said between chews on a greasy bone. "You said yourself that the female controls the brute, and that she seems to like you. I say we stay out of sight and try to rest for at least two more day globes."

"You didn't see Bolt. If Swift Nail hadn't jumped between us and Lil' One would only have pieces of my fur to remember me by."

"Exactly my argument. Bolt is like every stupid male, and jumps whenever Swift Nail swishes her tail. She will keep him in line."

Lil' One scrambled after a meaty rib in the corner, shifting the pile of garbage, and tumbling deeper into the dumpster. The other two cats watched him dig his way back to the top.

After catching his breath, Lil' One spoke up. "I thought Bolt was the ugliest thing I've ever seen, but if he tries to fight you, Wind, he'll be so ugly not even the snouters will want him around."

"Thank you, Lil' One, but I don't want to find out what might happen if Swift Nail turns him loose. Scowl, you may be right and I'm overreacting, but we have to be very careful."

"Believe me, my friend, Bolt has a short memory, if any at all, and will forget about this," Scowl Down said. "We'll soon resume our journey fat and rested and leave that ugly creature far behind. Now stop your worrying and eat before Lil' One buries us all."

Bolt was practicing his powers of persuasion with a pack of cats when the trio returned unnoticed and settled on a stack of old burlap sacks to the right of the front doors. Scowl and Lil' One lay down immediately for an afternoon nap, but Wind couldn't sleep. He hoped the old female was right, but he didn't believe that Bolt would forget about their encounter. As though she could read his mind, Swift Nail appeared beside him.

"Your friends are enjoying deep sleep, and Bolt is out exploring the wharves. This would be a good time for us to get to know each other better."

Swift Nail rubbed the side of her head and neck against his. "Why don't we go where we can be alone and you can tell me about your adventures?"

Her heavy perfume filled his nostrils, a wave of heat swept over his belly, and he followed her across the warehouse floor into the packing crate.

"Windrusher, you are an extraordinary cat and I am awed by the mission you have taken upon yourself."

He had told her of the search to find his Hyskos family; of the dream with Irissa-u, and of how they would soon continue their travels. Now he lay quietly facing Swift Nail, his heart beating rapidly.

"Could you not stay here with me for a night globe or two before traveling on? I could use an intelligent ally to assist me in what might be a very troublesome time."

"That wouldn't be possible," he said after a long pause. "I have committed myself to this journey and will be leaving well before another night globe rises. But I thank you for your hospitality."

Swift Nail sat straight; her two front paws close together, and studied him through half-closed eyes. Her tail floated from one side of her body to the other.

"You can repay my hospitality by helping me with a special quest of my own. Please consider doing this one thing for me before you leave."

Wind tried to make the connection between the cat he had seen interacting with Bolt and the quietly concerned leader before him now. "What is this special quest, and why do you need my help?"

"You may have heard the noise of Hyskos machines in the distance. Everyday they come closer, and I fear it will not be long before they are upon us. We must move the colony before it is too late and many of us are killed. You have proven yourself to be a resourceful cat and I can't think of another better than you."

She moved forward until the small gap between them was gone. Wind felt the tickle of her whiskers brushing lightly across his face. His head filled with the smell of her, he could feel the heat of her body, and his heart hammered in his chest. He stood abruptly and walked several paces away; his ears flickering like a humming bird's wings.

"What about your friend Bolt? Why doesn't he help you with this special quest?"

"Ah, Bolt," Swift Nail said with a quiet sadness. "Bolt has many redeeming qualities, despite his quick temper. This task, however, requires more foresight and imagination than Bolt possesses. It calls for an understanding of how a colony must sustain itself, and a sensitivity to the needs of each cat in the colony. You have proven yourself many times, and I would trust your judgment."

"As I said, I will not be staying long, but if it will help the colony, I will search the area for a suitable new home before I leave."

"Thank you, Windrusher, for not disappointing me. Let's not panic the other cats, so please, keep this to yourself. This includes your two companions, especially Lil' One, who is quite unrestrained when it comes to sharing his thoughts."

Swift Nail covered him with soggy licks, and Wind backed away trying to extricate himself from her attentions. Three steps and his buttocks hit an unyielding obstacle behind him. Slowly, he swiveled his head and there was Bolt standing like a boulder in his path.

Wind turned to face the creature, wondering how long Bolt had been lurking outside the packing crate. Had he heard their conversation? He remembered the last time Bolt had nearly attacked him and wondered if Swift Nail would stop him this time.

Bolt glared wildly from Windrusher to Swift Nail, his yellow eye gleaming malignantly. Wind tensed himself for the worst, but Bolt brushed roughly past him, pushing him aside like he was passing through a spider's web.

Wind teetered on wobbly legs before regaining his balance. His heart beat so loud he was sure the other cats could hear it pounding in his chest. When he felt he could move without falling, he quietly padded toward the stack of burlap bags.

The wind howled along the docks like a wounded animal. Inside the warehouse, Windrusher had decided to tell Scowl Down of his encounter with Swift Nail and the favor she asked of him. Lil' One was in a far corner sharing his tales with another group of enthralled cats. Swift Nail was right about his small friend, his natural enthusiasm made it difficult to keep secrets.

"It's best if I quickly take care of this business for Swift Nail, and we leave here as soon as possible," Wind said.

"But, I thought—"

"We can't take the chance, Scowl," Wind cut in. "It's not safe for Lil' One, for you or for me. Believe me, Bolt will not be held back much longer. I have a bad feeling about him."

Scowl Down's eyes slid away from Wind toward Lil' One, then faced him again with an audible sigh.

"You're probably right. Do you want me to go with you?"

"No, I'm taking Big Rock with me. He knows this waterfront like the whiskers on his face. I want you to stay here and make sure Lil' One doesn't get into any trouble."

Wind and Big Rock left the warehouse before the day globe appeared and moved briskly along the waterfront alleys. The five days of rest at the colony had left him lazy, and it felt good to be outside, pushing his body once again. With any luck, they would quickly locate a new home for the colony and leave this place behind.

They scouted the blocks south of the warehouse to see how close the Hyskos machines had encroached, then Wind and Big Rock retraced their steps and moved northward and west off the riverfront. It looked like the Hyskos were tearing down the entire riverfront, block by block, and in order to find a safe haven they would have to move away from the water.

Wind and his small guide searched one abandoned and decaying site after another; warehouses similar to the one the colony now inhabited, brick buildings with condemned signs across the front, and the basement of a former hotel.

Wind studied each one to be sure there was enough space for the growing colony, that it contained easy access for the cats, but not for potential enemies, and that it was close to food and water. The morning rapidly became afternoon, and Wind sensed that Big Rock was tiring.

"Thank you for your help, Big Rock," Wind said with a nod to his companion. "Swift Nail should be pleased with at least one of the places we found. Why don't we make our way back and perhaps find something to eat along the way?"

Bolt was lying quietly at the rear of the packing crate. The day globe had already passed the top of the sky and he left the box only once to care for his needs. He lay there fuming, letting the words run through his mind in an endless loop.

This quest requires more foresight and imagination than Bolt possesses.

Bolt understood that Swift Nail was manipulating Windrusher just as she manipulated him and all males. That was her way. Still, it was becoming more difficult to control the murderous thoughts caroming through his brain.

He had surprised himself by not tearing the whining fraud's ears from his ugly head when he emerged from his packing crate. If he had given in to his fury, though, he wouldn't have stopped until Swift Nail was part of the bloody carnage. As much as she may deserve it, he needed her more than he needed the taste of Wind's blood in his mouth. At least, that's what he told himself yesterday.

He had spent last night and today letting toxic visions of revenge sweep any rational thought from his mind. This is the day Windrusher dies, he decided, and not only the hero, but his two worthless friends, too. After that, no cat, including Swift Nail, will dare challenge me. Bolt leaped to his feet and went in search of his own quest.

Lil' One and Scowl Down moved outside to take advantage of the afternoon sun. A pack of young cats trailed after them, still hoping to hear more stories.

As he had many times before, Lil' One rose to the occasion.

"What is it you want to hear this time?" he asked.

"Your escape from the snouters."

"Tell us about running down the mountain during the storm."

"What about how you met Wind?"

The story of how Wind and Lil' One met was one of his personal favorites. In its many recitations, the shy and fearful kitten was now recast in the role of intrepid rescuer for the bumbling Windrusher.

Lil' One stood on a cement block acting out the story of how fate stepped into the lives of two very different cats that day in Avon. "I had just finished outwitting a stupid and ugly floppy-eared snouter when I heard my brother cat crying out for help. He was cornered by an army of vicious high-legged beings carrying huge sticks."

Scowl Down lay in a shaft of sunlight next to the warehouse. If she had to listen to this story again she would spit up a hairball. A nap was a far better choice, she thought, so she closed her eyes.

Cats parted in the wake of the monster cat shouldering its way through the warehouse. Bolt's massive head hung down and swiveled from side to side as his one good eye hunted for his prey in the shadows. A pulse in his temple next to his blind eye began ticking and he felt a wave of heat spread across his face and down his throat.

Moving like death's own emissary, the clicks of his claws echoing on the cement floor, Bolt went straight to the column at the far end of the warehouse where he first saw Wind and his friends. They were gone.

Abruptly, he moved toward the pile of rotting burlap bags near the front doors. There were any number of places where Wind could be hiding, but he would root him out and kill him. He took one measured step toward the back of the warehouse and stopped, his unmarked ear swiveling toward the sound.

He recognized the whining voice of the cat that called himself by the ridiculous name of Lil' One. Silently Bolt moved toward the doors, his senses on full alert. His pupil dilated in the bright sunlight as he squinted at his prey — Windrusher's young friend.

"There he was surrounded by Hyskos cutting off all his escape routes," Lil' One was turning the story into a melodrama of epic proportions. "But they didn't expect him to have help from above. That is when I appeared on top of the tall fence and called for Wind to follow me. 'I'll save you,' I yowled down to poor Wind whose days as a free cat were nearly over."

The other cats huddled together under Lil' One's makeshift stage, hanging on his every word like they were the Seven Laws delivered by Tho-hoth himself. None of them noticed Bolt until it was too late.

The brutish cat had heard as much as he could stand. It wasn't enough that Windrusher was finding favor with his female, but now this stunted Wetlos was standing there like the king of the colony with subjects at his feet.

The buzz in his ears amplified, rising to a mind-shattering frequency. Lifting his massive head, he leaped from the doorway in a huge arc smashing into Lil' One and they tumbled backwards together. A hideous hissing arose from the rolling bodies until, finally, they lay still with the monstrous cat sitting solidly on top of Lil' One.

Squeals of surprise arose from the young cats, most of them fleeing the terrible sight before them. The others were rooted where they stood, frozen into a state of paralysis.

A ferocious growl erupted from deep in Bolt's throat as he swiped one thick paw against the side of the small cat's head. A tiny bubble of saliva formed at the corner of Lil' One's mouth and blood seeped out of a cut at the base of his ear. He struggled to force out the tiniest of whimpers while staring wide-eyed at the terror before him.

Bolt's lips pulled back exposing the awful canine teeth. He sensed fear flowing from the young cat's body, and heard the small heart beating out what would soon be its final chorus of life. This insignificant piece of offal was not Windrusher, but the whiskerless kitten would have to do until Windrusher appeared. The thought gave him great pleasure as he prepared to rip out Lil' One's throat and pictured doing the same to Windrusher.

His mouth wide, teeth bared, Bolt's head descended toward the exposed neck. Scowl Down caught him totally by surprise. The hysterical charge tumbled Bolt off the young cat, and the old female was on top of him, claws flashing, an ear piercing howl echoing off the wharf. Bolt pushed himself to his feet shaking the furious female off his back like drops of water. Scowl Down slid across the rough wooden planking, scraping her nose and leaving tufts of white fur trailing behind. Pain shot up her sternum and spread through her side, yet she managed to stand and shakily stepped forward. Bolt was on her before she could take a step. One ferocious swipe of his paw sent her crashing back to the dock.

"Run, Scowl. Get up and run," Lil' One yelled.

Scowl Down stared dully at Lil' One, then turned her eyes to Bolt. The ugly cat was straddling her, and she saw the hate in his contorted face, saw her death mirrored in that one bright lemon drop eye.

"Go and find Wind, Lil' One. Hurry, find him," she managed to croak in a voice tight with panic. She watched him hesitate then disappear around the corner.

Powerful claws raked across Scowl's flanks then down her nose. Bolt's fury was building to a crescendo. He had allowed the young Wetlos to get away, and this half-dead female had attacked him in full view of the other cats. He savaged her ear with powerful teeth while his sharp claws ripped at Scowl's tender belly.

By now, nearly half of the colony's population was outside watching in stunned disbelief the brutality being committed on the old female. Swift Nail was among the last to find her way outside, and she arrived as Bolt sank his teeth into Scowl's neck, biting down unmercifully.

"Bolt," she cried out. "Stop, you're killing her."

At the sound of her cries, the cats emerged from their catatonic state and began howling and jumping on one another in fright. Bolt's mouth was still clenched around Scowl Down's throat when Swift Nail reached him. She clawed the unhearing Bolt on the inside of his good ear until he let go.

He whirled to face Swift Nail, a look of pure hatred on his face, a low guttural sound gurgling in his throat. Bloody spume ran from his mouth, and he lurched toward Swift Nail. One cat after another surged forward, actuated by the sight of Scowl Down's body and their loathing for the tyrannical brute. The yowling cats raced angrily toward Bolt, and he turned and ran for his life, his tail drooping between his legs.

Scowl Down lay limp and unmoving on the dock. She was on her back where Bolt had left her, one paw still up in the air, the other foreleg hanging limply across her bloody body. The side of her head was flat against the splintered planks, her eyes staring into the distance. Bursts of sunlight glinted off the water, and a sea gull swooped down, glided elegantly across the surface and flew away.

On the river, an enormous barge stacked with barrels floated by in silence, and the river grew indistinct as if a gauzy curtain had fallen over the scene. She dropped her eyes to the wooden plank. Even the wood looked fuzzy, and what was that liquid spreading out in front of her in a shimmering coppery pool?

chapter 20

LIL' ONE SAT in the alley, his chest heaving, blood dripping from his cut ear. He had run crying from the dock then stopped to catch his breath. While he was fleeing the inconceivable horror that had almost taken his life, racing away like the frightened kitten he was, Scowl Down was facing Bolt's anger. Anger that was meant for him.

He was a heartbeat away from feeling Bolt's teeth in his neck when old Scowl charged in and saved his life. What could he have done against the brutish cat, he asked himself over and over? No, Scowl was right, I have to find Wind. He looked nervously from his left to his right, mentally choosing the path to take, and started to his right.

Big Rock turned the corner at the same time and the two cats nearly collided.

"Lil' One, what happened to you?" Big Rock asked, alarmed at the sight of blood on his friend's face.

"Help me find Wind. Bolt tried to kill me. Scowl Down saved me, but I'm afraid—" The words tumbled out of Lil' One then caught in his throat when Windrusher appeared.

Windrusher ran furiously to the dock prepared for the fight of his life. The pile of cats surrounding his fallen comrade brought him to a sudden stop, and it took a moment for him to decipher the scene. Dozens of cats pressed around the prostrate body of Scowl Down. They stared in stunned silence as Swift Nail licked the horrendous wound in the old female's neck. She lay motionless in a pool of blood, her white hair now turning a startling shade of crimson. Her body was torn so badly, Windrusher froze at the sight. This couldn't be his old friend, the same Scowl Down that had shared their lives for the past two night globes. Not the grumpy old cat that chastised him for his follies, and tolerated Lil' One's pounces and pranks.

The circle of cats opened to allow Wind to pass through. Swift Nail looked at Windrusher with an expression of pure misery on her blood-splattered face. Even though he suspected the worse from Lil' One's brief description, the sight of Scowl's body and the look in Swift Nail's eyes took his breath away.

Scowl Down lay unmoving, completely framed by the drying puddle of blood. He squatted next to her, bending his head to hers. Wind saw the tiniest of movement from her chest and a pale spark of light in her eyes and realized she was still alive.

With Windrusher and Lil' One now at her side, the old female's eyes brightened in recognition, and Lil' One gently licked the stricken female's face.

"My f-friends," Scowl Down stammered in a ragged voice filled with pain.

"Save your strength," Wind replied softly.

"I'm sorry I can't follow your Path any longer, Wind," she murmured, spitting a globule of russet colored froth from her mouth. "Promise me..."

Her eyes closed and her body shook violently. Wind and Lil' One leaned in closer to their friend.

After another long pause, Scowl's eyes opened and she looked first at Lil' One then cut her eyes to Windrusher. In a voice so faint Wind had to put his ear next to her lips to hear, the old cat whispered, "Take care of Lil' One, he..."

She was still and a vast emptiness replaced the light in her eyes.

Slowly, very slowly, a sob made its way up the length of Lil' One's small chest and caught in his throat. It seemed like a noose tightened around his neck, cutting off his breath, causing him to gulp for air.

The sob finally emerged in the form of a long, low howl. He put his head down and butted the unmoving body, then lay still beside her, his head between his paws.

The sun slipped behind a bank of dark clouds, pushed away by a cold breeze that raked through their fur like a frozen comb. The cats of the colony silently moved behind the trio, as if standing guard on the three cats and their grief.

The tragic scene didn't have the same affect on Bolt. After running away from the pack of cats, he circled back, and was watching warily from behind a stack of mildewed and splintered pallets. Anger was joined inexplicably by a mounting sense of sadness as he contemplated what he had lost by killing Scowl Down. Windrusher was now the top cat in the colony. Windrusher had Swift Nail's affections. And, it was Windrusher that should be dead.

Hate and fury coursed through his body, and it took all his strength to stop himself from charging through the phalanx of cats to kill Windrusher. Normally, self-control was not a trait he admired, but he had learned a valuable lesson. All in due time, he told himself, all in due time. You have my solemn pledge, Windrusher, that we will meet again one day. And, believe me that will be your final day alive on this globe.

He turned, slinked silently down the alley, and padded away from the waterfront.

Windrusher spent the afternoon alternately blaming himself, and tending to Lil' One. He groomed the young cat methodically, licking the nasty cut along his ear until it scabbed over. Thankfully, Lil' One was not seriously hurt, at least not where it showed, but he cried for hours before falling into an exhausted sleep.

Wind paced the concrete floor in a silent rage. It was my visit with Swift Nail that caused this, I know it. How could I let this happen? Even after I warned Scowl Down about Bolt, I left her alone with him.

Wind's agitation finally subsided, he lowered himself to the floor, and rested his head across Lil' One's back.

Later, when they were both awake, Lil' One asked the question Wind had feared.

"Why?"

"This was Scowl Down's Way," Wind said. "She followed the Path of Irissa-u and proved herself a worthy cat by saving your life."

"So she will live forever?" Lil' One asked.

"If any cat deserves to live forever, shouldn't it be Scowl Down?"

The two friends huddled together throughout the evening, consoling each other and remembering their dead friend. After another long nap, they padded through the darkness of the warehouse, out the huge doors, and never looked back.

chapter 21

RAHHNA MUST BE GRIEVING, too, Windrusher thought. The day globe remained hidden behind murky skies casting a dreary pall over the city. It took the travelers days to find their way through the Hyskos village, dodging frenetic traffic, hiding from snarling snouters, and finding their way back on the mainland.

Fear became a constant partner, gnawing at Wind like the fleas that bled him and threw him into spasms of scratching and biting. Since leaving the nightmare behind, they were confronted with constant reminders that they were just two small cats in a Hyskos world.

Traversing hundreds of miles of enormous Hyskos villages and confusing highway systems took its toll on them. They moved mostly at night to avoid as much human activity as possible. Between the commuter towns, falling one upon the other like the results of some grotesque domino game played by giants, they encountered speeding freight trains and confusing highways littered with the two-eyed vehicles. Lil' One could not imagine why these high-legged beings were not content to stay in their homes. They always seemed to be darting from one place to the other.

It was nearly daybreak and they stood shivering in the median of an eight-lane freeway as an eighteen-wheeler blasted a wall of sand over the two cats. Wind squeezed his eyes shut, then looked to be sure his small friend had not been swept away.

They maneuvered across the other four lanes of traffic, and crossed a lightly wooded field toward higher ground. The trees were a welcome sight after weeks of hiking through the treacherous urban area. In the distance they saw a small farm, and heard the sound of a diesel tractor carried on the morning breeze. The sweet smell of clover and purple violets tickled Lil' One's nose and a tiny sneeze shook his head.

"Scowl Down would have loved this land, wouldn't she?" Wind asked.

Despite the welcome tranquility of the countryside, the thought of Scowl Down's death ached inside him like a hairball that would not go away and grew larger each day. More than once as they scrambled down city streets, through back yards and alleys, Wind unconsciously paused to give Scowl Down time to catch up with them.

Lil' One carried more than his share of grief for their lost friend, so he was surprised when the little tom responded to his rhetorical question. "She would have complained about the rocks hurting her paws, the bugs in the water, and the damp night air."

Wind looked at his small friend, fond memories of the cantankerous old female flooding back to him. "You're so right, Lil' One. The Holy Mother must surely have been surprised when she welcomed Scowl Down to Rahhna. Little did she know that there was so much wrong with the holy home, but now she has Scowl Down there to tell her so."

Lil' One was draped listlessly over the trunk of a lightning-struck maple tree. His eyes were closed and one foreleg was extended in front of him, the other tucked beneath his neck. At Wind's words, he jumped to his feet and bounded over to his older friend.

"That's true as a whisker," the young cat spluttered excitedly. "Only Scowl Down would find fault with the kingdom of Rahhna. Can you see Irissa-u chewing her tail while Scowl tells her how it can be improved?"

Lil' One butted Wind emphatically several times in the shoulder, almost knocking him off balance.

Windrusher groomed his small friend tenderly, licking him across the head and ears, careful to avoid his still tender ear. Lil' One hung his head and became quite still, and Wind sensed melancholy replacing the lighter mood.

"There will never be another cat like our old friend," Wind said. "We were fortunate to have her with us for so long. Her wisdom was there to help us when you were sick, to keep me upon the proper path, and she proved her friendship by giving her life to save yours."

Wind felt the knot in his chest dissolve and give way to a

powerful lightness that seemed to lift him off the ground.

"Just know that Scowl Down did more than most cats have done in their lives. She was part of our mission, and remains with us. She will always be your friend, and watch over you from the kingdom of Rahhna."

Wind resumed grooming Lil' One, then they lay down close to each other and watched the butterflies hovering above the violets.

Four eyes glowed in the dark of the woods absorbing every fractured scrap of light filtering through the trees. Even with their extraordinary night vision, several times better than the high-legged beings, the two cats often had to feel their way through the thick forest. They relied upon their sense of smell, hearing, and the delicate touch of their whiskers to help them navigate the woods.

Windrusher finally had to admit that even these senses weren't enough. Were they making progress or simply traveling in circles? He stopped and sat, his tail swishing rapidly.

"Lil' One, these woods have turned me into a whiskerless kitten. Each tree and bush looks like the other, and it seems like we're following our tails."

Wind bit furiously at a flea that was feasting on his shoulder. "Spphhh." He shook his head and tried to spit out some hair lodged in his upper lip.

"Perhaps we should just nap here until Rahhna returns so we can see our own feet. I'd hate for you to fall into a hole and…"

Wind realized that Lil' One had not responded to him and he couldn't see his young friend anywhere. "Lil' One," he bellowed. "Where are you?"

Only the sounds of night came back to him; the chirp of crickets, a slight rustling in the underbrush as some nocturnal creature scurried away. From overhead a haunting hoo-hoo-hoooo skimmed the tree-tops and dropped ominously to the forest floor.

Windrusher tensed, willing his eyes to see through the gelatinous gloom. "Lil', can you hear me? Answer me; this is no time for games."

Moving as quickly as he could in the blackness, Wind put his nose to the ground and searched for Lil' One's scent. He backtracked to the last place he remembered seeing his small friend and found his scent at the base of a large sweet gum tree. He continued sniffing around the tree, then stopped, unable to believe his eyes. Even in this dim light, he couldn't mistake the bushy question-marked shape of the tail that stuck out of the ground. He watched a moment as the buttocks shifted from side to side and backed out of the rabbit hole.

Wind was so relieved to see Lil' One, that he almost missed the soft swooshing sound above him. Startled, he raised his head to see huge yellow eyes hurtling down from the sky towards them. The round orange face was capped by two horny ears, but it was the shiny black beak and razor sharp talons that roused him to action.

Windrusher heaved himself toward Lil' One, propelling him backwards over a root. They tumbled together as the Great Horned Owl screamed out a growling "krrooo-oo," its talons cutting through the air just a hair's width from Wind's back.

"Quick, hide before the creature returns."

He prodded the small tabby forward out of the clearing and toward a tangle of bushes. They wormed their way deep inside the thicket, scratching their noses on the brambles, and lay quietly listening for the unsettling swoosh of wings.

Hours later, as the sky began to lighten in the east, the two cats cautiously nosed their way out of the bushes, studied the branches above them, and scurried away.

"It was just a baby rabbit, and I was sure I could reach him." Lil' One was explaining how he came to be in the rabbit's burrow.

"I wanted to surprise you with a tasty supper, but I couldn't fit down the hole."

Wind was still shaken at how close they had come to being prey to another night hunter. He licked quietly at a painfully cracked paw trying to forget the sight of those terrifying talons.

"What is wrong with you, Wind? You're not still worried about that great bag of feathers, are you?"

"No, it's not that. I was thinking how far we still are from my Hyskos family. If we don't find a swifter route we may wear down before…" His voice trailed off.

The early morning sun was scraping the night palette clear of burnt umber, replacing it with wide strokes of red ochre. Windrusher gazed at the woods around them, silhouettes of trees coming into leafy focus.

"You know I have favored staying out of the Hyskos villages and finding our way through this kind of country," he said. "There is danger there, but there is danger everywhere, and I fear that wandering through the woods and hills will lead us to ruin, not to the Path."

Lil' One jerked his head to one side like he had just seen something lurking in the bushes. Then he spun around chasing his tail. "The Path," he yowled. "The Path."

Wind cut his eyes to the twirling cat wondering what his poor Wetlos friend was doing. "Lil' One, are you trying to attract that flying devil again? What about the Path?"

Lil' One rolled over until he was looking Windrusher in the eye. "Listen to me before you call me a Wetlos, will you?"

Wind wondered if the little cat could now read his mind. "Yes, of course I will."

"What is the straightest, most direct way to get from one place to another?" he asked. Without waiting for an answer, Lil' One blurted out, "The Hyskos Path."

"Yes, but—" Wind began.

"Yes, and if we follow it we won't have to go through woods and climb rocks and cross rivers. We just do like the Hyskos vehicles and follow the black path."

Lil' One rolled over once more with excitement.

"I understand what you're saying, Lil' One, but there is great danger on the Hyskos path."

"That's the wisdom of it, don't you see? We don't have to be on the black path itself. We can stay on the side, safe from the Hyskos vehicles, and still follow it."

Lil' One sat with a satisfied expression on his face and waited for Wind to tell him what an excellent idea it was.

Wind thought for a moment, weighed his fear of the black path and the deadly vehicles against his need to find his family. He quickly made up his mind.

"Lil' One, I think that's an excellent idea."

chapter **22**

LIKE MANY EXCELLENT IDEAS, Lil' One's suggestion proved to be more difficult than it appeared. Staying away from the hurtling vehicles was relatively easy, and following the black path was far better than blundering through woods, climbing over and around hills. They picked up their pace and traveled during daylight hours as much as their exhausted bodies would allow.

The problem was the black paths themselves; there were so many shooting out in different directions, that they became confused. The landscape was braided by paths intertwined like the reeds in a straw basket.

Wind's internal beacon kept them on a general southwesterly track, but he couldn't be sure where the Hyskos' paths might lead. And each one was different. Some were narrow and seldom traversed, and they dashed across and followed alongside these without fear. Others stretched out beyond their vision and carried as many vehicles as hairs on their tails.

The two travelers studied the path carrying six lanes of traffic up and down the black ribbon of highway. They walked past a green sign with a blue and red shield designating it as I-80, and decided to see where it took them.

Three day globes passed, and they found a nearby hollow and prepared for a long sleep.

"This path has no end, does it? By my whiskers, I can't see it leading us in the direction of warm waters."

"That may be so," Lil' One replied obviously unconcerned. "But look how far we've traveled since we've followed the black path."

"What does it matter how far we travel if we're moving away from our destination?"

Wind found he was beginning to complain more these days. Several times, he caught himself sounding exactly like crotchety old Scowl Down.

"I'm too tired to think now. Let's sleep and then we'll decide what to do."

Windrusher rolled over and with that wonderful ability cats possess, went immediately to sleep.

Wave after wave washed over him, pulling him into the vortex of Akhen-et-u. The voices reached out for him and he felt himself reeling from one side to another as if he were a billiard ball caroming off the cushions. Slowly the tinny voices merged and he was able to plunge through a brief gap and introduce himself to the massive network of sleeping cats.

"Ah, Pferusha-ulis. We have all been waiting to hear of your latest adventure. What has happened since you left the colony?"

This was followed by a general uproar that almost overwhelmed him. Windrusher wasn't surprised. Each time he visited the Inner Ear more voices seemed to join the clamor, demanding details of his adventure. He kept his report brief, and highlighted the essentials of the past several weeks. After another outburst that included statements of disbelief and awe regarding their grueling travels and the frightening encounter with the Great Horned Owl, Wind detailed their travels along I-80.

"It is true we have made excellent progress on this Hyskos path, but my instincts tell me we are farther away from the warm waters than before we began following the great black path."

This time the babble of voices was more subdued, until a new voice emerged from the background.

"Trust your instincts, adventurer. My Hyskos family travels that path often as we live very close to where you are now. And you are correct. The direction of warm waters is below you and this will take you far toward the place where Rahhna goes to sleep."

"Aiyiii! So I was right, and we have worn away our pads for nothing," Wind said with more than a hint of self-pity.

"Don't despair. You have not done any harm, and you will soon come to a place where another great path crosses. Follow this one.

You and Lil' One have made us all very proud, Windrusher. May the Holy Mother continue to walk by your side."

Wind thanked them for their advice and fell away exhausted from the chorus of voices pressing in on him. He slept fitfully, with dreams of Swift Nail, Bolt, and Scowl Down chasing him through darkened woods filled with hidden traps. In one frightening scene, he followed Lil' One into a rabbit hole only to have the tunnel whipsaw violently and toss the two of them into the night.

He woke with a start, his ears flickering nervously, his mouth dry with the taste of fear. Lil' One was still sleeping, and Wind relaxed, drawing encouragement from the last voice he heard during his encounter with Akhen-et-u. They will make their turn toward the warm waters tonight, he told himself.

It was close to 10:30 P.M. when they saw the lights and the small building. The enticing aromas carried on the warm night breeze promised a story with a satisfying ending, and they followed their noses into the rest stop. A series of aluminum light poles, spaced every thirty feet through the parking lot, bathed the area with a jaundiced hue, casting eerie elongated shadows on the only vehicle parked in front of the rest area.

A line of picnic shelters stood empty in the night like ghostly cemetery vaults. Directly ahead was a shed with three snack machines and a path leading to a small concrete block building.

The parking lot was empty of the Hyskos traveling vehicles except for a white metal box with wheels. It was attached to another vehicle and parked sideways across several spaces between the restrooms and the picnic tables. The cats saw a light shining through the small windows in the side of the white contraption.

Wind and Lil' One eased closer to the picnic tables, looking cautiously from side to side to be sure they were alone. They were already familiar with the rest stops, having visited several and always finding tasty morsels left behind by the high-legged beings.

After satisfying themselves that there were no Hyskos in sight, the two cats scurried toward the picnic shelters. Lil' One led the way this time. Hunger drove him on, and he outraced his more cautious friend toward the closest trashcan. The small cat was atop the garbage can growling at the uncooperative lid when Wind caught up with him. Seeing that the lid was firmly ensconced on the can, Wind moved to the next picnic shelter.

He sniffed at another garbage can, and saw the lid balanced precariously atop a heap of trash. A rush of smells collided in his nostrils, confirming that there was more than enough food to satisfy their hunger, and he thanked the Holy Mother for this bit of good fortune.

Wind leaped on the garbage can lid, and it shifted under his weight exposing paper plates, a watermelon rind, and scraps of fried chicken. He plunged into the trash, the lid slid out from under him and crashed to the ground.

Minutes later, he raised his head from the trashcan and took a deep breath. His tongue licked wide circles around his mouth and he was about to dive back into the garbage when he heard a voice.

"Nice kitty. That's right, it's so good, isn't it. Here's some more for you."

The voice was soft and soothing, and brought back memories of Kimmy, his Hyskos female. Wind spotted a slim girl with very short hair the color of corn silk on the dirt path that led to the sidewalk. Dressed in a pair of cut off jeans and an oversize T-shirt, she was bent over, her hand extended, moving slowly backwards toward the parking lot. Wind's eyes followed the girl's hand and saw Lil' One eating a scrap of food.

The young female dropped another scrap on the ground; all the while talking to the little cat in a voice so comforting, even Wind felt himself relax. Lil' One looked at the girl with wide eyes that reflected the pale beams of the parking lot lights, hesitated as if trying to work his way through some puzzle, then scurried forward to eat the next nugget of food.

Wind watched unmoving and uncomprehending as this ritual was repeated several times, the pair now on the sidewalk moving farther away from the picnic shelters, closer to the boxy white vehicle parked nearby.

The girl carefully climbed the steps, opened the door so slowly it seemed to take forever, and eased herself inside. Wind watched the girl step into the box, a light above her head bathing her in a bright aura, blurring her features. Then she leaned forward out the open door and tossed more food to Lil' One while her voice seemed to offer a heavenly security that drew the little cat unconsciously toward her.

In that moment, the sound of highway traffic was suddenly muted. The greasy taste of chicken on Wind's tongue was replaced by a sour, metallic coating. It was that moment when the indistinct became distinct and the pieces came together for Windrusher. Clearly, Lil' One was being drawn into a trap that would take him away, perhaps forever.

Wind bounded off the garbage can and dashed toward the recreational vehicle. He tried desperately to warn his friend, but the cry rattled around in the arid patches of his throat, and emerged as a tiny gurgling sound. He reached the sidewalk just as Lil' One hopped on the top step enticed by another morsel of food.

The girl in the shorts and T-shirt saw the larger cat running toward her. A small smile played across her even features, and she reached down as if to drop another chunk of food at her feet.

Now, the cry finally broke free, and Wind called out his friend's name in a long grating wail. Lil' One paused before stepping through the open door. Windrusher was screaming his name and charging toward him at a full run. The sight made the hairs on his back standup in alarm.

It was too late. When he looked back, the girl reached down from inside the brightness, grabbed Lil' One by the nape of the neck and pulled him into the compartment.

Wind felt his heart fluttering in his chest as the younger cat disappeared. There was no time to make a conscious decision. Without hesitation, he hurtled the two steps into the Hyskos vehicle just as the door slammed shut behind him.

Both cats remained frozen in the overhead light. All of Wind's preconceived notions of a Hyskos vehicle were turned upside down. They weren't in a vehicle at all, it seemed, but inside a home. The oak cabinetry in front of him housed a picture box, and on the floor were bright area rugs. To his right was a green and white couch covered with little yellow flowers.

A sudden knock on the door startled Wind and he jumped into the air, then turned and ran toward an open room. Amazingly, he spied a bed in the small room and slid beneath it, followed immediately by Lil' One.

"Honey, are you in there," a woman's voice asked from outside.

The door swung open and a tall woman with reddish blonde hair and freckles stuck her head inside and smiled broadly at the child. "Baby, you need to turn off that light and go to bed. Your dad is about to take off and I don't want you bouncing around in here."

Moments later, assured that their daughter was safe in bed, Mr. and Mrs. Wilkins climbed into the cab of their navy blue Ford F250 and headed for home.

chapter 23

WILKINS MADE a lazy U-turn and pulled the Travel Star through the parking lot toward the exit to I-80 West. The glowing beams of the overhead sodium lights washed over the RV's fiberglass body, a parade of anemic colors playing across the roof until it passed into darkness.

A dense mass of Northern Bayberry bushes covered the southeastern corner of the rest rooms. The bushes screened a small pump house that controlled the irrigation system that kept the lawn green during the spring and summer. At this time of night, there was no one to admire the lushness of the lawn, or the aromatic green leaves of the Bayberry bushes. The only sentient being within one hundred feet of the bushes would never appreciate the wonders of nature's garden.

Especially not tonight.

Bolt slipped from behind the Bayberry and watched the Hyskos vehicle drive away with Windrusher and Lil' One aboard. The Setlos from the warehouse colony was a handsome cat compared to the bedraggled creature standing at the rest stop. He had lost ten pounds in the weeks since he was chased from the colony, and his skin hung like a fur serapé on his massive frame. His huge head seemed to hang even lower than before, highlighting the ugly red scar snaking its way through his ear and down his face.

The harsh lemon colored eye burned brighter than ever, and even though he witnessed their escape in the Hyskos vehicle, he still could not believe it. Bolt had chased his sworn enemy from town to town since that fateful day he killed Scowl Down, and his hatred rose by increments. Each day the emotion roiling inside him was ratcheted up another degree, as if he feared what might happen if he allowed all the repulsion and loathing he felt to tumble loose at one time.

Sometimes he thought the tales surrounding Windrusher might be true; that he had been picked by Irissa-u to fulfill some holy mission. But weren't these all kitten tales? The only mission this journeyer would fulfill was what Bolt intended to do to him once they faced one another.

Yet, how do you explain what he had witnessed?

He was so close to getting his bloody and satisfying revenge. He had worked it all out so carefully, the suffering he would bring down on Windrusher, the pain he would inflict. All too soon the worm-eaten fool would cower and beg him to end his miserable life.

That's how it should have been, and this was the place he should have found his revenge and tasted the cat's blood. He had slipped behind the bushes while they were occupied with the trashcans, and was waiting until they were both gorged and ready to nap. Who would believe a Hyskos female could spoil his plan?

Stunned by his failure, Bolt collapsed; suddenly weary from his efforts over the past weeks. After following the pair through the dangerous streets of several New Jersey towns, Bolt had lost their scent and wasn't sure he would ever find them again. Then he realized that Windrusher was too vain not to report on his mighty mission to his adoring fans awaiting him in Akhen-et-u. From that point on, he stayed plugged in to the Inner Ear as much as possible to hear any word of the traveler's progress.

Still, it was not an easy task. He had always been a day globe or two behind them, tracing their steps through alleys and storm drains. Backtracking when he went straight and they made illogical turns, and intimidating other cats for clues to where they rested. Then the trail went cold and he wandered without any real hope of finding them. That was when Wind made the mistake of being too explicit about his whereabouts on the Hyskos path. From that point, he was able to make tremendous gains on them.

And he had them in his sights, just a claw length away. What was he was going to do now? It was one thing to follow Windrusher when they used their own four feet, but how could he track him in a Hyskos vehicle, going who knows where?

Bolt's exhausted body wouldn't let him think past the disappointment and hunger he felt. Slowly, on legs aching with the pains of his travels, he walked toward the scraps that Wind had been digging through. First, I have to eat, he told himself.

He looked at the tempting garbage can, his lemon drop eye going out of focus as though he was concentrating on an internal question whose answer eluded him. Above him, precariously balanced from the rim of the green container, a wishbone dangled, swaying in the hot summer breeze.

chapter 24

CARROLL DENNIS WILKINS, named after an uncle who never returned from the Korean War, was known simply as Denny to everyone in Gallipolis. During the night, his wife safely asleep beside him and unable to nag him about speeding, he averaged seventy-two miles per hour, driving the Ford and the Travel Star nearly 400 miles closer to home. Somewhere around Hazelton, he turned south on U.S. 81 and was now passing Pennsylvania signs advising him where to stop for gas and food.

The sun was brightening the horizon off to his left, the light glinting in his side mirror. It was time to fill-up, but what he really needed was a cup of strong coffee and a place to take a whiz. He took the Tremont exit and pulled into the station with the big red sign not so much because of the welcoming Texaco star but because of the McDonald's next door.

Light filtered through the window shades and flashed across Libby Wilkins' face when the trailer slowed down and eased into the Texaco station. Suddenly wide-awake, she rubbed a hand over her hair, and called out to the two cats.

"Hey, are you guys still hiding under there?" she said in a singsong voice.

She dove to the side of the bed, hung her body over and pulled up the dust ruffle. Libby stuck her head under the bed and saw the shadows huddled together against the far wall. In the darkness, the girl caught the glints of light reflected from their eyes but couldn't tell the small multicolored tabby from the orange striped one.

"It's all right. You don't have to be afraid. You're going to love the farm, just you wait and see."

The two cats looked at her warily then turned away so she could no longer see their eyes. Libby jumped off the bed and ran to the refrigerator just as the Travel Star came to a stop. She returned to the bedroom with two cereal bowls, one filled with milk, the other with water, and slid them under the bed.

"You guys help yourself to breakfast. I have to break the news to mom and dad so we can get you some real food. I don't think potato chips will be too good for you." She slipped on her sandals and ran out the door.

Eleanor Wilkins reached out and wrapped her daughter in a huge hug, lifting her off her feet and kissing her on the mouth. "Did you enjoy sleeping alone in that big bed?" she asked.

At first glance, there wasn't much resemblance between the slim fair-haired girl and her mother, but as they walked to the gas pump, there was no doubt that these two were from the same gene pool. Arms swinging like a pair of Rockettes on parade, mother and daughter laughed and talked, their eyes crinkling with the same sly playfulness.

"How you holding up, big boy?" Eleanor Wilkins said, giving her husband a peck on the cheek.

Wilkins slouched against the truck, his eyes half closed beneath a sweat stained Stetson. He wore a pair of Wranglers and Timberland hiking boots. A white tank top bearing the gold and blue WV logo of West Virginia University stretched tightly across his chest. Despite signs of stomach muscles giving up yardage in the battle of the bulge, the rest of him looked as solid as a defensive end, which was the position he played with the Mountaineers and briefly with the Chicago Bears a hundred years ago, as he liked to tell people who commented on his heralded football career.

Wilkins pushed his hat up with a callused thumb and smiled broadly at Eleanor and Libby. "Baby, I'm ready for you to take this rig and let me get some sleep. First, let's go over to Mickey D's and order up some breakfast."

Between bites of her breakfast, Libby told them about the rescue of the two cats at the rest stop. Mother and daughter shared strong feelings about the protective role of the human race when it came to animals, and both had brought home so many strays that Wilkins called their farm the petting zoo. Wilkins was a dairy farmer and always concerned about his animals so he understood his family's love for nature's creatures. When it came to pets, however, he had always been a dog lover, and although he groused each time it happened, he was ready to share his 420-acre farm with the growing menagerie of wild and domestic animals.

After breakfast, they walked back to the Travel Star. Limping slightly on his bad knee, Wilkins nodded his head vigorously with a bemused expression on his face as if he had just heard the perfect punch line and wanted to commit it to memory. His Stetson eased slowly down with each assertive nod until it rested on the bridge of his nose.

"What's so funny?" Eleanor Wilkins asked her husband, pushing up the cowboy hat.

"I don't get it," he said looking from his wife to his daughter. "Even on vacation, in the middle of the night, miles away from the civilized world, you still manage to find strays to rescue."

He placed the same kind of emphasis on the word *rescue* as he might on the word *tofu* in response to a waiter's suggestion.

"Daddy, just wait until you see them. They're so cute, especially the little one. And they were so hungry. How could I let these animals suffer, when we can help them? That's what you and mommy always told me, isn't it?"

Denny Wilkins bent over and snatched up his daughter, holding her in the crook of one arm as if she were still an infant. "You are right, baby," he said, giving her a noisy kiss on the neck. "Let's meet the newest residents of the Wilkins' Petting Zoo."

While the Wilkinses enjoyed their breakfast, Wind and Lil' One cautiously emerged from under the bed and explored their new environment. Wind was standing on the kitchen counter and Lil' One was stretched out in an armchair when the door opened unexpectedly. The Wilkinses hurried inside and closed the door behind them; surprised to see the cats obviously making themselves at home in the Travel Star. Before any of them could say a word, Wind leaped from the countertop, slid across the slick kitchen floor, and dashed into the bedroom.

Lil' One stood on the armchair, his eyes wide with fear, watching the girl approach him. Libby was within two paces of the small cat when he jumped over the winged arm and followed Windrusher under the bed.

"Those two heifers couldn't be happier to see us, now could they?" drawled Wilkins. "I think they have the right idea, though. As soon as we get them some food and a litter box so they don't pee under our bed, I'm going to join them in the bedroom, if you don't mind."

Wind peered from under the dust ruffle, his green eyes glistening in the dimness of the shaded bedroom. The two cats had huddled together listening to the sound of the road below them and the occasional noise of the bed springs stretching as Denny Wilkins rolled over on the bed above them.

Windrusher padded silently into the living room. Light streamed through a large window behind the green and white couch, the sun flashing shadowy signals over the floor as the trailer whipped past a grove of trees. He jumped on the back of the couch and looked out the window in shocked amazement. The Travel Star was in the far right lane of traffic and Wind saw the Pennsylvania landscape stream by in a blurry montage.

Lil' One joined his friend and for a moment they stared silently out the window.

"This Hyskos vehicle is unlike any I have traveled in before," Wind said, remembering the panic attacks that struck him every time he would ride in the Trembles' vehicle.

"It seems a more comfortable way to journey than walking along the black path, wouldn't you agree?" Lil' One asked.

"Yes, but we are trapped in this…this rolling room, Lil' One. And we're moving away from the warm waters."

Wind's tail and ears vibrated with agitation then he flattened himself on the thick cushions atop the couch. Lil' One followed his friend's lead, and both cats stared through the window at the hodgepodge of billboards, gas stations, motels, and trees that passed like ghosts in the outside air.

After lunch at the Carlisle Cracker Barrel, Denny Wilkins slipped into the driver's seat and eased the Ford out of the parking lot. "Fasten your seat belt, put your tray in its upright position, and prepare for take off. Next stop, Gallipolis," he announced, stroking his wife's knee.

In the Travel Star, Libby Wilkins sat on the same couch the two cats had occupied earlier that day. She bounced a small yellow cylinder of cat treats up and down in her hand as though trying to gauge its weight. Then she shook it harder and the treats rattled around noisily in the can.

"Cleo and Theo, guess what I have for you?" she called out. "It's something really tasty, but you have to come out here and get it."

She poured a few of the heart shaped treats in her hand, walked to the bedroom, and waved the treats under the bed. The air was suddenly alive with hints of chicken, shrimp, and liver mingled with the yeasty smell of whole wheat bread. Wind's stomach gurgled, but he remained in his hiding place at the far corner of the bed.

To Lil' One, the smell was both new and old. He recognized some of the appetizing fragrances but others were so exotic and compelling that he automatically crawled toward the source of the smell. Wind growled a warning that halted the small cat. Looking back toward his older friend, he lay still, and rested his head on his paws.

Libby repeated her enticements several times, all the while speaking in soft soothing tones to the hidden cats. Each time, Lil' One inched closer to the foot of the bed. After the fourth try, the girl tucked the dust ruffle below the mattress, exposing the hiding place and dropped one of the treats on the floor next to the bed. She retreated to the middle of the living room and sat on the floor.

Seeing the bit of heart-shaped goodness proved too much for Lil' One to ignore. He dashed out, snapped up the treat, and returned to his position under the bed.

The small tabby had lived by his own wits until meeting Windrusher, and had developed a finely honed internal security system that alerted him to potential danger. That system was silent now. He could sense no danger from the Hyskos female despite the occasional growls coming from Wind. In fact, since they had entered the rolling room, this female had treated them with kindness, fed and cared for them.

Libby shook the can again then took another one out and threw it toward the bed. The small cat crept forward until he emerged from the darkness into the light of the rolling room. He halted there, his legs tensed under him prepared to dart back to the safety of the bed, his eyes cutting from the girl to the treat on the floor, then back to the girl.

Libby remained motionless, her legs folded, her hands planted on the floor. "You're safe here, my pretty little cat. Libby won't let anything hurt you. Go ahead and eat, its okay."

The girl spoke so softly it could have been the sound of a summer breeze blowing through the trees, or the lyrical tune of a songbird humming in the cat's ear. Lil' One edged forward, his belly flat against the floor, his tail tucked under him, as if trying to make himself even smaller than he was. All the while, his gaze remained fixed on the girl until he finally reached the treat and, after one final look, sucked down the snack.

Libby smiled broadly, slowly took another treat out of the can, and tossed it lightly in front of her.

Lil' One jerked at the girl's motion, then relaxed with a flicker of his ears. He checked again for danger signals, inched forward, and devoured the treat.

Windrusher had also emerged from under the bed. His earlier fears had given way to warm memories of his Hyskos female, and a life that seemed so distant it might have been part of a dream. Lil' One sat at the girl's feet staring up at her, and Wind remembered the almost mystical attraction a young cat had to its Hyskos.

The girl slowly put her hand out toward the cat. Lil' One's tail swished nervously, but he stayed where he was. The girl eased herself forward, her hand extended, still making those same incomprehensible, yet comforting, sounds until she was close enough to touch the small cat. Even from the bedroom, Wind heard the low purring as the girl gently rubbed Lil' One's head. She stroked under his jaw, ran her hand over his back and lightly down his tail and Lil' One rolled over on his side, purring even louder, kneading his head into the carpet.

She carefully stroked the cat's belly, and smiled. "I see. You're not a Cleo, you're a Leo," she said.

When the Travel Star pulled into the farm at Gallipolis later that night, Wind lay on the couch watching the Hyskos female sleep in the big easy chair. Her head was tilted back, and her eyes moved rapidly under the pale lids as if watching some internal movie. Wind saw a tentative smile play over the girl's mouth and her hand twitched slightly as Lil' One shifted in her lap.

chapter 25

THE MORNING SUN rose like a fiery spider, weaving fine cords through the early morning air. It flamed past the rolling hills of southeastern Ohio, past the bustling Ohio River, and roused an energetic rooster at the Wilkins' farm. Denny Wilkins was still asleep when the rooster crowed its noisy reveille outside his bedroom window. He groaned loudly and pulled the pillow over his head.

Eleanor sat on the small wooden deck outside the kitchen sipping coffee from a navy blue cup that was big enough to double as a soup bowl. She let her eyes drift over the fishpond, starbursts of light twinkling on the surface, then toward the milk barn where Jeremy and Earl, Jr. were still milking the seventy-two cows.

Counting the milking herd, calves, bulls, and dry cows, they had approximately 160 cattle to tend. This was a full-time job for at least three people, not counting her and Libby who pitched in regularly. Dairy farming was a family affair, and Denny would be back into his routine soon enough, but their son, Jeremy, had been in charge for the past week, and he could manage for one more day.

The life of a dairy farmer was an exhausting one filled with twelve-hour days of tending cows, storing and selling milk, and producing forage for the herd. Denny had nearly 320 acres planted with corn, hay, and sorghum. Most of that went directly to feed the animals, although he managed to sell some of his corn crop each year.

Eleanor took another sip of coffee and settled back in the old cane rocker. She savored these moments of serenity knowing they were rare. How did the summer slip away so quickly? In three weeks she would report to school to prepare for another year educating the young minds attending Samuel Finley Vinton High. That was her real job, although she spent nearly thirty hours a week, counting weekends, helping Denny with the farm.

"Mommy, guess who slept under my bed last night?" Libby yelled through the kitchen window, shattering the peace and bringing a smile to Eleanor's face.

"Come out here, young lady. Let me see if sleeping in your own bed made your hair grow."

Libby bounded onto the deck, a glass of orange juice in her hand. She threw an arm around her mother, rubbing her head against her mother's cheek.

"Yes, it seems to have grown a good inch since last night," Eleanor laughed. "Why I let you get that haircut I'll never know."

She reached out and brushed her hand over the girl's head with more than a hint of affection. "Tell, me, how did Theo and Cleo do last night?"

"Leo," the girl screamed. "Didn't I tell you that Cleo is a boy, so now he's Leo, like Leo the Lion. Pretty cool, huh?"

"Shhh, you'll wake your father. Did the cats sleep okay in your room?"

"Uh-huh," she said through a mouth of orange juice. "They're still under the bed, but they'll come out for food. I want to give them a bath today. They look like they've been rolling through the manure pile, and kind of smell like it, too."

"Libby, you do have a way with your descriptive phrases," Eleanor said. "I'll help you with the cat wash after breakfast, but you know you'll have to help with the milking this afternoon."

Libby nodded vigorously, looking toward the milking barn. "Can I drive the skid loader?" she asked.

"I think Jeremy has that under control, but they'll need your help with the wiping and dipping later. I don't know about you, but my stomach is sending me hunger deprivation signals. I'll get started on some pancakes, and maybe your father will be awake by then."

Wind crunched several mouthfuls of the dry food, licked his face, and studied the bedroom. It contained a four-poster bed with an oak chest in front piled high with pillows and clothes. An oak dresser with a mirror nearly covered with magazine clippings and a small desk completed the furnishings.

Wind heard Lil' One squeal and turned to see the multicolored tabby rolling on the bed as if he was playing in a patch of catnip.

"Come up here, Wind, I can almost taste the Hyskos female, her scent is so strong."

He rolled back and forth, one claw catching in the sheet pulling it over him until all that was visible was the tip of his curved tail.

"Sometimes you act as crazy as a Hyskos," Wind replied to the thrashing bundle beneath the sheet. He started to jump on the bed when the door swung open and Libby stepped into the room. Wind darted under the chair, and kept a watchful eye on the young girl.

"Hey, there. What's that hiding in my bed?" she said pulling the sheet back.

The young cat lay there suddenly very still looking up at Libby.

"How's my Leo this morning? Did you sleep good?" She rubbed the tabby's head and lightly touched his injured ear.

"You got yourself in a fight, young'un. I hope this wasn't your doin, Theo," she said looking at the big cat still crouched beneath the chair. "Nah, I'm sure you would have taken out whatever bully did this to your buddy. Am I right, Theo?"

Wind didn't know what the young Hyskos was saying, although he was sure she was speaking to him.

She pulled the small cat to her and held him in her arms like a baby. Lil' One's eyes went wide and his breathing constricted for a moment. He felt the warmth of the girl against his skin, heard the sound of her soothing voice, and relaxed. But only for a moment. When the Hyskos female stood up and tried to carry him with her, he twisted around frantically.

"I'm rushing things, huh?" She put the small tabby on the bed and stepped back. "I'll leave you alone for now, but you're going to get what I'll bet is your first bath in a long time. See you soon."

She waved at both cats and left the room.

Soon, the Wilkins family settled into their fall routine. Each morning at 4:30, Denny and Jeremy brought the cows in to the milk parlours for milking. Eleanor fixed breakfast and lunches, dropped Libby at Cushing Elementary and drove on to her job as principal of Vinton High. Afternoons, Libby ran into the house to check on her menagerie, and then helped her father and brother with the 5:00 P.M.

milking.

Life was amazingly good at the Wilkins farm and the hardships Windrusher and Lil' One faced during their travels now seemed like foggy wisps of a once vivid dream that fades in the light of day. Each night Lil' One slept cuddled next to Libby, and Wind curled up at the foot of her bed, his head facing the door.

Soon, another night globe had passed.

chapter 26

THE SAND ADHERED to every part of him, filling his nostrils and ears, stinging his eyes. His paws felt like they were weighted with stones and he struggled to move his exhausted body one single step, then another.

Overhead, the sun was a sulfuric hole in the frozen blue sky that liquefied the edges and seemed to suck the oxygen from the air. Shimmering waves of heat rose from the desert floor and Windrusher saw three figures silhouetted against the horizon.

As always, she was leading the way. She climbed the shifting sands of the dune; her proud, bushy tail held high, the sun's burning rays lingering on her polished gold and black coat like a mother caressing her new born babe. Unlike the three cats trailing far behind her, there was no hesitation, no slipping or falling, no pausing to gulp down mouthfuls of superheated air.

Even from this distance, he recognized the Holy Mother, Irissa-u. Surely, he was dreaming again, he told himself, knowing all along the difference between dreams and reality. He tasted the gritty sand coating his mouth, the scalding heat burning through his coat, the agonizing pain in his cracked and broken paws that sent tongues of fire up his legs with each step.

This was no dream.

Had he ever been so bone weary and so thirsty, even in the worst of his travels with Lil' One and Scowl Down? Behind him, his footsteps trailed into the distance across the burning desert floor like cuneiform writing on a scorched parchment.

Ahead of him, Irissa-u was almost to the summit of the dune, the other two cats still slowly trudging behind her. Wind licked his parched lips, feeling the grit on his tongue, and willed his body to move. If it was the last thing he did in this world, he would reach the top of that dune and be with the Holy Mother.

The sand gave way to rock and his footing became easier. He paused to catch his breath, his chest heaving with the effort of the climb. Windrusher closed his eyes and felt a cool breeze like the one that came off the Wilkins' fishpond in the evenings. He smelled the sweet lavender of the pasture and almost tasted the food in the bowl next to the refrigerator.

"By the head of Tho-hoth, let me rest and renew myself, then I'll join the Holy Mother," he murmured to himself.

Wind's head lolled back and rested against a rock. Then her voice cut through the haze that was dragging him away from this nether world of misery. "Windrusher! We're almost there. Don't give up now."

It was that same beguiling voice he recognized as belonging to Irissa-u.

Wind had no choice but to open his eyes and saw the Holy Mother scrutinizing him with an expression that mixed limitless mercy with the glory of triumph. Rahhna framed her in all her magnificence; its golden rays both bending around her, and penetrating through her, sending rivulets of fire down each of the fine hairs on her godlike body.

"Join us, Windrusher, and you'll have the answer you're seeking. Let me show you why we have endured this journey from the jungles to the desert."

The faces of the other two cats appeared at the edge of the dune.

"Come," she said turning away, "we will wait for you."

Time no longer existed in this world, so Windrusher could not say how long it took him to climb to the top of the dune. He dragged himself up those final feet, scratching for footholds in the loose rock and sand, and collapsed utterly exhausted.

The cool, wet strokes of her tongue washed away the spider webs of sleep that were enveloping his brain. Irissa-u licked his eyes clean, and nudged him to his feet.

"Ah, my Pferusha-ulis. I knew that I made the right choice when I asked you to join me on this holy mission." She walked toward the western edge of the dune and gestured toward the horizon with her head. "Look, do you see, Windrusher, how close we are?"

He peered down to where rocks grew into boulders. In the

distance, a dry valley walled with limestone cliffs bleached to a golden hue shimmered with layers of heat. Odd shaped peaks and outcroppings of erosion stood guard like lonely sentinels along the ridgeline. The sun played tricks on his eyes, shifting the shadowy shapes into awesome full-maned creatures, naked Hyskos' children, and bearded men.

"Just beyond that valley are the stone-walled Hyskos villages we seek." Her voice boomed inside his head. "They will embrace us, and treat us as gods, Windrusher." Now the voice was softer, leading him forward. "They will call me *Bast,* the cat goddess, building monuments to me, and our kind will grow beyond number, spreading throughout the globe.

"Will you be with us, Pferusha-ulis," she paused and stared directly into his eyes, causing a shiver to travel along his back. "Or will you be the lost follower?"

Wind's head was throbbing. The cliffs before him seemed to recede and fall into themselves until there was only a bright spot surrounded by darkness.

"You must make a decision and choose which direction to travel." Her voice was receding like the limestone cliffs. "One direction is very difficult, filled with danger and the possibility of failure. You will face threats that few cats can imagine; yet, if you succeed perpetual life will be yours. Windrusher will live in the minds and hearts of cats forever.

"The other is an easy road, my fellow traveler. There, you will find comfort, and all your physical wants fulfilled. You will live to be an old and fat cat. Few could fault you for choosing the easy road after the hardships you have endured. Only you can decide between the two."

Wind's mind was numb, and his head began to whirl dizzily. Instinctively, he stepped backwards from the edge of the dune, struggling to focus on Irissa-u's message.

"Which will it be, Pferusha-ulis? Follow me and stay on the Path, or...."

Irissa-u's words faded as she scrambled down the side of the dune, jumping from one rock to the next until she was on the floor of the dry valley. The shimmering layers of heat surrounded her like a glittering aura, and then parted in her wake. He watched until she disappeared, her glowing outline vanishing into the golden cliffs.

chapter 27

THE PAIR of Rhode Island Reds moved in an awkward ballet, pecking diligently at the kernels of corn. Heads down, the bright red wattles and spiked combs flapped as beaks speared nuggets of corn, and their beady black eyes looked around nervously.

Wind and Lil' One timed it perfectly. They rushed around the corner of the white clapboard farmhouse as the two plump chickens bobbed their heads toward the corn. It was a full-scale assault.

Pocahontas and Mulan, as Libby named the hens during her Disney phase, let out a series of discordant squawks and leaped a foot off the ground. The hens maniacally flapped their black tipped wings sending dark red feathers flying in all directions and fluttered awkwardly to the top of the split rail fence. There they sat swaying sputtering in agitation.

The two cats skidded to a stop where the Reds had been feeding moments before, and studied the ground around them as if suspecting the chickens had tunneled their way to freedom. The fowls clucked angrily at the playful felines, their long backsides twitching and their wings flapping disdainfully.

It was only then that Wind and Lil' One seemed to notice the angry Reds on the fence and gazed at them as if considering renewing their attack. Instead, they sniffed at the hard corn on the ground and returned to the deck to rest from their chicken-chasing escapade.

This was the newest game the two cats had invented to pass the time as they waited for Libby to come home from school. Each time it seemed like a new adventure to them and apparently to the unsuspecting chickens.

They lay on the deck; the fall air was redolent of freshly mown hay mingled with sharper barnyard aromas. Wind was reliving the vision of the burning sands in his mind. It could only mean Irissa-u wanted him to renew his journey. Wind needed to share his decision with Lil' One, but struggled to find the right words.

"The young Hyskos female will be home soon," Wind said with a flick of his tail against the worn cypress plank.

"Then we can visit the home of the smelly milk baggers and drink of their warm milk." Lil' One jumped to his feet and turned toward the milk barn, his nostrils sniffing the air for the smell of milk. Then he heard the chickens clucking and moved surreptitiously to the edge of the deck, poking his head around the side of the house.

"The fat feathered ones are feeding," he said excitedly changing the subject again. "Let's give them a scare and see how many feathers they lose this time."

Wind remained motionless, his eyes focusing on the distant pasture where a herd of black and white cows grazed. As if losing interest in the bucolic scene, he turned toward the front of the house and traced a line along the fence toward the open gate and dirt driveway.

"Lil' One," he finally said. "The Holy Mother has seen us through many adventures, and brought us to this fine place." He spoke slowly, picking each word carefully. "Here, the Hyskos treat us well, and we have grown fat and lazy."

Lil' One gave Wind a playful head butt followed by a lick. "You may be getting fat and lazy, old one, but I've become bigger and stronger."

He turned away from Wind, then spun around with his back arched, his legs stiffened, and his curled tail waving behind him like a battle flag. He thrust his head toward Wind's supine form with one eye closed and his teeth bared. A low growl gurgled in his throat.

Despite himself, Wind had to admit that this was a fair imitation of Bolt, and rolled over on his back in a sign of submission. "Oh, please don't hurt me you ferocious beast."

Then the roughhousing began.

It was while the two cats were rolling on the slick deck that Libby came running through the kitchen and threw open the back door. "Are you fighting again? What am I going to do with you two?"

She disentangled the two cats and swooped Lil' One into her arms. The girl sat in the rocker and settled the young cat in her lap. "I know you had a busy time here, but let me tell you about my day."

Libby ran her finger tips through the small cat's fur, smoothing out the errant tangles and dispersing the fine hairs with a fluttery motion of her fingers like she was releasing baby butterflies.

Wind watched the female Hyskos rocking back and forth with strong kicks of her small legs, all the while gently petting Lil' One and jabbering on in her unintelligible language. Lil' One's eyes were half closed and his head leaned against the girl's stomach.

Windrusher stepped off the deck and crawled into the cool shadows below the wooden platform. Long slivers of light creased the darkness, and he heard the soft voice of the Hyskos and the creaking of the cane rocker above him. He closed his eyes and an image of Irissa-u came to him. She stood alone on top of the sand dune, her body silhouetted against the molten disc of Rahhna. He could almost feel the desert heat, and a tiny shiver passed through his body.

It was a daily routine: Windrusher and Lil' One following Libby through her chores, feeding the chickens, rabbits and pigs, then into the barn for the milking. After a taste of warm milk, they normally returned to the house to await another meal. This afternoon when the girl ran to the house, Wind stopped Lil' One before he could follow her inside.

"Stay with me here, I must share something with you," he said.

They stood at the corner of the barn and watched the two high-legged beings close the barn doors and walk to the sink outside a utility shed where they washed their hands.

Lil' One was curious. "What is it?" he asked with a note of concern.

"I have told you about the Holy Mother and how she instructed me to undertake this mission."

Wind didn't expect an answer nor did he get one.

"Last night, Irissa-u spoke to me again. She said it was time for me to choose."

"What do you mean 'time for you to choose'?"

"Our travels have been very difficult, and because of that I embraced this place and stayed longer than...." Wind's voice trailed off.

Lil' One stared into the eyes of his friend looking for an answer to some question that still had not been asked. But Wind's eyes were diffused as if a panel of translucent glass had been raised between them. He turned away, staring at the road leading up to the farmhouse, then back at Lil' One.

"What I am trying to say is that it is time for me to resume my journey and find my family."

Lil' One exhaled sharply. "Do you mean now?"

"Yes."

"Nut-atna will be upon us soon, why not wait until the day globe returns?"

"No, Lil' One, this is the time. Already we have been here more than two night globes, and I indeed have become fat and lazy while we enjoyed this place. I must go."

The small tabby hung his head in silence, lost in his own internal struggle. He gazed toward the farmhouse and then back to his friend.

"You are right; we have remained here too long. I'm ready to go," he said with an air of resignation.

Wind moved closer and sniffed Lil' One politely, then rubbed his head gently against the smaller cat.

"You don't understand, my friend, I am going and you are staying here. It is my Hyskos family that is lost. You have found yours and the young female would be sad if you left her behind."

"But we are partners in your mission. Your Path is my Path?"

He sat down stubbornly in front of Wind as if to block him from moving.

"You have been as good a partner as I could ask for, but you are needed here to care for the Hyskos female. I must complete the mission on my own. That was the message the Holy Mother gave me in my dream. Besides, you have had more adventures than any cat could imagine."

Windrusher licked the silent cat affectionately, feeling the lumpy texture of the scarred ear on his tongue.

"You know I am right, Lil' One," he said softly. "Let me go now and wish me well."

Lil' One's mouth opened, his throat was tense and unyielding. Finally, he said, "Goodbye, and watch out for those Hyskos vehicles."

"Goodbye, Lil' One. Remember the Path and the Way."

Wind turned from his friend and walked briskly past the barn, past the watering trough, past the Ford F250 parked in the dirt driveway, and out the front gate. He paused briefly and looked at the small cat still standing by the barn, then began running down the road toward Gallipolis.

chapter 28

A SOUR SMELL hung above the docks like two-day sweat on a wool shirt. Wind approached the waterfront district of Gallipolis nearly two days after he left the Wilkins' farm in Springfield Township. It was a straight shot down State Road 160 from the rolling farmlands of Gallia County into the old river town that made the most of its historic past as the third oldest settlement in the former Northwest Territories.

Walking along SR 160, past land that may have belonged to early French settlers, Wind entered Gallipolis at 3:00 A.M., forty-two hours after he said goodbye to Lil' One. He wandered the empty streets until the smell of the Ohio River pulled him toward the waterfront.

Windrusher surveyed the public pier and boardwalk not sure what he was looking for, but knowing he would recognize it when he saw it. His travels provided him with lessons that served him well, and now his most urgent task was to find a way to cross the wide river.

There was another, more important, lesson that was vital to his success. Even though he was first frightened and later perplexed while riding in the rolling room, it taught him that the Hyskos method of travel was far superior to his own four legs.

The breeze off the water was brisk, and caused him to quicken his pace. Wind instinctively realized the heat of summer had given way to cooler days of fall. A voice in his head told him that perhaps in a night globe or less the air would turn colder and icy rain would fall from the sky.

Far away, a low rumble of thunder announced the imminent arrival of a morning rainstorm. As if in answer to the thunder, the soft thud of a heavy object bouncing off the ground caught his attention. It was followed by a harsh outburst, and several other Hyskos voices offering background counterpoint. Wind decided to investigate and edged toward the voices and the orange bloom of light.

He peered through an eight-foot chain link fence and saw a truck with its dirty silver trailer backed to a loading dock, its cargo door rolled up. Two fluorescent work lights attached to the dock's overhang bathed the area in a soft glow. Several men carried boxes from a warehouse to the truck while another was bent over a slatted crate that had spilled its load of corn across the cement platform.

The man bending over was so obese he was having trouble keeping his balance as he stuffed the corn back into the crate. A pair of clinging bib overalls with one shredded knee covered a torn and discolored thermal underwear shirt. Green shucks and yellow tassels were scattered at his feet and protruded from the top of the crate like exotic birds trying to escape a packed cage.

"Damn it, George, that's the second one you've dropped this morning. You know we're scraping to cover this order, and here you're throwing it around like we're swimming in corn. C'mon, pick it up and get your fat ass moving."

The man yelling at George shook his head with exasperation and looked at the clipboard in his hand. His black-rimmed eyeglasses glinted under the overhead lights, and he scratched at a patch of dry skin on his nose. He studied the flakes sticking to his fingertips and flicked them away like he was launching a spitball.

Wind watched the men make several trips inside the warehouse and back to the truck where they stacked the crates alongside other boxes. Finally, the man with the clipboard held up his hand and wriggled his fingers. "Okay, that's it for Winn-Dixie," he said, then turned to another man who had climbed down from the cab and joined him. "Harv, you're good to go. Didn't I say we'd have you loaded up in time to have that cup of coffee? How bout it?"

Harv clapped the other man on the back and nudged him forward. "After you, pardner," he said.

The two men climbed the four steps to the loading dock and brushed past the man called George who was leaning against the wall catching his breath. When they passed, George pushed himself forward and almost tripped over a single ear of corn at his feet. With a disgusted snort, he kicked it with the side of his foot like a soccer ball, sending it flying off the loading dock, then followed the other two men into the dark bowels of the warehouse.

Wind hurried through the open gates of the fence and stood nervously watching the building. The first drops of rain fell on his coat, and he warily approached the steps to the loading dock. Bounding up the steps, he peered into the warehouse and saw nothing but stacks of boxes and packing crates.

The rain was coursing down Wind's flanks now and he shook the water from his head, droplets of rain spraying out in all directions. He leaped from the loading dock into the open trailer, burrowing deep into the cargo of produce and wedged himself between two boxes.

"Man, we got this thing loaded just in time. Look at this rain."

The driver reached up, grabbed the grimy canvas strap, pulled the door down with a loud clang, and rammed the handle in place.

"See you on Wednesday, big guy," he said, and sprinted toward the cab.

Moments later the truck with Night Hawk Express stenciled on the side lurched forward and negotiated several turns in sleepy Gallipolis before turning onto Route 35 on its way to Charlotte.

The blackness inside the truck was a solid mass that seemed to envelop Windrusher, almost taking his breath away. Outside, the rain pelted down and lightning splintered the morning sky. Inside the trailer, Wind fought the panic that accompanied every bump in the road.

He remembered the rolling room that carried them to the farm, how it moved smoothly and rapidly through the countryside. The inside of that vehicle resembled a Hyskos home, but this one was stacked with boxes and crates. This is the same thing, he told the frightened voice in his head. All the Hyskos vehicles are different; some of them are small, while others are larger, like the rolling room.

His thoughts bounced from one fragment of the past to another desperately trying to make a connection, to see the complete picture. But it eluded him like an old jigsaw puzzle missing a dozen pieces. Somewhere in his struggles to solve the puzzle, the darkness and incessant vibrations combined to lull him to sleep.

Darkness also played a major role in a vivid dream taking place hundreds of miles away. In the dream, Kimmy saw herself lying on a double bed in a strange room. Although it was dark, the entire room was spread out before her, as if she were peering down through a skylight in the ceiling. Her small body was outlined on the large bed, and at her feet was a dark lump that she realized was Tony. Even in her sleep she felt a surge of joy at his presence.

Kimmy watched the peaceful scene of the two sleeping forms play itself out in her unconscious. Everything seemed so normal, so serene, but she was aware that something had changed and she grew uncomfortable.

She strained to understand the source of her discomfort. Was it that slight hum in the background? Within seconds, the hum grew into an intense droning and then to a deafening roar. In her dream, Kimmy sat up with a terrified look on her face and yelled for Tony, but her words were lost in the clamor.

Tony slowly raised his head and stared at the ceiling, as though he could see Kimmy observing him from her perch high above the bedroom. In that instant, the room rocked violently, and the cat was swept from the bed, like an unseen hand had reached out and snatched him into some black void.

Kimmy felt her heart beat in her chest as she viewed the nightmarish scene. The bed was pitching like a rodeo bull intent on hurling the rider from its back. The noise around her was incredible, pictures were flung from the wall, and furniture crashed from side to side.

Kimmy's moaning became louder and she willed herself to wake up. Before she could pull herself from the depths of the nightmare, the girl saw a blinding light suddenly appear in that black, twisting bedroom. Then everything was still and peaceful.

Kimmy stared in awe at a wavering translucent globe that pulsated and changed colors.

"Your pet is facing a grave danger, but be not afraid for he will survive and you will be together once again."

Surely, there was no mouth in that pulsating circle of light, yet she heard the eerie voice clearly inside her head as she slept, as though her brain had intercepted a radio signal.

"Tony is searching for you. Find him and bring him home."

The shimmering specter blinked out like the last ember in a

fireplace, and Kimmy awoke to find herself sitting up in bed, the words ringing in her head. *Tony is searching for you. Find him and bring him home.*

Her chest ached from the nightmare that was still so vivid she could taste the fear coating her mouth. Her father had explained that nightmares were tricks her mind played on her while she slept, and she would normally blame it on the pepperoni pizza she had for dinner, but this was different. If Tony was in danger and needed her help, she had to do something. But what could she do?

Windrusher was in the middle of his own troublesome dream. The moon hung against an early morning slate sky, and scattered around him were mounds of debris as if he had wandered into a junkyard. A familiar voice floated through the surreal landscape, breaking the abnormal silence. It was the voice of his Hyskos female, Kimmy, he thought, and she was calling his Hyskos name.

"Tony!"

The word came out as an elongated punctuation mark in the night. The voice was solemn and haunting, sounding like the first note of *Taps* played over an open grave.

Wind could not see Kimmy, but he sensed that she was trying to reach out to him, desperately trying to communicate with him. In the dream, he stiffened at the sound of Kimmy's voice, his ears swiveling trying to locate the source of the cry. He stood alone with only the trash and the fading sound of his name to keep him company.

Windrusher awoke with a start, the blackness pressing in on him, and he lurched forward against a crate of corn. The truck was braking and the grating of changing gears vibrated through him. He remembered where he was; locked in a huge Hyskos vehicle that, thanks be to Irissa-u, appeared to be taking him toward the warm waters, closer to his Hyskos family.

He stretched his cramped body as much as he could in the close quarters, trying to clear his head and make sense of the dream that still haunted him. Could it mean that his Hyskos female was in trouble and needed his help? There was definitely an undercurrent of terror clinging to the voice that called his name. More likely, she was trying to warn him of some hidden danger that might be awaiting him on his journey.

A loud gurgling deep in his belly directed his attention to more immediate concerns. His grumbling stomach reminded him he had not eaten since long before the last day globe appeared. Wind had no way of knowing how long he had been riding in the suffocating blackness, or how much longer before the light of Rahhna would shine on him again. He was hungry now, and he probably wasn't going to eat again until the Hyskos vehicle stopped.

The cat extended his claws and scratched at the wooden crate trying to ignore his complaining stomach. His body pulsed with the vibrations of the truck, and he realized there was nothing he could do but lay there and listen to the roar of the vehicle. Or he could sleep.

Sleep was always a good choice.

At 1:45 P.M., the Night Hawk Express pulled into the Winn-Dixie Marketplace on Alleghany Road in Charlotte. Windrusher awoke to the sound of the creaking roll-up door, and blinked as sunlight squeezed past the stacks of crates, pushing the darkness aside. Hyskos' voices made their way into the trailer, and he squinted nervously toward the open door.

At the sound of a box scraping across the trailer's bed, he instinctively pushed back against the crate of corn, but the protective walls surrounding him dwindled before his eyes. One by one, the boxes disappeared from the trailer until a high-legged being came into view. A young man with a grimy apron around his waist walked straight toward the two boxes where Windrusher lay. He felt his chest rise and fall rapidly, and wondered if the Hyskos could hear the thudding of his heart.

The crate to his left was suddenly lifted off the floor, and the direct force of the sun hit him in the face. Wind sucked in a shallow breath and exploded forward, running right between the surprised man's legs.

The man jumped back as the dark shape passed below him. "What the hell—" he yelled out, dropping the crate of corn and lifting one leg as if he expected the creature to run up his pant leg.

Windrusher leaped onto the loading dock and skidded to one side to avoid another man coming toward him. Frozen momentarily with a two-legged being behind him and another in front, Wind threw himself from the loading dock. He cleared a garbage can, and kept running leaving the two men scratching their heads in disbelief.

chapter 29

THE NIGHT AIR was crisp, and a crescent moon lit the cat's way. He walked for hours leaving the dangerously busy streets behind before finding a quiet residential neighborhood. The homes backed up to a suburban park with a small lake at its center. A tree-lined path circled the lake, punctuated by a series of wooden benches sitting under massive live oaks.

Windrusher moved silently through the park, each step a dull reminder that he hadn't eaten in more than a day globe. He stopped momentarily to sniff the cool air, catching a familiar scent that caused his left ear to flicker uncontrollably, then loped toward a tidy split-level home, secluded by a wooden fence, hedges, and tall trees. Following the scent of food, Wind jumped on the low wooden fence, and inspected the heavily landscaped yard. Red maples and wax myrtles fronted the fence on each side screening the home from neighbors. Arcing across the corners of the yard and flowing back toward the home were two gracefully curved flowerbeds filled with a rainbow of perennials and annuals.

A flagstone path meandered between the beds toward a cluster of azaleas and rhododendron, forming a semicircle around a young willow oak tree that was festooned with bird feeders. There, a lone Cape Cod chair sat amidst the shrubs, an oasis in the middle of the yard like a monument to solitude.

Windrusher took in the pastoral setting with a glance, but what he noticed most of all was the lack of any other living creature that might pose a threat, and a tantalizing smell from across the yard. He followed the flagstone path until it broadened into a patio. At its center sat a tile-topped table ringed by four ornamental iron chairs. Large terra-cotta pots crammed with red and yellow mums bordered the patio.

The hungry cat didn't care about the hours of backbreaking work that must have gone into landscaping this lovely garden retreat. Before him was the object of his search; two fluted glass bowls that could have been from a set of ice cream dishes. One of the bowls was half filled with brown nuggets of cat food, the other with water.

The thought that he would be eating another cat's meal barely entered Wind's mind. There were more than enough disappointments to go around. He devoured the food quickly, licking the bowl clean and inspecting the ground to be sure he hadn't left any of the tasty nuggets for the ants.

He sat for a moment, looking over his shoulder at the trees and neat hedge row that bordered the backyard. He had a feeling he was being watched, but aside from the moon shining through the branches of a Japanese maple, he seemed to be alone. Satisfied he was safe, Wind draped himself over the water bowl and slowly lapped mouthfuls of the sweet liquid.

That evening, Wind rested in the park, not far from the home where he found the food. The dampness and cold night air awoke him early and he stretched himself out before curling into a ball. He watched the sliver of moon fade into the morning sky and thought about the freezing weather he had left behind at the start of his journey. After many night globes of warm weather, the biting cold seemed to be returning.

Windrusher was not capable of selecting from the volumes of information that human children collect in their first few years of existence. The change of seasons was baffling, but he understood that if he couldn't find a swift route to the land of warm waters he might have to seek shelter nearby.

There were an abundance of dwellings available, and, if he wished, he was confident he could find a temporary home with one of these Hyskos families. With this last thought providing him a level of comfort and security, he tucked his head against his paws, and closed his eyes.

Two hours later, the sound of voices and stamping feet brought the cat to full alert. In the distance, two morning joggers padded along the dirt path, and Wind, listening to them fade into the distance, stretched himself, and opened his mouth in a gaping yawn.

He thought of the food he consumed last night, and looked forward to a return visit to the home and its garden. A full food bowl was always enticing, but there was something else about that Hyskos dwelling that drew him towards it like an old friend.

Cautiously, Windrusher approached the glass bowls, stopping several times to sniff the air. The intriguing scent of another cat hung over the back yard, growing stronger the closer he got to the food bowl.

This morning the glass bowl contained savory moist food that brought an involuntary and thankful meow to his throat before he caught himself. Like last night, another feline had been here before him, but the bowl was more than half full. Without giving another thought to why this gift had been left for him, Wind dropped his head into the bowl and furiously licked at the flavorsome morsels.

After traveling hundreds of miles, experiencing one crisis after another, Windrusher should have been prepared for what followed. He wasn't. The claws raked his right flank and his hunger was forgotten in the surprise of the moment.

"You are beginning to annoy me; you know that, don't you?"

The question was asked in a flat, nearly conversational tone that somehow mixed mirth and menace. The answer to the question was as obvious as the stinging along his backside.

He swung around, knocking the food bowl against the water bowl, the water lapping over the side, forming a small puddle around his back paws. The hair on his neck stirred as if it had a life of its own, and he prepared to defend himself from the annoyed cat with the sharp claws.

She stood there unafraid and unmoving, eyeing him, his rear paws soaked by the pool of water from her bowl.

"It's obvious you're lacking in manners. Are you also a poor Wetlos lacking the gift of communication?"

Windrusher stared open-mouthed at the creature before him. He gasped audibly, and for a moment felt he was drowning in the hot pools of sapphire staring calmly back at him. The red point Siamese stood with her hind legs slightly higher than her front legs, sleek, with a dusting of freckles across her nose, and an ivory coat highlighted by stunning tips of cinnamon.

"Ah, this must be your food, I suppose," Wind said, struggling to recover his composure, and losing the struggle.

"You suppose correctly, although from the look on your face, I wasn't sure if you knew the difference between a food bowl and a foot bath."

She cast her eyes down toward his paws still soaking in the puddle of water.

Wind followed the path of those laser bright eyes and for the first time noticed his wet paws. He stepped forward awkwardly, shaking his paws and brushing against the unmoving Siamese.

"Excuse my rudeness, it's just that I was very hungry and the food was sitting there—"

"That's right. It sits there until I eat it. But I am not a glutton like some Setlos creatures, and always save some for later in the day. Fortunately, there's more inside my Hyskos home."

The Siamese tilted her head toward the brick house, then turned abruptly and walked away.

"Wait. Please. I'd like to… Could you…"

Wind was stammering like a brainless kitten. Why couldn't he communicate with this cat? He hurried after the retreating Siamese following so closely the flame tipped tail slid across his face leaving a trail of heat.

Wind padded beside the young queen who pointedly ignored him. The red point's tail was up in the form of a question mark, her ears erect, her eyes straight ahead. He brushed against the Siamese just enough to slow her down, then moved in front of her.

"Let me apologize again for my rudeness. I realize I'm an intruder on your territory, but I'd like to explain if you allow me."

His face was only inches away from hers. She focused her brilliant blue eyes on his, and he had to summon every ounce of his discipline to keep from disintegrating into a mumbling bag of fur and bones. He inhaled and was overcome with the delicate sweetness of her scent. It caused his mouth to go dry and his tongue involuntarily did a strange dance, flicking repeatedly at the roof of his mouth.

The young queen sat down, her creamy tail wrapping itself around her feet. All the while her eyes, reflecting the clearest of azure skies, remained focused on his face.

"Go ahead," she said.

Windrusher looked blankly at the female for a moment, and then hung his head. Crestfallen, he turned away from the red point.

"No, go ahead and explain."

Wind turned back toward the young queen, and sat directly in front of her. He swallowed hard and politely sniffed the female's muzzle. "First, let me introduce myself. I am Windrusher, Pferusha-ulis, Son of Nefer-iss-tu."

Under the circumstances, he felt compelled to let this queen know that manners were not completely foreign to him, that he was a cat with a proper upbringing.

"And you are?" he asked.

The Siamese closed her eyes slightly, and then opened them wide. "Windrusher. Now, that's a name one doesn't hear very often. Sometime you'll have to tell me how you found your call name. I am Silk Blossom, Kalosisha-ulla, daughter of Bast-Ma-at."

She lowered her head ever so slightly toward the big-boned gray and orange tomcat in front of her as if giving him permission to speak.

Windrusher didn't hesitate. He told her the story of his journey to find his Hyskos family, beginning with their inexcusable departure leaving him behind with another family, and ending with his ride in the metal box that brought him to her. Wind did not include every detail, but he told her of how Irissa-u spoke to him in his dreams, and of his two traveling companions.

Silk Blossom sat quietly through the entire story, only interrupting him to clarify a few points, and once, when he told her of Scowl Down's death, she nuzzled him gently.

When he finished, Wind lay down at her feet. The story of his epic struggle was difficult for even him to believe, and he was sure Silk Blossom—what a wonderful name—would certainly consider him a teller of tales if not worse.

He wouldn't blame her if she sent him away, and he prepared himself to move on.

The young queen gazed upon the prostrate form of the cat at her feet. She bent and licked the top of his head several times and when he looked at her, she turned away from him with a flick of her tail. "Follow me; I have something to show you."

Silk Blossom walked to the side of the split-level house where a pair of French doors opened on to the patio. One of the doors was slightly ajar and she pushed against it with her head, and Wind saw several overstuffed chairs and a brick fireplace inside.

"I'm not sure what I would do in your place, but I understand your feeling of loss. This is my home and I would miss it terribly if it were taken away from me. I've been with this Hyskos family since I was a kitten, and can't imagine another life."

"It is a fine home, Silk Blossom, and I'm certain it will remain yours for as long as you wish."

"Most of the time, I prefer to stay inside, but I am allowed to sun myself on the patio, and this door is open for me to come and go when one of the high-legged beings is home." Silk Blossom rubbed the side of her head against the doorjamb. "That's why they sometimes put my food outside. Fortunately for you, I'm not inclined to overeat."

She leveled her sapphire eyes at him once again.

"Yes, I was fortunate. As are you to have such a home," he said, meeting her stare.

"Agreed, but think of the adventures you've lived through. That would be something."

A low growl formed in Wind's throat and he stared directly into those bottomless blue pools.

"Listen to me," he said. "Once I left the shelter of the Hyskos, I learned how difficult it was to survive on my own. When Irissa-u sent me on this mission, I had great visions of how I would soon find myself adored by cats everywhere for my heroic feats. Instead, I found not glory and praise but hunger, danger, and fear. Appreciate what you have here, for there are multitudes of cats that would quickly take your place."

Wind lowered his eyes, wondering if he had impressed this lithe young beauty.

"You are right, of course. This is my home and I would never leave it, but cats must dream."

Silk Blossom turned again, swishing her tail across Windrusher's muzzle. She walked regally toward an islet of sun on the patio, her behind bobbing gracefully with each step, and sat on the warm stones.

Wind stood mesmerized as she walked away from him. When she cut her eyes toward him, he felt a feverish wave pass through his abdomen, and his tongue did its strange dance inside his mouth. His paws felt like they had grown roots, and with some effort, he joined the young red point in the circle of sunlight.

"I suppose that now you've eaten, you'll be on your way," she said.

"There's no rush, is there? I am still weary from my travels and besides it will soon be too cold to continue my journey."

A slight breeze blew through the backyard, and both cats looked at the maple tree, watching the lower branches wave gently. The leaves showed distinct highlights of gold and orange, painting the first strokes of autumn across their leafy landscape. A muddy brown female cardinal sat on an upper branch whistling a high-pitched series of notes that seemed to end with a question. Soon, its showier mate flew over and joined it, and the question was answered.

Wind spent the remainder of that day sleeping in the boxwood hedge. He had an unobstructed view of the backyard from his vantage point, and watched for the young queen's return between catnaps. Later that evening he spotted her slipping through the French door. She jumped into one of the chairs and turned several times before finding the most comfortable position. Windrusher waited until his heart slowed to a nearly normal rate, then walked over to be close to her.

"Frank, look, there it is. I told you I saw another cat hanging around earlier today." Terri Lowery stood at the French door waving her arm toward her husband who was engrossed in the evening news.

Lowery pushed himself off the recliner with beefy arms and peered over his wife's shoulder at the big gray and orange cat sitting close to the Siamese. In his hand was a martini, straight up with three green olives.

"I'd say our girl has a beau," he said, taking a sip of the martini. "Have you seen it around here before? Maybe it belongs to one of the neighbors."

"No, I'd remember that one. You don't think Bitsy is in any danger, do you?"

"Nah. They seem to be hitting it off pretty well. Why don't we let him hang around? Bitsy could use the company."

Frank Lowery was built like a fullback ready to lead the way through his opponent's defensive line. In reality, Lowery was the gentlest of souls; a banker who read poetry, was an excellent ballroom dancer, and avid gardener. He was also the person who brought the tiny bundle of cream and amber home more than a year ago. He named her Elizabeth B, after his favorite poet, and Elizabeth B grew into Bitsy.

"Well, I'm certainly not going to let him come in the house," she said. "He can hang around tonight, but if he's still here in the morning, I'm calling animal control."

chapter 30

LOWERY WATCHED as much bad news as he could stomach, switched off the television, and walked outside seeking the peace his backyard always brought him. He made a quick side trip to the garage, found a ten-pound bag of sunflower seeds, and carried them out to the yard with him. After filling the three bird feeders, he lowered himself into the cushioned Cape Cod chair and waited for the gardens to work their serene magic on his psyche.

He inhaled the aromas from the bushes and flowers, watched a pair of doves pecking at the sunflower seeds, and quickly forgot about the pressures of the day. Lowery had spent countless hours shaping his yard into a secluded haven and he wasn't finished yet. Next spring, the plan called for digging a garden pond with a small waterfall. He relaxed just thinking about the soothing sounds of moving water.

Lowery was slipping into the first stage of a twilight sleep when the insinuating sounds of a cat vocalizing pulled him back to wakefulness. It wasn't Bitsy's distinctive meow, which she used to get their attention, so it must be the cat Terri was worried about. Reluctantly, he rose from the low wooden chair and walked around the azaleas toward the patio.

Bitsy was stretched out on one of the patio chairs and the strange cat was sitting at her feet, as though it was standing guard. Lowery smiled and walked slowly toward the patio so as not to frighten the cat.

"Hey, guy, what's shaking?" he said quietly.

He took another step toward the cat, then kneeled down to be closer to the animal's height. Lowery stretched out a hand and wished he had some food to offer Bitsy's gentleman caller.

The cat studied the big man, looked around the yard warily, and then back at the kneeling man.

"Don't worry, I won't hurt you."

Lowery stood up and moved closer, his hand still extended. Bitsy hadn't moved from atop the chairs' flowery cushion. He sat in the chair next to Bitsy and gently reached down and scratched the gray cat on the head. It purred audibly, and rubbed its muzzle against Lowery's leg.

"Well, aren't you a sweetheart?"

He continued scratching the cat and then picked it up and put it in his lap. The cat stuck out its legs stiffly for a moment, looked around wide-eyed, and then relaxed.

"There you go. Here's a nice soft lap for you." He began stroking the cat's fur until he felt the hard muscles soften under his hand, and the purring start up again. "I wonder who you belong to, big boy. Someone must be very sad that they lost you."

The cat rubbed its head against the big man's thigh, and then turned to look at him as if asking why he had stopped scratching his head.

At dinner that evening, Frank Lowery told his wife of his experience with the visiting tomcat.

"This isn't a feral cat. He's very affectionate, very comfortable with people. You should have heard him purring when I was petting him. And he's a good looking cat."

"That's fine. I'm sure animal control will find a good home for him," Terri said.

"Bitsy seems to really like him, and you know she's pretty particular about other cats in her territory. Remember the commotion she made when the Hardy's cat got in the yard last month? The fur was really going to fly if that coward hadn't turned tail and run back to his own yard." Lowery smiled at the memory and took another sip of his wine.

"Frank, it sounds like you're lobbying to keep this cat. Tell me I'm wrong, please."

"What would it hurt? We've got this big house to ourselves. Buddy's in his last year at Chapel Hill, and another cat will be good company for Bitsy and for us."

He took his wife's hand, lifting it to his mouth and licking her palm the way he used to do when they were first dating. It drove her wild then, and it still did. Terri pulled her hand from his and wiped it on her husband's sleeve.

"You're disgusting, you know that?" She smiled despite herself and Lowery sensed victory.

"Yes, but I'm your disgusting hunk," he said. "Let's do this, we'll put him on probation and see if he's civilized enough to live with the Lowery's. We can let him stay in the garage for now, then if he demonstrates himself to be brave, clean, and reverent, and a good Republican, we'll let him use the inside litter box."

"What if he's carrying some disease?"

"I'll call Dr. Hall tomorrow and get an appointment."

Terri Lowery shook her head. "It looks like we're going to have two hard-headed males in this household once again," she said.

Dr. Stephen Hall, DVM, spent ten minutes with Lowery's newest pet, a large gray and orange male domestic, temporarily called John Doe Lowery on the patient's record sheet. He took a vial of blood, examined his eyes and ears, listened to his heart, felt for any strange lumps or contusions, and probed his other openings.

The technician held the cat firmly, but it remained quiet except when Dr. Hall forced its mouth open to check out his teeth. Even then, it only growled briefly then whimpered and was quiet.

Later in the lobby, Frank Lowery and Dr. Hall had a short conversation.

"Looks like you've got yourself a healthy boy here," Dr. Hall said. "I'll have to wait for the blood work, but I'd say he's in pretty good shape. My nurse will call if anything pops up, but I doubt it."

"That's good news. I had a feeling this guy didn't have any problems. Just look at him. Looks like he works out, doesn't he."

"Yeah. Speaking of working out, you might want to consider having him neutered so he doesn't work out too much."

"Since he was obviously a house cat, I thought they already fixed him."

"Not this one. But give us a call and we'll make an appointment for you."

Lowery knew that sterilization was the best policy, but then he thought about Bitsy. Elizabeth B was a legitimate beauty, and she had all the papers to prove it. People were always raving over the red point, and when she was eight months old Frank decided to breed her and provide a litter for their friends. Terri didn't share Frank's enthusiasm, thinking about the chaos five or six kittens running around her house would create, but Frank convinced her they wouldn't stay around for long. When Bitsy came on heat last spring they matched her with a suitable mate.

Nothing happened, to Terri's relief. No pregnancy, no kittens. Since the tom had sired other litters, the Lowery's assumed poor Bitsy was barren. Probably nothing to worry about, Lowery thought, but we'll keep an eye on them the next time Bitsy starts feeling frisky.

Fall spread its colors throughout Charlotte, and the trees flew their brilliant autumnal banners as the shorter, cooler days of October paraded past in quick time, one season merging into the next.

Windrusher's two-week probation period was spent in the garage where he slept in a box draped with an old towel. The cat that was once known as Tony, later as Theo, now had another name. Frank Lowery wisely gave naming rights to his wife.

Terri spent days considering the possibilities, including Chippendale and Bauhaus, but finally decided upon Feng Shui. She was currently studying this ancient Chinese practice to incorporate it into her interior design business, and it seemed to her to be the perfect name. Frank cringed when she told him, but bit his tongue and secretly called him Fang.

By mid-November, with the temperature averaging fifty degrees, Windrusher was welcomed into the closed society known as the Lowery family. To his mind that meant he could spend even more time with Silk Blossom. The young queen had an amazing effect on him; whenever she was near his thoughts cascaded into a confusing jumble that made him forget his epic mission, his former friends, and his original Hyskos home.

Lowery sat in one of the stuffed chairs in front of the brick fireplace, enjoying the heat emitted by the gas log, and nursing his second martini. Terri sat in the other chair looking at her husband with a bemused smile on her face.

"I guess we should be honored to be included," he said.

"Don't take it that way, hon. At least we'll be together for Thanksgiving. Aren't you excited that we were invited to meet Jessica's parents? It certainly sounds serious."

Lowery held the cool glass against his cheek, and smiled at his wife.

"You are absolutely right, dear. And I'm an old poop. It's just that I get so caught up in having the family together for the holidays, and this will be the first time in I don't know how long that we're not home for Thanksgiving dinner."

Terri moved over and sat on the arm of his chair. She cradled his head in her arms and kissed his bald spot.

"You are a sentimental old poop. That's what I love about you. We'll be together for Thanksgiving, just not in our home. Plus, we'll get to see your brother while we're in Raleigh."

"But what about Bitsy and Fang?"

"Bitsy and Feng," she corrected. "What about them? Harriet will be happy to come by and feed them. We'll only be away for three days, and we've certainly taken care of their dogs enough times, haven't we?"

She gave a tug on his arm, and he followed her into the dining room grumbling under his breath like a pouting child.

chapter 31

"I SWEAR SHE KNOWS we're going away," Lowery said, zipping closed the suitcase. Silk Blossom rubbed against his leg, a low, rumbling purr filled the bedroom. She shadowed his every move, circling his legs like a toy train.

"You are the cutest thing, Bitsy. You know that, don't you?"

Lowery bent to pick up the Siamese and she rolled over on her back. He laughed and stroked the cat's belly. "Oh, poor baby doesn't want us to go. We'll be back in a few days and Mrs. Nichols will be sure your food bowl stays filled, so don't you worry."

Terri stood in front of her closet listening to her husband, and had to smile at this burly block of a man talking baby talk to their cat. She shook her head and surveyed her clothes one last time to be sure she hadn't forgotten anything important.

Wind awoke from his post breakfast nap just as the Lowery's departed for Raleigh. He sat up and licked a forepaw. He could tell something was different, but he wasn't sure what it was. It wasn't the sound of the Hyskos vehicle driving away, that happened on a daily basis and he was accustomed to the high-legged beings coming and going regularly.

No, this doesn't involve the Hyskos. He cocked an ear toward the open door and heard the faint crooning of another cat. Could that be Silk Blossom?

He jumped from the bed and ambled into the kitchen where a pungent odor struck him, sent a wave of heat coursing through his limbs, and stopped him in his tracks. Wind was released from his temporary paralysis by the unmistakable cries of Silk Blossom vocalizing in a way he had never heard.

He hurried toward the living room. With each step the odor became stronger, the strange crooning sounds of Silk Blossom louder. He felt a curious tightening between his legs, and an obsessive desire to be with the Siamese.

The Lowery's had pulled the sheer drapes closed over the French doors except for a six-inch gap that allowed a slash of midday light to cut across the dim living room. Wind followed the column of light to the floor and saw a writhing lump in the middle of the Oriental rug. It was Silk Blossom rolling back and forth, the light playing across her fur.

She purred loudly and contorted her body in a manner that both frightened and fascinated Windrusher. He stood in the doorway captivated by the sight of the young queen rubbing herself against the rug, all the while crooning in the most seductive voice Wind had ever heard.

He rushed to the twisting red point, afraid she was hurt, afraid she was not. It proved to be a mistake. Silk Blossom leaped at him, spitting and growling, one claw slicing the air inches from his face, the other ripping across his neck. He quickly retreated to the edge of the rug both confused and aroused. Motionless, he watched the female, her eyes closed, writhing on the floor. Wind's body told him that something very important was happening, but he was too perplexed to do anything but sit and watch the young queen twisting and crooning her song of seduction.

Silk Blossom gazed alluringly at Windrusher through hooded lids, as if calling to him to join her on the rug. Each time Wind looked into those eyes he was compelled to move to her side, but each time the entranced female turned on him fiercely.

Instinctively, he understood he was part of an ancient mating game that had certain rules, and penalties were assessed when the rules were ignored. He didn't know what prize awaited him if he followed the rules, but there was no doubt that Silk Blossom controlled the outcome of this game.

Windrusher heard a strange chirping sound then realized it was coming from his own throat. In response to the noise, the red point's purring became even louder. Watching her movements carefully, Wind observed how often she looked away and when she closed her eyes.

He inched toward the agitated queen, moving only when she couldn't see him, and froze in place before she looked back.

Could it be that the Siamese was unaware of his surreptitious approach? He didn't see how that was possible, but continued scurrying forward. Moving. Freezing like a statue. Watching carefully to stay out of reach of those razor sharp claws, he was soon sitting next to Silk Blossom.

He was aware of his own heart beat, and the muscle at the root of his tail twitched involuntarily. Silk Blossom suddenly stopped the writhing movements and the loud purring. She stared at Windrusher, her sapphire eyes bright with lust.

Without thinking, Wind leaped.

chapter 32

THE CAT Terri Lowery had named Feng Shui rubbed his muzzle against the corner of an old Dr. Pepper crate. Inside the box, five tiny kittens clambered over the Siamese trying to find a nipple. She lay there quietly as they nursed. In the three weeks since she gave birth to the kittens, she had learned so much about them, and about herself.

She gazed warmly at the nursing kittens, amazed at their differences. The two nearest her head were creamy bundles of fur that had the distinguishing cinnamon highlights of a red point. The next two were larger and had taken longer to deliver. They provided a dramatic contrast to their sisters with their dark mottled coats and lighter stripes. The last one nursed as far away from the others as possible, and there was no mistaking who his father might be.

"I think they need their rest, don't you?" Lowery said. He picked him up and carried him into the living room, closing the bedroom door behind him.

"You proved us wrong, Fang, so I guess we'll have to be sure that doesn't happen again." Lowery sat in front of the fire with the big cat in his lap. He stroked the cat's back as he spoke.

Terri came in from the office carrying several manila file folders. "Are you talking to yourself again?" she said.

"I know you're just looking for an excuse to trade me in on a younger model, but I wasn't talking to myself, I was talking to the cat."

He made a sweeping gesture with his hand like Vanna White displaying a letter.

"Oh, that's much better," she said with a laugh. "I hope you were telling him what a bad boy he was to take advantage of our sweet little girl."

"I did, and you know what he said?"

"I'm afraid to ask."

"He said a guy's gotta do what a guy's gotta do."

"Well, this guy's done as much as he's gonna do," Terri said, shaking her finger in the cat's face.

"Don't be too harsh on my man, Terri. At least we know there's nothing wrong with Bitsy. Think of it as a practice run."

"It's the last run he's going to make, and maybe Bitsy, too. I don't think I want to go through that again. You need to make an appointment with Dr. Hall to be sure Feng doesn't have anymore impure thoughts."

Terri sat in the chair next to her husband's and opened one of the folders in her lap.

"What's that you've got?" he asked.

"I thought I'd get an early start on our taxes so we don't end up needing an extension like last year."

"I know I tend to put things off a bit, but its only mid-February. We have two months to worry about the taxes. Let's go to Bonterra's for dinner, and you can whisper sexy tax talk in my ear."

He reached over and scratched lightly on his wife's arm, his fingers tracing tiny concentric circles on her sleeve. She noted that it was the same motion he had been unconsciously making under Wind's jaw just moments before.

The cat took that opportunity to jump from his lap, walk to the French doors, and look outside. Twilight filtered through the trees bathing the patio in amber tones that matched the rust colored leaves coating the brown grass.

Windrusher sat on the flagstone patio and studied the yard he had come to know so well in the past few months. The stones were cold beneath him, although it seemed like the air was warmer than it had been the last time they allowed him outside. He noticed the oak's branches with their coating of green promising new beginnings.

Change was in the air.

He sniffed the ground at his feet, tracking a scent that was probably one of the many gray squirrels that populated the Lowery's backyard. Wind followed the squirrel's scent through the azalea bushes to the back of the yard thinking how attached he had become to this home during the past five night globes.

A vision of Silk Blossom intruded itself in his thoughts, as she often did. He felt he could reach out and touch that magnificent creamy coat with its indescribable hints of cinnamon on her tail, ears and paws. Then there were her eyes. Each time he looked into those bottomless sapphire pools he was struck with the same feeling. They seemed to promise eternal pleasure, yet they were so distant and unforgiving.

So much had happened to him since his Hyskos family left him and set in motion the series of amazing events that brought him to this place. Nothing could take from him the memory of those adventures or the friendships he made along the way. But Silk Blossom was the culmination of everything in his life and she had such a grip on him it was frightening.

Windrusher settled on the stone path and watched the last rays of Rahhna retreat behind the fence. He struggled to remember what Irissa-u had told him in the dream. It was so long ago, and after all, it was only a dream, wasn't it? A fuzzy picture came to him of the golden goddess standing on a high dune. In the distance were cliffs of limestone with their eroded pillars standing guard over the desert.

As if a gauzy curtain had been ripped away from across his memory, Wind remembered exactly what Irissa-u told him. *It was time to choose*, she said. But that was another time, a time before he found this home, this family.

Before he found Silk Blossom.

This mission began because his Hyskos family left him behind. Wasn't that the most tangible demonstration that they no longer wanted him as part of their family, he thought, pushing Irissa-u's words out of his head.

This family cared for him and, more importantly, they wanted him.

What would he gain by resuming his dangerous journey? Only uncertainty, peril, and the possibility of failure. Irissa-u had promised him that. Here he had comfort, security and companionship. These were certainties.

Windrusher dropped his head to his paws and closed his eyes. He tried to picture the face of his Hyskos female, and the young girl called to him as if from a great distance. Slowly, she moved forward, but he still could not see her face. Was this the high-legged being who cared for him, the one for whom he had endured so much?

He shook his head to clear the throbbing that emanated from a spot directly over his left eye, and the image of the young Hyskos faded away like a wisp of smoke. In its place was a picture of Silk Blossom. She was lying in the box, her radiant eyes imploring him to stay with her.

The vision in his head expanded, like switching to a wide-angle lens, and they were no longer alone. Crawling over the recumbent young queen and spilling over the box and onto his feet were five tiny kittens.

Lowery brought the cat he called Fang into the house before they went out to dinner. Wind went directly to the laundry room where his food bowl was kept and, even though he wasn't hungry, chewed on a mouthful of the crunchy pellets. Alone with his thoughts, he continued to eat until he heard the soft padding of the young queen's feet behind him. He turned to find Silk Blossom standing so close he nearly bumped into her.

"Are the kittens sleeping?" he asked feeling awkward and ungainly in her presence.

"Thanks be to Irissa-u. Let them nap peacefully and give me time to rest," she said wearily.

The Siamese bent over the water bowl and lapped slowly.

She was exhausted. Silk Blossom had lost all of the weight she gained while she carried the kittens, and her ribs furrowed down each side and lost themselves in a belly that swayed when she walked. Her nipples were pink and raw, sandpapered by the kitten's constant nursing.

He waited for her to finish drinking, and together they walked to the bedroom where she inspected the kittens closely. Four of the kittens were curled up with each other making it difficult to discern one's tail from the other. A ball of dark gray and orange fur was inserted between the others, his head resting on the back of one of the creamy kittens.

"They are special, aren't they?" she asked.

"They have no choice in the matter considering who their mother is," he said.

The kittens would need every bit of Silk Blossom's attention for at least two more night globes. All her energies would flow in their direction; discipline, feedings, teaching survival skills. These were all the things a mother passes along to her young, if they are fortunate enough to hold on to her for that long.

The two cats stood silently lost in their thoughts, then left the kittens. In the living room, Windrusher and Silk Blossom lay down on the Oriental rug. Images of another time together on this rug snapped through his mind like a series of flash cards, and he shook his head as if trying to shake water off his whiskers.

Sleep was just a blink away, and the insistent yelps of hungry kittens could call her at any time. She closed her eyes welcoming the sweet peace that even a short nap would bring.

"Are you awake?" Wind asked.

The exhausted red point opened one eye reluctantly and cocked an ear toward the tom. "Yes."

"I wanted to say that I've watched you with the kittens and you are a good mother. They are fortunate to have you to care for them."

Silk Blossom twisted her neck and yawned. "Isn't that what mothers are supposed to do? Care for their young, I mean."

"Yes, of course. In my journey, however, I have met so many cats damaged for their entire lives because they grew up without a mother to instruct them." Wind thought of Lil' One and looked toward the guest bedroom where the kittens slept. "You would be surprised how many are left alone even at this young age."

Silk Blossom wasn't sure what answer was expected from her. All she could envision was the blessed sanctity of sleep, and Wind was keeping her from that. Her ears straightened with a sudden irritation that surprised her. This male could sleep from globe to globe if he wished. Her days were endless feedings, sleep fractured by ceaseless interruptions. A constant awareness that five lives depended upon her nurturing skills.

"Let me sleep before they awake. Unless you think you can nurse them." She lowered her head to her paws and was instantly asleep.

Wind watched her sleep, the slight rising of her chest, an occasional twitching of her ears. He left her asleep on the rug, walked to the French doors. Outside, the vague outlines of the trees blended into the blackness of the night sky. Off in the distance, the glow of the night globe beckoned to him.

chapter **33**

WINDRUSHER MADE his decision long before Terri Lowery returned home from work on that Tuesday afternoon the third week of February. He was standing in front of the French doors when she came in through the garage.

Earlier that day, Wind spent time with Silk Blossom. He was with her as much as she would allow, even slipping into the back bedroom when she slept, inhaling the fragrance that was uniquely hers. The kittens were now able to climb over the sides of the crate, and they explored every corner of their new world. Together, he and Silk Blossom, watched with pride as they wrestled and tumbled across the floor and under the bed.

It felt like the weight of Rahhna was lifted from his back when he accepted Silk Blossom and the kittens as part of his life. He had experienced so much during his journey; exhilarating triumphs, profound fear, and tragic loss. But that loss had brought forth new life and a new home. It was beyond his understanding, but he gave thanks to the gods for allowing him to be part of it all.

In his way, he also gave thanks to Silk Blossom. She was a determined mother, a firm disciplinarian, and totally immersed in her new role. "Your patience is amazing," he said to her that afternoon.

He watched her carry the kittens back to the crate countless times, gently picking them up by the scruff of their necks, and licking them tenderly.

"I would not have the patience." He felt he was repeating himself. "They will grow to be remarkable cats, like their mother. You should be proud."

She didn't respond, but continued grooming the kittens

"I have been fortunate to live a life filled with more adventures than most cats will ever see." His voice trailed off. "It's been my time with you, in this Hyskos home, though, that has made me happier than I can remember."

Silk Blossom's laser eyes burned deeply into him for a moment then turned back to her kittens.

He had agonized over his decision for days, judging the distances and directions of his life, like a student working on an algebra problem, until he was finally comfortable with the solution.

"What I'm trying to say is that my travels are over. This is where I want to stay, with you in this home."

The tired queen looked at him with eyes that were strangely flat, as if those bright blue windows to her soul had suddenly been shuttered and locked.

"I know," she said.

Windrusher stared, waiting for more. When she remained silent, he said, "You know. Is that all you have to say?"

Silk Blossom carried one of the kittens to the box and returned Wind's gaze.

"No, that is not all. I was hoping you would decide to leave on your own, and I could spare you from this."

Wind was stunned. He sat down unsure he was hearing what his brain was interpreting. "What are you saying?"

The red point let out a deep sigh and flicked her lovely tail several times. "Windrusher, you have your life and I have mine. This is my home, and now I have responsibilities that consume me. This will be my Way from now on, and I must take it seriously."

She paused to look at the box of kittens and sat beside him. "Our friendship has been dear to me, but both of us know that your place is not here, but out there. It is what Irissa-u has told you, and it is what you must do."

Unsure of what to say, he rose and nuzzled the side of her head, inhaling the intoxicating aroma of her body.

She shook her head belligerently and pulled her lips back exposing her long teeth. "No," she said, the word catching in her throat. "Don't you understand, I don't want you here."

He was standing by the French doors when Terri Lowery entered the room. She placed her purse and a lavender tote bag on the coffee table.

"How long have you been standing there, Feng Shui?" She crossed the room to stand beside him, ran her hand over his muscled back, then straightened and looked into her backyard. Green buds lined the branches of the willow oak, and the red bud was preparing to erupt in a rosy homage to spring.

"It's a beautiful afternoon," she said, pulling the door open. "You might as well go out and enjoy it for awhile."

Windrusher followed the flagstone path to the back of the yard, his legs feeling stiff and heavy. He paused by the boxwood hedge, glanced at the low fence behind it, and turned for one last look at the home he was leaving.

In the corner, by the French doors, two glass bowls sat awaiting a visit from the cat of the house. Wind's eyes swept past these reminders of his introduction to the cat who melted his heart with one piercing look, past the open door, the sun glinting off the window panes, past the trees bursting with spring growth, and back to the fence.

Hidden behind the living room's gossamer drapes, Silk Blossom watched Windrusher disappear over the fence. She blinked to clear the watery blurring that suddenly clouded her sapphire blue eyes and returned to the back room to care for her kittens.

chapter 34

LEON JACKSON was dragging.

Winston-Salem was his third stop in two states, and he still had 400 miles to his last delivery. He looked at himself in the side mirror as he climbed out of the cab, and thought he was still in pretty good shape for a sixty-four-year-old man who had been loading and unloading furniture for thirty-six years. His dark skin was still virtually unlined, only the coarse gray whiskers and thinning hair providing clues to his real age.

He thought he cut a real fine figure in the company coveralls, and straightened them as he stepped down, treading lightly on his left leg. The coveralls were the color of deli mustard with the company's overlapping triangle logo in bright red over his breast.

Yes, he thought, he was in pretty good shape for the shape he was in. Jackson looked in the mirror once more to assure himself that was the case. Of course, the mirror didn't show the immense belly that rode his waist like a rodeo rider, or the hip bone that was so porous he expected he could sift flour through it.

At least the company provided him with young bucks to do the heavy lifting, but he wondered if it was worth it since it took most of his energy to keep them from tearing up the furniture or hurting themselves. There was no way he could have been so stupid when he started out in this business or he would never have survived. At least that's what he told himself.

"Hold on a minute," he said in a gravely baritone that reminded everyone of Louis Armstrong.

The young man wore the same mustard colored coveralls, but they were a size too small and stretched tightly across muscular thighs. He stood at the rear of the van, his hands poised to swing open the two doors. At the sound of Jackson's voice he turned and stared sullenly at the old man.

"Before you get too carried away, let's be sure this here's the place and where the apartment is at. You don't wanna hump all that stuff and find out we're on the wrong block or there's no one home to let us in. Right?"

Jackson looked at the manifest and limped toward the manager's office leaving his young assistant leaning against the truck.

Ten minutes later, he returned. Edison watched the old man limp along the curving sidewalk, flipped his cigarette on the ground, and waited for Jackson to tell him what he was doing wrong.

"We're in luck. Apartment 12-A is right around the corner, and he's there waiting for us. Let's get moving, we might make it to Montgomery tonight, and I know a sweet barbeque joint that will make you think you done gone to heaven."

He tucked the manifest into his back pocket and waited while Edison swung the steel doors wide. Together they pulled the ramp down and set it into place. Edison climbed up the ramp, his large thighs threatening to tear through the coveralls. He thought about how much he hated barbeque and reached toward the heavy quilt covering a dresser.

"No, let's save that for later. We want to bring the boxes in first, you oughtta know that by now."

Jackson shook his head at the young man, and Edison felt the heat radiating across his face and clenched his jaw until his mouth ached. He wasn't sure he was going to make it through this run without kicking the old man's ass. He turned toward the row of identical cardboard boxes; each one coded with an identifying sticker, squatted in front of one of the larger boxes, and slid his hand along the side.

The scream took him completely by surprise. Then came the pain. It sounded like the cry of an angry mountain lion; at least that's what he told Jackson and anyone else that would listen, including the doctor at the walk-in clinic.

Edison stumbled backwards when he heard the piercing cry, and saw a black head with large fangs protruding from the open mouth. Pain seared his hand and he fell on his bottom, using his feet to scoot himself away from the boxes.

"What's wrong, Tyrell, you need some help?" asked the big man with the Louis Armstrong voice.

Jackson peered into the shadows watching his helper sliding across the trailer bed on his butt like it was on fire and he was trying to put it out. He grabbed the handrail with his right hand, planting his right foot on the steel bumper, and swung his gimpy leg up on the trailer bed. He stood there swaying slightly wondering if Edison was having some kind of fit.

A large black cat suddenly leaped from the shadows, stopped at the old man's feet, lifted its oversized head, and fixed Jackson with a malevolent stare. Jackson stared back not believing his eyes.

The cat opened its mouth and spit a wicked hiss through long, brown teeth. The old man instinctively threw himself back, away from the creature. The hip with the disintegrating pelvic socket slammed against the trailer and his other leg slipped from the bumper.

Jackson hung from the rail by one arm, cursing through the pain in his hip, and watched the black cat streak down the ramp and around the corner.

Later, Jackson would swear that it was a devil cat that had cut Edison. He got a good look at that black devil and he never wanted to see it again. He could still see that one yellow eye piercing him with its evil gaze. It gave him the shivers.

chapter 35

BOLT WAS on the loose again.

He ran blindly past the first L-shaped unit of two-story apartments. Past the stone planter filled with weeds, beer cans, and two dead juniper bushes. Past the rows of dented green garbage cans chained together like a six-pack of beer.

Past the second apartment unit and out of sight.

It felt good to run free. Free from the confinement of the Hyskos vehicle with its putrid smells of high-legged beings permeating the air and the piercing noise that kept him awake for most of the ride.

How long had he been running his paws bloody chasing after Windrusher? How many times had he arrived at a place ready to take his revenge only to find the whiskerless worm was gone?

Bolt thought back to that dark night at the rest stop. After tracking Wind and Lil' One for so long, over so many miles, he finally would end their miserable lives. He watched his two enemies from behind the Bayberry bush, nearly overcome with giddiness. They would pay dearly for shattering his happy world, for separating him from Swift Nail, for the terrible life he had been forced to live tracking them across the countryside.

Then, his exhilaration crashed to a depth of despair he had never felt before. In disbelief, he watched the two worthless creatures scramble into the Hyskos box and drive away.

What could he do now?

Bolt gorged himself on the remains of the garbage at the rest stop and slept through the night. With morning light the thoughts of revenge again coursed through him, and he swore that only his own death would ever stop him from killing Windrusher.

In the months following the two cat's escape from the rest stop,

Bolt walked numbly across hundreds of miles of farmland, following a general southerly course that he hoped Wind would take. It was at another highway rest stop near Aurora, West Virginia that Bolt finally came to the same realization as Windrusher and rode in his first Hyskos vehicle.

The rusted and dented pickup truck sat alone in the parking lot as if the other vehicles feared contamination. The truck's bed was heaped with cast-off furniture including an old kitchen table and three mismatched chairs that might have been rejected by Good Will. A tattered blue tarp coated with blobs of ancient paint covered the furniture.

Bolt saw the truck and instantly made a decision that changed his life. He jumped onto the fender and quickly burrowed beneath the tarpaulin. Minutes later he was flying down Federal Highway 219 toward Elkins, West Virginia.

Bolt had to admit that this was much easier than attempting to follow Windrusher on foot. Through the Inner Ear, Bolt learned that Windrusher was no longer at the farmhouse, but he didn't know where he was going. If the braggart stayed true to form, though, he would eventually tell every cat plugged into Akhen-et-u all the details of his *mystical journey*. And once Windrusher arrived at another destination, the creature was too vain to keep it to himself.

Lying in the truck bed, surrounded by furniture, Bolt tried to imagine what it must be like living in a Hyskos home. Unlike many cats that spent their days coddled by the high-legged beings, he had never felt the warmth of acceptance, or any Hyskos touch, except in anger.

The gaunt cat was exhausted by his travels; he shut his good eye, and fell into a deep sleep. Bolt awoke with the acrid stench of gasoline in his nostrils. The harsh glare of sunlight hit him like a hard slap, and he blinked to clear his head. Momentarily confused, Bolt felt himself snatched up by the scruff of the neck. The next moment he was roughly pushed into an empty pet carrier. The door clanged shut.

"Well, looky what we have here." The voice twanged with the sound of the West Virginia hills.

Bolt growled and lunged at the metal grate, his mangled ear flopping against his head. He was trapped. There was nothing he could do but sit and look through the bars at the grinning high-legged being.

The man admired the brutish cat and smiled through a mouth missing two teeth. "You are an ugly critter, aren't you? I'd say you've been in your share of fights, tough guy. But you probably gave as good as you got. Right?"

Jimmy Lee Higginbotham understood giving as good as you got. He had been in more than one barroom brawl, and the missing teeth were only the most visible sign of his drunken furies. His slumping left shoulder was the reason he finally went on the wagon. Thanks to the four-inch blade that sliced through tendons and nerves, Higginbotham couldn't raise his arm above his head without agonizing pain. That put him at a disadvantage as a house painter.

Higginbotham scrunched up his rubbery face and kneaded his aching shoulder. He couldn't wait to see his wife, but would be happy if he never saw her mother again. Which was hard to do since they were living in the old bat's house.

Higginbotham held the pet carrier at waist level and waved to his wife. "Hey, Lou Anne, look what I brought you."

Lou Anne stared at the creature in her pet carrier. She bent over to get a good look and recoiled at the sight. The matted black hair covered with gaping white scars, the mauled ear, the dripping white eye, the horrible scars across the animal's flattened face, and that evil lemon-colored eye, were a potent combination for the hardiest of souls. And Lou Anne Higginbotham had never been described as hardy. Her stomach twisted and she turned away from the animal.

"Good Lord, Jimmy Lee, what the hell is that?"

Higginbotham laughed nervously, and put the carrier down at his feet.

"What does it look like? It's some poor cat down on its luck. Kind of looks like me, don't you think?"

Lou Anne was a spindly woman with light brown hair tied back with a red bow. She had high cheekbones and a nose that sat slightly off center in her almost attractive face. "Jimmy Lee, you know I like cats as much as anyone, but something's not right with this animal. Are you sure it's safe to keep it around the house?"

"Of course it is, sweetie," he said. He turned toward his mother-in-law and gave her a gap-toothed smile.

"Here, you take a look, Mrs. Johnson, and tell Lou Anne that it's just a beaten up old cat."

Lou Anne's mother stood behind her daughter, as if she'd found the only shady spot in an arid desert. The older woman moved hesitantly to one side to get a better view of the object of their discussion. Her eyes were red from the stream of smoke rising from the cigarette tucked tightly in the corner of her mouth. A network of shallow brown troughs creased her face and furrows ran down her lips when she pursed them, which she frequently did. She stared wide-eyed at the cat, made the sign of the cross over her bony chest, blew out a cloud of smoke, and returned to the house without saying a word.

Higginbotham watched Mrs. Johnson's retreat then turned to his wife, giving her a tight-lipped smile. "Baby, it was sleeping in the back of the truck. I thought you'd want to see it, at least feed it until its back on its feet."

He put his good arm around her shoulder, giving it a tiny squeeze. "I know how you miss your other cat."

"I don't know, Jimmy Lee. That thing scares the bejeebers out of me. You can put it on the back porch for now, but keep it in the box, I don't want it running loose."

The cat stayed in the box for five days before Higginbotham talked Lou Anne into letting the cat have the run of the back porch. They kept the food bowl filled, and left the cat to itself. It spent most of the time hiding under the moldy day bed, coming out only to wolf down the cat chow and occasionally use the litter box.

Lou Anne made only one attempt to befriend the feral cat. One morning, she bravely stepped onto the back porch, pulling her wool sweater tightly around her slim shoulders. "Come here, you black dragon," she said with false bravado. "I've got some goodies for you."

Lou Anne kneeled down and dropped some cat treats at the edge of the day bed. Despite her fears, she cooed kindly to the brute, just as she had done with all her cats. She chattered on for a minute without hearing any response. Thinking it may somehow have found a way out of the room, she lowered her head to the floor and peered into the shadows.

The unholy glow of the creature's yellow eye jolted her backwards, just in time to avoid the swipe of its razor sharp claws.

After that, Lou Anne refused to enter the back porch. Higginbotham tried to laugh it off, but he had to admit that he wasn't particularly fond of the cat, either.

After two months with the Higginbotham's, Bolt's weight was back to normal. He felt the old strength surging in his limbs, and he was growing accustomed to the shelter and security of life on the back porch.

That was about to change.

A crash of thunder woke the old woman. She rolled over and looked at the little Gruen alarm clock that had been on her nightstand for at least thirty years. It was 3:35 A.M. The lightning flash cast shadows across her drapes and she groped for her robe. This was as good a time as any, she thought.

She entered the back porch, and walked directly to the outside door without looking to see if the black cat was anywhere in sight. She pushed the door open and felt the cold breeze hit her in the face like a blast of air conditioning on a summer's day. In the distance, a black thunderhead suddenly glowed with the eruption of sheet lightning.

Mrs. Johnson could smell the storm on the horizon. Rain was coming. It was coming soon, and it was coming hard. She slid an old milk can in front of the door, propping it open to the outside chill, and hoped the cat was smart enough to leave a place he wasn't wanted. A double strand of lighting splashed orange and yellow molten lava against the night sky and the old woman turned her wrinkled face toward the sky.

That's good, she thought. Maybe the good Lord has something waiting for that devil cat.

chapter **36**

WIND WAS WANDERING blindly around the Carolina countryside in a fog bank of self-pity and conflicting emotions. The smells and images of Silk Blossom clung to him like the burrs in his coat.

He berated himself endlessly for being so foolish as to think she wanted to spend her life with him. His chest ached when he thought of how he must appear in her eyes. In those magnificent sapphire eyes.

After days of self-pity, he came to realize that there was nothing he would have done differently. He would always treasure their special relationship, but there were some things that could not be changed. From past experiences, Wind understood that there are times when the gods determine a different course than he would take if left the choice. It happened when his family left him behind. It happened when poor Scowl Down was killed. And now it happened again.

There came a time when it became clear that Silk Blossom was right, that he needed to move on and fulfill the mission Irissa-u had set before him those many night globes ago. Instead of wandering consumed with self-pity, he determined the proper direction and resumed his journey.

Windrusher wasn't ready to face another Hyskos city and carefully made his way around Columbia, South Carolina. Following the black path southward until it merged with Highway 321 outside Columbia, he carefully picked his way through the strips of woods and clearings that paralleled the roadway.

Fresh blooms of gloriosa daisy, red corn poppy and purple coneflower blanketed the roadsides with waves of color, but Wind was only dimly aware of the spring greenery and trudged stubbornly ahead. There was only the present that mattered. This step he was taking.

And the next one.

And the next.

Windrusher kept his eyes focused on the ground in front of him. He walked through fleeting patches of darkening shadows and faint light as a scudding bank of clouds raced across a fading night globe. Morning was close to breaking through the grasp of night, and off to the cat's left, a reddish glow suffused the darkness.

His ears were the first of his senses to send warning signals to his numb brain. The low roar came from behind him and he whirled to face it. He was still frightened no matter how many times he heard and saw the screaming links of silver boxes invade the landscape like demons infesting his dreams.

Wind ran to a nearby thicket of loblolly pines and hunkered behind the largest. Just below him, down a shallow embankment, the thing flew through the early morning darkness. He felt the gusts of hot air whipping through the trees, propelling dirt and gravel as if thrown by an invisible hand.

He had encountered this Hyskos marvel before in his travels, but this was the closest he had ever been and he stared hypnotically as car after car whizzed by kicking up sparks like clouds of fireflies. The shiny boxes glittering with windows were the first to fly by. These were followed by a string of huge steel containers with strange markings on their sides. Interspersed were low platforms stacked with oddly shaped containers.

With a dying shriek, it slowly receded until Wind could no longer see or hear it. He waited until he was sure it was gone and made his way down the embankment. Carefully, he picked his way through the underbrush onto a flat bed of stones intersected with oily beams of wood.

Windrusher crossed the gravel bed; the stones crunching under his feet reminded him of the sounds he made chewing the hard pellets of food the Hyskos put out. He approached the steel rails and stared curiously at the sight of the parallel tracks stretching out of sight.

He surveyed the tracks, listening intently for the screaming beasts, then leaned over and sniffed curiously. Wind wrinkled his nose and exhaled sharply as the stink of sulfur and creosote assaulted him.

Windrusher moved away and sat down. He scratched savagely at a fleabite on his flank, and replayed the sights and sounds he had just witnessed. It didn't seem possible, he thought, but behind some of those windows, flittering by like ghostly reminders of things left undone, there were the heads of high-legged beings.

Yes, it had to be, this was another Hyskos vehicle.

The passage of time was marked with each punishing step the cat took. He limped perceptibly from a thorn that bit into his paw and resisted every effort he'd made to dig it out. Windrusher no longer resembled the well-groomed heavyweight feline he'd become during his days with Silk Blossom. Now, his coat was matted and spiked and his skin was stretched taut across his ribs.

His hunting skills helped keep him alive throughout his travels, but now he seemed to have lost the patience needed for pursuing his prey. Fortunately, the high-legged beings threw out enough food to keep him alive, and he continued on his southerly course.

Sometime during the past three day globes, Windrusher found himself veering further away from the black path and following the stone and steel path of the railroad tracks. The screaming vehicles still alarmed him, but he was fascinated now that he understood what they were.

He plodded along a narrow clearing between the gravel bed to his left and the line of telephone poles standing like staunch sentinels in the morning mist. To his right lay a sprawl of greenery overgrown with palmettos and pine.

Wind had been on the trail for hours, and he noted the rising day globe washing the horizon with hues of rose and gold. The sight of the brightening morning lifted his spirits, and now he was certain he was getting closer with each step. Although he was exhausted, the knowledge filled him with exhilaration and renewed strength.

Windrusher edged toward the tangle of bushes and trees. A thirty-foot Black Locust tree, festooned with gray-green oval leaves, stood surrounded by scrub oak and palmetto. In the distance, fading down toward the highway, was a field of ragweed with spikes of tiny green bells waving in the morning breeze.

He worked his way through the bushes looking for a protected spot and felt the brittle branches snatch at his fur. Beneath the towering Black Locust, Wind found a bed of soft white sand and made several looping turns before dropping on his belly.

He was in the midst of pulling his legs under him when the piercing *caw* of a crow caught his attention, and he turned to see the black bird rise heavily from a telephone line. A sudden shiver coursed through his body, causing his whiskers to vibrate, and Wind jumped to his feet. He sniffed the sweet Carolina air, rich with spring flowers and the first blooms of ragweed.

It was none of those floral aromas, however, that caused the hairs on the back of his neck to rise and his tail to stiffen. He could not see it yet, but the foul odor carried on the morning wind told him that it was close by.

Windrusher's ears swiveled at the crunch of leaves on the edge of the undergrowth. Silently, he pushed his way through the bushes and squeezed below the overhanging fronds of a palmetto.

The bluetick coonhound rushed through the trees baying like a bugle. With tail held high, the well-muscled body crashed through the scrub oak and the baying turned into a coarse chopping bark.

Windrusher backed out from beneath the palmettos keeping the bushes between him and the approaching snouter. The coonhound sniffed at the base of the tree where the cat should have been napping, and traced Wind's scent toward the clump of palmettos.

Wind crept silently through the underbrush until he was outside the ragged rectangle of greenery. He heard the dog snuffling and rooting in the bushes like a wild hog foraging for roots and acorns. It wouldn't be long before the snouter tracked him through the bushes, and he fought the fear that threatened to paralyze him.

Windrusher considered his options: Should he run toward the highway, perhaps hiding himself in the thick stalks of ragweed, or stay close to the trees? The sharp chopping barks were getting closer now and Wind circled away from the frightening noise. There was little chance of outrunning the snouter, and once the enraged animal cornered him it would be over quickly.

All of his protective instincts were engaged. Adrenalin coursed through his system and he prepared to fight for his life if necessary. He was so intent on avoiding the fetid smelling creature approaching from directly in front of him that the menacing growl behind him took him totally by surprise.

chapter 37

WINDRUSHER WHIPPED his head around and saw another snouter just feet away. The dog's mouth was drawn back into a hideous grin, the yellow canine teeth dripping with spittle. Oozing open sores trailing long ribbons of slime pocked the dog's listless brown coat.

Wind instinctively arched his back and stiffened his legs as though he were standing on tiptoes. His fur stood out giving him an even larger appearance, and he turned broadside toward the disgusting creature while hissing ominously. Wind's striking green eyes narrowed and hardened into dense obsidian globes.

The two animals faced each other, the snouter returning Wind's stare and adding a growl deep in its throat like the final moments of life itself. Wind looked into the snouter's flat black eyes. Fishlike scales surrounded them, and the skin around its mouth and eyes was taut with stress and anticipation. Then a subtle change came over them, and the big cat saw indecision play across the watery pupils.

The growl faded into a gruff whine, and Windrusher chose that moment to lash out. With an explosive spit, he raked his claws swiftly across the snouter's muzzle and down its nose. The mangy animal yelped loudly, throwing a foreleg over its bleeding muzzle, then turned and ran.

Windrusher's heart beat thunderously in his chest as he watched the snouter retreating toward the railroad tracks, its wiry tail tucked firmly between its legs. The cat breathed deeply and relaxed his legs and back. He thought back to the time he defended Lil' One from the snouter and realized how fortunate he was to be alive. Either one of these smelly snouters could have ended his life with one bloody bite.

The bawling bark of the bluetick snatched him back to the present. The domed and broad skull was pointed directly at him as the hound raced around the bushes. The coarse coat gleamed in the white glare of the sun, and in that bright light, the cat saw flecks of black, blue, and tan.

It was too late to run from the hunting dog. The hound's blood was up, and a fleeing cat could only be construed as one thing—food. Wind took the only course open to him, and crashed blindly through the bushes, back toward the towering Black Locust tree.

He felt the hot slathering breath of the bluetick close behind him, the choppy barks jarring him like a chainsaw. Windrusher squirmed between and under branches, gaining precious seconds, then broke through to the small clearing. The hardwood tree stood like a beacon of hope and he leaped at the dark ridged bark with fully extended claws. In moments, he was ten feet above the ground to the first branch.

Wind sat for a moment, his chest heaving, the sound of his heartbeat ringing in his ears. Below, the coonhound braced its muscular legs against the trunk and rasped a desperate bark at the treed cat. The dog's dark brown eyes seemed to plead for the cat to come down and play another game of hide and seek.

Windrusher kept watch on the hound not sure if it was able to climb after him. He stopped paying attention when it became evident that the snouter was no more able to scramble up the trunk of the Locust tree than it could fly.

The warmth of the mid-morning sun filtered through the oddly aligned leaves and lulled Wind into a light catnap. When he awoke, the sun was directly overhead. Nothing moved below except a few desiccated leaves shifting position in the breeze.

Windrusher scrutinized the cluster of bushes, the scrub oaks, and the palmettos. He surveyed beyond the thicket, toward the highway, back toward the railroad tracks. The snouters were gone; he had outwitted the small-brained, smelly creatures once again.

He lowered himself down the trunk, his claws clinging to the furrowed ridges of the bark. About halfway down, Wind hesitated. Did he hear something, or were his fears taunting him? He rotated his ears toward the imagined sound and heard the faraway rumble of an approaching train.

Convinced he was safe, Windrusher retracted his claws and

dropped to the ground. He slid in the loose sand and sat quietly for a moment. The stink of the snouter was unbearable. It permeated the air like cigar smoke in a closed room. Pushing quietly through the underbrush, Wind stood silently listening for any hint of danger. His tongue licked his parched lips and fluttered in the air momentarily, tasting the invisible currents.

It was time to resume his journey, and, hopefully, find something to eat. Curiously, he was filled with an excitement for hunting once again, and he pictured himself stalking a plump rodent or unsuspecting squirrel. He prudently decided to lose himself among the field of ragweed, at least until he was well out of sight of this spot, and loped away from the thicket toward the highway hoping to find his breakfast hidden in the foliage.

Wind was only a few feet into the weeds when he heard them. The shrill baying of the coonhound mixed with the higher-pitched yelps of the diseased mongrel. The big tom couldn't see them from amidst the ragweed but his ears told him they were below him near the highway.

And they were getting closer.

He wasn't secure in the field of weeds since the snouters obviously had his scent. For the third time that day, Windrusher ran for his life. He broke through the ragweed and raced away with the chilling howls of the dogs closing in behind him.

Wind scrambled up the embankment toward the railroad tracks and heard the thunderous roar of the screaming Hyskos vehicle vaulting down the tracks less than one hundred feet away. He poured every ounce of energy that was left in his fatigued and stressed body into his legs even as his mind calculated the geometry of survival.

His only chance was to reach the tracks and cross them before the snouters. If his luck held, the rumbling row of silver boxes would block his pursuers. If not? He shook off any thoughts of the alternative as his front paws clawed at the sharp gravel.

Behind him, the shrieks of the snouters were so close he felt their vile spittle landing on his shoulders and neck. He refused to look concentrating on the steel rails before him, and trying not to slip on the shifting rocks. His feet touched one of the blocks of oily wood while his back paws churned for purchase in the gravel, kicking up stones in the face of the coonhound.

The rumble of the train had become a series of ear-splitting detonations that exploded in his head and threatened to sweep him down the embankment. Wide-eyed with fright, Windrusher saw the locomotive bearing down on him in a curtain of smoke and fire like some demonic force from a nightmare world.

He felt his tail sweep across the snouter's muzzle and feared he was just moments from feeling the deadly teeth sink into his back. Ahead of him, he faced instant death under the wheels of the screaming behemoth. Swallowing his panic, Windrusher leaped across the first rail into the very face of the locomotive.

chapter 38

"Where's Kimmy? We've got to get moving."

Gerry Tremble paced the floor with steps too short for his long legs, like he was struggling to keep stride with a smaller person. For the fourth time he pulled back the cuff on his white shirt and checked his watch

Amy sat quietly, twisting an embroidered handkerchief between her thumbs and forefingers. She watched her husband pacing back and forth in their living room.

"Will you go see what's holding her up, Amy, please," he said.

"We have plenty of time, Gerry. Why don't you and GT pull the car around and I'll go get Kimmy?"

She rose from the couch, smoothing the wrinkles from her black dress, and walked through the family room to Kimmy's bedroom. The twelve-year-old sat on the edge of her bed, head down, holding a single patent leather pump in her hands.

"Honey, is everything all right?" Amy asked.

Kimmy looked as if she had been awakened from a deep sleep.

"I was just thinking about Grandpa Stu, and how much I'll miss him."

"Oh baby, we're all going to miss Grandpa Stu."

Amy sat down on the bed beside her daughter and hugged her tightly. "Aren't we lucky that we were able to spend this last year with him, though? We have so many memories that we'll keep with us forever."

"He was sick for a long time, wasn't he?" Kimmy asked, still holding the shoe.

Amy smoothed her daughter's hair back from her forehead. "Grandpa's illness probably began years ago. That's why they kept asking us to come down here and help them with the hotel," she said, taking the shoe from her daughter's hand and putting it on her foot.

"Let's see how you look," she said, pulling the girl to her feet.

Kimmy wore a black jumper over an ivory blouse, and Amy thought she was the most beautiful child she had ever seen. "You are beautiful, your grandfather would be so proud of you. Let's go now, we don't want to keep dad waiting any longer."

Captain Stuart Tremble's friends and business acquaintances were many and the Crystal River Presbyterian Church was nearly full. This was Kimmy's first funeral and she sobbed quietly while the minister prayed, the choir sang, and her father tearfully remembered his father—the decorated Navy pilot, entrepreneur, hotel owner.

In the days following the funeral, Tremble returned to the hotel and lost himself in his work. Amy did the same at the hospital, and GT rejoined the high school baseball team. Kimmy returned to school as well, but nothing was the same. Her mind drifted during class, and her friends noticed she wasn't quite the boisterous and vivacious tomboy she was before her grandfather's funeral. It was not lost on the Trembles either.

Amy knocked on Kimmy's closed door and asked if she could come in.

"I guess," Kimmy said.

She closed the door behind her and observed her daughter propped up on her elbows on the bed. Stella, the black Lab, lay on the floor right below the girl. The dog lifted its broad head and whipped the floor with its tail when it saw Mrs. Tremble.

Kimmy was staring at a photo scrapbook.

"What's wrong, Kimmy? You haven't been acting like yourself this week."

"I don't know. Everything seems different since grandpa died."

Amy sat on the edge of the bed and gently ran her hand over Kimmy's back. She glanced at the open scrapbook expecting to see a picture of the girl's grandfather. Instead, there was a snapshot of Kimmy holding her cat up to her face and grinning like a Halloween pumpkin.

"I know you miss grandpa. We all do. It just takes time before the pain goes away." She continued stroking the young girl's back. "That's a great picture of you and Tony," she said gesturing toward the scrapbook.

Kimmy snapped the covers closed so hard that two of the pictures flew out. She pushed them aside and put her head down on the comforter. Stella barked abruptly at the sound and jumped to her feet. Not seeing any likely intruder to lick into submission, the Lab turned twice and settled back on the floor.

"What is it, baby? Can I do anything to help?"

Kimmy sobbed quietly, the tears rolling down her cheeks, branding the yellow comforter with patches of dampness. "It's Tony," she said finally, her voice muffled against her arm.

Amy hesitated a moment, trying to adjust to this change in direction. "Tony? I'm sure he —"

"No." Kimmy turned over on her side and glared at her mother through red-rimmed eyes. "No, he's not all right. Something bad is happening to Tony and he needs me."

"Oh, Kimmy, we don't know where Tony ran off to after he left Stacy, but I'll bet he's with another family and they're taking good care of him."

Kimmy shook her head violently, and looked at her mother as though the older woman was from a foreign land and spoke a different language. "You don't understand. I've dreamed about Tony, and I know he's trying to find us. I'm afraid if we don't help him something bad will happen." The girl threw herself into her mother's arms, pressing tightly against her.

Amy thought carefully before she answered. Her nurse's training conjoined with her motherly instincts prompted her to stop the pain, yet try to understand its source. She gently held her child by her arms and pushed her forward so she could look in her face.

"You know, honey, sometimes when we're very upset about something, like Grandpa Stu's passing, our mind tries to help us by finding something else we can worry about. Does that make sense?"

"It's not that way, mommy, really," Kimmy insisted with another shake of her head. "I am sad about Grandpa Stu, but I dreamed about Tony before grandpa died, and I know he's in danger."

While fixing dinner that night, Amy told her husband about the conversation with Kimmy. Tremble listened carefully. He sipped from a glass of Diet Pepsi, and tried to make sense of what his wife was saying.

"I'm not a psychologist, but I think this is what they call displacement behavior," she said.

Tremble scrunched up his face and shook his head.

"You know, it's when a person's behavior is really a way of protecting them from something else that is so painful they can't deal with it."

A glimmer of understanding crossed Tremble's face.

"In this case," she continued, "I think Kimmy is so upset by Stu's death that she's obsessing about Tony."

"Well, why Tony, of all things?"

"I know it seems strange, especially since she wasn't that upset when Tony ran away. But, remember that Kimmy is no longer the little girl she was back in Bloomfield. Tony is part of her happy childhood, and it's a way for her to cling to that happy time while working out her emotions."

Tremble's forehead furrowed with concern. "I don't know, she's always been a stable kid, has her head on straight. At least for a pre-teen. Do you think she needs counseling?"

"No, certainly, not at this time. Let's just be very supportive, and I'm sure she'll come around."

chapter **39**

WINDRUSHER ROLLED down the side of the embankment, the roar of the train vibrating in his chest, and nearly bursting his eardrums. He looked back to see if the two snouters had followed him over the steel rails, but only saw the chattering wheels of the speeding monster sending up sparks and smoke.

Thanks be to Irissa-u he wasn't flattened beneath the rolling Hyskos boxes. Still, there was no time for analysis or celebration. He forced his legs to move, to take him away from the endless links of mammoth vehicles. While the train remained as frightening as it was unfathomable to him, it had saved his life, and some inner voice was telling him it could still prove very helpful and not to run too far away.

He set a course that paralleled the tracks, put his faith in his internal compass and trusted that he was indeed traveling in the right direction. Without that trust, all the efforts he made over the past night globes would be wasted and that was too horrible to contemplate.

Moving southward, Wind sometimes followed the black paths, sometimes trekked through the scraggly buffer zones of pine, maples, and scrub oaks. Always, he stayed close enough to the railroad tracks to hear the howling blasts echo through the night until they became part of his daily routine. He watched each one with equal fascination, convinced that they would play an important part in his travels.

Twenty-two days passed in Hyskos time before Windrusher stumbled upon the train station. He had left the black path behind to follow the unending steel threads that carried the mammoth vehicles. The night sky reflected the faint glow of a waning moon that played over the leaves of the trees lining both sides of the track. Waves of nocturnal music covered the night with the incessant chirping of crickets and the expectant mating trills of frogs.

Windrusher approached a highway overpass and one of the noisy linked vehicles, moving very slowly, clanked by. On the other side of the overpass, the steel ribbons split apart, and, like rust-colored vines from a single stalk, grew into three separate tracks. The tracks crossed over each other and continued in roughly the same direction.

Wind stopped at the intersection of tracks momentarily puzzled and wondered which of the steel rails to follow. In the distance, a glaring bank of lights whisked away the darkness and he saw silhouettes of high-legged beings moving about.

Cautiously, he moved closer to the harsh blaze of lights and almost tripped over a wide cement platform that jutted out at his feet and continued as far as he could see. In front of the platform, like a gigantic phosphorescent snake biding its time before its next meal, stood the silver boxes. Puffs of white smoke emerged from beneath the locomotive, and even though it was not moving, the train emitted a sense of incipient chaos, as if it could leap to life at any moment.

A pre-cast concrete shelter ran the length of the platform, resting upon a row of faded mauve colored steel I-beams. Hanging below the overhead shelter was a sign that might as well have been written in Egyptian hieroglyphics to Windrusher, but if he could read the large black letters, he'd realize where he was.

SAVANNAH

High-legged beings disappeared into the belly of the grinding monster as he watched. Wind scurried to the steel rail fence that surrounded the brick building adjoining the platform and tried to make sense of it.

It was late in the evening, and perhaps twenty-five people were there to catch Amtrak 89 for Jacksonville. Some of them talked quietly among themselves, suitcases at their feet. Others walked directly to the passenger cars and climbed aboard.

A man in a dark blue suit checked tickets and pointed to the various cars. "All aboard," he yelled.

None of them seemed to notice the dirty cat lurking in the shadows behind the fence. Windrusher slipped through the fence and slinked over to one of the support beams, hiding himself between the chipped beam and a chrome-plated luggage cart. From this vantage point, he watched as high-legged beings climbed the few steps and disappeared into the vehicle, only to reappear behind the windows. Through it all, the blue-suited Hyskos paced up and down the platform.

Harold Logan opened the tarnished railroad watch for the third time in the past five minutes and clicked it shut. It was his job to keep the train on schedule, and he was good at it, as his twenty-two-year record as a conductor demonstrated. He was also good at keeping his eyes open, and Logan spotted the stray cat hiding behind the beam in Zone 8. He clicked the watch closed and dropped it in his pocket. Nonchalantly, he made his way toward Zone 8.

Windrusher considered the scene before him and wondered once again if he was indeed lacking the sense of a floppy-eared snouter. Was it even possible for him to find a way on to this terrifying Hyskos vehicle? An insinuating voice in his head kept telling him this was too dangerous, that this was the most foolish thing he had ever attempted. He disregarded it and rushed from behind the column toward the closest open door. There he was met by the tall Hyskos in the blue suit.

"Whoa, where do you think you're going, you little sneak?"

The conductor stood directly in front of the steps leading up to the silver box. He stuck his leg out toward the animal as if trying to push it aside. Wind crouched defensively, his rear down on his haunches prepared to leap in any direction, and stared at the man wide-eyed.

"You go crawling under that thing and you'll end up a train pizza. Go'wan, get," Logan said and stamped his foot.

Wind bolted away from the blue-suited man, dashing between the legs of a large woman in a flowered dress. He ran down the platform, his nails clicking against the cement, dodging another Hyskos that suddenly emerged from a walkway below the platform. Ducking behind the concrete wall that surrounded the underground walkway, he caught his breath.

Windrusher poked one green eye and a fuzzy gray ear around

the wall and peered along the length of the platform. A series of light bulbs in gunmetal gray casings stared down from the protective shelter like dead fish eyes. The conductor checked his watch again and called out several times in his unintelligible speech.

Wind's ears pricked up at the rush of noise suddenly echoing around the terminal. A burst of smoke erupted from the first silver box, and two more high-legged beings hurried to enter the vehicles.

The Hyskos checked the platform behind him, and waved to a porter who leaned out from one of the last passenger cars. Wind scurried along the wall and froze in place against the rough concrete. He held his breath and when the Hyskos in the blue suit looked away he ran again, careful not to let his claws click against the floor this time.

Wind's heart raced. The insufferable voice in his head returned, but this time it screamed at him to do something, because the success of his mission depended on him finding his way into the frightening vehicle. He dashed forward and hid behind the rusted wheel of a flatbed freight cart that looked like the remains of an ancient Conestoga wagon.

Above him, the public address speakers blared: "Last call. Boarding for Jacksonville, Daytona Beach, New Smyrna Beach, and Titusville. All aboard."

Another burst of smoke swirled along the platform spreading an acrid scorched metal smell. Windrusher pictured the long line of boxes springing to life and rolling down the tracks. He heard the roar of the train; saw it disappearing into the distance until it was a tiny black spot trailing smoke. After all he had been through, to come so close, it was going to leave him behind and there was nothing he could do about it.

That was when the old woman slowly made her way past him. She leaned heavily on a quad cane that was painted with blue bells and butterflies, and clutched the handle of a shopping bag with her free hand. A leopard print purse, nearly the same size as her shopping bag, hung precariously from the same arm holding the cane.

With a great effort, the woman raised the cane to eye level and held it there as though hailing a cab. "Wait up, you're not leaving without me," she shrieked in a voice that sliced through the growing din of the locomotive.

The conductor turned and inhaled deeply at the sight of the woman shuffling toward him. He willed himself to smile. He was a professional, after all.

"That's okay, ma'am. We're not going to leave you." Logan gritted his molars, hoping it still looked like a smile. "Let me give you a hand."

Logan hurried to the woman and relieved her of the shopping bag. He wanted to push her along, tell her they were almost two minutes behind schedule, but instead took her elbow in his hand and ambled beside her at the same furiously deliberate pace.

They finally approached the first car. "Can I see your ticket, ma'am?"

"Of course you can, young man, it's in my purse."

Both of them stopped as the old woman wrestled the purse from her arm. Logan eyed the capacious bag then gazed wanly toward the train. When he turned back one corner of his lower lip was pinched between his teeth and his jaw was working it like a wad of snuff.

To his great relief, the ticket was right on top and she presented it to him with a little twist of her wrist as though it was an invitation to a country club ball. Logan checked the car number and took her arm again.

"Thank you, ma'am," he said, holding on to the ticket. "Your car is right down here. Let's get you aboard and make you comfortable."

The conductor and the elderly woman inched their way toward the fourth car. Watching from behind the column, Wind could not believe his good fortune. The Hyskos seemed completely occupied with the female, and he was moving farther and farther away from him.

Wind surveyed the length of the walkway one more time, and silently dashed up the steps of the nearest silver box. He found himself in what looked like a small room with doors on all sides. Directly in front of him the door was split in half; the bottom half closed and the top latched back so he could see the black night sky nicked with phosphorescent flakes of faraway stars, like votive candles shimmering through a gauzy curtain.

The metal door on his right was closed tight, but the one to his left was propped open. He entered and stopped in the center of a long aisle bordered by rows of seats. Windows ran the full length of the transportation box, and high-legged beings sat looking out into the night.

Windrusher stood in the aisle unsure of what to do next. He jerked his head from side to side desperately searching for a hiding place. The rows on either side of him were empty, and he darted under an unoccupied seat, squeezed himself into a tight ball in the far corner, and waited for the huge vehicle to take him on the next stage of his journey.

chapter 40

WIND'S HINDQUARTERS shifted beneath him when the box lurched forward. He dug his claws into the carpeting, his muscles tense with fear and anticipation. The floor hummed with a throbbing that vibrated through every cell in his body, and his breath caught in his throat like an unseen fist had clenched his windpipe. His pulsating heart echoed in his ears so loudly he was afraid one of the high-legged beings would hear it above the clatter of the train.

And there was that fickle, infuriating voice again. This time it was telling him to run, to leave the dark, noisy force pressing in on him. It took all of his will to ignore it, and he called up memories of all the Hyskos vehicles he had endured, the noisy rides, the confined spaces. This was the same thing, he told himself, only the vehicle was different.

Wind forced his mind away from those early memories of the small Hyskos vehicle he was forced to ride in as a young cat. He was not the same cat. His experiences proved that there was nothing to fear by these Hyskos vehicles, and everything to gain. Very slowly his breathing returned to normal.

It became clear that observing these convoys from along the tracks was certainly different from being inside. Outside, it seemed like a great wind would blow him away if he stood too close to the tracks, and the screams of the fiery monster in the night shook the woods around him.

There were no screams here, only a constant rattle that oscillated through the floor. It surrounded the cat and soon became as much a part of his world as his own whiskers.

Amtrak 89 would make the trip from Savannah to Jacksonville in two hours and fifteen minutes, arriving at 1:43 A.M. Many of the passengers were dozing in the dim light, heads bobbing slightly with the rhythm of the train. At the rear of the car, hidden from the sleeping passengers, the cat relaxed and let his body sway with the perpetual shaking. Soon his eyelids felt the tug of blissful sleep and he became one with the rattling box.

Like an autumn leaf spiraling to the ground, Windrusher dropped into the welcoming embrace of sleep. Gone was the anxiety and turmoil that wracked his waking body. He was safe now in the soothing nest of the Sleep Mother, Hwrt-Heru, assured of waking with renewed energy.

Lil' One and Scowl Down appeared to him in his dreams, grooming each other below a sycamore tree bathed in the rose-hued light of sunset. They were replaced by Silk Blossom nursing four of her kittens while the fifth, the tabby with the dark gray fur ringed with orange stripes, scrambled over the side of the box and ran for the open door.

And there was Kimmy, his Hyskos female, holding out her hand to him, calling his name.

In his dreams, he allowed her to run her soft hand across his back and knead the roll of skin at the base of his skull. She pulled him up by the scruff of the neck and his dream crashed in around him. Wind was no longer dreaming. He was wide-awake now, spitting and hissing as he swayed in the grasp of the blue-suited Hyskos.

"Well, I tried to tell you that this wasn't where you belonged," the conductor said.

Logan held the cat out in front of him careful to avoid any claws that might be aimed his way. In his other hand, he held an empty canvas mail sack. Ignoring the tom's protests, he pushed it into the sack and pulled the rope tight.

Across the aisle, an elderly man with a mottled face the color of week-old tomato juice leaned in to get a better look.

"Thanks for letting me know about my friend here, sir. You have good eyes," the conductor said with a wink to the old man. "He gets a free trip to Jacksonville, and after that I'm sure there's a place that can offer him bed and board. At least for a few days."

Logan turned and walked down the long aisle carefully holding the sack out from his body like a ticking bomb.

chapter 41

THE WOMAN in the green scrub suit walked purposefully along the quiet hallway ignoring the trail of bright blue paw prints veering from the floor and up the wall next to the door marked Cat Adoption Center. She knew where she was going and what needed to be done.

The adoption wing wouldn't open to the public for another ninety minutes and the halls of the Jacksonville Humane Society were quiet except for a few staffers making early morning rounds. She entered the room and immediately heard familiar greetings from some of the forty-five inhabitants. Through the walls, she heard barking, which indicated that one of the technicians was visiting the kennels. It was common to hear barking even here in the Cat Adoption Center, where the vocalizing tended to be much more subdued.

When the facility opened its doors to visitors, the room would take on an air of anticipation as animals and humans reached out to each other in a never-ending pas de deux. The daily dance of cats searching for a way out of their cages and people seeking a sign amidst the meows and wide-eyed stares continued unabated. The two-legged dancers were hoping for a magic spark of recognition that this cat is worth taking home, worth their love. The four-legged ones offered all they had for the chance to be rescued, their unconditional love, their very lives. Some people asked permission from the volunteer on duty to hold one of the animals that caught their eye; many others walked through and left without touching or being touched.

All of this would happen soon, so the woman in the scrub suit had to take care of business quickly. She walked along the triple-stacked row of cages, three to a row, thirteen across, which covered one entire wall of the small room.

Absently, she scanned the cages, and heard soft meows from several of the dozens of felines in the room. The young, friendly ones craved attention and sat at the front of the small cages waiting for someone to stop. The woman peered into cage fourteen where three smoke gray kittens lay intertwined in sleep. Everyone loves kittens; they wouldn't be here long. Next to them, a small champagne colored domestic meowed politely and stuck its paw between the shiny steel ribs of the cage door.

The woman paused and scratched the cat's head. "How are you this morning, Montgomery?" she inquired, bending over to look directly at the cat. "I'll bet this is the day some lucky family takes you home. You just wait and see."

She disengaged her hand from the soft, imploring paw and moved on to cage number six. The sign hanging on the front of the cage referred to it as Cattery 6 and contained the inhabitant's pertinent information. Similar signs hung on each cattery, and a fortunate few also displayed a small HOLD sign indicating that the animal was in the process of being adopted.

According to this sign, Cattery 6 housed Buster, a longhaired domestic mix male that had been with the Humane Society for three months. Buster had received all its inoculations, was two and a half years old, and had been neutered. The sign said that Buster was looking for a home with a *patient adult willing to win this headstrong boy over with lots of love.*

The longhair lay on its side on the Metro section of the local newspaper near the back of the cage. The cat was primarily black with patches of white on its chest and rump, and it looked at the woman through slotted, untrusting eyes that never wavered.

Buster was a large cat, and fully stretched out he filled up most of the twenty-four-inch by thirty-two-inch cage. The cat's back pressed against a small aluminum foil pan that held clumps of soiled litter. A red plastic food and water dish was pushed to the front of the cage door.

"Hey, Buster, I guess you're tired of this place, aren't you," the woman said quietly, pulling up the rod that held the cage door in place. "Sorry it didn't work out for you, big guy."

The black longhair jumped to its feet at the sound of the cage door opening and backed up as far as it could, one foot stepping into the litter pan. The woman moved her left hand against the wall just out of reach of the longhair's claws. The cat hissed and turned toward the empty hand. With a practiced sweep, her right hand shot out and grabbed the frightened cat by the scruff of its neck. She pulled it out, dragging the newspaper and tipping the food bowl out onto the floor.

"It's okay, Buster, you won't feel a thing. I promise."

The woman held the cat firmly to her chest. "Shhh, it's all right. I'll take good care of you."

She spoke lovingly to the cat long after it stopped struggling, then pulled open a thick door marked "Employees Only" at the back of the room. It was painted a soft aquamarine like the concrete block wall, and it closed behind her with a whoosh of air abruptly shutting off her consoling murmurs as she took Buster on the last walk of his life.

Two rows down from number six, in Cattery 27, Windrusher cringed in the corner of the tiny cage, the sour taste of fear coating his tongue like a suffocating layer of fog across a landfill. He recoiled at the sound of the closing door, the sight of a Hyskos carrying away another animal.

It was a sight he had seen too many times. During the past week, eight cats had disappeared through the aquamarine door in the early morning hours, some of them whimpering, shaking with terror. It wasn't lost on him that none of them had returned, although new cats occupied their cages within hours.

Wind thought back to his brief ride aboard the long Hyskos vehicle. It should have been an adventurous ride that brought him closer to Kimmy and the rest of the high-legged beings that cared for him. His adventure came to an abrupt end and ended here in this cage surrounded by cats of every age, size, and color.

This is how it happened.

Lennie Wollski closed the door on the last cage and pushed the steel gray utility barrel against the block wall. He leaned his hefty frame against the barrel and wiped his forehead. Even though the room was kept at seventy-six degrees, he spent yesterday afternoon on the roof of his house patching shingles, and his skin felt like it was covered with hot ash.

Wollski pulled an oversized green bandana out of his back pocket and gingerly patted his naked scalp, tinged scarlet by the hot Florida sun. Wringing out the bandana, he tied it around his head, leaving his seared pate peeking through like a halved melon sitting on a produce counter.

He volunteered each Tuesday and Thursday mornings at the Humane Society, coming in at 9:00 A.M., an hour before visiting hours started. He cleaned the litter pans, filled the water bowls, and assisted visitors with the cats. Wollski did his best to make sure none of them left empty-handed.

May had brought unusually hot weather to North Florida, and Wollski slumped into one of the chairs. He wore a pair of threadbare khaki Bermudas and a damp T-shirt adorned with a sly looking alligator drinking a Bud Light. He pulled the shirt away from his substantial stomach pumping it up and down like a limp bellows hoping to build up a current of cooling air.

The door suddenly opened and a tall, smiling woman entered the cat adoption center. She wore a white blouse tucked into tailored navy blue pants and held a cat carrier in one hand. Wollski jumped to his feet.

"Mrs. Tibbetts. How nice to see you this morning," he said.

Mrs. Tibbetts took in Wollski's shirt and green bandana in a glance and arched an expressive eyebrow.

Wollski nervously wiped at his damp forehead and swept the bandana off his head.

"Lennie, here's a new one for you. Let's put it in Cattery 27." She held the carrier toward Wollski. "This guy's special, so treat him right, okay?"

"Yeah, he looks like a special kind of cat. One that just got himself a new place to live." He took the carrier and held it up to eye-level to get a better look at his latest charge. "What makes him so special?"

"Believe it or not, he sneaked aboard an Amtrak train in Savannah, but the ride didn't turn out quite the way he intended," she said.

"Huh," Wollski answered.

"Conductor grabbed him and turned him over to the station

master in Jacksonville."

Mrs. Tibbetts scanned the rows of cages quickly, then looked back at Wollski who seemed confused. "The station master happens to be my neighbor, so he brought him over to me this morning rather than calling animal control. At least, he'll have a shot at adoption with us."

Wollski shook his head thoughtfully. "I hope so, but he's awfully big, you know."

Mrs. Tibbetts pursed her lips and nodded. "We're really pressed for space now, literally tripping over kittens." She looked at the cat in the carrier, then brightened. "But remember, this isn't an ordinary cat, Lennie. He stowed away on a train. What a story you can tell about that, right?"

Wollski gave her a huge smile. "You're right, Mrs. Tibbetts. C'mon big guy, I have a clean penthouse waiting just for you."

Mrs. Tibbetts turned to leave, then turned back, eyeing the volunteer in his soggy T-shirt with the beer bottle on it.

"Was there something else, Mrs. Tibbetts?"

"Yes, Lennie. I wanted to thank you for all the hard work you do for us. We really appreciate it."

chapter 42

AFTER A SEVEN-DAY waiting period to see if anyone claimed him, Windrusher was taken to the clinic and tested for feline leukemia and rabies, then inoculated when the tests proved negative.

Eight day globes had come and gone since he was brought here. During that time, no one had expressed any interest in taking him home, and Wind forced himself to focus on his quest to find his Hyskos family and the young female that cared for him. There had been times in the course of his journey when he struggled to recall the girl's face, and his harrowing experiences seemed too bizarre to be real. But that was no longer the case. The longer he remained imprisoned in this cage, the sharper his vision became.

Now, an increased sense of urgency pulled at him, adding to his desire to escape. A tickling sensation gnawed at him, hanging tantalizing just outside of reach, that something wasn't quite right—aside from the fact he was locked in a steel box in a small room housing dozens of other felines crying to be let out—and Kimmy was at the center of it. Wind felt the physical presence of the girl, reaching out to him as though she was the one who needed his help.

"Oooh, look at these, daddy. They're so cute."

The voice came from down the row of cages. A girl of five or six knelt in front of a pair of tiny brown tabby siblings that were almost identical. The girl stuck her finger in the cage and squealed when one of the kittens pushed against it and purred loudly.

"They are cute, honey, but we're only looking for one cat today, and it wouldn't be fair to separate a brother and sister, would it?" He took his daughter's hand and pulled at her gently trying to move her away from the cage with the two kittens. "Let's keep looking, there are lots of others here," he said.

The girl resisted his pull for a moment then let herself be led away. The man stopped in front of Cattery 27 and gawked at the large tomcat inside.

"Look, Deb. This one's name is Tiger." He picked the girl up and held her in front of the cage. "Doesn't he look like Tony the Tiger?"

"Uh-huh," the girl said. She stuck her finger through the cage door and rubbed the cat's nose. "I think he likes me, daddy?"

The man nuzzled his daughter on the back of the neck. "I'm sure he does, sweetheart, and why wouldn't he?"

The girl wriggled wildly and the man put her down. She moved to the next row of cages and jumped up to get a better view of the champagne colored cat. "Daddy, daddy. What's this one's name?"

He looked at the sign and read it. "Montgomery. It says that he's sweet and loves children, especially little girls named Deb."

Deb jumped up and down squealing. "Can I hold him, daddy?"

A young volunteer in a Race for the Cure T-shirt appeared next to them.

"Montgomery is a very special kitty," she said. "Why don't you sit over there and I'll bring him to you. Have you held a kitty before?"

Over the next four days, the Humane Society placed eighteen cats with new owners, but during that time, they also accepted thirty-four additional cats, twenty-seven of them less than two months old. Wind watched cats of all ages leave the center with their new Hyskos families. He sensed the love and security filling the small room when this happened, but there was a different feeling when the Hyskos female in the green scrub suit made her early morning visits. Each day she took away two or three felines, and even though she spoke calmly and held them carefully, once they were taken out the back door those cats never returned.

There was nothing to do but sleep and Windrusher huddled deep within himself. Thousands of tinny voices swirled around him threatening to drag him down and bury him beneath the unremitting waves. He waited patiently until an appropriate break and after the ceremonial introduction described his plight to the Inner Ear.

"Windrusher, it has been so long since we heard from you. I was afraid your mission had come to an unfortunate end."

The familiar gravely voice stabbed through the background noise

"Short Shank, it has been a long time, my wise friend, but I have been busy," Wind said.

"You have followed the Path set out for you by Irissa-u, I know, and now you're so close to fulfilling your mission. Cats everywhere will praise your name when you find your family."

Wind allowed himself to be momentarily seduced by Short Shank's flattery, then remembered where he was. "They can save their praise for a cat that Tho-hoth blessed with more wisdom than myself. Unfortunately, I may have come to the end of my Path." He quickly told them of his circumstances.

"Your Path continues on, Pferusha-ulis, until you complete your journey. This is only a temporary stop. You have proven yourself resourceful and will overcome this setback," Short Shank said encouragingly. "After all, you are well-fed and secure so gather your strength until you return to your journey."

"There is something wrong here. I'm sure that bad things are happening, even though I can't see them."

Wind told the Inner Ear about the woman and her morning visits.

"Windrusher, if I may interrupt," another voice introducing himself as Twisted Tail, entered the conversation. "You are right to be fearful. I live not far from where you are, and was imprisoned by the Hyskos for two night globes. Fortunately, I was taken away by a kindly family, but others suffered different fates."

Wind listened intently, stirring nervously in his sleep. "Yes, I feared this. What did you learn?"

"During my stay, many cats who had been there longer than I were taken away through that back door and I believe they were destroyed." Twisted Tail's voice trailed off.

"How do you know that?" Windrusher asked.

"I would communicate with one of them, Bright Foot, through Akhen-et-u, but that stopped after he was taken through the door."

The noise level jumped dramatically pulling at Wind from all sides.

"Yes, but Windrusher has only been there a short time," cut in Short Shank abruptly.

"That may be so, but it was understood that during certain times when many cats are brought to this place they must do away with the older cats to make room for the newcomers," said Twisted Tail. "You have said that many kittens are filling the cages around you. Just beware, that is all I can say."

Voices battered him with questions and suggestions, leaving Wind exhausted and more confused than when he entered the Inner Ear. He excused himself and embraced the sweet escape of sleep.

Windrusher awoke to the quiet before dawn. The adoption center was dark and he heard only the breathing of a few nearby cats. He stretched as well as he could in the small cage, then arose and chewed on a mouthful of pellets while mulling the final remarks made by Twisted Tail. The cat was telling the truth, and unless he found a way out of his prison, he would become a cautionary tale for stubborn kittens, not the heroic legend he had created in his own mind.

The door scraped open and Wind's ears pricked up at the sound. The overhead fluorescents came on and the woman in the green scrub suit approached the rows of cages. She murmured her greetings to the cats, reaching through several of the doors to rub heads and bellies.

She bent over a cage in the row next to Cattery 27 and looked in on four tiny kittens that had arrived the day before. They were all sleeping, piled haphazardly one upon the other. She smiled and moved to the next row.

"Hey, how are you feeling today, Biscuit?" she asked, looking into Cattery 26 right below Wind's cage.

Windrusher stared at the top of the high-legged female's head and held his breath. There was a small patch of white spiking up in the back of her freshly combed black hair, like a lightning bolt in the night sky. If only there was a way to will her to move on, to take her deadly morning errand to another room, at least to a cage far from his.

The woman straightened and looked directly into Windrusher's eyes. They held each other's stare for a moment until the woman reached up to the cage door. Wind whimpered and scurried back.

"It's okay, Tiger," she said, and fingered the sign on the front of the cage. "We haven't done a very good job selling you, have we? Too bad. You're such a smart boy, and comfortable with people."

She gazed at the rows of cages full of kittens and slowly shook her head.

Wind was fixated on the woman's hand as it moved toward the rod to the right of the cage door. His green eyes grew wider the closer she came; a muscle twitched near the root of his tail. This will be the day, he told himself. The day he learned what was on the other side of the back door.

chapter **43**

THE WOMAN in the green scrub suit leaned her hand against the cage door.

"We're going to give you a few more days, Tiger. Maybe even put you on television Friday morning," she spoke slowly as though to a lip reader. "There's surely someone out there looking for a big, strong cat like you."

Wind missed his opportunity to be on the Pet Patrol Friday. Late Thursday morning Lorene and Linda Hawkins entered the Cat Adoption Center looking for an adult cat. It had been a slow morning, and Lennie Wollski was happy to see the young women. It was obvious they were twins, even though one had short hair and the other's was tied back in a long ponytail.

Lennie walked over to the women prepared to answer any questions. "Let me know if I can be of any help," he said. "Are you looking for anything in particular?"

Linda Hawkins swung her head toward Wollski, her blond ponytail flipping around her long neck. She smiled at the round man with the bald head. "Oh, hi," she said cheerfully. "My sister and I are just looking right now. We lost our cat a few months ago—"

Lorene Hawkins was at her side now. "Kidney failure," she added.

"We had Duke of Earl since we were little girls," Linda said.

Lorene was nodding her head like one of those plastic birds on a spring bobbing in front of a glass of water. "Uh huh," she said. "He was thirteen years old."

Wollski rested an arm across his substantial stomach. The other hand was knuckled against his cheek, his forefinger and thumb unconsciously tugging at his ear lobe. He looked from one girl to the other trying to keep up with the story.

"When Duke died we didn't think we wanted another cat, at least not for a while."

"You know, they become part of your family and you can't replace family, can you?" said the shorthaired girl.

Linda Hawkins nodded agreeably at her sister, and then continued. "We drove in to Jacksonville today to do some shopping at Regency Square."

"We live in Keystone Heights and like to come to the big city once a month or so," Lorene said with a self-deprecating smile on her lips.

Wollski returned the girl's smile then turned back to the one with the ponytail.

She didn't disappoint him. "So, we said why don't we go by the Humane Society and just see what they have."

"Can't hurt, can it? That's what I said," added Lorene.

Lennie Wollski took a deep breath and jumped in before Linda could say anything. "I know that Duke will be hard to replace, but let me show you a very special cat."

He took both girls by an elbow and moved them down the row of cages. They stood before Cattery 27 and he pointed with pride at the big cat inside. "You won't believe how smart this bad boy is."

The Hawkins twins looked at Wollski then peered into the cage at Windrusher. Windrusher pushed eagerly against the cage door, allowing a long purr to build up in his throat.

"As far as I know, this is the only cat in the world smart enough to catch a train," Wollski said.

The girls leaned in closer to the cat. Linda reached up and scratched Wind gently on the nose while Lorene scratched the soft spot under his jaw.

Wollski told them the story of the cat's journey from Savannah to Jacksonville, stressing the bravery and intelligence the feline must possess to do such a thing. He paused and both girls turned to face the round man. He smiled broadly at them.

"And I'm convinced that the reason Tiger made this incredible journey," he paused again for dramatic effect, "was so he could be here when you two lovely women came looking for a new cat."

The twins giggled and gave him a little push on his shoulders, then turned back toward Cattery 27.

chapter **44**

IT WAS almost 5:00 P.M. when the Hawkins twins parked alongside their lakefront duplex in Keystone Heights. The air was hot and humid even in the shade of the live oaks surrounding the two-story unit. Clumps of silvery Spanish moss hung from the lower branches like cascades of limp, feathery boas from an aged stripper's neck.

The duplex faced Lake Santa Fe, one of the largest lakes in North Florida, although a three-year drought had evaporated tens of thousands of gallons leaving boathouses and fishing docks resting on a wide band of dried mud. Determined boaters now trailered their boats over fifty feet of lakebed before reaching enough water to float the boat free.

Lorene climbed from behind the wheel of the old Honda Accord, swiped at the swarming Love Bugs, ran around to the passenger side, and heaved on the door like she was trying to pull the car across the yard.

Inside, Linda had thrown her shoulder into the door and nearly tumbled onto the ground as the door swung open. She held on to the door handle and awkwardly pulled herself out of the car. "We've really got to get that door fixed…"

"One of these days," Lorene completed her sentence and laughed.

Linda opened the back door and dragged a cardboard box across the seat. It was covered with nickel-size air holes, and she hefted the box in her arms. The word "Tiger" was written in neat block letters across one flap of the box, and someone had drawn a line through the word and written "Amtrak" just below it.

"We're home, Amtrak," the shorthaired Hawkins twin said into the box, then whirled around as if twirling a dance partner.

"Linda, let's get him inside before you make him sick."

Wind was released on the gray tiled floor of a large screened porch that ran across the back of the duplex. Linda and Lorene busied themselves filling the litter box, food and water bowls. The cat carefully watched the sisters from the top of a faded rattan couch in the corner of the porch.

"Look, Lorene," Linda said, pointing to their new pet. "That's where Duke liked to take his naps."

They both approached the wary cat. Lorene sat next to Wind, and calmed him with soothing strokes. "Welcome to our little world, Amtrak. I hope you like your new home and your new name," Lorene said. "I believe your days of train-hopping are over, though."

While Lorene and Linda Hawkins prepared dinner, Wind prowled the screened porch curiously. He sniffed the couch, the matching easy chair, the plants, even the litter box. The lingering scent of another cat intrigued him and he searched suspiciously to find its hiding place.

Satisfied there was no other cat around, Wind jumped on the concrete block kneewall surrounding the room and scrutinized the outside world. The expansive yard, dotted with cabbage palms, maples, and live oaks, flowed into a sand pine forest that blocked the horizon. Wind saw the day globe perched over the trees, casting great blocks of shadows toward the duplex.

The gods have smiled on me again, Windrusher thought. It could have been me carried away through that back door, yet here I am even closer to my own Hyskos family, living with two kindly high-legged beings. He felt sad for the cats that remained behind at the shelter, sadder still for those who would never have a home like this one. Surely, there would be disappointment and sadness for these two Hyskos when he left them, but he had no choice.

Wind eyed a green anole resting on the screen above him. Its head was raised, mouth open as if tasting the air. The cat stared in fascination at the long-tailed lizard and watched it extend a pink dewlap several times then scurry away.

Yes, this was a fine place to rest before the next stage of his journey.

The sun broke over Lake Santa Fe casting fractured splinters of light across the blue water. A soft blanket of mist clinging to the shoreline would soon be chased away by the heat of the sun. Windrusher stood at the sliding glass door and watched a Great Egret flap its snowy wings and drop from its perch on an oak tree branch, gliding to the shallows in search of breakfast.

Wind enjoyed his life here, but it was time to move on. His days of living with the Hyskos had taught him many things, and one of them was how to beg. The cat padded to the open door of Linda's bedroom and leaped on the bed. He smelled her strong scent under the sheet, and butted against her side, meowing plaintively. Seeing no movement from the female, he repeated his morning wake-up call.

Lorene rolled over and reached out for the cat. "Okay, okay, I get the picture." She gave the cat a hug and released it.

"Who needs an alarm clock with you around?" she said to the back of the cat scrambling out the door.

Lorene stumbled sleepily into the kitchen and poured a cup of Science Diet in a plastic bowl. "Here you go, Amtrak," she said, "eat up."

Lorene yawned broadly then retreated toward the bathroom to take a shower while her sister was still in bed.

Wind ate a few mouthfuls then walked to the other bedroom. He peered into the darkened room and saw the shape of the other high-legged being lying on the bed. Leaping on the bed, he trotted purposely across the pillows, barely missing the girl's head, and began meowing loudly until the female rolled over. Wind scrambled down and stood in the doorway continuing his strident vocalizing until he heard a reaction from the Hyskos.

"Can't you let me sleep?" Linda pulled the pillow over her head.

The cat jumped on the bed and meowed again.

A muffled voice came from under the pillow. "Ahh, Amtrak, I don't have any classes this morning, please let me sleep."

He meowed again, this time louder.

Linda sat up and looked at the cat through bleary eyes. When she swung her legs over the side of the bed, Wind rushed from the room and waited at the front door. He began whining as she approached, looking pitifully at the high-legged being.

"Come on, Amtrak, let's get you some food so I can get back to bed," she said walking past the cat.

Wind remained rooted behind the door. The female returned from the kitchen with the food bowl in her hand. "You've already been fed, haven't you?" She turned her head toward the bathroom door and heard the water running in the shower. "That's a sneaky trick. You got her up to feed you, then you got me up."

Wind meowed loudly and looked at the closed door.

Linda shook her head impatiently. "You want to go outside and use the sandbox? Fine," she said. She pulled the chain lock back and opened the door.

"Linda can let you in when you're ready. I'm going back to bed."

chapter 45

AN AFTERNOON THUNDERSTORM blew west over the Oklawaha River and whipped the clouds across a Florida sky suddenly as black as a snake's eyes. Rain puddled on the ground around the cat and soaked through to his skin. Still, he continued to walk, just as he had for the past two weeks.

The pattern was the same; a sun-splashed, humid morning gave way to the sudden furies of an afternoon downpour that punished the countryside with torrents of rain and frightening explosions of thunder. Then it would fade away, turning the dirt beneath the cat's feet into a marshy bog that made each step a struggle.

When he was fortunate to find an open culvert or overturned tree, Windrusher waited out the storms. Protected from the elements, he invariably gave thanks to Hwrt-Heru, the goddess of sleep, and plunged into her renewing embrace for a long nap. But these times were rare, and instead, like this day, he trudged through the rain, through the mud, a solitary, besotted creature, and hoped the storm would soon vent itself.

Exhaustion was his constant companion. The miles wore on his paws, strained his joints, and leached the energy from his body like a blood-sucking parasite. He awakened from his naps with a penetrating soreness in his muscles that transformed him into a limping, almost decrepit version of himself. Wind walked slower, each step sending needles of pain up his legs.

He had always been able to overcome the aches and pains of his travels by resting his body and renewing his spirit. Now, even sleep seemed to be working against him. Disquieting visions invaded his dreams and unleashed dark forces he didn't understand. Windrusher believed the nightmares were simply a result of his exhaustion, but only through sleep could he take advantage of the healing powers of the unconscious.

Shortly after the day globe passed overhead, Wind tramped through a lush pasture looking for a place to sleep. He kept his distance from the majestic four-legged beings that did their best to ignore the cat crossing their territory, tossing their manes with an occasional whinny.

He stopped at a small pond and drank deeply of the warm water, then continued up a small rise shadowed by sweetgums and cabbage palms. A light wind ruffled the palm fronds while wispy swirls of cirrus clouds billowed overhead. Wind marveled that there was so much beauty everywhere he went. He tramped circles in the long grass beneath a sweetgum tree and lay down, tucking his front paws under him. He felt the fatigue pass through his body into the ground below him and closed his eyes.

Sleep engulfed him, and he floated on a bed of blackness before plunging deeper into the refreshing arms of Hwrt-Heru. Windrusher barely twitched at the first flash of lights that exploded across the dark landscape of his unconscious like bursts of lightning over a ridge of mountains.

The flash illuminated a jagged avalanche of debris falling toward the sleeping cat. In his sleep, he moaned and tried to cover his head, but his moans were drowned by the sounds of a thousand furies screaming at him to run away.

He is asleep; he knows he is, yet there he is trying to run from the oncoming destruction, the winds buffeting him from side to side. A new scene flashed through his unconscious and he is back at the warehouse dock with the colony of cats. The pitiful form of Scowl Down reached up with impotent paws to hold off the crushing weight of the black behemoth. Wind watched the gruesome tableau from above, looking down on Bolt's broad back and Scowl Down's head twisting to the side

Scowl Down's head turned and she looked directly at him with those terrified yellow eyes. It seemed like the old female was trying to say something. Then, the tortured cat was swept away in a splash of blood and Wind was pulled into a blackness rent with patches of starlight. Piles of debris were heaped around him, and he heard the roaring scream, like a passing train, fading in the distance.

Windrusher awoke with a start. His heart pounded like he had been chased through the forest by a vicious snouter. He felt cold and damp, unsure of where he was. There wasn't any question he was awake now, but why could he still hear those horrible moans? Then he realized they were coming from deep inside him.

chapter 46

AMY TREMBLE gazed across the table at her husband, and silently gave thanks for the way their life had turned around. Even in the dim lighting of the Crystal Grille, she saw strength and self-assurance etched in his face. It was a look she recognized from their years of marriage, but one that had been replaced by frustration and hopelessness after losing his job at Colonial National Bank.

A vase of miniature orchids sat on the edge of the table, and right beside it, a votive candle cast flickering shadows over the menus. For just a second, in that shimmering glow, she thought she could see the same impetuous man she had fallen in love with so long ago.

The move to Crystal River was a turning point in their lives and it seemed inconceivable they had resisted it for so long. She unconsciously jerked her head slightly in reaction to the thought. Instead of grabbing at this life preserver extended to them by Gerry's father, they kept struggling to make it on their own. That was then, she thought. Now, we seem to have everything we ever wanted. Amy put her hand out and caressed her husband's arm.

Gerry looked up from the menu he was studying and smiled at his wife. She met his smile and held her wine glass up to him.

"Happy anniversary, honey," she said.

"Twenty years, can you believe it?"

Amy shook her head and gave her husband's hand a squeeze. "It's been a wonderful twenty years, Gerry. Thanks for everything."

"No, no, thank you," he replied and clinked the wine glass.

Amy expected that. He was so predictable sometimes. She let her eyes wander around the nearly full restaurant, the mahogany paneled walls, the crystal chandeliers, the waiter hovering not too far from their table. She shook her head when the waiter caught her eye and began to approach them. Of course, they would keep a special watch over the boss's table, she thought.

"It all seems like a dream, doesn't it?"

"What does?"

She lifted her hand from his and twisted it slowly in front of her, the fingers curling delicately outwards.

"All of this. It's a dream. Think about where we were just over a year ago: losing your job, the debts, the car accident, and the biopsy," her voice trailed off. It had been months since she even thought of her breast cancer scare.

Gerry put down his wine glass, reached out, and ran his fingers gently along his wife's jawbone. He looked into her green eyes and took her petite hand in both of his large bony ones.

"Sometimes dreams do come true, don't they? I've been lucky the hotel is doing so well, and I want to thank you for supporting me while I figured out what I was doing. You are happy here, aren't you?"

"Yes, of course I am," she said. "And I'm so proud of you. You came in here knowing so little about the hotel business, and you've done so well. Everyone tells me you're a natural at this."

"You can thank my father for that," he said. "He built this hotel into one of the best on the West Coast, and he was a great teacher. I just needed to stay out of the way and let everyone do their job."

Amy smiled broadly. "You're always so modest, but you know you've been able to keep the hotel and restaurants nearly filled while the others are struggling."

"Well..."

Amy reached across the small table and gave her husband a gentle push on his shoulder. "Well, nothing. Admit it. You're a marketing genius."

Gerry looked down at the table and shook his head modestly. "Okay, I admit it. I'm a marketing genius."

Amy smiled and picked up her wine glass, tilting it slightly to one side. The rich dark liquid flowed toward the rim of the glass, the candle reflecting golden highlights on the bowl. She sipped the merlot slowly, tasting its fruity flavor on the tip of her tongue, and looked directly at her husband.

"Everything does seem to be going right for us, Gerry. I love our new house, and my job. And the kids have adapted well to life in the wilds of Florida."

"GT is doing great, but Kimmy still seems to be down in the doldrums, doesn't she?" he asked.

"That's what I wanted to talk to you about. She's still fixated on Tony. I thought about getting her another cat, since we have the space now. But I think she may be a little homesick."

"You want to take her back to Bloomfield for a visit?"

Amy canted her head slightly and pursed her lips. "That's one way to do it. But I was thinking it would be nice to invite my sister and her family down here for a visit. I would love to see Jeannie, and you know how close Kimmy and Stacy were. You can show off your hotel to Tom, take him golfing. What do you think?"

Tremble grinned broadly. Amy was aware that Gerry had envied Tom Warren's success, especially after he lost his job. With his successful transition into the hotel business and their lovely new home on the golf course, she figured he would jump at the chance to play the gracious host to his brother-in-law.

"Well," she said.

"You're brilliant. We have plenty of room for them, lots for the kids to do around here. Why don't you give Jeannie a call tomorrow?"

The corners of Amy's mouth lifted slyly in a mysterious Mona Lisa smile.

"I was hoping you'd say that. Jeannie and I talked this afternoon, and they'll be here next month, June 27, to be exact."

chapter 47

SARAH KILCREASE bent over and pulled the weed out of the rose bed with a vicious yank that almost threw her off balance. Her formidable backside was pointed at the neighbors, or at the neighborhood to be more accurate, the checked cotton of her shorts pulled so tight the small orange checks were now rhomboid-shaped squiggles.

She put her hand in the small of her back and straightened with an audible moan. Sweat beaded on her forehead under the floppy brimmed tennis hat, pooled briefly at her sparse white eyebrows and coursed down the wrinkled planes of her face. Her thinning hair was plastered on the back of her neck like a newspaper against a curb in a heavy downpour.

Sarah Kilcrease was seventy-nine years old, a retired auditor with the IRS who survived two bouts with cancer, endured a triple bypass operation, had lost most of her hearing, took fourteen tablets a day for high blood pressure, cholesterol, osteoporosis, and arthritis, and had buried her husband of fifty-one years just three months earlier.

She was a survivor, as her doctors always told her. Unfortunately, she could not say the same for Jake.

They had moved south to Belleview, Florida after their retirement to be close to their daughter in Ocala, and purchased an expensive manufactured home in Boca Grande Park. Boca Grande Park! Mrs. Kilcrease always laughed when she thought of the sign at the front entrance. Boca Grande, after all, meant big mouth in Spanish.

Still, it was a peaceful life among the hibiscus, live oaks, pine, and palm trees, with a generous mix of younger families and retired couples. She thought of the many hours spent in her cushioned chaise, sipping tea and reading while Jake tended to his precious roses. Mrs. Kilcrease regarded the flower garden tenderly, and blinked back tears recalling that it had been almost three months since she buried Jake. She took stock of the rose bushes, deciding which blooms to bring with her when she paid a visit to the cemetery.

The old woman took the red, white, and blue bandana from around her neck and soaked it with the garden hose trickling at the base of the Hybrid Tea. The wet bandana felt good against her parched skin, and she stood there a moment with her eyes closed, the damp cloth pressed against her forehead, as if trying to divine some deep, unfathomable mystery of life.

That's when she heard the sound for the first time. She kept her eyes closed not sure where the plaintive whimpering originated or if her still grieving mind had created this heart-tugging lamentation from two branches scraping together.

Mrs. Kilcrease opened her eyes and spotted it on the edge of her property; the most bedraggled cat she had ever seen. Skin hung loosely on the large-boned feline, reminding her of the pathetic condition Jake was in during his final days.

The cat meowed once again, fixing her with a steady gaze from bright green eyes that never left her face. The cat was in bad shape. Aside from being underweight, it stood with its front right leg cocked as if it was having difficulty putting any weight on it.

"Oh, you poor thing," she said.

She stepped toward the pitiful-looking cat then stopped when the animal turned apprehensively, as if to run from her. Mrs. Kilcrease froze.

"I know you're hungry," she said in a quiet voice. "You wait right there and let me see what I can find for you."

Mrs. Kilcrease disappeared inside the house, and reappeared a minute later with a saucer of milk and a slice of ham she had torn into small pieces. She set them on the edge of her patio and watched the cat lap up the milk, and make short work of the ham.

"That's a good girl," she murmured, not sure if it was a male or female. "How about some water?"

The cat was still there two hours later. It lay in the pine straw next to Belinda's Dream; one of Jake's favorite rose bushes, and gazed fondly at Mrs. Kilcrease sitting in her chaise lounge. A sudden squawking overhead caused them both to look up. A mockingbird pursued a large crow over the live oaks. The crow beat its wings furiously trying to escape the angry bird and after a few evasive maneuvers flew off with the mockingbird close behind.

The old woman had seen these territorial disputes many times, yet remained impressed that the much smaller mockingbird was seemingly fearless and willing to take on any foe, sometimes even the two-legged variety, to protect its nest.

I guess we'll never know how large a heart God's creatures have, she thought. Mrs. Kilcrease smiled at the cat lying in a pool of sunlight, but she was thinking about Jake.

chapter 48

WINDRUSHER PURRED loudly. He lay on the old woman's ample legs while she scratched behind his ears. First one ear then the other. She was watching the picture box and laughing at the unintelligible antics on the screen. Wind felt her legs jiggle under him with each laugh.

This was a favorite position for both of them, and the big cat felt more comfortable in her lap than he could remember feeling in some time. Wind had lost count of the number of times the Hyskos had brought him into their homes as though he were a missing relative. But there was something special about this home. He felt a tug on him that almost rivaled the compulsion he had to find his original Hyskos family.

In the nearly three weeks since he found his way to the woman's yard, Windrusher had grown attached to the old female. The pains in his legs had faded, and he regained the weight he lost on the road. His coat gleamed with a healthy luster, and he was content to stay with the old woman as long as she wanted him.

Curiously, a memory of Scowl Down and Lil' One came to him. The three of them were in a grove of trees on a shady hillock. Rahhna was slipping below the horizon, bathing the clouds with gossamer bands of pink and orange. A clear brook trickled behind them, and Scowl Down stood silently as though absorbing the tranquility of their surroundings.

"This is a fine place, isn't it?" Scowl Down said.

She was speaking mainly to herself, as she looked at the peaceful scene below her, but in saying those words, she was trying to convince her two friends that perhaps there was more than one place a cat could call home. Scowl Down was a wise friend, and yes, he thought, this is a fine place.

The big cat opened his eyes and gazed at the old Hyskos woman, still enjoying the picture box. Fleshy pouches hanging from the woman's chin shook as she laughed, and she looked at the cat in her lap, noting he was looking at her.

"I hope you're enjoying this as much as me," she said and continued combing her fingers through his fur.

Wind thought she had a kindly face, for a high-legged being. He tried to picture his young female Hyskos, the one who had cared for him so long ago and so far away. She was the one waiting for him to return to her, yet he found he could no longer see her face clearly. It troubled him and he concentrated harder to bring the girl's face into focus.

Eventually, her face emerged from the gauzy film that covered Wind's memory and he wondered if she really did need him, and if she would miss him if he didn't return to her. Windrusher flicked his tail and tucked it alongside his body. He shifted position slightly on the old woman's lap finding just the right mixture of soft comfort and support.

Wind cleared his head of past associations knowing that if Irissa-u intended for him to find his way home, he would. Otherwise, this was as fine a home as a cat could have. Soon, he felt himself floating away, like a dandelion seed caught in a warm afternoon breeze, and reached out and embraced sleep.

"Right. That's great. We can't wait to see you guys either," Amy said into the phone.

Tremble leaned over the granite counter top watching his wife intently, trying to interpret the conversation going on at the other end of the phone line. He looked past Amy at Kimmy sitting on the couch supposedly reading, but obviously listening to the conversation between her mother and her Aunt Jeannie. He gave Kimmy a little smile then turned back toward his wife.

Tremble raised his eyebrows and inclined his head toward Amy, holding out a hand with the palm up as if to say he was waiting for more information. She waved him off impatiently.

"I know you'll enjoy Silver Springs." She shot her eyes toward her husband and shrugged her shoulders. "We'll see you tomorrow night. Love you."

"Silver Springs?" Tremble asked incredulously after Amy hung up the phone.

"That's right, Silver Springs. You know Tom. Seems his parents took him there when he was a kid, and he wants to show Stacy and Jeannie what a grand place it is. Besides, it's on their way to Crystal River."

Tremble shook his head in disbelief. "But Silver Springs? And it's not exactly on the way."

"It's not that far out of the way, Gerry, just up 301. And they'll probably be here before dark tomorrow. Don't worry, it gives us a little more time to make sure the house is clean and the wine is chilled."

Amy reached out and grabbed the back of her husband's neck, pulling him toward her. She gave him a loud, wet kiss. Tremble reddened slightly and shifted his gaze briefly toward his daughter in time to see her make a face.

"All right, it's their vacation," he said. "The Tremble Arms will be at their disposal whenever they arrive, and I'll be on my best behavior."

Amy twisted her lips into a wry smile and nodded as if to say she had heard that before. Then she waited for the last word from her husband.

He didn't disappoint her. "But can you believe he's taking them to Silver Springs before they come to see us?"

Windrusher groped his way through the swirling cacophony of noise inside his head. Fragments of conversations from thousands of discordant voices clamored around him. They prodded and pulled at him from every side then dropped away as if he was on a swiftly moving conveyor belt passing through a mammoth room crammed with cats.

This was the first time in nearly two weeks his subconscious had connected to the Inner Ear. Instantly, he was immersed in the ancient tension that preceded communication, haunted by the fear of being lost in this confusing tunnel of babble and never finding his way out. At the appropriate time he plunged into a gap and introduced himself, closing with the traditional supplication, "Lend me the wisdom of oneness that only Tho-hoth could provide through his gift of Akhen-et-u."

Wind was soon bombarded with questions demanding to know details of his latest adventure, or misadventure as it may be. Quickly, he assured them he was well, and described his life with the old Hyskos female.

Before he could continue his story, a familiar voice interrupted. "You're living with an old Hyskos female? That doesn't sound like the daring adventurer I've heard so much about."

The voice was like an electric shock that galvanized every nerve cell in his body and left him tingling with both pain and pleasure. Even in his sleep, a sharp vision of sapphire blue eyes radiating out of a lithe young body left him limp with desire.

"Silk Blossom, is that you?" he blurted out.

"I'm pleased that you haven't completely forgotten me, Windrusher. You are doing well, it seems."

"There have been times I was certain I would never feel Rahhna's heat again, but the Holy Mother has smiled on my mission and protected me."

He was acting like the runt of the litter trying to impress his littermates, he thought. Why does she have this effect on me? "How are the kittens?" he asked.

There was a long pause and for a moment, he was afraid she was no longer plugged into the Inner Ear.

"The kittens are growing quickly, Windrusher. It's kind of you to ask. Fortunately, for me, the Hyskos are feeding them now and I have more time to rest. Which is why I have only now been able to visit Akhen-et-u to learn of your travels."

"It is always good to hear from you, Silk Blossom, I—"

"Take care of yourself," she cut in before he could finish. "You are so close to completing your quest. You made many sacrifices; it would be a shame if you gave up before you found your Hyskos family."

Silk Blossom's voice was abruptly lost in a rush of noise that closed on him like the walls of a collapsing cave.

"Silk Blossom," he called out.

There was no response. She was gone, and all he had left was the memory of her words, and the image of the lovely Siamese red point that he would carry with him forever. Wind could no longer concentrate on the bedlam swirling around him, the weight of his efforts, plus the shock of hearing from Silk Blossom crushed him and dragged him into the depths of exhaustion.

He excused himself and let his subconscious travel down its own path where he relinquished all control and was quickly enveloped in the serene cocoon of sleep.

"It was a scorcher today, folks. Humidity was suffocating and reached almost one hundred on the heat index. I know everyone has their air conditioner running at full throttle, but I have some good news for you. Believe it or not there's a cool front moving down through the panhandle right now that should reach us by 10:00 P.M. and provide a little relief for tomorrow."

Mrs. Kilcrease was watching the weatherman point to the animated arrow moving through Northwest Florida into the central part of the state. He doesn't look much older than seventeen, she thought. What could he know about weather? As a matter of fact, she was certain that none of them knew a thing about the weather since they usually were wrong as much as they were right.

The teenaged weatherman wore a linen dress shirt the color of whole wheat bread with a matching tie that gleamed under the studio lights. Mrs. Kilcrease couldn't be sure, but it looked like his yellow and brown suspenders were covered with sunbursts and umbrellas.

The weatherman turned smartly from the chroma-key map to the camera, in what Mrs. Kilcrease assumed the child meteorologist thought was a mixture of savvy and authority. She thought he looked constipated.

"No, you don't have to go to your attic and pull down your winter clothes again," he said. "But we might get some thunderstorms and some lightning strikes so plan to stay indoors tonight. Of course, we can really use the rain, can't we? So, the five day forecast looks like this...."

"I'll be asleep for two hours by 10:00 P.M., so let it storm," Mrs. Kilcrease said to herself and turned the channel to Fox so she could catch the rest of *King of the Hill*."

chapter 49

IT WAS actually 9:30 P.M. when the cumulonimbus clouds gathered southwest of Belleview. The front raced south from the panhandle, as the weatherman had predicted, driving cool, dry air ahead of it.

By then, Mrs. Kilcrease was fast asleep, just as she had predicted. She was a creature of habit, and after a sip of brandy—just to help relax me, she used to tell Jake each night until it became a standing joke; now she said it to the cat she called Crackers—she folded back the thick comforter until it was only a burgundy colored twenty-inch band at the foot of her bed, and crawled under the pink sheet. She found the sagging mattress somehow comforting and reached out and patted the pillow next to her. It was the same queen size bed she and Jake slept in every night since they purchased the mobile home and moved to Boca Grande Park.

"Goodnight, Crackers," the old woman said to the cat.

Wind stood on the bed and idly scratched at the bedspread before settling down at the old woman's feet. It was 8:08 P.M. and within minutes, the big cat heard a shrill bray that sounded slightly like the call of the Pine Woods Treefrog. It had taken Windrusher several nights to determine the noise was coming from the old female and not from some night creature that had found its way inside to keep them company.

Wind now found the snoring soothing and relaxing. It had the same effect on him as the brandy did for Mrs. Kilcrease, and he soon was drifting on a buoyant cloud toward deep twitchless sleep.

At 9:35 P.M., Windrusher awoke to the muffled sounds of thunder. His ears flickered and he stared into the blackness of the room in nervous anticipation. The thunder faded, and he relaxed, looking at the large sleeping form filling nearly half the bed. He yawned broadly and went back to sleep.

Minutes later, at 9:47 P.M., rain and marble size hail slashed across Boca Grande Park. A blaze of light flashed behind the closed bedroom blinds followed almost immediately by a horrendous clap of thunder. Windrusher was instantly awake, his eyes wide, his ears pointed toward the window. Above him, he heard the rain and hail slam against the metal roof, sounding like a fusillade of machine gun fire.

The big cat whimpered and glanced at the old woman. She remained fast asleep, her massive chest rising and falling, her froggy snores muffled by the wind hissing around the mobile home.

Windrusher felt pressure building above his eyes and at the base of his skull. Something large and hard caromed off the side of the mobile home and he whipped his head around to the wall behind him. The hissing noise of the wind was suddenly engulfed by a grinding howl that clawed at the structure like a beast from hell.

The frightened cat remained frozen on the bed. All of his instincts were screaming at him to run away, to hide from this horrible nightmare. Try as he might, he couldn't get his legs to move. Could not command them to carry him from this screaming madness that was now lashing the trailer with rain and wind.

A bedroom window splintered with a deafening crash, sending shards of glass flying through the room. The blinds tore free from the wall and clattered onto the bed just a foot from Mrs. Kilcrease's head. A metal garbage can, its lid still firmly attached, flew through the broken window followed by sheets of wind-driven rain.

"Lord Jesus, what was that?" the old woman yelled.

Mrs. Kilcrease sat up in bed just in time to see the garbage can slide across the floor and bounce off the dresser. Before it stopped rolling, a pine tree branch, as big around as one of her legs, tore through the roof like it was made of soap bubbles, and impaled itself in the floor next to the queen size bed.

The old woman screamed and covered her head with the pillow.

Wind's heart felt like it was about to burst from his chest. The room vibrated to some frenetic rhythm, and it suddenly heeled over to one side like a sailboat tacking in the ocean. The mobile home hovered in the air then plunged back to the ground with a grinding crash. Mrs. Kilcrease was flung from the bed and bounced against the far wall. She groaned loudly, rolled over once, and then collapsed in a sodden heap by the door.

Outside, a huge black mass of dense clouds hung over the area like an avenging demon. From its belly, a twisting, heaving stovepipe of energy sucked up billowing storms of dirt and debris. The massive funnel cloud was nearly three-quarters of a mile across and it moved to the northeast at fifty-five miles per hour.

The tornado snapped a row of utility poles lining 301 outside Boca Grande Park, flinging them to the side and leaving electric lines arcing across the highway. Sparks danced over the rain-whipped blacktop as the wind shrieked overhead. A massive water oak creaked ominously then slowly released its grip on the earth and crashed down across the road, its ancient roots pointing up like the toes of corpses ready for burial.

Stop signs, car hoods, lawn chairs, concrete planters, and branches flew through the air in an incredible procession of destruction. The heavier objects moved in slow motion compared to the others, bounding off trees and rolling into the field beyond thousands of feet from where they were picked up.

The tornado cut through the trailer park like an invisible scythe, slashing and ravaging everything in its path. Automobile horns blared out and mixed with shrieks of pain. The trailer behind Mrs. Kilcrease's seemed to launch itself from its foundation and flew one-hundred-feet over the mobile home next to it, crashing end over end into a third home near the community pool. The two of them embraced each other then flattened into a single five-foot pile of sheet metal.

The wind exploded through Sarah Kilcrease's mobile home, shattering the walls and peeling the trailer's roof back like the top to a sardine can. Windrusher felt himself sucked from the bed, the comforter whipping around him. He heard the old Hyskos female scream, then the dark force catapulted him, gasping and struggling, through the open roof into the chasm of the night.

In the next day's newspaper, scientists would call this one of the worst tornado disasters to hit Florida. Classified as an F-3 tornado on the Fujita scale with winds over 200 miles per hour, it would be written that the tornado lunged drunkenly from point to point, caroming off buildings, hurling parked cars, and churning a massive path of destruction for twenty-one miles.

Shaken eyewitnesses would be quoted as saying it "sounded like a runaway freight train," and give thanks for miraculous escapes. The sheriff declined to provide names, but said there were at least fourteen people dead.

All of that and more was discovered when the harsh, Florida sun rose in the morning.

chapter 50

FIRE AND RESCUE crews rushed in from Ocala, Gainesville, and even Orlando to assist the tiny Belleview volunteer fire department.

In the space of eighteen minutes, the monster tornado left a debris trail twenty-one miles long that cut through a shopping center, a new middle school, two blocks of a residential neighborhood where the county judge lived, and, of course, Boca Grande Park.

Fortunately, Belleview was not heavily populated, and the tornado vented much of its fury on miles of wooded fields. The funnel cloud's path slashed a swath through a nearby pine forest, leaving it looking like giant feet danced a dizzying polka through the timber. Surrounding trees stood as mute witness to the devastation, some of them cracked and splintered, others stripped of their leaves, the bark peeled back from the trunks. One grizzled veteran of World War II said it reminded him of the woods surrounding Bastogne after weeks of enemy artillery barrages.

Rescuers had to cut through the fallen trees barricading the roads in order to reach Boca Grande Park. It took them two hours. The sound of chainsaws was deafening in the night. As men worked to trim the branches, tow trucks with hydraulic winches hauled the trees to the shoulder of the road. Then the night air was rent by the sounds of sirens descending on the ravaged trailer park.

The Department of Transportation loaned the sheriff's department a half-dozen generator lights. The light poles were ratcheted up to their maximum height and the bulbs cast a pale sheen over the area, giving everyone a gray sallow complexion, the noise of the generators adding to the confusion.

Art Schilling joined the knot of volunteer firemen, sheriff's deputies and other assorted rescuers at the entrance to Boca Grande

Park. He drove there in his pick-up truck as soon as he got the call from the fire chief.

"Be careful in there," the fire chief was saying. "We think the power is off, but don't take any chances. You don't want to be the one to find out that a power line is still hot. And I don't want to be the one to call your mama with the bad news."

The men nodded solemnly in agreement and looked past the chief at the devastation that once was Boca Grande Park.

"So, watch where you step, and let's help these people. We'll get the most seriously injured out, help the others with first aid. Okay?"

The men moved purposely two by two down what was once a tree-shaded road into the trailer park. Schilling looked unbelievingly at the piles of debris and wondered if they would find anyone alive. Directly in front of him, a mobile home was flattened like an empty beer can someone had stomped on. A few others were tilted crazily on their sides.

Another home had the roof peeled back and the walls sagged out at strange angles. Next to it sat a long, bricked trailer that was nearly intact except for a few gaps in the brick veneer, and a piece of skirting missing along one side. As if to prove the random nature of the tornado's violence, a bicycle leaned against the porch railing as though a kid had just run into the house for a peanut butter and jelly sandwich and would dash out at any moment.

The crew worked through the night, following the screams into the twisted piles of metal and sheetrock that once were homes for families with children, homes for retired couples and individuals. The park manager was among the fortunate ones unharmed by the twister and he assisted the rescuers by identifying the homes and the number of people who lived in each one. He also helped to identify the dead.

The tornado that savaged Belleview the night of June 26 left a total of sixteen dead, although a seventeenth person would die two days later of a heart attack. Thirteen of the victims resided in Boca Grande Park.

Firemen eventually uncovered six bodies inside the two trailers that collided and came to rest by the pool. The pool itself was so thick with flotsam from the catastrophe that one fireman actually walked across it.

Three other people were found outside among the piles of trash. Apparently, they had been running from their trailers hoping to find safety outside. A falling tree hit one, the other two died of head injuries. Numerous people sustained cuts from flying glass and were treated on the spot by the EMTs, while another dozen required hospitalization for various injuries.

There were also stories of miraculous survivors like the man who was blown out of his trailer and across his yard, "flopping along like a tumbleweed," as he told the television reporters the next day. He was unhurt except for a skinned elbow.

Firemen also found a seventeen-month old boy walking beside a fence at the rear of the trailer park. The boy, who was sucking his thumb, was dressed only in a diaper, and seemed to be enjoying his walk. With the help of the park manager, rescuers located his trailer, and found his parents; one dead and the other unconscious.

Then there was the elderly woman found in the wrecked trailer with the missing roof. The woman was covered with cuts and bruises and had apparently suffered a broken leg. The EMT that wrote up the report said she was dazed and incoherent, and as they loaded her into an ambulance, "She asked for crackers," he later told one of his buddies.

The night seemed to last forever, and Schilling was both mentally and physically exhausted. When the sun finally added its illumination to the tragic scene, he got his first real look at what was left of Boca Grande Park. The piles of rubbish reminded him of a landfill. Scraps of clothing and furniture mixed with the detritus of people's lives: photo albums, shoes, books, broken dishes, chair legs, all intermingled with pieces of paneling, concrete blocks, car parts, boards with nails stabbing through them, and crushed vegetation.

Schilling shook his head in amazement that anyone lived through the destruction. He rubbed the stiff muscles on the back of his neck and rolled his head around in a circle. Even the trees that were still standing could not escape completely undamaged. Most were missing leaves and the remaining branches were decorated with bright strips of yellow and pink insulation, bed sheets, and newspapers. He noticed the sycamore tree next to his parked truck, and saw a twisted and torn burgundy comforter in the crook of a branch fifteen feet off the ground.

The fireman stared at the comforter. Was it moving? After the night he just had, he wasn't sure of anything. Schilling walked to the tree and examined it closely. A section of the bedspread was wedged between the trunk and the branch, the rest of it wrapped tightly around several limbs. He suddenly realized that there was a lump under the burgundy material, and it was definitely moving.

Schilling ran to his truck, retrieved the aluminum extension ladder, and leaned it against the tree. Several of his co-workers stopped to watch him, and wandered over to see what was happening, finally understanding that they were witnessing another miraculous survival story. They yelled encouragement to Schilling, and others hurried over to the tree to watch the rescue, including one of the first TV videographers allowed into the park. He pointed his camera at Schilling.

The fireman pulled the bedspread free of the branches, carefully holding the lump in one hand so it wouldn't fall. As he did, he heard whimpering sounds from beneath the comforter and clutched it to his chest.

"That's okay, I have you," Schilling said. "You're safe now."

He slowly backed down the ladder, cradling the tattered comforter and the frightened victim in one arm. By this time, a second TV reporter was shooting video of the rescue, and the other firemen were all pushing in to see what Schilling had brought down from the tree.

The whimpering grew louder and Schilling carefully pulled the folds of burgundy material from around the wriggling thing in his arms. The head of a large gray and orange cat broke free from the comforter. Green eyes flashed in anger, and the cat opened its mouth widely letting out a scolding meow at the same time that Schilling sneezed.

chapter 51

"THE WATER is crystal clear, and there's about twenty of these beautiful mermaids swimming around like fish, doing all kinds of tricks. You'd swear they were real mermaids except for the air hoses hanging down."

Warren realized he was overdoing the hype, but he couldn't help himself. The mermaids were about the only thing he remembered from that terrible boyhood vacation that took them from one end of Florida to the other, trying to squeeze in every major tourist attraction possible. It was the last time he visited the Sunshine State.

The excruciatingly long drive from Massachusetts was bad enough. He and his brother, Chester, were crammed into the back seat of the old Chevrolet along with a suitcase and several bags of souvenirs they bought at their many stops. His father had planned the Florida vacation like a military campaign. This was to be the *ultimate* Florida vacation, he stressed to his family, and they would enjoy it.

In the space of three days, they visited the St. Augustine Alligator Farm, drove to Silver Springs, rushed to stare at the Bok Tower for a few minutes, then hurried to Weeki Wachee, and finally to Cypress Gardens for the water ski show. That was just the top half of the peninsula.

His mother talked incessantly on that part of the trip, as if trying to fill the space between them. Later, the conversations from the front seat became shrill, and the pauses extended, until, finally, somewhere near Ft. Lauderdale, they stopped talking altogether. The original plan was to continue on to visit Key West, but his father turned the car around after a breakfast in which his mother spent the entire time in the car crying.

It was the last vacation they took before they joined the ranks of broken American families and became just another depressing statistic.

"Beautiful mermaids, huh? So that's why you're so excited about this trip," Jeannie said, giving a wink to her daughter in the back seat of the rental car.

Warren glanced briefly from the road to his wife in time to catch the wink.

"Certainly, not as beautiful as you, dear, although I have to admit I've never seen you in a fish suit. But I can tell you, they really made an impression on this eleven-year-old boy."

They had left the Winter Garden motel after a late breakfast. It was later than Warren wanted to get away, but Jeannie was suffering from morning sickness, and she needed time to settle her stomach. They had just confirmed the pregnancy last week and Jeannie was looking forward to surprising her sister with the announcement when they saw them that evening.

When they arrived at the Orlando airport the night before, along with hordes of other tourists, they picked up the Yukon SUV from Hertz and drove through town, past the Lake Buena Vista and Disney World exit.

"Are your sure we'll be going to Disney World," Stacy asked, eyeing the highway sign with the famous mouse ears.

"You bet we will," Warren assured his daughter. "Don't you want to go with Kimmy?"

"Sure, but what if we don't get a chance?"

Warren glanced into the mirror at the girl that was looking more like Jeannie everyday. Thank God, he thought, that she didn't take after me.

"I promise you, honey, that if that doesn't work out, we'll leave a day early so we can all go to Disney World. Hey, don't you think I want to see Mickey, too? Not that it will be as exciting as the mermaids…"

After stopping for a late dinner, they checked into the motel. Stacy was almost instantly asleep, so they muted the audio on the television while Jeannie read and Warren traced his route up 301 on a Florida map. A special breaking news alert came on with a brief story about a tornado touching down in Belleview, but neither of them was paying attention.

Schilling placed the shaken cat along with the burgundy bedspread in the front seat of his truck. He sneezed loudly, pulled out a handkerchief, and blew his nose with a honk. It didn't take long for his allergies to kick in. He needed to get rid of this cat, but he couldn't release it in this disaster area, could he? Maybe they would find the owner, but for now he had no choice but to leave it in his truck.

He tucked a corner of the bedspread over the cat and held his hand on its back. The animal was shivering as if it was cold, and he realized it was still in shock. "Can't really blame you, kitty," he said. "You rest here while I go back and help with the cleanup. You never know, what else we might find in a tree."

Windrusher tried to reconstruct what happened when he awoke to find the home he shared with the old Hyskos female falling apart around him. He remembered the windows collapsing, the glass flying, the tree falling through the roof, and the entire room shaking so hard the big female was flung from the bed and bounced crazily on the floor. Through it all, he was frozen with fright, unable to save himself.

Then the dark force scooped him off the bed, along with the bedclothes, and hurled him through the air as though he were a hairball spit out of some giant's throat. He recalled crashing into something hard and unyielding, then nothing. Nothing, until he awoke and found himself smothering in this blanket, and tried desperately to find a way out.

That was the last thing he remembered until the Hyskos male retrieved him from the tree and brought him here. Wind licked his sore shoulder, and wondered if this was another one of Irissa-u's tests to see if he was worthy of remaining on the Path. No, the Holy Mother was not a Setlos and would not cause harm to another cat. At least he didn't think she would.

The drone of chainsaws and shouts of Hyskos broke through his thoughts. He looked at the small gap in the window, his ears twitching, aware of the noise around him for the first time. Wind tried to reconcile the noise and the bedlam that occurred last night with the peaceful picture he had of his days with the female high-legged being. His traumatized mind was having a hard time making the connection.

Wind pulled himself off the comforter and winced from the pain in his shoulder and leg. He stood on the pickup's seat, stretched his neck toward the passenger window, and stared at the remains of Boca Grande Park.

He couldn't believe what he was seeing and raised himself against the window to get a better view. All around him were piles of garbage and crushed structures that used to be Hyskos homes. Uprooted trees had fallen against vehicles and stacks of metal and wood were strewn everywhere.

High-legged beings sifted through the trash piles and cut the trees with noisy tools that slashed through thick branches like a claw ripping through flesh. Windrusher collapsed on the seat, unable to fathom what could have caused such immense damage. In the back of his mind, he realized how close he had come to the end of his Path, and was thankful to be alive.

Thanks be to the Holy Mother and all the gods, he thought. Once again, I have survived the perils of the Hyskos world. Still, an emotion akin to human guilt was worming its way into his brain, and he shook uncontrollably, the muscles along his back flexing spasmodically.

It seems everywhere I go disaster follows. Now, it has struck here and possibly harmed the good-hearted Hyskos female. He recalled the kindnesses she had extended to him; taking him in when he was near collapse, feeding him, nursing him back to health.

Windrusher hoped the dark force that struck this little village during the night did not hurt her. He lowered his aching body and flattened himself against the comforter. A faint scent of the large female clung to the bedspread, and he pressed his head into it and closed his eyes.

chapter 52

KIMMY TREMBLE opened one bloodshot eye, looked at the clock on her shelf, and groaned. She didn't feel like getting up and playing tennis. Her head throbbed and her eyes felt like they were full of oatmeal after a night of tossing and turning. Kimmy enjoyed the summer tennis camp, but there was no way she was going out and hit balls this morning.

Amy Tremble entered the bedroom and stood over Kimmy's bed. She was dressed in her uniform.

"Hey, sleepy bones, aren't you getting up today?"

Kimmy's head was turned toward the wall. "I don't feel so good," she said.

Amy sat down on the side of the bed and touched her daughter's forehead.

"What's wrong, Kimmy, are you catching something?"

The young girl turned toward her mother with a tiny groan. "I didn't sleep very well, and I have a headache."

Mrs. Tremble held the girl's face in both hands and looked into her bleary eyes.

"I don't think you have a fever, but let's not take a chance. I'll get you a couple of Tylenol and you rest today. You don't want to get sick with your cousin coming to visit tonight."

She kissed Kimmy on top of her head, and left the room, returning a minute later with a glass of water and two tablets.

Kimmy sat up, leaning on one elbow, and swallowed the tablets. "Maybe the headache will go away, and I'll ride my bike over to the tennis courts," she said.

Amy shook her head vigorously. "I don't think so. You need to get as much rest as you can, young lady. I'm only working half a day, so I'll check on you when I get home, dad will be home around 3:00, and GT is spending the day with his soccer buddies. That gives you a day to yourself, and I expect you to do nothing more strenuous than sleep."

She leaned over, tucked the sheet under the mattress, and fluffed up the pillow. Gently, she pushed the girl down on the bed, giving her daughter a sympathetic smile.

"Nurse Tremble has prescribed bed rest as the best medicine. You understand?"

"Yeah, I understand."

"Good, I'll see you this afternoon."

Kimmy heard her mother's car drive away, and rolled over on her side trying to get comfortable. Was she being a baby? Her right temple throbbed as though someone was banging out a hip-hop beat with a set of rubber mallets, but she couldn't stand the thought of being sick during Stacy's visit.

She remembered the last time she saw her cousin. It was more than a year ago in Bloomfield when she left... That's right, when she left Tony with her. And then what happened? Tony mysteriously disappeared.

Kimmy gritted her teeth and made a face against the pillow. No, no, no, she scolded herself. That was not Stacy's fault, so forget about it. She trusted her cousin as much as she trusted her brother. Well, maybe a little more.

Ninety minutes later, Kimmy awoke from a nap that seemed to have cleared her head and brightened her spirits. She yawned loudly, and realized she was hungry. Nurse Tremble didn't say anything about starving yourself, and she headed for the kitchen. Sitting at the kitchen counter with a bowl of corn flakes and sliced bananas, she reached over and turned on the small television set next to the microwave oven.

"...and, as you can see by this dramatic video, the tornado devastated this trailer park in nearby Belleview."

Kimmy chewed her corn flakes and gazed with mild interest at the scenes of destruction. The camera tilted down the side of what was once a large mobile home. It was flipped on its side, and a huge slice was missing from the roof, as if someone had taken a can opener to it.

Kimmy shook her head, and got up to pour herself a glass of

orange juice.

The picture cut to a shot of a local television personality standing in front of the Boca Grande Park sign. Her brown hair was cut short and she wore a Navy blue jacket over a red dress. She held a microphone up to her mouth.

"A spokesman for the Belleview sheriff's department told Channel 9 News that thirteen people died here last night when that killer tornado struck central Florida."

The reporter was replaced by a young police officer who looked like he had been up all night. A graphic appeared at the bottom of the screen identifying him as Sgt. Hank Belton.

"The tornado ripped through three sections of the county, but this was the hardest hit," The sergeant said. "We had members of the fire department, emergency medical technicians, police, and other volunteers here within hours to help bring out the most critically injured."

While Sgt. Belton spoke, the picture switched to a series of quick cuts of rescue personnel carrying people to waiting ambulances and administering first aid to the injured. Then the news reporter reappeared.

"It was a terrifying night for these residents, many of whom lost their homes, and, some, tragically, their lives."

Kimmy swallowed her vitamin pill with the last of the orange juice and began clearing off the counter. She really was feeling like she could play tennis, but she remembered what her mother said.

"Fortunately, there was some good news mixed with the bad. Volunteer fireman Art Schilling was more than a little surprised when he climbed a tree to rescue this victim."

Again, the reporter disappeared and was replaced by a man on a ladder high up a tree. The man seemed to be untangling a torn bedspread from the branches of the tree and then carried it down the ladder. The camera moved in on the lump under his arm, and the head of a cat appeared. The camera's microphone picked up the cat's meow.

"This cat may have used up more than one of its nine lives, but it can thank Art Schilling for bringing him back to earth safely. This is Rebecca DellaRossa reporting live from Boca Grande Park in Belleview, Florida."

Kimmy Tremble stood frozen in disbelief staring at the television screen. She shook her head slowly as if trying to convince herself that what she had witnessed was the result of her earlier headache. It didn't make any sense, though. How could Tony be here in Florida, in Belleview, wherever that was?

She ran into the office with its floor to ceiling bookcases and pulled out the National Geographic Atlas of the World. Quickly turning the pages of the big book, she found a map of Florida on page thirty-one. It took her a few minutes of scanning the hundreds of tiny words dotting the map, but she finally located Belleview. Her mouth fell open as she looked at the map and saw that Belleview and Crystal River were perhaps an inch apart on the map.

"No way," Kimmy said to the map.

Now, she was truly perplexed. She had left her cat in Bloomfield, Connecticut in April of last year. There was no way he could have traveled, what: 1,200, 1,500 miles? And how could he get within fifty miles from where she was right now?

Kimmy began questioning herself. It happened so quickly, maybe she was wrong and it was another cat that looked like Tony. I mean cats sorta look alike, don't they? And I was feeling kind of down and thinking about him this morning, so maybe my head is messing with me.

Unsure of what she really saw, Kimmy went into the family room and turned on the large screen TV set. She switched channels until she found another station carrying news of the disaster. More of the same scenes of destruction passed in front of her, plus video of the damaged shopping center. The scene switched to Boca Grande Park, and finally there was a shot of the fireman holding the burgundy comforter against his chest. He was surrounded by a circle of men and women who cheered madly when the cat's head emerged. The camera zoomed in on the cat just as it meowed loudly.

Kimmy slammed her palm on the cushion. "That's him," she yelled out jubilantly. "That's my Tony!"

The exhilaration faded as quickly as it appeared. It was obvious that Tony was safe, but how long until they send him to animal control or just turn him loose? What could she do? I guess I should call mom and tell her, Kimmy said to herself, stepping toward the phone. She stopped with her hand in midair above the telephone.

There's no way mom is going to believe I saw Tony on TV and he's in Belleview after being thrown into a tree by a tornado. Come on. That's too much for anyone to believe, and if I hadn't seen it myself I wouldn't believe it.

Then she remembered the scary dream. The details were fuzzy now, but there was no doubt in her mind that Tony was in danger and needed her. She told her mother about the dream and she didn't believe her then, why would she believe her now?

She saw it all with a new clarity: the dream was a warning that Tony would be swept up by that horrible tornado, that he was in real trouble, and I was the one he turned to for help. So, it's up to me. But how can I get to Belleview, even if I knew where this Boca Grande Park was? There was no end to the questions cropping up in her mind, what she needed, however, was answers.

Kimmy ran into the office and sat down at the computer. She clicked the Internet icon and typed Belleview, FL into the search box. Instantly a page of websites appeared with *Florida > Belleview >* listed at the top. Kimmy clicked on that and a page with links to various Belleview businesses appeared, including real estate and rentals. Before long, she had the address for Boca Grande Park.

Next, she found the listings for taxicabs in the local phone book. This is where it was going to get tricky. She had to convince them to take her to another city forty or fifty miles away. Everyone made fun of her deep voice, telling her she was going through the change. Maybe she could make it work for her.

She cleared her throat and dialed the first cab company in the book.

"Yes, I hope you can help me," Kimmy said trying to sound as adult as possible. "Could you possibly take my daughter to Belleview?"

She was prepared with a lame story about a sick grandmother who was looking forward to her visit, but the voice on the other end of the phone wasn't looking for conversation. It informed her that it was going to cost seventy-five dollars.

Kimmy gave the operator her address, and hung up the telephone. That was too easy. Now, all she needed was seventy-five dollars. She had about fifteen dollars saved for her next CD purchase; that left sixty. In her parent's bedroom, Kimmy found five ones on the dresser.

She really felt bad doing this, but she was sure they would understand. Well, maybe not, but she didn't have time to sort it all out right now.

Her dad kept his keys and wallet in a small jewelry box in the top drawer of the chest of drawers by the closet. Two new $20 bills were tucked into one of the pockets of the box along with a pile of quarters. She grabbed the bills and counted out four dollars in quarters. Quickly she did the math and realized she still needed eleven dollars, and time was running out. Kimmy searched the room one last time, scrambling through the nightstand drawers and looking in her mother's extra purses, where she did find three more dollars.

Only eight to go. In her room she retrieved the fifteen dollars, wriggled into a pair of jeans and a clean shirt, then ran to GT's room. "I know he has money squirreled away somewhere around here," she said aloud, looking at the mess that was her brother's room. She examined the cluttered desktop, covered with sports magazines, a stack of baseball cards, and an assortment of paperback books.

Kimmy rifled through the magazines, yanked out the desk drawers and even searched under her brother's mattress. No money. Where could it be?

She looked under the bed and aside from wadded up clothes he had obviously kicked there instead of dropping them in the hamper, there was only a single running shoe with the toe torn open.

Kimmy couldn't believe her brother's slovenliness. She was about to move to the closet when she glimpsed something inside the dirty Nike. She pulled it out and smiled. Wasn't it just like GT to use an old shoe as his bank? Crammed inside the shoe was a wad of bills totaling forty-eight dollars. She pulled a twenty from the stash, jammed it into her pocket with the rest of the money, and hurried to the front hall just as the taxi driver blew the horn.

Kimmy rushed down the walk toward the waiting cab, her heart beating wildly. She didn't know how she was going to pull it off, but she knew she wouldn't return home without Tony.

chapter 53

THE MORNING SUN blinked briefly through strips of gray flannel clouds cloaking the sky over Boca Grande Park then retreated. Even without the direct sunlight, the temperature had risen dramatically over the past three hours along with the humidity. The rescue personnel, still looking for tornado victims, felt like they were working at the base of a waterfall.

Inside Art Schilling's pickup truck, Windrusher was now fully awake. After sleeping deeply for two hours, he awakened to the heat that was building in the cab, and the noise of nearby vehicles. Wind shuddered as he remembered the fearsome strength of the dark force that had ripped the old Hyskos home to shreds and sent him hurling through the air.

Now, he was imprisoned in another Hyskos vehicle that might take him further away from the old female, from his own family. Wind put his paws against the passenger window, and began meowing loudly and insistently.

While Windrusher was asleep, Schilling called his wife to let her know he'd be home in a couple of hours. He started to tell her about the cat he rescued from the tree, but she informed him that she already saw his daring rescue on TV that morning.

Schilling returned to the truck and saw the big cat propped against the window. He opened the door carefully, scooped it up, and sat on the edge of the seat, holding the cat in his lap.

"Hey, partner, you feeling better, now?" he asked, running a hand over the cat's back, and feeling a sneeze coming on. "I'm not sure what I'm going to do, but someone will surely want a TV star like you."

Around him, fresh crews filed into the park and tired volunteers, their faces streaked with dirt and perspiration, were leaving. A large man in fireman coveralls stopped at Schilling's truck. His muscular shoulders were slumped forward like he had an invisible hundred-pound sack draped across them. He swung a half-full bottle of Gatorade from one hand, and held his helmet with the other.

"Quite a night. I can't remember when I've been so tired," he said, leaning against the cab next to the open door.

"You calling it a day?" Schilling said.

The man unscrewed the top to the bottle of Gatorade and gulped it loudly until there was only a mouthful left. He held it out toward Schilling who shook his head.

"Yeah, I've got to get some sleep before I fall down. What about you, champ?"

Schilling nodded and continued stroking the cat. "In a few minutes. Hey, you want a cat?"

The fireman shook his head, smiling broadly at Schilling and the cat.

"That was something," he said. "I understand you two made it on TV this morning."

Schilling returned the smile and nodded. "Louise said she watched it, and most of the time they were focused on my butt coming down from the tree."

"Well, at least they got your good side," the fireman said. "Good job, Art. I'll catch ya later."

The fireman tossed the empty bottle onto a nearby pile of trash, heaved himself off the truck, and walked away with slow, measured strides.

Schilling was completely drained of energy. He leaned his head back against the seat and closed his eyes, keeping his hands tightly over the cat.

Wind eyed the Hyskos and thanked the Holy Mother once again for sparing his life. Surely, I have lived a charmed life, more than any cat could ever expect. How many times did I tell myself that this was nothing but a fool's journey? There is no reason why I shouldn't be just another piece of worm meat instead of sitting here with this high-legged being.

Schilling felt the cat tremble under his hands and opened his eyes.

He started to rise from the seat, and sat back heavily, as if his legs had been cut out from under him.

"Damn. I guess I'm more tired than I thought."

Windrusher sensed the exhaustion in the Hyskos holding him, and he relaxed in his lap once again. Outside, other high-legged beings rushed back and forth, some carrying equipment, others searching under the jagged strips of sheet metal. In the background, chainsaws and sirens collided with shouts and the whine of generators. Wind's mind echoed the confusion around him, but mostly he was thankful to be safe. He knew it was because of this high-legged being who had plucked him from a tree.

Schilling's breathing took on a deep, steady rhythm and his hands fell limply to his side.

Windrusher stared at the sleeping Hyskos then out the open door. He understood there was a decision to make. By some miracle he had survived the brutal forces that devastated everything in his sight. Perhaps it was time to admit this foolish quest was not to be and find another Hyskos family.

He had fought his way through all of the barriers thrown in his path, and now, when there was a chance to put the danger and hardship behind him, he realized he couldn't do it. The decision surprised him. There was only one family that was truly his, and he couldn't stop until he found that family. Wind leaped from the man's lap, and ran for his life through the chaos and destruction that was now Boca Grande Park.

The taxi driver took county road 491 out of Crystal River then picked up state road 200 into Ocala. That trip took less than an hour. When they got to Ocala, the driver, a young man with a sparse blond goatee and two earrings, told Kimmy they would switch to 301 South and it would be another twenty minutes or so to Belleview.

Kimmy tried to remain calm during the drive, which seemed to take forever. She was thankful the driver didn't have much to say. Instead, he listened to a rock station, keeping time by tapping his fingers on the steering wheel.

South of Ocala, the traffic began to slow, and Kimmy became impatient. She thought about her mother coming home and not finding her in bed. Kimmy left so quickly she didn't have time to leave a note, not that she could actually explain what she was doing, since she didn't understand it herself. The sheer lunacy of her actions had sunk in during the taxi ride, and all of her doubts returned.

"You're sure this Boca Grande Park is on 301?" the driver asked.

"Uh, that's what grandmother said. You have the address."

"Right. Guess we'll run into it in a bit so keep your eyes open."

Windrusher sprinted madly across the trash-strewn trailer park desperately trying to ignore the frenetic activity around him. He stopped at the base of a live oak tree and caught his breath. The tree was stipped of its leaves, and branches hung down at peculiar angles. Wind heard voices coming toward him and scurried behind the tree just as two high-legged beings carrying equipment passed him on their way to a waiting truck.

The sound of chainsaws and wailing sirens seemed to grow louder, and his ears swiveled wildly at the noise that attacked him from every side. He instinctively moved southward toward the highway that ran in front of Boca Grande Park.

It was 9:30 in the morning and traffic was backed up in both directions along U.S. 301. Florida Highway Patrol officers and sheriff deputies manned barricades and directed rescue vehicles in and out of the devastated park, as they had all night. During the early morning hours, traffic was detoured around the site, but now most of the fire and rescue people were gone, and the police allowed the stream of cars and trucks to resume their use of 301.

Kimmy's taxi inched along. "This is a real mess," the young driver said, pulling at his goatee. "I hope this doesn't take all day, I have to get back to town before noon." He glared at his passenger as if it was all her fault.

Kimmy saw the flashing lights from the Highway Patrol cruiser ahead of them. "I think we're almost there," she said.

chapter 54

WINDRUSHER LAY HIDDEN behind a hedge of red hibiscus bushes that miraculously remained untouched by the tornado's scathing winds. The bushes lined the southern end of the driveway to Boca Grande Park and extended around the corner along Highway 301. Behind him was the shattered trunk of a young pine tree and a pile of crushed branches, needles and brittle, brown cones.

Two black and yellow vehicles were lined up on the side of the road, blue strobe lights flashing. A pair of tall Highway Patrol officers stood in the middle of the road directing traffic around orange cones, while a chunky sheriff's deputy kept an eye on the emergency vehicles entering and exiting the trailer park.

The sun finally burned away the hazy film of clouds, leaving a clear azure sky that at any other time might have recalled a day at the beach, the smell of salt and sun tan lotion, the taste of a cold beer. Today, the sky reflected the quiet passivity that follows natural disasters, standing only as mute witness, neither approving nor disapproving of the scene below. The air around Windrusher was heavy with the flowery aroma of the hibiscus, but a fetid scent was building from within the piles of garbage left behind by the tornado.

This stretch of 301 was once a shaded canopy of overhanging live oak branches, festooned with spidery webs of Spanish moss. On this day, after the killer winds ripped a mile long patch through the wooded park, the highway was bright with unhindered light that flickered and danced on the windshields of the passing cars, and coruscated in sudden flashes off the Highway Patrolmen's aviator sunglasses each time they turned.

Wind stuck his head between the willowy branches of the hibiscus and eyed the bumper-to-bumper traffic passing before him.

It seemed to be moving faster now as the uniformed Hyskos tried to hurry the gawking drivers past the ruined trailer park. His family was somewhere on the other side of the black path, but he feared he would end up beneath one of the vehicles if he attempted to run across it now.

He backed out of the bush and sat in the relative shade of the toppled pine tree. He wrapped his tail around his paws, and decided this spot was safer than most, and the wisest course of action was to wait.

"Oh, man, it looks like they had a hurricane here," the taxi driver said.

The path of destruction was easy to follow. Huge oaks lay on their sides, fresh cut branches glistening white in the sun. A string of utility poles were snapped in half, and repairmen were working on the lines that trailed behind them like a family of remora clinging to a dead shark.

"There was a tornado," Kimmy said flatly.

Then she spotted the Boca Grande Park sign next to the patrolman's cruiser.

"This is it," she yelled. "Let me out."

The driver turned in his seat and looked at the girl. "Are you nuts, kid? I can't let you out in the middle of the road."

Kimmy pulled the money out of her pocket, and threw it over the front seat. Before the driver could object, she pushed opened the cab door and rushed into the lane of traffic. The heat and humidity almost took her breath away. Flashing lights blinked in her peripheral vision, and overhead she heard the *whomp, whomp, whomp* of a low-flying helicopter. Kimmy ran blindly toward the trailer park, ignoring a policeman who waved at her as though he was swatting at moths, his mouth moving angrily.

She dodged in front of a surprised driver who stomped on his brakes to avoid her. Then she was on the shoulder of the road shouting for Tony, adding her voice to the tumult ebbing and flowing around her.

Windrusher thought he heard a familiar sound, but dismissed it after it faded away and the only sounds he heard were the Hyskos vehicles. He rubbed his sore shoulder against the sculptured pine bark, and shook his head to ward off a swarm of gnats that were flitting in and out of his ears.

There was that sound again. This time to his right, beyond the tangle of pine and oak branches that had been trimmed from the fallen trees and piled up to form a dense wall of vegetation. The sun glared over the top of branches, sending bright fingers of light poking through the openings.

Wind stood motionless, staring into the radiant mound of branches. He caught a brief glimpse of something that moved in front of the brush pile, but now it was stationary and he thought the shadows were playing tricks on his tired eyes.

Then he was sure he heard a familiar voice, and it was calling his Hyskos name.

"Tony."

The name hung in the air and his heart surged with joy. This was the voice of his Hyskos female. One foot moved forward toward the voice. At that moment the shape in the shadows stepped into the light.

"You never thought you would see me again, did you, Windrusher?" asked Bolt.

chapter 55

"GOOD LORD, will you look at that," Jeannie Warren said, pointing at the devastated landscape to her right.

The Warrens were stopped in a line of traffic almost one hundred feet from the entrance to Boca Grande Park. A Highway Patrolman stood in the roadway blocking their lane waving a red and white rescue vehicle onto the highway. It sped north, emergency lights flashing, siren blaring.

Their ride up 301 was leisurely until they passed Summerfield and traffic started backing up. That was an hour earlier, now they were at the epicenter of the damage, waiting for the five cars in front of them to be allowed past the roadblock.

Warren stared at the spectacle of ruin and managed chaos before them. His lips tightened into a hard grimace and he shook his head as if denying responsibility for the disaster. "This is terrible."

"Oh, those poor people," Jeannie replied. She rolled down her window and the sound of chainsaws, emergency vehicles, and a hovering helicopter flooded into the car. "Can you imagine what it must have been like?"

"How far away is Crystal River?" Stacy asked from the back seat.

Jeannie picked up the map and examined it, then held it toward her daughter. "It's not really that close, honey. I'd say it's fifty miles west of us."

Stacy hung over the front seat and looked at the map in her mother's hand. "I guess Kimmy is lucky they don't live any closer, huh?" she said.

Warren glanced at his daughter and gave her a half smile. "You're right about that, honey. When something like this happens, the best thing is to be as far away as possible."

"Bolt."

The word caught in Wind's throat. He watched the hulking cat approach through the columns of light with his peculiar rolling gait augmented by the addition of a pronounced limp in his hind leg. Bolt's backside dipped obscenely with each step, and light reflected off the hundreds of tortoiseshell flecks in his scarred and matted black coat.

Windrusher stared in astonishment as Bolt stopped just inches away from his face. He felt heat radiating from the cat's massive body. His breath smelled like rancid meat left in a closed garbage can for a week, and Wind expected to see maggots crawling out of Bolt's dead eye.

"You seem surprised to see me."

Wind caught his breath and forced himself to look into that bright yellow eye. "I…I am surprised," he stammered.

His mind was tumbling trying to sort out the possibilities, trying to make sense of the fact that the animal that killed his friend was standing in front of him. He felt like that young cat, so many night globes ago, caught in the beams of the Hyskos vehicle. Frozen, confused.

How many night globes had it been since he last saw Bolt, how far had he traveled from that colony of cats by the waterfront? "How could it be that—"

"That I found you?" Bolt interrupted.

"Yes."

Bolt made a sharp hacking sound in the back of his throat and watched Wind jump.

"You were a foolheaded Wetlos from the very beginning," he spit out. "So filled with yourself and your *magical* mission. You think no other cat could travel great distances?"

He leaned his massive head forward until their noses touched.

"Obviously, you're wrong."

Windrusher saw the puckered crimson scar furrowed through Bolt's ear and across his eye. A vein throbbed on the side of the creature's neck, and he moved forward again, pushing the smaller cat backwards against the shattered pine.

"No, the real question is not how I found you, which I'll be happy to share, but why I even bothered," Bolt said.

An image of Scowl Down's body lying in a bloody pool flashed through Wind's mind with such graphic detail that he fought to control his emotions. The animal before him was responsible for the death of a loyal and loving friend. Adrenalin poured into his system and every nerve in his body screamed for revenge, to lash out with claws and teeth and cause the same pain and damage to Bolt as he had to Scowl Down. Just as quickly, the rage left his body, pushed aside by the reality that any battle between the two of them would surely lead to his own death. He was too close to his final destination to allow that to happen.

"And why did you go to all this trouble to find me?" Windrusher's tail twitched indecisively, his ears flickered and turned away from Bolt.

"As I said, you are not the only cat that can have a mission. After that gang of putrid snouter droppings chased me away from the colony, you became my mission. I made a pledge that one day I would find you and kill you."

Perhaps it was the light, but a three dimensional grid seemed to settle over Bolt's bright yellow eye like a flat, dead scrim shrouding whatever spark of life might be contained inside his body.

"The thought of watching you kick and squeal and bleed, then die like your worthless old friend, was all the encouragement I needed to stay in the hunt," Bolt said.

The blood pulsed in Wind's ears. If he was going to survive this encounter, he had to derail Bolt's fury, at least until he could find a way to escape with his skin intact. "Your tracking skills are impressive," Wind said, edging away from the murderous cat.

Bolt flicked out a scabby paw that caught Wind behind the ear. "You made it easy for me to find you," he hissed.

Windrusher focused on the yellow eye and tried to ignore the throbbing in his head. "What do you mean?"

"The *great* Windrusher was chosen by Irissa-u herself to undertake a journey that would make him a hero to all cats. Isn't that the story you told to every cat that would listen?"

He hit him again on the other side of the head as if to make sure he was paying attention. "And you couldn't help play the hero and announce your progress to the Akhen-et-u at each stop you made."

Bolt's head was tilted slightly as if he were having trouble holding it straight. A line of scummy fluid traced a dark stain from the corner of his sightless eye down his cheek. Wind blinked several times to clear his head. A muscle in his thigh began to twitch.

"You're saying that you found me because of my visits to the Inner Ear." Wind was incredulous.

"It was nearly as good as following your scent. I almost had you and the little Wetlos once, but you managed to escape in a Hyskos vehicle. But I want to thank you for teaching me how to use those vehicles to travel. Your boastings helped me find you, and you always had to rest. That gave me even more time."

Bolt pushed his flat face against Wind's sore shoulder and Wind staggered back a step.

"You're such a pampered weakling that you were forced to beg help from the high-legged beings and rest your puny body."

It had taken so much effort for Wind to get to this place. He had endured and he had sacrificed, but he had stayed on the Path. He attributed his good fortune and persistence to the Holy Mother. What powers, he wondered, did this ugly cat possess to follow him all the way from Swift Nail's colony?

"Your persistence is remarkable," he said.

Bolt raised one paw toward Windrusher, the claws fully extended.

"And my persistence is about to be rewarded, you miserable buttworm. Prepare yourself to meet the Holy Mother, or whatever foolish ghosts you worship."

He opened his mouth wide, pulling back his lips and exposing the deadly teeth that had torn open Scowl Down's throat. A terrible screech seemed to erupt from deep within Bolt's bowels and he crouched low preparing to leap upon the prey he had followed halfway across the country.

chapter 56

"I DON'T CARE why you're here, young lady. I told you not to cross that road, are you trying to get yourself killed?"

The Belleview sheriff's deputy had Kimmy by the arm and was pulling the protesting girl toward his patrol car near the trailer park's entrance. Blue lights flashed across the bars on the roof of the car. He opened the back door and pushed her inside.

"You stay right here until things slow down a little, and then we can sort this all out." He gave the girl a stern look. "Do you understand?"

Kimmy nodded meekly at the officer. "Yes, sir."

He left the door open and walked to his post alongside the orange cones cutting his eyes toward her then toward the traffic.

Kimmy's stomach tightened into a hard knot. She realized this was one of the most stupid things she had ever done, and she had done lots of dumb stuff, especially today. This wins the prize, though. Stealing money from her own family because she imagined she saw Tony on television.

Even if it was Tony, the tornado was last night and he's probably long gone. I guess mom and dad will forgive me because that's what parents do, but I'm twelve years old, and I should know better. And it's not going to help if I get arrested, and they have to bail me out of jail.

The deputy was directing traffic, his back to her, and he was waving a line of cars into the far lane around the cones. Kimmy glanced over her shoulder at the Boca Grande Park sign only twenty feet away, then back at the deputy. He can arrest me if he wants, she told herself stubbornly. I didn't come all this way to sit here and wait.

Kimmy stepped out of the car and shifted to the other side of the sedan trying to keep it between her and the deputy. She walked deliberately along the shoulder of the road toward the entrance, the sounds of car horns and police whistles behind her, and fought the urge to run. She was only five feet from the sign when the deputy turned around and saw her.

"Hey," he yelled from across the street. "Where do you think you're going?"

He ran toward the driveway attempting to cut her off.

Kimmy jerked around, her eyes wide with fright. She tripped over a branch and staggered backwards into the hibiscus hedge lining the road.

Windrusher felt strangely calm, as though the unfolding confrontation with Bolt was happening to another cat and he was watching it all through a window. Or perhaps, it's another one of his dreams and he will awaken at the foot of the old female's bed. She will fuss over him and bring him food and water.

Wind saw the muscles tense along Bolt's flank, heard him hissing and spitting. He wasn't asleep, and this was no dream. The sirens and chainsaws receded into the background, the grating voices of the high-legged beings seemed to stop abruptly, and he felt a tic plucking the skin at the corner of his eye.

Each of his hairs stood out from his body and he braced himself for the brutish cat's attack. If this is how it is supposed to end, he thought, then for Scowl's sake, let me give him a good fight.

The bushes behind Bolt shuddered and crackled suddenly under the weight of the twelve-year-old. Kimmy shrieked loudly and Bolt jumped around to face the intruder.

In that instant between the thrashing noise in the hibiscus bush and Bolt turning away from him, Wind decided that instead of fighting for his life, the wiser choice would be to run. He crashed through the hedge onto the shoulder of the highway, and hesitated before the oncoming vehicles.

The clamor of horns and sirens hit him like one of Bolt's paws; he stared momentarily at the long line of traffic, then over his shoulder at the bushes. There was no time to debate options, either he waited to be torn apart, or he put the black path between them. He tried his best to ignore the third and most likely option, since that involved his life ending smashed beneath the wheels of one of the vehicles.

Windrusher darted through a narrow gap between two vehicles, hoping the Holy Mother was still with him. He heard the sound of bushes parting, then something that caused him to stop in mid-stride on the deadly black path.

"Tony!"

Kimmy screamed his name as he dashed past her and into the road. She rushed to the edge of the highway where the policeman was impatiently waving at the drivers staring at the trailer park and not at the road.

She followed the frightened cat on to Highway 301, plunged in front of a large car whose driver leaned on the horn, hit the brakes, and screeched to a stop just inches away. Kimmy pushed herself off the front of the hood, and raced across the road calling for Tony to stop.

Bolt broke through the hibiscus bush just as Windrusher scampered across the black path. The Hyskos girl startled him by following the cat and yelling. Like all cats, Bolt could not understand what made the high-legged beings do the strange things that they did. He did understand that he might not have another chance to rid himself of Windrusher if he let him get away once again.

I have not followed him across the globe just to let him disappear again and become the house cat of some fat, old Hyskos, he thought.

The blood pounded loudly in Bolt's ears, and his chest heaved. He steeled himself to dash across the highway. No more talking when I get hold of you, Windrusher. The only sounds will be the gurgles of your blood spilling out of your pitiful body. He lifted his massive head, his good eye shifting rapidly, and ran as fast as he could across the path.

The sound of the screeching tires came as a complete surprise to Bolt. He turned his head toward the skidding vehicle in time to see the huge black tire sliding toward him in slow motion. His eye fastened on the long dark grooves circling the tire like they were rings of black acid eating into the surface. He smelled the pungent stench of burning rubber and saw wisps of acrid smoke rise from the pavement.

The tire moved so slowly, that for a moment Bolt thought it would never reach him, and he was safe to pursue Windrusher across the black path. Then the tire caught him on his left shoulder and pulled him under like a swimmer caught in a riptide. His bright lemon drop eye grew wide with the realization that he was not going to catch Windrusher today. He closed it and the Yukon passed over him.

chapter 57

"Is EVERYONE all right?" Warren asked.

Two of the cars behind the SUV collided when he slammed on the brakes, and he felt a jolt pass through the vehicle. After seeing that both his wife and daughter were unharmed, Warren climbed out of the Yukon to see what he had run over.

He had been looking at the awful tornado damage when Jeannie nudged him and pointed toward the patrolman. The officer's face was red, and he was waving his arms furiously trying to get the big SUV moving. Warren gave the officer a sheepish grin and a shrug of his shoulders as if to say he was sorry for not paying attention, then stepped on the gas. He was swinging around the first orange cone, picking up speed, when the small dark body flashed across the road in front of him.

Warren raised his foot from the gas pedal and thrust it down on the brake, automatically throwing his arm out to stop his wife from slamming forward even though she was wearing a seat belt. He felt the slight thud of the Yukon's tire pass over something, followed immediately by the shock of the impact from the car behind him.

"Oh, crap," he thought. "Maybe I should have bought that extra insurance."

Windrusher was running full tilt when he hit the patch of gravel on the side of the road. His feet slid out from under him and he tumbled tail over whiskers into what was left of a telephone pole. He lay there gasping for air, his shoulder throbbing, his eyes closed before finally struggling to his feet. He expected to hear the mocking sound of Bolt's voice at any moment and feel the pain of his razor sharp teeth on his throat. The awful vision ended with the bloody remains of his splayed body on the side of the path, and he wanted to be as far away from that mental image as possible.

Screeching tires and the crash of vehicles riveted Wind's attention back to the black path. Moments before he faced a vicious and painful death at the claws of Bolt, was it possible that now he might be free? His mind couldn't grasp the truth of the gruesome scene before him as he stared at the shapeless black mass protruding from beneath one of the vehicles. Was that pulverized and bleeding body really Bolt or was his mind playing tricks on him again?

Either way, he had a mission to complete. Wind dashed into the woods thinking that he wouldn't let anything stop him from finding his family. Behind him, Wind heard car doors slamming, the shriek of a police whistle, and the shouts of high-legged beings.

He ran twenty feet into the woods and realized that one of the shouts he heard was the name his Hyskos female called him.

"Tony."

Wind stopped abruptly. His ears swiveled like a radar dish and he heard the voice again carrying over the confusion on the black path. She was close now, her footsteps crunching on the wet leaves and broken branches.

"Tony, don't be afraid. It's me. It's Kimmy."

Windrusher stopped and his whiskers quivered and arched forward as though they were reaching out for the safety of the forest ahead of him. He recognized that voice, and it was calling the name she called him. It was the voice of the Hyskos female he had been searching for since she left him behind so many night globes ago.

He slowly turned and saw the girl bent over, head down and breathing hard. She abruptly sat back, hitting the ground hard and covering her face with her hands. Windrusher hesitated, he couldn't be sure, it looked like his Hyskos female, but she was bigger than he remembered. It's a brainless notion anyway, he finally told himself and prepared to continue running.

Kimmy's legs shook and she gasped for breath thinking how close she came to being hit by that car. Then, seeing her cat run away was almost more than she could take. Kimmy's legs gave way and she sat on the damp ground with a groan. She raised her head and saw the cat she called Tony turn away from her and began crying.

"Oh, Tony, Tony," she choked, and put her hands up to her face.

Windrusher heard his name again, this time with a sad, plaintive tone that forced him to turn back and stare at the Hyskos. She was still sitting on the ground, her hands covering her face, her knees drawn up tightly. Sunlight bloomed from her blond hair and cast a gauzy shadow over her legs.

Something about the young female melted Wind's defenses, and moved him to push aside his fears for the moment. He cautiously put one paw forward, paused; sniffing the air for danger, then took another step. Ever so slowly, he edged closer to the young female until he was no more than a cat's length from her. He stopped and listened to her disconsolate sobs, her scent was strong now, evoking memories of playful days when he was a much younger cat.

Wind took one more tentative step, meowed meekly, then saw her wipe the tears from her face and look directly at him.

Kimmy beamed at the cat and threw her arms out. "Tony, it is you. It is you," she cried.

Kimmy was sitting in the back seat of the Yukon next to her cousin, Tony was asleep on her lap, and they were on their way to Crystal River. The Warrens sat mesmerized as Kimmy told them the story of the TV news report and Tony's rescue.

"He was all wrapped up in a quilt or something and had been blown into a tree."

"No way," Stacy said.

"Can you believe it? Then a fireman hauled him down, and when they showed his head peeking out from under the quilt I almost spit up my corn flakes."

Jeannie Warren laughed and shook her head. "What in the world was he doing down here in Florida? And so close to where you live."

"It's weird, isn't it?" Stacy said.

Kimmy ran her fingers lightly through her cat's fur, gazing thoughtfully at her pet. She knew that Tony had been looking for her, waiting for her to come to the rescue like some comic book hero. A thought hit her and she jerked her head up, a look of surprise and delight on her face. "I just thought of something," she said. "Look at Tony."

"What," Stacy said loudly, causing Wind to open an eye and peer around the car.

"Don't you remember he hated riding in cars? He would go bananas, even in the carrier. I could never hold him like this; he'd be bouncing all over the place and clawing me to pieces."

"That's right."

"Look at him now. It doesn't bother him at all," Kimmy said with an incredulous shake of her head.

"What do you think, Tom?" Jeannie asked. You've been awfully quiet over there. Are you still thinking about that poor cat you hit, or brooding about the ticket you got?"

Warren shook his head. "Oh, I was just thinking that we won't get a chance to go to Silver Springs and see the mermaids."

Kimmy leaned forward, making sure she didn't upset the cat. "There are no mermaids at Silver Springs. You mean Weeki Wachee Springs. We went there last summer, and it's not very far from Crystal River."

Warren glanced into the mirror at his niece, a puzzled expression on his face. Suddenly, his eyebrows shot up and he laughed. "That's right, it is Weeki Wachee Springs."

EPILOGUE

IN THE WEEKS following the tornado, Windrusher barely had time to reacquaint himself with the Tremble family before his notoriety made him a national celebrity. A front-page story in the *Citrus County Chronicle* was headlined "Miracle Cat Survives Killer Twister." A picture of Kimmy holding him was spread over three columns, and the story played up the mystery of the cat that traveled from Bloomfield, Connecticut to Belleview, Florida in search of its master.

The Associated Press picked up the story, and for a week, the Trembles' phone rang constantly with requests for interviews by area and national media. His picture appeared in newspapers and magazines ranging from the *Star* to *People*. Network crews came to the Tremble home during the second week and rolled cables, lights, and cameras into their living room for an early morning appearance on the *Today Show*.

Wind was content to lie in Kimmy's lap during the interview; his eyes closed against the bright lights, while his female Hyskos answered Katie Couric's questions. Although Katie was in New York, the living room was filled with strange people twiddling with equipment and making odd signals to one another.

Fifty miles away, Sarah Kilcrease reclined in bed in the rehabilitation unit of Belleview General. Her broken leg was in a full-length cast, and she ran through the channels of the small TV above her bed while she waited for the doctor's visit. This was the day she would be discharged, and her daughter was coming to take her to her home in Ocala. Her fingers froze on the remote when she saw the close-up of the cat on the little girl's lap. She raised the volume level to its highest setting to hear what they were saying, just as Katie

Couric asked the girl how she felt when she realized the cat at the tornado site was her long lost pet, Tony?

"Crackers," Mrs. Kilcrease sobbed. She had believed Crackers was dead, and tears streamed down her cheeks as she watched the interview. It was a remarkable story. Maybe not worth losing her home and breaking her leg for, but still remarkable. She dabbed at the tears, relieved and suddenly proud that she had played a part in bringing Tony and her family together.

Hell, it nearly killed me, she thought, but I'm still here, and Crackers is home where he belongs. Sometimes things have a way of working out, don't they...? She was about to say "Jake."

"Goodbye and good luck to all of you," Katie Couric said at the end of the interview from the studio in Rockefeller Center. "And a special goodbye to a very special cat. I have a feeling we haven't heard the last from you, Tony."

As if on cue, Windrusher looked directly into the camera, hunched his back, stretched as if he was waking from a three-day sleep, and yawned extravagantly.

He soon grew accustomed to the outlandish behavior of the peculiar Hyskos that came to his home. Windrusher didn't understand all the fuss, nor did it seem unusual to him, since cats believed the high-legged beings existed in a world that was both incomprehensible and somewhat foolish. Still, he appreciated the pampering his Hyskos female accorded him; it only strengthened the bond that existed between them. Everything he had experienced had been done for her, and in his mind he had improved the female's life as much as his own by returning to her and his Hyskos family.

Wind was never far from the events of his fourteen-month journey, and learned to live with the pictures of his past that appeared to him from time to time. Even in his sleep, Wind sniffed his old friends, did battle with ancient enemies, and saw the faces of those kindly high-legged beings that took him in and nurtured him to health. They peered out of the warped visions of his dreams, serious, unsmiling faces each in turn silently judging him: The Hyskos family at the farm with smelly milk baggers stood mutely, Lil' One cradled in the girl's arms; Silk Blossom's family came next and there was the gentle male sitting in his favorite chair, an expression of loss on his face; the female sisters who rescued him from the cage of death were there, too. Their usually happy faces were always sad and confused in his dream. Most often, the old woman appeared to him, offering love and the comfort of her lap. The dream ended with a grinding crash that left her writhing on the floor, lonely and in pain.

None of them had asked anything of him. There were no conditions to the comforts they offered, but he had coolly walked away from each of them, except the old woman, to pursue his quest. He invariably awakened from these dreams feeling drained and somehow diminished.

On this day, six months after Wind was reunited with his family, he entered the large living room, now encrusted with red, green, and gold holiday decorations, and found his favorite sleeping place on the couch. He settled on the white blanket Kimmy put out for him, groomed his fattened belly, and surveyed the tall tree standing in front of the picture window. Long strands of golden garlands crawled around it, a pile of presents heaped below. On the wall above him were pictures of the Hyskos family, and he stared briefly at the newest one of his young female holding in her lap the cat she called Tony.

Wind breathed deeply and carefully examined his right paw. He licked it, then wiped it across his ear once, twice, three times. His eyes grew heavy, and he tucked his paws against his body, wrapped his tail around them and rolled his head into his chest. Sleep came quickly and he drifted in the peaceful currents, tasting of the ripe fruits of his unconscious. Soon he was in that nether world where the past blended with the future and gods walked the earth.

A soft, lavender light covered the village and the sun hovered above a row of low saffron colored buildings. Windrusher padded down a narrow lane staring at the houses on either side of him. They were constructed of individual bricks of mud and straw probably left out in the hot rays of the day globe to bake. A warm breeze blew out of the west, kicking up puffs of chalky sand at the far end of the dirt path.

Odors of garlic and baked fish hung in the air, and he heard strange Hyskos voices chattering around him. Low on the horizon floated the faint outline of a complete night globe shimmering like a faded silver dollar in the glow of the pink and lavender streaked sky.

Wind moved slowly as though his feet were sticking to the hot sand. A pair of dark shadows darted between the houses to his right, and he stared at the retreating shapes. His eyes adjusted to the waning light, and dozens of cats came into focus, some lounging in doorways staring brazenly back at him.

Far off in the distance was the peak of a great stone pyramid, but standing before him was a solitary shape that seemed to glow under the last rays of Rahhna. Again, he heard the familiar voice pulling him forward, and the strange feeling of his mind deserting his body as though to better view the scene that was unfolding around him.

"Pferusha-ulis, you've come back to me," the words arrived not through his ears but from within his head.

The burnished gold of her fur shimmered in the fleeting lavender light, and she waited patiently for him to approach. Waves of serenity washed over him with each step, and soon Wind was standing next to the Holy Mother.

She gazed into his eyes with the love of eternity shining through them, and he worried that his legs would fail.

"Did you see them, Windrusher?" Irissa-u asked.

He looked down as though the clues to her question were scattered in the dust at his feet. "See them?" he repeated.

Irissa-u swished her tail and hundreds of green and yellow eyes pierced the darkness. Moments later, the cats pushed through the shadows and stood silently in a circle around them. His mouth dropped open at the scores of cats that seemed to have appeared from the walls of the buildings. He looked from the circle back to the Holy Mother.

"Many night globes ago I promised you a great adventure if you followed me. I told you how cats spread across the stone kingdom, and how we came to be revered in all Hyskos villages. We journeyed together, those many generations ago, Windrusher, and now cats multiply like the grains of sand beneath your feet.

"You are the bravest and most loyal of all my followers. By your efforts, cats understand what it means to follow the Path and if you believe with all your heart, you will find the Way."

Irissa-u rubbed the top of her head against Wind's neck then licked his face gently. He shivered at the touch of her tongue, and felt an unearthly peace pass over him that he had not felt since he nursed at his mother's breast. Dropping to his knees, he bent his head under the majestic queen's grooming.

The grooming stopped and Windrusher looked at the Holy Mother through eyes that were suddenly moist. She was staring at the distant horizon, and spoke as though addressing the mammoth mass of stone in the desert. "I will be going soon, Pferusha-ulis, for there is still much to accomplish to protect cats in all parts of the Hyskos world."

Windrusher blinked and moved closer. The broad face of the night globe rose behind her, the wind shifted and blew clouds of dust around their feet, and he felt his face flush hotly. "How can I help you, Irissa-u?" he asked.

She was still staring at the desert sky. Wind's heart thumped in his chest, he held his breath and waited for her response, afraid she had already given it.

Slowly, she turned her head to him, and Wind lost himself in her golden copper eyes. There was no mistaking the soft glow of love reflected there.

"Ah, my Windrusher," she said softly. "You have a life of pleasure and security with your Hyskos family. Enjoy it, you've earned it. Return to them, and they will keep you secure for the rest of your days."

"But…" he stammered.

Irissa-u tilted her head slightly as though she heard a noise that was meant only for her ears. "You will always be with me, Pferusha-ulis, and I with you." The stately queen turned with a swish of her dark tail and strode toward the stone pyramid.

Windrusher felt like he was cast adrift in a vertiginous sea, swirling dizzily, caught in the grip of a dangerous undertow.

"Tell me, Holy Mother," he screamed at her retreating back, "will I see you again?"

Irissa-u stopped and gazed warmly at Windrusher. She stood for a moment, the enormous silvery night globe gleaming like an incandescent curtain behind her, and parted her lips as if to reply. Wind waited to hear her voice once again, wanting to hear that another adventure awaited him when he awoke. Instead, the Holy Mother turned and walked away from the village, striding purposefully into the cold desert night.

Windrusher saw the brilliant gold and black highlights shining off her back then melt away as she became one with the shadowy landscape.

Author's Note

While *Windrusher* is obviously a work of fiction, certain locations in the book are real. Although there was no mention of a sterilization procedure during Windrusher's stay at the Jacksonville Humane Society, all pets adopted from this facility are indeed altered. Feline overpopulation is an immense problem in this country. Too many people allow their unaltered cats to roam and breed, or even abandon them when they move. This leads to the shocking statistic of approximately seven million cats euthanized each year because no one wants them. Please help save lives by spaying or neutering your companion animal.

FELINE GLOSSARY

Akhen-et-u Also known as The Inner Ear, this ancient communication tool allows cats to speak to one another while deep in sleep. Not every cat is fortunate enough to be plugged into this feline Internet (See Wetlos). Windrusher uses it to help him complete his mission.

Buttworm Strong pejorative, a disparagement usually hurled in anger.

Call Name A name a cat takes for himself. Often selected for some physical attribute, the surroundings where it spent its early days, or even a boastful exaggeration meant to impress other cats. Windrusher found his call name in a dream that later came true.

Day Globe The sun, Rahhna, and the time it takes for the sun to rise—one day.

Floppy-eared Snouter A dog, also a derisive term as in "doesn't have the sense of a floppy-eared snouter."

Hairless Idea A screwball idea, not worth considering.

Hwrt-Heru Goddess of sleep. A maternal presence believed to renew the energies and spirits of cats while they sleep.

Hyskos An ancient cat term for humans, also known as high-legged beings.

Irissa-u The Holy Mother, a mythic goddess who led seven followers from the jungles to the city of the Hyskos. Legend has it that most cats are descended from these first disciples of Irissa-u.

Kalosisha-ulla Silk Blossom in ancient cat language.

Mother's Name A cat's official name that traces the lineage of the cat through its mother's family. For example, Wind is the Son of Nefer-iss-tu.

Night Globe The moon. Also refers to the period of time it takes for the moon to ebb and wane—a full month. Hence, Windrusher's almost impossible journey of twenty night globes or a journey of twenty months.

Nut-atna The god of night. Oversees the comings and goings of night creatures.

Path Feline rules to live by. Cat legend has it that if cats follow the Path, they will be reborn and eventually brought up to Rahhna to live with Irissa-u and the other gods. That is the Way to eternal life.

Pferusha-ulis Windrusher in ancient cat language.

Rahhna The sun, also known as the day globe. Legend has it that the gods live on Rahhna.

Rahhnut The keeper of the day globe, also known as Rahhna.

Setlos A very bad cat.

Tho-hoth God of Wisdom. Tho-hoth is given credit for creating the Akhen-et-u.

Wetlos Cats unable to communicate via the Akhen-et-u. Often looked down upon by other cats.

About the Author

Along the way, Victor DiGenti has worked as a radio announcer, produced award-winning TV documentaries, written for newspapers and magazines, and produced a nationally acclaimed jazz festival. He's also executive director of an organization working for the welfare and protection of abandoned, feral, and homeless cats. DiGenti lives in Florida with his wife and seven rescued cats.